"In *Charlie and the Angel,* Ms. Handeland gives us a riveting romantic adventure!"

—*Rendezvous*

HEAVEN ON EARTH

"Are you crazy?" Charlie growled. "This thing's loaded. You could have blown your head off. Or worse, you could have blown my fool head off. What are you doin' out here, Angelina?"

She couldn't answer, could only shake her head helplessly. He was right. She could have killed both of them. She who had vowed not to hurt a living soul. She had to get back to the convent before she broke every tenet she held dear.

"Angelina?" Charlie's voice sounded at once confused and curious. He reached out and touched her face.

The contact of his warmth against her icy flesh soothed away the lingering fright. Instead of pulling away as she should, she allowed him to brush his fingertips up and down her cheek.

Heaven and hell. Ice and fire. How could so many things be contained in one man's touch? He was temptation in all forms, and she couldn't summon the strength to resist.

She turned her head into the caress, suddenly aching for more of what she didn't understand. Charlie stepped closer, cupping the side of her face in his large palm. He was going to kiss her, and suddenly she wanted to be kissed more than she had ever wanted anything in her life.

Other *Leisure* and *Love Spell* Books by
Lori Handeland:
SHADOW LOVER
SECOND CHANCE

LORI HANDELAND

Book Margins, Inc.

A BMI Edition

Published by special arrangement with Dorchester
Publishing Co., Inc.

Printed in the United States of America.

Digest format printed and distributed exclusively for Book
Margins, Inc., Ivyland, PA.

For my parents,
Beverley Jo Miller—who showed me, by example,
"Never give in!",
Robert "Buck" Miller—who showed me an artist
at work,
and
Judy and Dennis Handeland—who showed me how
to raise little boys into incredible men.

Prologue

"Open the safe and hand out the money or there'll be one dead engineer."

Silence met the demand. The band of outlaws glanced uneasily in their leader's direction. He shrugged and fired, watching without emotion as red blossomed across the front of the engineer's shirt. The man crumpled to the ground.

"We're gonna start pickin' passengers now. Shootin' 'em one by one until you open up."

Hearing the threat, women screamed from within the train. The leader flinched and swung his gun toward the sound.

A bolt slid free, drawing the outlaws' attention back to the car in front of them as the door slipped slowly open. Within minutes, ten men, all wearing black masks and broad-brimmed hats that obscured their features and hair, galloped through the waving grasses of Texas. Nine howled the rebel yell. The tenth, mounted on a massive white horse, merely rode and smiled with satisfaction.

Revenge was sweet.

Chapter One

North of San Antonio, 1875

Angelina Reyes screamed.

But there was no one left alive who cared. Her terror merely amused her attackers even more than the dead bodies littering the ground around them.

"You will scream with pleasure before I am through with you, senorita." The leader of the trio of murderers advanced, his cruel black eyes narrowing in anticipation. Angelina stumbled backward in her haste to get away. Spinning, she prepared to run. She wouldn't give up without at least trying to escape.

Hampered by long, heavy black skirts, she had run no more than a few faltering steps when the two other attackers stepped in front of her. Their leader grabbed her around the waist and flung her to the ground. Grunting, he followed, pinning her down on the dry dirt with his body.

She couldn't breathe; she couldn't see. Biting her lip hard enough to draw blood, Angelina centered her mind on that self-inflicted pain. She forced herself to concentrate, to focus on the here and now. Panic swelled within her, threatening to strangle any chance she had for survival. Alone, with only herself to depend on, she did not dare surrender to the near mind-numbing fear. She must fight for her virtue and her life. She had learned as a child that the Lord helped those who helped themselves. The time had come to put that adage to a test.

The two men not directly involved in her violation seated themselves a few yards away to watch the sport. While they shouted their encouragement and suggestions between swigs of whiskey, their leader grew bored with her struggles and slapped her—once, twice, three times.

The world wavered in front of Angelina's eyes. For a moment she forgot her resolve to fight and lay motionless. The shriek of rending cloth as her dress was ripped from neck to waist revived her. With all her might, she brought her knee up between her attacker's legs.

His breath whooshed from his lungs in surprise, sickening her with the rancid smell. She shoved his unresisting body away and rolled to the side. Then she was on her feet and running, this time with her heavy skirts held high.

"Get her, idiots!" shouted the leader, his voice thick and choked with pain.

Angelina ran. With every step she expected a large, heavy hand to latch on to her shoulder. Fear engulfed her again, threatening to choke off what little air she could draw into her burning chest. The terror lent her speed. She reached the top of a short rise before one of them caught her. She jerked away from the groping hand, and for a second she ran free once again. Then she stumbled forward, pitching headfirst into nothingness. She hit the ground hard enough to stun herself. Then she was rolling, rolling, rolling until she reached the bottom of the hill. Her attacker landed on top of her. He wasted no time continuing what his leader had begun. Angelina's stomach roiled as he pressed his fetid mouth to hers. His fingers fumbled inside her ripped bodice.

"Get up."

A rasping whisper came from somewhere behind the man. Angelina jerked her head away and tried to see who spoke from an area just beyond her sight. Had one of the others followed them down, intent on having her first? No. She could swear she had never heard that voice before.

Her attacker either did not hear the order or chose to ignore it, for he continued to foist damp kisses across her chin and down her neck. Angelina flinched away from his roving mouth, praying with all the fervor within her that the man who stood just out of her sight was a gift from God.

"I said, get up. Slowly. Keep your hands where I can see 'em."

Angelina was certain she had never heard this voice before. She would remember the eerie, graveled tone until the day she died— which she hoped would not be as soon as she'd thought. Someone had arrived to save her. God was indeed helping the not-so-helpless today.

This time her attacker heard and obeyed the rough command. Perhaps because this time the words were punctuated with the sound of a gun being cocked. He got up slowly, as ordered, and Angelina squinted into the blinding sun.

Her savior rode a white horse, and he rode alone. A broad-brimmed hat obscured his features, but his silhouette revealed him to be tall and heavily muscled. The pistol cradled in his hand seemed as much a part of him as the long fingers casually curled around the butt of the gun.

Angelina swallowed nervously.

A gunshot rang out from the rise above them, spurting a cloud of dust at the feet of her savior's horse. Startled, Angelina glanced upward. The two remaining attackers stood at the top of the hill. Before she could cry out a warning for her rescuer to beware, two more gunshots echoed. The men rolled down the hill and landed in a lifeless heap at the feet of the massive white horse. The animal leaned down and sniffed them once before raising its head. Obviously having encountered dead bodies before, the horse had little interest in two more.

"*Madre de Dios,* do not shoot me, senor," the last attacker begged in a high-pitched whine. "You can have her. I will not fight you."

The man on the white horse turned his head, and when his gaze met that of the attacker, the other man paled and closed his mouth abruptly. Her rescuer turned toward Angelina.

"You can get up now, ma'am. He won't move. Sounds like he wants to keep his body parts in the same condition he has 'em in right now." The rasp of his voice added an even deeper threat to the words. Her attacker nodded swiftly in agreement.

Angelina sat up, but found she couldn't get to her feet. She began to shake and couldn't seem to stop. She had seen dead men in her life, but until this morning she had never seen anyone killed before her eyes. The cold finality of the act repeated over and over, first on her friends and then on her enemies, stunned her. She closed her eyes and uttered a swift prayer for strength and guidance.

When she opened her eyes, the man on the horse had swung his leg over the saddle. He slid easily to the ground, never removing his gaze from the prisoner or allowing the gun in his hand to waver. "Stay right there," he said to the attacker, who again nodded his understanding of the order. The man seemed to have lost his voice along with his courage.

Angelina's breath caught in her throat as her savior moved closer, then reached out to assist her. He wore the typical uniform of the Texas cowboy—Levi's, dark, dusty boots and a long-sleeved shirt. He wore no spurs, an omission she'd never encountered before. A kerchief hung knotted around his neck, available to pull over his nose and mouth when the trail dust became too thick. Angelina raised her gaze from the kerchief to her rescuer's face, but his hat still shaded his features, and she could not see his eyes. That fact made her nervous, but she firmly reminded herself he had just saved her life. She should not feel so threatened by him.

Unless, of course, he had killed the other men so he could have her for himself. The thought sent another trickle of fear through her, and she fought the urge to cross herself. Showing her fear was a weakness she could ill afford. She had at least learned that much from living with her father.

Angelina looked up at her rescuer again, squinting to see past the shadow obscuring his face. Her mother had always told her that eyes were the windows to the soul. A glimpse of this man's soul would be welcome at that moment.

"Relax," he whispered, and at the sound of his voice she froze. "Never raped a woman in my life. I ain't aimin' to start with you." He flexed his fingers in invitation.

Tentatively, Angelina placed her hand in his palm, clutching the torn remains of her bodice together with the other hand. His fingers closed over hers, swallowing her hand in his. His warmth encased her icy flesh, yet she shivered, then caught her breath when she was yanked unceremoniously to her feet.

The man glanced over at her attacker, who had not moved, and nodded in approval. Turning back, he removed his hat. Hair the color of spun gold, shot through with a vein of silver, spilled past his shoulders. Angelina looked for the first time into the face of her savior.

"Lucifer fallen," she whispered and took a step away. Her palm came up to rest against her racing heart.

Exquisite. There was no other word for the unearthly beauty of the man. His skin had tanned to a rich golden tone that only accented his angelic hair. He had a bump on his nose that told of a former break and a small scar over his right brow. Those small imperfections only served to create a masculine air in the midst of otherwise perfectly hewn features. Angelina suspected she beheld an angel until she gazed into his eyes.

The pits of hell, she thought. He has been there and survived.

Angelina had never seen such cold black eyes. She hoped she never would again. He had just shot down two men, and yet she could detect no emotion in their fathomless depths.

His full mouth tilted up in amusement, though nothing so frivolous shone in his gaze. Suddenly aware she was staring, Angelina flushed with embarrassment.

"Get that reaction from most women," he said with the same smile that did not reach his eyes. "But you look a bit young for my taste."

Ignoring her frown of reproval, he turned away and retrieved a rope from his saddle. Quickly and efficiently he tied up his prisoner.

"What will you do with me?" the man asked.

"Nothin'. If you behave, I'll send someone back from the next town to getcha. If not, you can rot for all I care."

"You can't leave me out here alone, trussed up, without a horse and a gun," the man said in disbelief.

"You didn't have much care for the lady." Her rescuer nodded at Angelina without looking at her. "I don't have none for you. Be thankful I'm lettin' you live. Goes against my nature to be so generous. But I get the feelin' she's seen enough killin' for one afternoon."

He turned away from the man and approached Angelina. Despite her resolve not to be frightened, she clutched her dress together tighter and took a another step backward. He loomed so tall next to her tiny frame. He might look like an angel, but she knew danger when she saw it. Even though he had done nothing but help her, something stirred in her when she looked at him. Something akin to fright—or another emotion she didn't know how to name.

"Who are you?" she whispered.

He stopped dead in his approach, but did not answer her for a long time. He merely stared at her with his obsidian eyes until she wanted to scream in his face just to get a reaction.

"Charlie Coltrain," he rasped and nodded his head once in greeting.

She returned his impartial nod. "Angelina Reyes."

"Coltrain?" the bound man exclaimed. "Hey, ain't you the one—"

"Shut up," Charlie snapped in a voice as cold and threatening as the northers blowing into Texas every winter.

The man shut up immediately, but Angelina opened her mouth to question Charlie. Before she could utter a word, he turned on her and asked harshly, "What are you doin' out here alone?"

"I-I'm not alone. Or at least I wasn't until this morning." She took a deep breath against the sudden flutter of panic overtaking her at the remembrance of that morning. "These three set upon my party and killed everyone but me. I'm sure I would have met the same fate as well if you hadn't happened along. I must thank you, Mr. Coltrain."

He shrugged. "I don't take to gettin' involved in other people's business, but I couldn't go by and do nothin'." He nodded at the rise. "The rest of your folks up there?"

"Yes." Up to that moment she had been too concerned trying to save her own life to have a chance to mourn her friends' untimely deaths. Despite the warm Texas breeze, Angelina hugged herself against the sudden chill of her skin. A choked sob escaped her lips at the thought of the six murdered men and women at the top of the hill.

Charlie glanced at her with a frown. "You're not gonna fall apart on me now, Miss Reyes, are you? We've got to bury your people before nightfall or every wild animal in ten miles will be circlin' us."

Angelina nodded, knowing that what he said was true. Swallowing the tide of grief inside her, she took a deep breath and led the way up the hill.

The carnage that awaited them was worse than she had imagined. All six lay where they had fallen, in a malformed semicircle around the still burning wagon.

"Is there a shovel anywhere in this mess?" Charlie asked, showing no emotion at the blood and fire before them.

"I'll get it," she said quickly and walked around the wagon, needing to get away from the sight if only for a moment. Memories of what had occurred earlier in the day threatened to overwhelm her; the screams of the dying and the jeers of the godless men who had attacked her and the others rang in her ears. The acrid stench of smoke burned her nose, and she was grateful for it—grateful she didn't have to smell the blood and the death.

Angelina spotted their supplies still in a heap, where the murderers had thrown them before setting the wagon on fire. She went down on her knees next to them. For just a moment she gave in to the terror that she had kept at bay for the past few hours in order to save her life. Tears ran in hot streams down her cheeks as she cried silently.

"Got a problem back there?" her rescuer asked.

Angelina hurriedly wiped away her tears and sniffed back the remnants of her sadness. She did not wish to share her grief with a stranger, especially one who had not even flinched at the carnage on the other side of the wagon. "No," she called, pleased her voice sounded so strong and even. "I'm fine. I'll be right there."

Closing her eyes, she uttered a short prayer for strength. Her friends deserved to be buried in the best way she could manage. As Mr. Coltrain had said, she could not fall apart now. She stood slowly, conscious of the aches and bruises covering her body from the rough treatment of her attackers. Angelina took a deep breath and pushed the pain from her mind to reside with the terror she had no time for now. Bending to tug the shovel free of the pile of supplies, she noticed her headpiece on the ground nearby, tossed aside in the midst of her struggles.

After freeing the shovel, she leaned over and picked up the scrap of cloth, placing it back on her head and securing it as best she could. Her torn bodice presented another problem. She could not continue to hold the material closed, and all her clothes and those of her friends had been burned with the wagon. Angelina shrugged and reached under her black skirt. With quick and efficient movements she removed a petticoat and tied the undergarment around her shoulders to resemble a shawl. Not exactly the height of fashion, but more modest than a gaping bodice.

Angelina returned to find Coltrain gazing at the bodies now lined up in a row for burial. He shook his head in disbelief.

"Two priests and four nuns," he muttered as if to himself, staring all the while at the people at his feet.

"Is there a problem?" Angelina asked.

Slowly he raised his gaze to her face; then his eyes focused on the material covering her hair, and his frown deepened.

"What the hell is that?" Charlie growled, realizing that Angelina was a nun. He shook his head and struggled with the first threat of laughter to come his way in years.

The sweet young girl—who had the curves of a courtesan, eyes and hair the color of the earth beneath his feet and skin like the finest cream—was a damned nun.

She stared at him now with a mixture of fear and wary trust he had already begun to hate. He was no hero—just a man in the wrong place at the right time, as usual. But he was no monster either. She didn't need to cringe every time he made a fast move in her direction, though seeing the carnage she had lived through already, he understood her fear.

"Why didn't you tell me?" he asked, pointing at the cloth covering her luxurious brown hair.

"Tell you what?"

"That you're a nun, Miss Reyes. Or should I call you Sister Angelina."

"I am not a nun, at least not yet. I'm merely a postulate. I've been with the sisters for only a year."

Charlie shrugged. Nun or nun-to-be, it was all the same to him. Either way, he needed to get rid of her and get back to work. He had headed out from the cattle drive to check into the smoke on the rise. He had not planned on shooting two men and burying six people before returning to the herd.

The job was the first honest work he'd had since leaving Mosby's command in '65, ten years earlier; he didn't plan to lose it after only one week on the trail. He was too old to continue on the path he'd followed since the war. What had once been a way of life he felt justified following to gain his revenge now haunted him during his dark, lonely nights. But did he have what it took to live the straight life?

Charlie grabbed the shovel from Angelina and went to work. By the time he finished burying the dead and Angelina finished mumbling and kneeling next to the mass grave, the sun had disappeared below the horizon and darkness settled softly over the land.

"Can you ride?" Charlie wiped the sweat from his brow with the back of his hand.

She nodded. "I was brought up on a horse ranch just outside the city of Chihuahua. I rode before I could walk."

"Good. We'll have to ride tonight. I'll take you to the nearest village and then head on back to the drive I left." He turned away to round up the horses.

Her soft voice drifted to him on the warm April wind and he halted. "Please," she whispered. "Help me."

Charlie glanced over his shoulder with a frown. So far she had impressed him with her strength in the face of hellish trouble. Now she sounded so much like a frightened little girl, he winced. He had no use for whining, clinging women. "I am helpin' you," he said and turned away from her pleading gaze. "I'll get you to a town. You can get in touch with your family or your convent from there."

"No. Please," she said again and moved closer, stopping just behind him.

His shoulders itched, and he shifted irritably. She stood too close to his back. He should ride away and leave her where she stood. Her soft pleas twisted his stomach and reminded him of the guilt that had been his constant companion for too many years. Things were much easier before he gained a conscience.

A light, insistent touch on his shoulder startled Charlie from his thoughts. His entire body stiffened at the contact, every muscle tightening in readiness at the sudden visions of past horrors. Charlie spun around and grabbed Angelina's wrist, then yanked her against him. She cried out in fear. Her heart beat against his chest like the wings of a tiny captured bird.

"I don't like to be touched without warning," he growled, angry at himself and at her for making him reveal his weakness.

He released her abruptly. She stumbled back, and he cursed himself for the inner terrors that made him who he was.

"I-I'm sorry," Angelina stuttered.

"Don't be, Sister." He rubbed his forehead, searching for a way to erase the sudden ache in its center.

"I'm not a Sister," she said sharply.

"Right. I forgot. What did you want?"

"Ah, I—"

"Come on. Out with it. I've got to get a move on."

Chewing her lower lip in consternation, Angelina hesitated for another moment. Then the words started tumbling from her mouth in a rush. "I want you to take me to the Sisters in Corpus Christi. They need me there as quickly as possible. They're sick with fever. When we were attacked, we were on our way back from nursing another order of Sisters in the north. Now I'm the only one left with the Sisters of the Incarnate Word and Blessed Sacrament who has the required nursing skills. They could all die without me."

"You heard what I said." He shook his head. "I have to get back to the cattle drive. I need that money."

"I can pay you," she said in the same rushed tone. "I'll pay you twice what they would."

Charlie hesitated, wondering where a nun would get such money.

"Three times," she blurted.

"You'll pay me three times what I'm getting to work on a three-month drive to take you to the coast?" Charlie asked skeptically. "Where would you get the money? I thought you nuns took vows of poverty—among others."

"I'm not a nun yet. My family can pay. I'll have them send the money anywhere you ask once we reach the convent."

Charlie turned and walked over to his horse. As he stroked the animal's neck, he thought about her offer. He figured he would have to sign on for at least two drives, and add that pay to what was left of the money he'd saved from the days thieving with the Coltrain Gang in Missouri, to afford the ranch he had always dreamed of. If he took Angelina's offer, he could have his dream before winter with money to spare.

But he had not gotten to the age of 37 in his profession without smelling trouble a mile off. Angelina Reyes was trouble.

She needed him. Lord, how he hated to be needed. The last woman who had needed him ended up dead.

Montana beckoned. Peace, quiet, his own place to be alone with the ghosts of a lifetime.

Charlie sighed. Hell, he was an old outlaw and she was a young nun. What could happen?

"All right," he said. "I'll take you."

And hope to God I don't regret it.

Drew Winston stood before Horatio Jones, Headquarters Officer for the Texas Rangers.

"Capt. Winston, I realize you feel responsible for the engineer's death. But no one suspected those thieves would travel away from Dallas to continue their robberies. I can't spare an entire detachment of men to chase after an outlaw who has surely by now reached Mexico, where we can't touch him."

"He hasn't gone to Mexico, sir. At least not yet. I have it on good authority he joined a cattle drive out of San Antonio, headed to New Mexico on the Goodnight-Loving Trail. Give me a week. I'll catch him. I swear."

The captain sighed. "I sense there's something more to this than you're telling me, Captain. I hear you've been out for this man's blood since you came to Texas. But the Texas Rangers are not here to fight personal battles. We're in the business of law enforcement."

Drew ground his teeth in frustration. "I realize that, Captain. This man killed a civilian on my assignment. I want him found and I want justice. That's all."

"Hmm." Jones eyed him with suspicion. "Regardless, I can't spare a detachment right now."

Drew hesitated, trying to think of some way to get the officer to agree to his terms. No two-bit outlaw years past his prime was going to continue to elude him. He had wasted valuable time tracking the man to Texas. Once there he'd found it nearly impossible to learn the whereabouts of a single human being in the vastness of the state. Once the Texas Rangers were reinstated in 1874 after being disbanded in 1871 due to lack of funds, he'd joined up and made use of their law enforcement system to search out his quarry. Now that he'd finally found the outlaw, the same system was getting in his way. But Drew Winston would get his man. No matter what he had to do.

"Sir, I respectfully request permission for a two-week leave."

Jones narrowed his eyes and stared at Drew so long and hard that Drew had to stifle the urge to look away. Finally, the officer gave a short nod.

"All right. I can see I'll get no decent amount of work out of you until this is settled. I'll send your men out on patrol with your second-in-command. Just do the job and get the hell back here."

"Yes, sir." Drew turned away, barely able to contain his sigh of relief.

Shutting the door of the office behind him, Drew pulled a crumpled piece of paper from his pocket.

"Wanted. Dead or alive," he read aloud. "For robbery and murder."

Drew stared at the picture he held in his hands. He would get this guy one way or another. Even if the outlaw spooked and skipped over the Rio Grande to Mexico, Drew would be right on his tail. Since he was officially on leave, he didn't have to obey Ranger policy and stay on the Texas side of the river. He could follow the same course as any citizen. And a dead-or-alive bounty knew no boundaries.

Drew's gaze flicked down to the name printed below the sketch, a name that whispered through his dreams every night. The name of the man who had burned his home and murdered his fiancee.

Charlie Coltrain.

Chapter Two

"Please. I can't sleep here." Disgust laced Angelina's voice.

Charlie also heard a hint of panic that hadn't been there before. She had been unusually calm in the face of such events, and he expected a breakdown at any moment. Looked as if the time had arrived.

"Why not here?" He looked around. The hill was a good place for a camp, the slightly elevated position giving them a better view of the surrounding area. Not too far out of San Antonio, they stood in the midst of hill country—plenty of thick grass, green trees and rolling hills. He'd passed through other parts of Texas on his way down from Missouri, and this area was definitely the best looking. Nope, he couldn't find fault with the view. Charlie sniffed the air and frowned. Smoke from the smouldering wagon could be a problem, but since the thing had been on fire for hours and hadn't attracted any attention, he figured they would be safe for the night.

"I can't sleep on the same ground where my friends died. This earth is soaked in their blood. I-I've got to get away from here."

Charlie sighed and rubbed his eyes. He hadn't thought of that. He had slept on blood-soaked earth so many times in his life such things no longer mattered to him. But he could see where the woman might have a problem with it.

He squinted into the increasing darkness. Good night vision had always served him well, especially during his years as one of Mosby's Rangers, then later as an outlaw leader. But he wasn't a youngster anymore, and he couldn't depend on his physical talents to last him forever.

"There," Charlie said and pointed. About a quarter mile away another ridge loomed, as easily defensible as the one they were on, with the added bonus of being away from the smoking remains of the wagon.

She nodded and flashed him a grateful half smile. She bent to gather their supplies together. Her movements were hampered when her makeshift shawl loosened and she had to readjust the petticoat around her shoulders.

"Interestin' shawl you've got there. Maybe you ought to change clothes before we move on," Charlie said.

Angelina stiffened at his reference to her undergarment, then slowly straightened. Without turning, she answered him. "I'm afraid items so unimportant as religious habits weren't removed before those men set the wagon on fire." She reached up a slim, elegant hand and touched the ridiculous scrap of material covering her hair. "As a postulate I am required to wear a veil only to attend chapel, but I brought this one along so I would have some protection against the sun. As for clothing, I'll have to make do with what I have. Perhaps if you have a needle and thread, I can repair the damage to my dress once we make camp."

"Maybe so," Charlie said gruffly, irritated at himself without knowing why. What was it about this woman that had him more on edge than he'd been in years?

"Listen, Sister, don't you want to cry or somethin'?" Charlie asked, reverting back to his earlier concern.

She glanced at him over her shoulder with a frown. "Why would I want to do that?"

"Well, most women would be cryin' and carryin' on for hours after somethin' like this. You just keep on goin'."

Her face took on an expression of serenity. "Crying and carrying on won't bring them back. They would, however, prevent me from doing what I have to do. God tells us to trust Him in all things. I have to trust that His hand guided what happened today for reasons of His own."

Charlie snorted and nodded at the fresh grave. "What reason could He have for this?"

"His reasons are not for us to know."

She sounded so certain, so at peace, so calm that Charlie almost envied her. Then he frowned darkly at his thoughts.

Envying a nun. Hell and damnation. What next?

Charlie turned and strode toward the horses, leaving her to gather the remaining supplies. After choosing the best horse for Angelina from the assortment of outlaw and church animals, Charlie divided what meager supplies remained from the wagon between that horse and his own.

With a smack on their rumps, the rest of the animals ran off into the gathering darkness.

The bound outlaw screamed obscenities as they left. Charlie flinched at some of the more colorful words, wondering if he should have shot the man after all. However, a glance at his companion revealed an unruffled profile. If she wasn't embarrassed, he certainly had no reason to be. Soon the voice faded into the moonlit night.

Charlie was glad to see she hadn't lied about riding well, though the true test would come the following day when they had to ride long hours in the hot sun.

When they reached the ridge and made camp, she helped without complaint and proved to be a good cook over an open fire.

He watched her as she tidied the remains of their meal, then poured them each a cup of coffee. She moved with an uncommon grace that intrigued him, heavy skirts swirling in a tantalizing hide-and-seek pattern around her ankles. Her hair, if allowed to flow free from that ridiculous nun's hat, would reflect copper highlights in the glow from the fire. Her eyes were lovely—warm and expressive in her small, heart-shaped face. Her skin, the color of honey, reflected a heritage of criollo ancestors—the Spanish aristocracy born in Mexico.

She stopped in front of him, a mug of steaming coffee in each hand. Holding his out, she leaned forward slightly to offer it to him. As she did so, her torn dress, twisted shut with her petticoat into a haphazard knot, slowly unraveled. Ignoring the cup she held out to him, Charlie watched the slow-motion tumble of the stark black-and-white cloth.

She remained motionless, almost as if she could stop the inevitable if she were only still enough. But she lost the battle. The bodice gaped open to reveal a plain cotton chemise, also slightly torn, but not nearly as much as the dress.

Charlie caught his breath. She wore no corset. A smart idea in the spring heat of Texas, especially with the heavy black dress and petticoats she wore. But was the lack a normal practice for a would-be nun? Her breasts were well developed, straining against the worn cloth that bound them. Definitely not the body of the child he considered her to be.

His gaze flicked up to hers, and she met it calmly with a hint of irritation in her eyes. He had to give her credit. She could have dumped the hot coffee in his lap and clutched her dress together like the outraged nun she aspired to become. Instead, she stared him straight in the eye and made him feel as though he needed his knuckles, or something else, rapped with a ruler. Her spirit had taken quite a knock during the events of the day, but he could see it coming back with a vengeance as she became more at ease.

"Mr. Coltrain, you've agreed to take me to Corpus Christi. For pay, I might add. That makes you my employee. I expect you to treat me with respect."

He took the coffee from her hand, accidentally brushing her fingers with his own. The slight contact tingled long after their flesh no longer touched. He frowned, wondering what on earth ailed him. Never in his long history with women had he been this jumpy.

"You can't blame a man for admirin' beauty, Miss Reyes. If you don't want me to look, you'll have to do somethin' about that dress."

She spun away, her skirts twirling a punctuation to her anger. Retreating to the other side of the fire, she sat down and sipped her coffee before answering.

"I'll need a needle and thread, Mr. Coltrain."

"Charlie."

She raised her eyebrows in question.

"If we're goin' to be travelin' together you may as well call me Charlie. Never answered to nothin' else. At least nothin' I could repeat for your ears, Miss Reyes."

"Very well. You may call me Angelina."

"Sister Angelina?"

"No. Just Angelina will be fine."

"You know, somethin's been botherin' me about you."

She glanced up, startled. But he had to admire her. Her voice didn't reflect anything when she asked, "What could be bothering you?"

"You're from Mexico, obviously Mexican, though I can see you're not a peasant. Still, I'm wonderin' why you speak English so good, better 'n me and hardly any accent."

Angelina took another sip of coffee before answering. "My father insisted all his children learn English and speak the language fluently. He brought in a special tutor for just that purpose. We only speak English at our home."

"Why?"

"He has visions of grandeur, my father. He wants to be a great man in Chihuahua—the greatest. He knows the United States is powerful." She shrugged. "He plans ahead. Now"—her tone turned brisk; she obviously had had enough discussion on her family—"if I could borrow that needle and thread, I'll take care of the problem with my dress."

"That brings me to another problem, Angelina," Charlie said, enjoying the sound of her name on his lips. "I don't have any."

"You don't have a needle and thread," she repeated incredulously. "How can you travel without them? What if you tear your clothes?"

"Well, I've never been good at mending. So I usually have a friend take care of such things for me."

Her brow creased. "A friend? I don't understand why a friend would do your sewing for you."

Charlie almost smiled at her innocence. "Not just any friend. My lady friends seem to enjoy doin' that sort of thing for me."

"Oh." She ducked her head and took a quick sip of coffee. Charlie was sure a blush graced her cheeks. "I see. Well, that is a problem then."

"I have an extra shirt, and you should probably put on a pair of Levi's as long as you're changin' clothes. You'll be able to ride easier. They'll be too big, but I can rig somethin' up till we get to the next town and buy you somethin' to wear. That should be tomorrow if I figure right."

Angelina sipped her coffee and stared into the flames. He could see her struggling to make a decision. Finally her lips tightened with resolve. "I'm sure the Sisters would consider me scandalous to wear men's clothing, but I don't see any choice. At least until we reach a town and remedy the situation. Besides, I've been told a nun needs to be pragmatic. So I'll accept your offer, Charlie, and thank you for it."

Charlie nodded shortly and got to his feet.

Tossing the remains of his coffee into the fire, he went to his pack. He returned to the fire a few moments later and handed her the clothing along with a piece of rope.

"To hold up the pants," he said in response to her puzzled look. He nodded to the horses, who grazed nearby. "You can change in peace behind them if you want."

Her grateful smile knotted his stomach. What was it about this woman that made him want to grind his teeth in frustration? Perhaps her innocence and trust, which contrasted so sharply with his own guilty soul and suspicious nature. She got under his skin and stuck there like a burr beneath a saddle.

He turned away and strode to the other side of the fire. Throwing himself down on the ground, he stared into the flames. He'd been without a woman just too damn long. Charlie looked up. Angelina stood outlined in the flickering light for several moments. He was half afraid she'd join him and ask what was wrong. Instead, she surprised him with another question.

"Your voice," she said softly. He tensed, already knowing the question that would follow. "What happened?"

Charlie sighed and rubbed his throat, torn between telling the truth and risking the return of nightmares he had long tried to bury or cooly informing her that his voice was none of her business. The latter worked with most curiosity seekers, but he didn't think Angelina had asked for curiosity's sake.

"Took a rifle butt in the throat during the war," he said, struggling against the wash of hate that always engulfed him when he remembered the long-ago agony. "Damn Yankee must have broke somethin' inside. I've talked like this ever since."

Angelina didn't prattle the usual response that he was lucky to be alive with the use of all his limbs. Instead, she stared at him through the flickering flames for a long moment, then closed her eyes. Her face became calm and serene.

He sucked in a breath through his teeth in realization. She was praying for him.

Too late, he thought. Poor kid, you're too late to save this man's soul.

Finally she opened her eyes and smiled sweetly. Charlie's heart turned over at the innocence and trust on her face. Then she turned away and disappeared into the darkness.

Charlie looked up at the stars and let out a long, strained breath.

He was too old for this.

The sun shimmered directly above, dancing on Angelina's head with the ferocity of a mountain lion. Charlie didn't possess an extra hat. He had gallantly offered his, but when she had put the hat on her head it had fallen down over her eyes. As a result, she was forced to wear her veil. Designed for deference in chapel, the material provided little protection against the sun.

They traveled all morning in near silence, Charlie answering her every attempt at conversation with a growl. His voice being what it was, the guttural rumbles sounded exceptionally fierce, and she eventually lapsed into confused silence.

The only men she had any experience with were family members or priests. Those relationships had not equipped her to handle a man like Charlie Coltrain. Though he had been nothing but kind to her, his size, his voice, his outright virility frightened her. But after spending 20 years with six older brothers and a bully for a father, she would not allow fear to get the better of her. Instead, she masked her emotions with the calm piety she had learned at her mother's knee. Turning to God in times of strife had never failed her, and she had no doubt she could continue to rely on Him in all things.

Angelina glanced over at Charlie. He was staring at a nearby outcropping of rock with intense interest. Squinting against the sun's glare, she studied the rock formation. Seeing nothing, she turned back to Charlie with a question on her tongue.

Without warning, he suddenly launched himself from his horse. He knocked her to the ground and covered her body with his own. Seconds later, a gunshot rang out, and a bullet ploughed into the dirt near their heads.

Charlie reached up and grabbed the trailing reins of her horse, his mount having continued on down the trail after Charlie had jumped from his back. He yanked on the reins, and to Angelina's amazement, the animal obediently lay down on the ground in front of them. She thanked God they had brought one of the outlaw's horses, which obviously knew how to behave in a gunfight.

"Stay here, behind the horse," Charlie hissed. "Keep your head down."

Without waiting for her answer, he rolled away, over and over through the dirt, firing his gun in quick succession at the outcropping of rock. He was totally exposed to whoever had shot at them. It was only a matter of time and bullets before he was hit.

Charlie stopped rolling and lay still. Had he been shot? Angelina's throat ached with tension, and she stared at him, her gaze frantically searching for some movement, some sign of life. Other than the first shot, she hadn't heard any further gunshots fired from behind the rock. But maybe she had missed the sound in the explosion of bullets from Charlie's gun.

"Charlie?" she called and her voice shook.

No answer.

All her attention focused on his still form. She had to get to him. To make sure he was all right. To help him if he wasn't.

Without a care for her own safety, she jumped up and ran across the hard ground that separated them. He lay so still, her heart thumped hard and painfully at the wall of her chest. Her breath rasped loudly in the alarming silence.

Bending down, she reached out and clasped his shoulder. Not a second later, her back slammed into the dirt. Charlie's large, hard hands pinned her wrists to the ground next to her head, and his face hovered only inches from hers.

Angelina flinched at the anger in his black eyes. She had forgotten that she was never to touch him suddenly. Her mistake.

"Didn't I tell you to stay put?" he asked, his broken voice absurdly loud and threatening in the glittering afternoon sunlight.

"You didn't answer when I called you. I thought you were hurt." She took a deep breath. "Praise God, you're not."

"I'm fine. If he was alive and I'd answered you, he would have shot me. I didn't think you'd come runnin' over here." He frowned at her, an expression she was coming to dread, and squeezed her wrists a bit for emphasis. Angelina winced. Charlie glanced toward the rocks. "I must have hit him right away, or we'd both be full of holes lying out here like lame buffalo."

Angelina waited, but he made no move to get up. His weight pressed on her, heavy though not altogether unpleasant. Her brothers had often pinned her to the ground when she'd been a child, then spit in her face. She'd detested that. They had known it and, as a result, had pinned her down as often as they could. Somehow, the weight of Charlie's body did not make her want to buck and kick and scream for freedom as she had all those years ago in Mexico. She felt something else entirely—a tugging warmth deep inside, though her skin tingled with a sheen of cool sweat. Maybe she was coming down with fever herself?

Angelina looked at Charlie and raised her eyebrows, tugging a bit at her wrists. He stared at her. His gaze wandered over her face and settled on her lips. Suddenly her mouth seemed too dry. She licked her lips, then flinched at his harsh intake of breath.

What was the matter with him? Had he taken a knock on the head when he'd rolled through the dirt?

She shifted beneath his weight. Startled at the sound of his groan, she exclaimed, "Charlie, are you hurt?"

Without replying he suddenly rolled to the side and got up, yanking her to her feet. When he let go, her legs were unsteady, and she reached out a hand for support. But Charlie had already turned away and strode toward the outcropping of rock. Angelina stumbled a bit, then recovered her balance.

"Wait," she cried and ran after him.

He paused, but did not turn toward her. When she caught up to him he had just reloaded his gun, his obvious ease with the weapon a welcome sight.

Together they approached the rocks. He motioned for her to remain behind him, then crept around the corner. Almost immediately he straightened up, and the taut readiness eased from his body. Looking over his shoulder, he nodded for her to join him.

A man lay on the ground, a gun still clutched in his fingers. His lifeless eyes stared up at the intense blue sky.

"Do you know him?" Angelina whispered.

Charlie uncocked his gun and returned it to his holster. "Can't say that I do from this angle. Doesn't mean he didn't know me."

"What do you mean by that?"

Charlie ignored her, walking over to calmly rifle through the dead man's pockets.

"Nothin'," Charlie said in irritation.

"What are you looking for?"

"Somethin' that might tell me why he shot at us."

"Robbery?" Angelina suggested.

"Doubt it. These days thieves rob trains and stages. Banks if they're real brave. More money for their trouble. Don't pay to wait on deserted trails, hopin' someone might come by. When someone does, he's most likely as poor as the thief." Charlie stared at the dead man again, then shook his head in disgust. "No, he was after me. Just wish I knew why."

A sudden thought came to Angelina, and she stared at him long and hard before voicing it.

"Are you wanted, Charlie?" she asked uneasily.

His gaze swung back to her. She wanted to back away from the cold emptiness in his black eyes. Her mind ran rampant with suspicions. What did she know about him? He had saved her life, but that was no assurance he didn't have his own designs on her. Especially since she had told him her family had enough money to pay him for helping her. He could easily kidnap her and hold her for ransom. If he did, by the time she got to the Sisters in Corpus Christi, they might all be dead of the fever.

Angelina stared into Charlie's eyes without flinching. She would not let that happen—not if she could help it. She wanted an answer and she would have one.

"Well," she said, "are you wanted?"

Charlie's mouth twitched, and Angelina's eyes widened in amazement as he began to laugh. The noise emanating from his mouth sounded more like coughing because of his damaged throat, but the expression on his face reflected his amusement.

"What's so funny?" she demanded, her fear of him forgotten in a sudden flash of anger.

"You asked me"—he paused to catch his breath, chuckling a few more times as though he couldn't help himself—"you asked me if I was wanted."

"I did. And I'd like an answer. I don't see anything funny about it."

"Well, Sister, I've been wanted and I've been wanted. If you're talkin' about women that's one thing. If you're talkin' about the law then that's another."

"You know very well I'm not asking about women," Angelina said, her face flaming.

Seeing her discomfort, Charlie looked as though he might start laughing again. Her angry scowl appeared to give him pause. He swallowed deeply and cleared his throat.

"Yeah, I've been wanted by the law. But not lately. I haven't done nothin' in the past five years that would make a stranger take a shot at me. Hell, I've been hidin' out in San Antonio so long I figured most lawmen up and forgot I was alive."

Angelina's face, which had only a moment before been flooded with heat, suddenly felt as drawn and cold as a winter sky. "What have you done?" she asked in horror.

"I told you," Charlie repeated, his voice tight with irritation. "Nothin' lately. Now let's get on to the next town and find out what's goin' on."

"After we bury this man, of course."

"What?" Charlie looked at her in amazement.

"We can't just leave him here."

"Why not? Sister, I can tell you for sure he wouldn't have buried us."

"Nevertheless, we must bury him."

"No." Charlie turned and walked away.

"What do you mean no?" she said to his retreating back.

He stopped, turning slightly to address her. "I mean just that. I only buried the two yesterday 'cause I didn't want animals hoverin' around our camp. I will not break my back buryin' a man who just tried to kill me. You can preach, and pray and prophecy at me all you want, Sister, but I ain't gonna do it, no how." He resumed his purposeful stride in the opposite direction from her.

Angelina stared after Charlie for a moment, then hurried to catch up with him. She reached out to grab his sleeve, then remembered what had happened the last two times she'd touched him without warning. Instead, she ran until she was directly in his path and stopped. She gazed up into his face, his criminally beautiful face, and all her doubts returned. What on earth was she going to do? She was out in the middle of nowhere with a man who admitted to being wanted by the law several times in his life. She remembered a lot of the outlaws from the states often hid out in Texas. For all she knew, he could be Jesse James. She forgot about the murderous stranger who needed to be buried as her fear of the man in front of her returned full force.

"Who are you?" she asked.

His brow creased in confusion. "Have you had too much sun, Angelina? We've got to get you a hat in town. I told you. Charlie. Remember? Charlie Coltrain."

He spoke slowly, as though she were an addled child. Angelina's fear gave way to fury. She had trusted him, prayed for him, believed in him. She deserved the truth.

"I know what you said your name was. But are you telling the truth? For all I know you could have been another member of that gang of men who attacked our wagon." Angelina caught her breath as a memory arose unbidden. "Come to think of it, that last man knew you."

She started to retreat, her gaze darting around the open area for a place to hide.

"No, you don't." Charlie reached for her. In one fluid motion, he grabbed her and yanked her to him. She struggled, kicking and hitting, but he held her easily. She could never match his strength, so she gave up the attempt and went still. Satisfied, he continued. "Angelina, listen to me. I admit I did a lot of things I'm not proud of. I had my reasons. I wasn't lyin' when I said I was on a cattle drive. I plan to buy a ranch in Montana. I just want to be left alone with my cattle and my horses. Is that too much to ask?"

Angelina tilted back her head and searched his eyes for the truth. Usually so cold, his black eyes appeared earnest. She stared into their dark depths, and sudden peace flooded her as he met her gaze without flinching.

"No," she said slowly as she continued to stare into his eyes. "That isn't too much to ask."

Often in the past, in times of stress, she had sought truth from a source deep within. Once again she drew on that source for guidance—and she knew Charlie did not lie. "Our Lord forgave Mary Magdalen. What you've done is between you and Him. I have no right to judge you."

Charlie let out a snort of laughter and released her. "Mary Magdalen. Well, I must say I've never been compared to someone of her persuasion before, though I've been acquainted with quite a few." He slanted his head to the side. "The Lord forgave her, you say? Well, then, maybe I have a chance at heaven after all."

"Don't blaspheme."

"Sister, you ain't heard nothin' yet," Charlie grumbled as he went to retrieve his horse.

Years of habit die hard. As they neared the outskirts of the small north Texas town, Charlie automatically stuffed his shoulder-length hair up under the crown of his hat. He couldn't count the times he'd been recognized because of the strange silver-gold shade of his hair. Life would have been a whole lot easier if he'd gotten rid of it. But once, long ago, he'd promised someone he loved he would never cut his hair. He'd broken a lot of promises in his life—this was one he could keep.

The town they entered was like hundreds of others on the Texas frontier, not really a town, though the people who lived there liked to think of it as such. Usually a name was applied to any gathering of a saloon, general store and stagecoach stop. A hunk of wood stuck into the ground on the outskirts of this particular gathering read Bakerstown, probably after some long-dead founder of the local whiskey mill.

A few people came out of the buildings lining the dusty trail that served as a main street and watched their approach. From beneath the wide brim of his hat, Charlie observed everyone and everything in sight. He was on edge, though his tension didn't show. Being shot at for the first time in five years had brought back all his latent survival skills full force. The years he had served with Mosby's Rangers during the war had trained him well in guerilla fighting, and he'd honed those skills later with his own gang in Missouri. Remaining calm at all times and never trusting anyone had kept him alive in many tight situations.

They stopped in front of a small general store and Charlie dismounted. He moved to help Angelina from her horse. She had taken off her nun hat, as he had come to think of it, which was probably a good idea. The odd combination of men's clothes and a nun's veil would surely draw attention he didn't want. Depending on what he found here, he wouldn't want either of them to be remembered later should anyone come asking.

Angelina slid from her horse without his assistance, and together they entered the small store.

Inside, Charlie blinked quickly to adjust his eyes to the dimness. One hand rested on his gun; the other hovered near Angelina's arm just in case he had to yank her from harm's way and shoot a path out the door. As his eyes focused, he sighed in relief. The store was empty.

"Ahem."

Charlie turned quickly. One of the men who had come out to observe their approach stood in the doorway.

"You folks lookin' to buy?" the man asked and slid behind the counter with a wary look at Charlie's loaded Colts.

"Yes, sir," Charlie said, coughing to disguise his voice. Next to his hair, his voice gave him away too easily. He took Angelina by the arm and, with a smile at the store owner, drew her aside to whisper in her ear.

"Buy a hat and whatever we need for food." He shoved some money into her hand. "You'll have to wait to get some other clothes. I don't want to hang around anywhere until I know why we were shot at."

Angelina nodded and went to deal with the owner. Charlie wandered around the store, wondering how they could get the information they needed without revealing too much. Several yellowed pieces of paper tacked to the wall near the back caught his attention. One sheet was still uncreased, not yet torn. Charlie moved nearer to read it.

"Hellfire," he muttered.

Wanted Dead or Alive
Charlie Coltrain
For Train Robbery and Murder
Outside Dallas, Texas on April 1, 1875
Bounty of One Thousand Dollars

Charlie didn't need to read anymore. A quick glance toward the front of the room showed the store owner still occupied with Angelina. Charlie yanked the poster from the wall and stuffed the paper inside his shirt. While his mind raced, he continued to peruse the other wanted posters as though nothing had happened.

April first? The cattle drive had left San Antonio on April twenty-eighth. On the first he had been in town waiting to leave. He could have robbed a train outside of Dallas and made it to San Antonio by the twenty-eighth. But he hadn't.

The problem was, someone had. And that someone must have looked and acted enough like him so that a dead-or-alive bounty had been issued in his name. Not that such a bounty was a new experience for him, but he'd at least done something those other times to warrant the treatment.

Her shopping completed, Angelina beckoned to Charlie. They carried the purchases outside and tied them on the horses. The store owner watched closely, but did not act as though he were suspicious. Charlie pulled the brim of his hat lower over his eyes. As long as he kept his hair covered and his mouth shut, he might get out of town alive.

"Where you folks headed?"

The man had followed them outside and looked at Charlie expectantly. Charlie smiled and shrugged, glancing at Angelina.

Her brow creased in confusion, but she answered the man. "Corpus Christi."

"You from there?"

"Yes . . . uh . . . no. I mean . . . I am."

"Oh, you visiting family then?"

Charlie coughed again and muttered, "Yeah."

The store owner smiled. "Wife's family, huh? Well, I don't envy you." He shook Charlie's hand. "Have a good trip and keep an eye out. There's supposed to be a murderer on the loose in these parts. Been so many bounty hunters through here lately you'd think it was a train station. You watch the missus, you hear? Right smart idea havin' her dress like a man. Up close you can see she's a woman, but from afar you'll be safer that way."

Charlie nodded and got on his horse. To his relief, Angelina remained silent and allowed them to get out of town before she started asking questions.

"What on earth came over you?" she demanded.

He shrugged, wondering how much he should tell her. She had been frightened of him after she learned he'd been wanted in the past. What would she think if she saw the wanted poster? For murder, no less. Then again, maybe he should show it to her and scare her off. She was in danger because of him. Maybe he should send her back to town to wait for the next stage. Still, traveling with her was a good cover. The store owner had believed them to be man and wife. Others would think the same.

"Charlie?" Angelina broke into his thoughts. "Why wouldn't you talk to that man back there? Did you find out why we were shot at?"

Charlie sighed. She had to know. Slowly he reached inside his shirt and withdrew the wanted poster. He reined his horse to a halt. Angelina did the same and he handed her the paper.

Her eyes widened as she read the words.

"What is this?" she asked.

"You can see what it is, Angelina. I'm wanted—dead or alive—for murder and train robbery. With that kind of reward, every bounty hunter and lawman in this state and a few others will be after me." He looked behind them, squinting against the late afternoon sun to see if they were being followed.

"But you didn't do it."

He jerked his head back in her direction so fast his neck creaked in protest. "What?"

"You didn't do this. You wouldn't."

"What makes you think that?" he asked, dumbfounded at her certainty.

"You're a good man inside. You saved me, twice in two days. An evil man wouldn't have troubled himself."

"Angelina," he said, then drew a deep breath, uncertain of how to deal with such unwarranted faith in him. God, she was so young. "I've robbed and I've killed in my life. I admit, this time I didn't do it. That doesn't mean I haven't done it before."

"I told you, what you've done in the past is between you and God. It's what you do from now on that matters."

"I could go back to bein' what I was. Easy. I've only had an honest job for a week, and I'm already wanted again. May as well go back to robbin'. The pay is better, the work is easier and I'm damn good at it."

"But you won't," she assured him serenely.

"Quit sayin' that!" he shouted, losing his temper for the first time in years.

"Why? I'm only telling the truth."

"You don't know anything about me. I've done whatever I pleased all my life and damn the consequences. It's just been luck and skill that's kept me from hangin'. You should be runnin' back to that town as fast as you can. Get away from me, Sister. I'm nothin' but trouble."

Incredibly, she smiled. His jaw tightened as it did whenever she looked at him in just that way. He'd only been with her a few days and already his mouth ached. If he had to save a woman, why did it have to be the one woman in the world who could drive him to the point of insanity?

"Let's go, Charlie," she urged. "The Sisters need me. Once I get there, you can go to the sheriff and explain you weren't the one who robbed that train."

"Right. And he'll believe me. You've obviously never had any dealings with my side of the law, Angelina. With a dead-or-alive bounty of one thousand dollars, I'll be shot long before I get near any sheriff."

She opened her mouth to argue, but he continued right over her protests. "Anyway, there's been a change of plans. Texas isn't healthy for me anymore. We're on our way to Mexico, Sister."

Charlie couldn't help but smile in satisfaction as Angelina at last fell silent. For a would-be nun she was awful mouthy.

Chapter Three

Charlie had to be joking. Mexico? Angelina would not go back there. She had left her father's hacienda a year ago for the convent in Corpus Christi, vowing never to return. God had called her to the life she now led by showing her the golden angel in her dreams. She belonged with the church. She had chosen the church. In Mexico she was no more than chattel.

"No!" she shouted, startling herself with the force of her anger. "I won't go back there."

"What's wrong with you?"

"You said we were going to Mexico."

"I did. Nothin' wrong with your hearin', Sister."

"I'm paying you to take me to Corpus Christi. I must get to the convent. People need me there."

Charlie looked at her as if she'd lost her mind. "I'm wanted in Texas. Over the Rio Grande, the law can't follow me, though the bounty hunters won't be so particular. If I stay hid long enough, they'll eventually give up. Then I can come back, use a different name and find out what the hell is goin' on."

"I am not going to Mexico," she said slowly and clearly, fighting against the panic rising within her at the thought. "Not now and not ever again."

She kicked her horse into motion. Smiling inwardly at the look of surprise that flashed across Charlie's face, she left him and his mount in the dust.

Angelina let her horse have its head for several minutes. Then she risked a glance over her shoulder. Charlie wasn't following her. Instead, from what she could see, he seemed to have turned off the trail and headed west—toward the Rio Grande and Mexico.

She heaved a sigh of relief. If he had chosen to, he could have caught her easily with that massive white horse. The animal looked as though it had been bred for speed as well as stamina. Though obviously a glorious animal and the best of the crop from the outlaws who had attacked her, Charlie's mount would have outrun her horse without much effort.

At her command, the horse slowed to a more sedate pace. Angelina looked around her. Unfortunately they had been headed out of Bakerstown in the direction of Corpus Christi. To return to the town and take the stage, she would have to turn around and go toward Charlie. Though he had been riding west, she didn't trust him to keep heading that way.

Well, she would just have to travel on to the next town by herself. She was on a well-used trail, and she had most of the supplies. She could make it.

Angelina glanced uneasily at the darkening sky. She would have to make camp alone or risk continuing in the dark. She hoped there was an extra gun in the saddlebags. A repeat of yesterday's experience would not be welcome.

Before night fell completely Angelina slipped from her horse and hunted through the supplies. She discovered a lethal-looking pistol that must have belonged to one of the outlaws. Only two bullets remained. A thorough search of the bags revealed no more ammunition. Well, two would have to do. If her luck held out, she wouldn't need any.

The lengthening shadows made her nervous. If she made camp, she would have to stay up and keep watch anyway, so she decided to continue riding through the night in hope of reaching another town by morning. All she needed to do was stay on the trail so she wouldn't get lost. She should be able to cope with that.

A coyote howled in the distance, and her horse skittered nervously. The eerie sound seemed to emphasize her isolation. Patting her horse's neck, Angelina murmured nonsense to try to make them both feel better.

The night was cloudy with no visible stars and only a slight shaft of moonlight penetrating the murkiness. She gazed up at the sky a moment, then shivered at the chill pervading the air since the sun had disappeared.

"Amazing how dark the night can be when you're the only human within miles," she told the horse. The animal tossed its head as if in agreement and she continued, soothed by the sound of her own voice. "Amazing how the silence can press on you when the only sound is your own rapid breathing and the impatient snort of your horse."

Angelina had never been alone in her life for more than a few minutes at a time. She had been raised in a household with six brothers, not to mention the countless servants, and there had always been someone nearby. Once she escaped to the convent, even more people filled her life.

"To be perfectly honest," she told her companion, "and honesty is something I strive for, I find solitude highly overrated."

Clip-clop, clip-clop, the horse walked in a soothing rhythm. The muffled sound of hooves on the dirt trail lulled Angelina into a near sleep. She didn't know how long she dozed. Then suddenly she sat up straight, her heart pounding in fear.

Had she almost fallen from the horse? No. She still sat upright and secure in the saddle. If not a near fall, then what had awakened her?

Angelina listened intently, reassured by the steady clip-clop. Then she heard the sound. In the distance still, but coming ever closer—the heavy thud of galloping hooves.

How many? How close? Who?

Her mind shouted questions as her heart raced. She had heard Indians could tell the number and speed of approaching riders quickly by putting an ear to the ground and listening. She had no such ability. In fact, she had no knowledge whatsoever of how to survive alone. She bit down on her lower lip and fought against the panic. Oh, why on earth had she ever left Charlie?

Angelina looked around for somewhere to take cover, but could see nothing useful for hiding both herself and a horse. Remembering what Charlie had done when they were shot at that morning, she dismounted and led her horse into the grass. She hated to use it in such a manner, but the animal was the only cover available. Standing behind the horse, she shakily withdrew the pistol from her saddlebag. She uttered a short prayer that whoever was riding hard and fast on her tail was headed somewhere farther ahead and would pass by her without a glance. If she were very lucky, all this fear would be amusing in the morning.

The steady thud of hoofbeats drew so close she could barely distinguish between the pounding of her own heart and the beat of the hooves in staccato rhythm.

Suddenly a horse burst from the darkness; a rider crouched low over the mount's back, at one with the animal. The flying hooves appeared to soar above the ground, like the mythical beast Pegasus.

Angelina shrank back as they thundered near. She pointed the gun in their direction, though her hand shook so much she would never be able to hit anything if she needed to. Time slowed to a near standstill as the horse and rider came toward her—closer and closer. Her eyes watered with the strain of peering through the night. The image in front of her misted. Wavered. Then the hoofbeats were upon her. All the rider had to do was turn to the side to see her crouched behind the horse.

Instead, the apparition soared past her and raced down the trail without pausing in its mad flight. Angelina's knees buckled and she sank to the ground, expelling the breath she had held for far too long. She didn't know how long she sat in the gently waving grass, waiting while her heart returned to its normal rhythm. Finally she rose and leaned her forehead against her horse's neck, petting the sleek animal for reassurance.

"Thank You, God," she whispered and uncocked the pistol.

"You'd best thank me, Sister," a gravelly voice directly behind her ear said.

Angelina shrieked and spun around, bringing the gun up as she turned. Strong, callused fingers wrapped around her wrist. She flinched from the pressure and dropped the gun into a waiting hand.

Charlie let her go long enough to open the chamber on the gun and glance inside. "Are you crazy?" he growled. "This thing's loaded. You could have blown your fool head off. Or worse, you could have blown my fool head off. What are you doin' out here, Angelina?"

She couldn't answer; she could only shake her head helplessly. He was right. She could have killed both of them—she who had vowed not to hurt a living soul. She had to get back to the convent before she broke every tenet she held dear.

"Angelina?" Charlie's voice sounded at once confused and curious. He reached out and touched her face.

The contact of his warmth against her icy flesh soothed away the lingering fright. Instead of pulling away as she should have, she allowed him to brush his fingertips up and down her cheek.

Heaven and hell. Ice and fire. How could so many things be contained in one man's touch? Charlie was temptation in all forms, and she couldn't summon the strength to resist.

Angelina turned her head into the caress, suddenly aching for more of what she didn't understand. Charlie stepped closer, cupping the side of her face in his large palm. He was going to kiss her, and suddenly she wanted to be kissed more than she had ever wanted anything in her life. She tilted her chin upward.

"Damnation," Charlie swore and dropped his hand. He turned and strode a few feet away, stopping with his back to her.

"Charlie?" Angelina asked and stepped toward him.

"Don't," he rasped, his voice sounding more damaged than usual. "Just stay over there, Angelina. Just stay the hell away."

"Why?" she demanded, though she did as he said. "What have I done?"

"You haven't done anything. It's me. All me, as usual."

"I don't understand."

"No, you don't understand, and that's the problem. I know very well what I'm doin' and I shouldn't be doin' it. I'm old enough." He laughed ruefully. "Hell, I'm long past old enough to know better."

"You're not old," she said softly.

"What would you know about it? You're what? Eighteen?"

"Twenty. Though I don't see what age has to do with this."

"No, you wouldn't." Charlie sighed, then turned back toward her, his body rigid with tension. "We'll have to make a cold camp—no fire. I think whoever that was who rode past is long gone, but I'm not takin' any chances. I heard him comin' down the trail and got out of the way. Then I heard you rustlin' around over here. Lucky for you that guy was stirrin' up enough noise on his own and didn't hear yours. But if he was lookin' for me he could be back."

Angelina stared at him. Why was he acting as though nothing had happened?

"Why are you here, Charlie?"

He was silent for a moment; then he let out a breath that was halfway between a laugh and a snort and shook his head. "I don't know. I would have been a lot nearer the border by now, but I couldn't leave you on your own."

"Why?"

"I honestly don't know. I've never met a woman who was more trouble than you, Sister, and I'm not one to stick around where there's trouble. Tomorrow I'll take you to town and get you on a stage to Corpus Christi."

And though that pronouncement should have set Angelina's mind to rest about her future, she was only more confused at the sadness that washed over her.

Long after Angelina had fallen asleep, Charlie stared into the fire. Why on earth had he come after her?

She was pious. She was irritating. She was innocent.

Hell, she was just plain trouble.

He had to get rid of her tomorrow. For that one moment when he had touched her, and she had innocently responded, a sudden and surprising lust had almost killed his common sense. Where such feelings had come from he had no idea. If anyone had told Charlie the day before that he would be lusting after a child in a nun's habit, he would have shot that person on the spot.

Angelina truly wanted to be a nun. He could see the devotion in her eyes, hear it in her voice whenever she talked about the Sisters, the convent and God. He didn't understand that devotion, but he respected it. He would do nothing to destroy her dream.

His gaze was drawn back to her as she slept—so beautiful, so pure. He ached just looking at her. With all the things he had seen and done in his lifetime, his soul was so black he didn't deserve to breathe the same air as Angelina Reyes. Maybe that was at the root of his sudden and unreasoning attraction to her. Never in his life had he encountered someone so at peace with herself and her place on the earth. She fascinated him.

Charlie sighed and gazed up at the stars. His mind already overflowed with memories of deeds he must live with for the rest of his life; one in particular haunted him more than the others. It was that event, more an accident than a crime, which had set him on the path to Montana. Though he had a reputation as a dangerous outlaw, he had never killed anyone who hadn't needed killing. Until the stage accident. With that blight on his soul he did not need any more—especially one with the name Angelina Reyes, eternal innocent.

By the time the sun tinted the horizon pink and orange, Charlie had rousted Angelina from her makeshift bed, and they were back on the trail.

Midafternoon arrived before they reached a town. Blue Creek boasted more amenities than Bakerstown. A saloon with rooms for rent, a sheriff's office and a whorehouse all lined the main street, next to a large general store. They left their horses at the livery stable behind the saloon, and

Charlie walked Angelina to the store.

"Get a dress," he ordered gruffly. "You can't wear my clothes back to the convent. You'll give the good Sisters apoplexy."

Before she could answer, he strode away to search out stage departure times and purchase her a ticket. Since early that morning a familiar itch had tickled the back of his neck. That itch meant someone was on his tail. And whoever it was was getting closer. He needed to get Angelina out of the line of fire so he could think straight. Then he could hightail it to Mexico.

"Charlie Coltrain, as I live and breathe," a female voice declared.

Charlie froze. His hand went immediately for the gun at his hip. A thousand-dollar bounty could be collected by a woman as well as a man. Slowly he turned.

"Luanne." Charlie breathed a sigh of relief at the sight of the tall, buxom blonde leaning in the doorway of the whorehouse. He and Luanne went way back—all the way to their childhoods in Missouri. Luanne would never betray him.

She approached with a sliding grace all her own. "Honey, I thought you were long dead."

When she stopped only inches away, her cheap perfume invaded Charlie's senses. He coughed. Before he could recover, she wrapped her arms around his neck and kissed him hard and deep and long. Once, such a kiss would have been all the invitation he needed to yank Luanne into his arms and carry her up the stairs to whatever room was empty.

Once. But no more. And certainly not today. Ignoring her puzzled expression, he pulled away from Luanne.

The warning itch had returned, stronger this time, almost painful. He slapped the back of his neck. His skin stung with the impact—and something else. Charlie turned to stare down the street toward the general store.

No sign of Angelina. She must have gone inside. No one watched him, except for Luanne, who wisely kept silent, knowing him well enough to see he was on the alert.

Finally he turned back to her, though his neck burned fiercely.

"Honey, I've never seen you this jumpy. Can't say that I blame you though, what with that wanted poster tacked up all over town and that Yankee Ranger looking for you."

A familiar surge of hatred swirled through Charlie's gut. He ignored it, knowing he had to keep his emotions in control or risk making a deadly mistake. "Yankee?"

Luanne nodded. "Strange, isn't it? Thought all them Rangers was from Texas. But not this one. He was in here last night, askin' all sorts of questions. Knowin' how you feel about Yankees 'cause of your ma and all, I played real dumb. Since he couldn't get any information out of me, he left."

"No," Charlie said, "he didn't." Amazed at how quickly his neck ceased burning now that he knew the source of the irritation, Charlie grabbed Luanne's arm and hustled her inside. While he learned all she had to tell, he would feel better with his back to a wall and the door at his face.

"Honey, you don't have to drag me. You're welcome in my room. It's a little early for business hours, but I'm always willing to accommodate a friend."

"Not now, Luanne," Charlie said absently, then went behind the bar and helped himself to a glass of whiskey.

"Since you're pourin' cowboy cocktails, pour out another for me," Luanne ordered.

Charlie shrugged and did as he was asked. After picking up the two glasses, he carried them to a table with the best view of the door and took the chair that placed his back to the wall. "Tell me about this Ranger. Tell me everything and make it quick."

Angelina had just stepped inside the store when she heard someone call Charlie's name. Curious, she peered out the front window and watched as a brightly dressed woman, revealing more chest and stocking-covered legs than Angelina had ever seen displayed in public in her life, threw her arms around Charlie and kissed him. They spoke for a few minutes, and then Charlie grabbed the woman's arm and dragged her inside. Angelina was not so naive that she didn't know where they were going—and what would occur once they got there. What surprised her was the shaft of pain shooting through her chest at the realization.

So, he's a man. Her father and her brothers had always boasted about a man's needs. Such boasting was usually followed by a trip to town. Now she had seen for herself the type of woman who fulfilled those mysterious needs.

Angelina turned away from the window and wandered around the store aimlessly. She was supposed to be picking out clothes for her trip to the convent, but she couldn't focus her attention on the task. Her mind kept returning to the image of Charlie kissing the woman. What would it feel like to be the woman in his arms? The woman in his bed?

Angelina straightened up sharply, her spine rigid at the direction of her thoughts. What on earth had made her think such sinful things?

Forcing her mind away from Charlie, Angelina strolled to the small selection of ready-made dresses at the rear of the store and tried to find something that fit.

Another customer entered and spoke with the clerk. Angelina continued with her shopping until she heard the name Charlie Coltrain mentioned.

Slowly she returned the dress she had been looking at to its place and turned. A shelf stacked with bolts of cloth stood between her and the two men speaking. If she moved closer, she could hear clearly, but they could not see her.

"Can't say that I know anyone by that name," the clerk responded.

"Big man," the newcomer said. "Rides a white horse."

Angelina frowned at the sound of the voice, devoid of the slightly Southern twang common to Texans. Instead, this voice was clipped and flat.

Yankee, she thought. Why has he come all the way to Texas looking for Charlie?

"Lots of men ride white horses," the clerk returned.

"If you saw this one you'd remember. He's got long hair of a peculiar color—gold and silver. And his voice—well, if you heard him speak you'd know for sure you were talking to Charlie Coltrain."

Angelina flinched at the accurate description. She had to get out of this place and warn Charlie. Her gaze darted around the back of the store and lit on a door behind the dresses she had been perusing. Slowly she sidled toward the exit.

"Saw a man come in on a big white horse a while ago. Went toward the livery stable."

Angelina didn't wait to hear any more. She bolted through the back door and ran as fast as she could across the street to the place she had last seen Charlie. She burst through the front door of the Blue Creek whorehouse, shouting, "Charlie!"

She stopped short at the sight of Charlie and the woman he'd kissed sitting companionably at a table, drinking and chatting. At her abrupt entrance, Charlie leapt to his feet, drew his gun and pointed the weapon in her direction. When he saw her he scowled and put the gun back in the holster at his hip. "Dammit, Angelina, don't do that. I could've shot you."

She ignored him. "I just overheard a lawman, or maybe he was a bounty hunter, talking to the man at the store. They didn't see me, but I heard them. He's looking for you, Charlie. I think you'd better get out of town."

"Yep, I was just goin'. Luanne here told me my face is plastered all over the finer establishments of this town."

Angelina spared a glance for Luanne and flushed at the look of avid curiosity in the woman's eyes.

"Charlie, who's the kid?" Luanne asked. "Too old to be your daughter." She frowned. "Hell, she can't be your woman. Ain't she a little young for you?"

"Shut up, Luanne," Charlie growled. "She ain't my woman. I'm just takin' her to the convent."

"She's a nun?" Luanne's voice cracked with suppressed laughter.

"Not yet," Charlie bit out. He frowned at Angelina, then walked past her to peer out the window. "Damn," he said conversationally.

"What?" Angelina said, flustered at the lack of emotion behind his curse.

"Man's headed this way. Must be our Ranger friend."

"Go!" Angelina practically shouted, tugging on his arm. "We'll stall him somehow. Just go."

Charlie turned toward her with a look of wry amusement. "You willin' to lie for me, Sister? I'm touched."

"Stop it," she hissed. "He might kill you and you think it's funny. Are you crazy?"

"No, just used to the situation. The only way to keep on livin' is to kill them before they kill you. That is, if you can't get out of town quick enough."

Her heart started to beat so fast Angelina feared it might explode. She couldn't understand how Charlie could stand in front of her with no emotion on his face while he calmly discussed killing a man or being killed. She wanted to shriek and stamp her feet and beat on his chest. She wanted to do anything that would make him listen to her and get out of harm's way.

"Would you two quit jabberin' and get upstairs," Luanne broke in.

"Why?" Charlie and Angelina asked in unison, still staring at each other intently.

"Because I have a plan that should keep my place from gettin' shot up along with the two of you. Get up there and get in bed."

"Excuse me?" Angelina asked. Breaking eye contact with Charlie, she looked at Luanne in amazement.

"Just do it."

Angelina glanced back at Charlie, who looked longingly at the front window while he fingered his gun. He wanted to shoot it out with that lawman, but she wouldn't allow that to happen. She would do whatever she had to do to keep someone from getting killed, especially if that someone was the man who had saved her life.

She grabbed Charlie's hand and tugged. "Come on. We can at least give her idea a try."

Charlie continued to hesitate and she yanked on his hand again. Finally, with obvious reluctance, he allowed Angelina to lead him toward the stairs.

"Never thought I'd have you takin' me upstairs in a whorehouse, Sister," Charlie observed.

"Quit teasin' the girl and get up there, Coltrain," Luanne ordered. "Get under the covers and stay out of sight. You"—she pointed at Angelina—"get out of those horrid clothes. Take off everything but your chemise and get in bed, too. I'll send one of my men up to help. You'll have to pretend he's a customer. Think you can do that?"

Angelina began to understand what Luanne had in mind. The plan could work, if she did her part.

The thud of boots on the plank walk outside made the decision for her. She nodded and raced up the stairs, holding tight to Charlie's hand.

With no time for shyness or modesty, Angelina yanked off her clothes and kicked them under the bed. Charlie was already under the covers. She lifted the blanket and hesitated when his gaze focused on her scantily covered breasts.

The door opened behind them. How had that lawman gotten past Luanne so quickly? She whirled. Fear closed off her voice.

The man in the doorway grinned at her, exposing large white teeth. Sporting a bare chest and long red drawers, he was a mountain of flesh-toned muscle.

"I'm Joseph. Heard you needed a little help."

Footsteps on the stairs made him glance over his shoulder. He frowned and stepped inside, shutting the door behind him.

"No time to talk. Get in bed."

Angelina did as she was told. Joseph joined her on the other side, squeezing Charlie in between them. Despite her fear, Angelina was comforted by the warmth of Charlie's body pressed to her side.

Joseph reached up and yanked the pins from her hair just as the door crashed open. Angelina let out a convincing shriek of surprise and turned to face the intruder.

He was big and tough, like the longhorns she had seen throughout Texas. Those cattle could survive nearly anything and thrive. This man would, too.

He walked into the room as though he owned it and stopped a few feet away. Angelina tilted her head back to get a look at his face.

"Miss," he said in greeting and removed his hat.

His hair hovered between blond and brown, as though it hadn't yet made a decision which color to be. But his eyes were as blue as the Texas sky on a blazing hot summer morning.

Handsome, she thought. Maybe too much so. He was used to getting his way. But not this time, she vowed.

"Who the hell are you?" Joseph roared.

"Drew Winston."

At the sound of the man's voice, Charlie stiffened against Angelina's side. She bit her lip to keep from crying out, afraid for a moment that he meant to leap out and shoot the man where he stood.

"I don't care what your name is," Joseph said. "What are you doing in here?"

"I'm looking for a man. Tall with gold hair."

"Well he ain't in here as you can see," Joseph snarled convincingly. "Now get out. She's paid for an hour, and I want all my time."

"Care if I look around?" The lawman's sharp gaze scanned the room as he spoke.

Joseph pulled himself up straight, making his muscled chest and arms look even more impressive as he glared at the intruder. "Hell, yes, I care. Don't need no audience. Now get."

"Calm down, mister. Maybe he came in here before you did and hid."

"And maybe he got out the back way while you were foolin' around in here."

The sound of horses running hard down the main street drifted through the open window. Drew Winston stiffened and crossed the room.

"Damn, there he goes." He turned and nodded in Angelina's direction. "I apologize, miss." The Ranger strode from the room.

Angelina held her breath, listening as he clattered down the stairs and out the door. Beneath the covers, Charlie shifted impatiently. His hair brushed her hand, and she shivered, stifling the urge to reach down and tangle her fingers in the golden strands, then release them one by one. She chewed on her lip to stifle a groan. Where had all these worldly desires sprung from?

Joseph rambled over to peer out the window. "He's leaving. You can come out now."

Charlie whipped the blanket off his head and sucked in a deep breath. His gaze locked with Angelina's, and the corner of his mouth twitched upward in a wry imitation of a smile. Her heart still raced so fast she didn't have the enthusiasm to return the expression.

How could he look so relaxed? They had come close to getting caught. But of course he had been on the run for most of his life. This was her first experience with evading the law.

Some of her doubt must have shown in her face, for Charlie reached out and brushed a loosened hair away from her brow with a surprisingly gentle gesture. Then, as though disgusted with himself, he muttered something, more likely than not a profanity, and got out of bed.

Luanne appeared in the doorway.

"Who's he following?" Charlie asked.

"One of my bartenders on your horse." She motioned for Joseph to leave. After nodding a good-bye to Charlie and Angelina, he did. Luanne continued. "My man'll lead him away from town, lose him and double back here so you can jump on Gabe and get lost."

"I hope your man can handle Gabe. You know how he is."

"I know how all your horses are. Don't worry. I told him not to wear his spurs. He won't hurt your precious Gabe."

"Gabe?" Angelina asked.

"My horse. I don't like to use spurs on my horses. Makes 'em spooky."

Angelina nodded. Another bit of information she'd been wondering about. "You named your horse Gabe?"

Luanne smiled. "Actually he named the horse Gabriel. He names all his horses Gabriel, after the angel."

Angelina frowned. "That's blasphemous."

Charlie groaned. "Hell, Sister. I wasn't much more than a kid when I started. Now it's just a habit."

"That's true," Luanne put in, her sharp gaze flicking between the two of them with interest. "When we were young, Charlie got so sick of people tellin' him he looked like that angel he started callin' his horse that. As I recall, he said he was as much an angel as a horse's a—"

"Luanne," Charlie barked, cutting her off mid-word. "I don't think we need to go into that."

Luanne glanced at Angelina, and her lips quirked in amusement. "No, I suppose not. Wouldn't want the Sister to think any worse of you, would we?" She looked Angelina up and down in speculation. "I suspect I'd better find you some clothes, girl. You can't go around wearing Charlie's things forever. I'll see if I can scrounge up somethin' to eat while I'm at it."

"Thanks, Luanne," Charlie said.

"Don't mention it. Old friends have to stick together."

She left with a lingering smile in Charlie's direction that left no doubt in Angelina's mind what kind of old friends Luanne and Charlie were. The surge of jealousy within her surprised and shocked Angelina. Such worldly emotions were not for her.

She really had to get back to that convent.

"Angelina." Charlie sat down next to her on the bed and took her hands in his. She looked up and was immediately lost in the black depths of his eyes. "Thank you for helping me. You didn't have to."

"Yes, I did."

She found herself fascinated with the length of his eyelashes. No man should have eyelashes that long, she thought irrelevantly. It's almost sinful.

In some distant corner of her mind she knew she sat on a bed, half clothed, in a whorehouse with an outlaw. She should be swooning with shock at her outraged senses. Her mother would certainly have fainted hours ago. Instead, faintness of a different type took over.

Unable to help herself, Angelina reached out and touched Charlie's hair as she'd wanted to do only moments earlier. Soft, just as she'd imagined, the color so strangely beautiful she understood why he kept it covered to avoid detection.

Sinful, her mind taunted. You're sinful. He's sinful. The pleasure rushing through you is definitely sinful.

Angelina hesitated for only a moment and then, for the first time in her life, ignored the voice of reason and listened to the feelings.

Her fingers trailed down the side of his face, and she marveled at the contrast of his unshaven cheek with his silky hair. He watched her, his body held rigidly still.

When her fingers reached his throat, she traced the skin there, unmarred despite the injury hiding beneath the surface. He captured her hand and held it.

"Did I hurt you?" she whispered, wide eyed.

His lips tilted into the half smile she had come to recognize. He raised the captured hand to his mouth and pressed a heated kiss to the middle of her palm.

"You make me ache, Angelina. You make me hurt so deep and so hard I can't breathe past the pain."

With a muffled curse, he pulled her toward him, slowly, watching her for any sign of resistance. But Angelina didn't want to resist. She went to him willingly, glorying in the touch of his work-roughened palms cradling her face.

His lips on hers were gentle, as though he were afraid she might shatter. And she was shattering—shattering with a need so new and so great she shook with its force.

Returning the kiss, she twined her arms around his neck, arching against him in an instinctive reach for the forbidden.

He stiffened with surprise, and for a moment she feared he would pull away. She clutched him tighter, caught in the midst of desires she didn't understand, but could not fight.

Then she was falling—falling back onto the bed as the warmth of his body covered her own.

Chapter Four

The world narrowed until there was only the sensation of Charlie's mouth, hard and demanding, upon Angelina's. Any thoughts she'd had of right and wrong, of chastity and honor, of any tenet she'd believed in since the day she'd known she had a calling were thrown into disarray at the tumult of feeling that invaded her mind and body.

The bed, so soft at her back, contrasted with his body, lithe and hard against hers. Her cambric chemise gave no protection against the rough texture of his Levi's, and the bite of his gunbelt into her flesh. She knew she should be afraid, but she wasn't. This was Charlie. Her savior. God had sent him to help her. She could trust Charlie.

When his tongue grazed her lips, she drew in a sharp breath and unknowingly gave him the access he sought. He stroked her teeth and tugged on her lips with shocking intimacy. When she stiffened, he gentled her with soft murmurs and kisses. Her eyes drifted closed, and she relaxed into his embrace.

Tentatively she kissed him back, touching her tongue to his with a feather-light stroke. He groaned and shifted, pressing his lower body against hers. His large, warm hand rested on her hip. He molded his fingers to the curve and urged her closer. She couldn't help herself. She arched against him and brought her fingers up to tangle in the bright gold of his hair.

"Well, isn't this a pretty sight?"

At the sound of Luanne's voice, Angelina's eyes snapped open. Charlie's face, so close to hers, wore an expression of chagrin. She struggled to slide out from underneath his body, but he would not move. Instead, he sighed deeply and lowered his forehead to rest against hers. His hair fell forward, brushing her cheeks and mixing with her own dark tresses, shielding them both from prying eyes.

"Hush," he whispered for Angelina's ears alone, and his breath swept across her lips. "I'll take care of her." Without moving he said, "Get out, Luanne."

"I brought the Sister—" Luanne paused to snort derisively. "I brought *her* some clothes."

"Put 'em down and get."

"But—"

"Now, Luanne," Charlie snapped, his voice rough with tension.

Angelina flinched as the door slammed. Charlie raised his head and gazed down into her face. She could still feel every inch of his body against hers. Her cheeks grew warm at the realization of how she must look to him, to Luanne—and, most importantly, to God.

"Please let me up," she whispered as mortification flooded her.

Charlie stared at her for another moment, his handsome features distorted into a frown. He looked at her as though he couldn't quite remember who she was or why they were in the position they were in. She shifted uncomfortably under his weight, and his face tightened as he closed his eyes. Then suddenly he rolled off her and she was free. When she turned her head to look for him, Charlie stood at the door.

"Get dressed," he told her gruffly. "Now. We leave in ten minutes."

Before she could answer, he opened the door, and then she was alone.

Angelina lay on the bed, staring at the ceiling. What on earth had come over her? She had no excuse, no explanation. From the moment Charlie's mouth had touched hers she had been unable to think—she had only been able to feel.

With a sound somewhere between a laugh and a sob, she got to her feet. She wouldn't think about that now. She didn't want to think about it. She had to get dressed. With an almost physical effort she pushed thoughts of Charlie's touch from her mind.

A dress lay folded at the foot of the bed. Angelina grabbed the garment and shook it loose with a sharp snap. She raised her eyebrows. Where on earth had Luanne found such a dress? Though clean, it had obviously seen better days. The color of the much washed material hovered between brown and cream. The shape resembled nothing so much as a large burlap sack with a hole cut in the top for her head and two sleeves attached.

With a shrug, Angelina yanked the garment

over her head. The material settled against her body and covered her to the floor. She heaved a sigh of relief. It felt good to be adequately clothed once again. Though Angelina hadn't thought it possible to find a dress uglier than the black one she'd just discarded, Luanne had accomplished the feat. Angelina had to admit she was relieved. She had been half afraid Luanne would return with a brilliant red satin gown, suitable for a dance hall but never a stagecoach trip to Corpus Christi. Then what would she have done?

A knock sounded on the door. "Just a minute," she called and reached up to twist her hair into a tight bun. She glanced around the room for her pins, spotting some atop the table in front of a mirror. Crossing the floor, she secured her hair and began to turn away. A flash of red caught her eye and Angelina peered closer. A ribbon, some beads and a pair of earrings lay in a jumble in the center of the table. She reached out and stirred the brightly colored array with her fingertip. When she raised her hand, the ribbon hung from her knuckle.

As a child, she had always loved pretty things—especially pretty red things. Her mother, at the mercy of six boys, countless ranch hands and her husband, had indulged the only other female on the ranch. Angelina's closet had been filled with a rainbow of dresses. She wore a different ribbon in her hair every day. Her mother had made all her dolls equally colorful clothing.

Thinking back on such frivolity, Angelina had to admit its silliness. Still, she would always be drawn to bright beauty. Such desires could be buried, but never forgotten.

The knock on the door was repeated, this time

louder and with more impatience. She continued to stare at the ribbon, mesmerized by the silkiness of the fabric.

"Angelina." Charlie's voice preceded him by a mere second as he opened the door and walked in.

She dropped the ribbon with a guilty start, and her gaze flicked up to meet his in the mirror. He frowned and strode across the room, stopping just behind her to peer over her shoulder. His breath brushed the loose tendrils at the back of her neck, and she shivered.

Charlie stared at the assortment on the table; then his eyes met hers in the mirror. His held a twinge of amusement.

"Not much fun being a nun, is it?" he asked.

"My life's work isn't supposed to be fun. It's supposed to be rewarding. And it is." She purposely looked away from the mirror, then stepped out of range of his seductive body heat. When she reached the door, she glanced back at him.

Charlie watched her, curiosity in his eyes. "What's your life's work, Sister?"

"Teaching and spreading God's word," she recited.

"Hmm. Ever thought of doin' anything else?"

"No. The church is my calling. I've known that since I was ten years old."

"Really? I wonder how a ten year old knows her own mind. I sure didn't at that age. Hell, I don't even know it now." He shrugged. "Well, I admire you, Sister. Too bad you couldn't do the things you mentioned without wasting yourself on the church."

She stiffened. "I don't consider God's work wasteful."

"I didn't say that. It just seems to me that you could do all those things you mentioned and still enjoy bein' a woman."

"I do."

Charlie smiled, slowly, knowingly, the first true smile she'd seen upon his lips. Angelina stared, transfixed, amazed at how such an expression lightened his countenance.

"I don't think you do enjoy bein' a woman, Sister." Charlie's voice drew her attention away from the contemplation of his handsome features. "Not the way you could if you'd wise up, look inside and see what you really want to do with your life."

"What would you know about my life?" Angelina was angry. She who had striven so hard over the past year to control her worldly propensity toward fury.

"I know that underneath that nun's costume there's a livin', lustin' woman just beggin' to get out. You forget. I've tasted those lips. You aren't meant to be a nun, Angelina."

"I forget nothing. Just because you forced me to kiss you doesn't mean I enjoyed it."

Charlie snorted. "Right."

Angelina bit her lip, calling upon all her hard-won internal strength to keep from shrieking at him. She had learned the hard way, growing up with six brothers, that yelling at a man never did any good. It only made them more self-righteous. If you ignored their taunts, they were the ones who ended up infuriated.

"I'll just be on my way to wait for the stage now," she said, pleased with the calmness of her voice.

She reached for the door. Just as she began to open it, Charlie's fingers clamped down on hers.

"You aren't goin' anywhere, Sister." His voice was gruff with anger, and she stifled a smile. She'd gotten to him—worked every time.

Then the sense of his words penetrated her mind, and she jerked her hand from his as she turned around. He was close, too close, behind her. She shrank back against the door, attempting to put some distance between them. It didn't work. He was so large, so muscular, so male. His very presence in a room was intimidating.

Charlie saw her instinctive movement away from him and frowned, then stepped back. Angelina breathed easier and straightened away from the door.

"What do you mean I'm not going anywhere?"

"Well, I shouldn't have said that. You are goin' somewhere."

Angelina smiled.

"You're goin' to Mexico with me."

Her smile faltered. "No. We already had this discussion. I'm going to Corpus Christi on the stage."

"Not anymore. You've helped me escape capture. That Ranger will be after you as well as me. The only way you'll be safe is in Mexico. I'll take you to your family."

"No!" Angelina heard the rising panic in her voice, but she couldn't seem to stop it. "Put me on the stage. Please. Then you go on. I'll be fine."

Charlie shook his head. "I can't do that. The Ranger saw you, and so did everyone else in this town. If he can't find me, he'll hunt you down. If he's in a real nasty mood he could put you in jail—or worse."

"I'm a woman of the church. He wouldn't dare."

"God, you're young." Charlie ran an impatient hand through his golden hair. "Men dare a lot—especially with a murderer on the loose and a sizable bounty for his capture. You'll be safe with me. I'm not so sure about the Ranger."

"Why?" Angelina demanded.

"Why?" Charlie made an exasperated sound. "Because I don't know him—"

"No, not that." Angelina stamped her foot in anger. "Why do you care what happens to me? Last week you didn't even know me. Pretend it's last week."

Charlie's face softened, and he took a step toward her again. Angelina tensed, but this time he didn't back off. Instead, he reached up and stroked a finger down her cheek, staring into her eyes with a rueful expression.

"Can't do that, Sister. Now that I've got you, I can't let you go. Wouldn't be gentlemanly. And if there's one thing us Southern outlaws are, it's gentlemen."

"You're not funny," she said, trying to sound stern, but only managing to sound breathless instead.

"I know. Neither is goin' to jail." He took his hand away from her cheek, and his face hardened. "You're comin' with me, Angelina. By your own will or mine, you're still comin'. It's your choice if I bind and gag you or not."

"You wouldn't." She gasped.

"No? Try me."

They stared at each other, brown eyes at war with black. Charlie had obviously had more experience with showdowns, for he never gave an inch. After several minutes, Angelina sighed and looked away. She knew when to surrender.

And when to regroup for the next battle.

"I thought you'd see it my way," Charlie said. "Let's go. Luanne's bartender should be back with my horse soon. Then we've got to get a move on in case that Ranger comes back this way."

"Is there a church in town?"

Charlie, who had been on his way out the door, paused abruptly. "Huh?"

"A church. You know, a building with a cross on top?"

"I know. Why do you want one?"

"I want to go to confession."

"Now?"

"Right now," Angelina said firmly. "I must." When Charlie continued to stare at her as if she had just escaped from a lunatic asylum, she stepped toward him and whispered, "Please. You must understand that I need to confess."

"Aw, hell." Charlie stomped out into the hallway. "If it means that much to you, let's go. I'll tell Luanne to send the horses over to the church, and we'll leave from there."

Angelina smiled. "Thank you, Charlie."

He never heard her thanks, having already turned and stamped away, heading downstairs as he shouted for Luanne.

Angelina tried to avoid watching as the woman bid Charlie good-bye. But she couldn't help taking a peak. Her face flamed. Luanne's lithe body was pressed intimately to Charlie's as she twisted her fingers in his hair and kissed him deeply. To his credit, Charlie didn't return the embrace, but he did return the kiss. When Luanne pulled away, he smiled and stroked the back of his hand up and down her cheek.

"Thanks for the help," Charlie said.

"Anytime. When you get rid of the lawman, and the nun, come on back. I'll show you what I've learned since the last time."

Charlie shrugged and nodded. He looked up and met Angelina's gaze. She averted her eyes, embarrassed to be caught ogling like a child.

"Seen enough, Sister?" Charlie escorted Angelina to the door, keeping her behind him until he glanced up and down the street. With a nod, he led the way outside.

"Too much." Angelina sniffed. "Do you enjoy such public displays?"

Charlie glanced at her, and her entire body grew warm at the suggestive tilt of his eyebrows. "I enjoy displays like that anytime—public or private. Though I must admit the private display we had earlier was more my style."

"Please, if I'm going to travel with you, that can't happen again."

Charlie turned away and led her down the main street toward the church at the edge of town. Without looking at her he asked, "Didn't you like it?"

Angelina hesitated. What should she say?

"Come on now, Sister. You're not goin' to lie to me, are ya?"

She sighed. No, she couldn't lie. "I'm not saying I didn't enjoy the kiss. But it was wrong. For both of us."

"I don't know about that."

"I do. There can be nothing physical between us. If I'm going to travel with you, though it's against my will, I must have your promise you won't touch me in that way again."

"You've got to be kiddin'."

"I assure you, I'm not."

"I was afraid of that," Charlie mumbled.

They reached the church and stopped in front of the doors. Charlie reached out to open one for her.

"No," she said and reached out to still his hand. "You must promise me you won't try to seduce me away from my vows."

With a swift movement, Charlie turned his palm upward, capturing her fingers in his. Angelina gasped and tried to tug herself free. He held on and brought her hand to his lips. One by one, he kissed each fingertip, then released her. Angelina's heart was pounding so fast she barely heard his whispered answer.

"All right. I promise not to seduce you, unless you ask me to."

"Wh-what?"

"If you want me to touch you, you only have to ask, Angelina. Ask and you shall receive. Isn't that how the saying goes?"

"I won't ask."

"No, you won't ask." The corner of Charlie's mouth tilted upward. "You'll beg."

His taunting words and the confidence in his tone caused a resurgence of her earlier anger, and she reached past him to jerk open the door to the church. He chuckled and followed her into the cool, silent interior.

At their entrance, the village priest appeared. He hurried down the aisle, pausing in front of them to frown at Charlie's gunbelt.

"Senor, this is a house of God. No such weapons are necessary."

"I'm just escortin' the lady. I'll wait back here." He pointed to a pew next to the door.

After a second's hesitation the priest nodded

his assent and turned to Angelina. "How can I help you, senorita?"

The priest's bald head was ringed with a circle of gray hair. His face, tanned by the Texas sun and lined from age and exposure to the elements, was open and friendly. His voice held a hint of an accent, just as hers did. Immediately she felt a bond with this man. She understood the church and the people of it. The uncertainty that had plagued her since she'd met Charlie disappeared, and she smiled in relief. "I wish to make my confession, Father. I am a postulate with the Sisters of the Incarnate Word and the Blessed Sacrament in Corpus Christi. My—a—he—" She gestured helplessly at Charlie, who smirked. Why did he seem so much larger and more dangerous within the confines of the sacred building? She looked away and focused her attention back on the priest. "He's taking me to my family in Mexico for a few weeks. I wish to confess before we go on the trail."

"Of course, my child. Follow me."

Angelina did so eagerly. Though she would have to confess her sinful desires for Charlie within the confines of the confessional, that was entirely different from explaining him in the middle of the church.

She entered her side of the enclosed structure and crossed herself. "Forgive me, Father, for I have sinned," she said, the familiar words giving her solace as they always did.

She barely heard the answer of the priest, so familiar was she with the ritual.

"I have lusted in my heart and in truth," she admitted. "Never before have I felt these emotions. I don't know what to do."

"You must be strong. Fight your weakness. Remember your devotion to God that brought you to your convent. You are young yet. There are many years ahead of you in which you must remain faithful to the promises you will soon make. Do not give in at the first sign of temptation."

Angelina sighed. That was her problem. She had never been tempted before. It had been so very easy to remain chaste when she'd never experienced the burn of desire.

"My child?" the priest asked. "Is the man who brought you here the one of which you speak?"

"Yes, Father."

"Hmm. Very worldly. He can't be good for you. Why are you with him?"

"I-I have no choice." Angelina paused, uncertain of how to explain.

The priest spoke into the strained silence. "God has a reason for everything He does. Perhaps you should search for His reason in this. God wants something of you. Pray and listen to God's voice from within."

"Yes, Father."

Angelina finished her confession with only half her attention, the desire to submit to God's will at war with her reluctance to return home. She soothed herself with the thought that her father would undoubtedly send her immediately back to Corpus Christi. He didn't want to see her any more than she wanted to see him, and the few hours she could spend with her mother would be worth the trouble.

It was obvious, for reasons unclear to her, that God wished for her to return to Mexico. Whenever she tried to go her own way or tried to convince Charlie to deliver her to Corpus Christi, some disaster descended upon them and forced her in the direction of Mexico.

She would take the priest's advice and pray for guidance, as well as patience and obedience. But despite her calling, her training and her genuine devotion to God's work, Angelina didn't know if she could force herself to return to her father's house without a fight.

Charlie watched Angelina exit the confessional. She looked different from when she'd gone in. He frowned and studied her more closely. What was it?

She walked down the aisle toward the back of the church, and when she reached him, she stopped and looked up. She smiled, the expression lighting her entire face and shining through her eyes.

Charlie's heart contracted. Why would she look at him like that? As though he were the most wonderful man on earth in her eyes. Hell, he'd done nothing to warrant such an expression. He'd nearly destroyed her greatest dream by taking her innocence on a whorehouse bed. If it hadn't been for Luanne coming in when she had, he wasn't sure if he could have stopped himself from finishing what he'd started. There was something about Angelina that had him more on edge than he'd ever been in his life. He'd never been drawn to virgins. He'd never had one that he could remember. So it couldn't be her innocence he lusted after. Or maybe he was just becoming even more depraved in his old age. He was disgusted with himself.

"Charlie?"

Angelina's voice broke into his thoughts. She still stared at him with happiness shining from her face.

"What happened in there? You look—" His voice drifted off. He didn't know how she looked—at peace, calm, tranquil. Feelings he had no notion of.

"I talked with the father and he made some things clear to me."

"You think he'd like to make some things clear to me? Like how I ended up with a bounty on my head when I didn't do nothin'."

"I'm sure if you wanted to confess, he'd be happy to listen."

Charlie snorted. The very idea of confessing his sins was laughable. There wouldn't be enough time left on earth for that confession.

"I think I'll pass, Sister. Spare the good father from havin' a seizure." He paused and listened.

Horses approached at a sedate pace. Waving Angelina behind him, Charlie went to the door and peered out. The sky was beginning to darken with approaching night. But he could still make out a man astride Gabe, another horse trailing behind. Nodding to Angelina, Charlie opened the door just enough for the two of them to slip outside.

"Any trouble?" Charlie asked as the man stopped the horses and dismounted.

"Nope." He handed Charlie the reins. "That Ranger sure can ride though. If it hadn't been for your horse, he might've caught us. Helps that he's not familiar with the territory around here. Lost him about two hours ago."

"Much obliged for your help."

"Forget it. I'd do anything for Luanne."

"Me, too," Charlie replied absently while checking his stirrups.

"Well, if you mean that, then stay away from here, mister. She don't need any trouble."

Charlie paused and glanced over his shoulder. The other man shuffled nervously. Charlie sighed. How many times in his life had he been told not to return to a place? He couldn't remember. For some reason, this particular warning grated on him.

"Charlie isn't trouble."

Angelina's voice, firm and sure, interrupted the angry words that lay like iron atop Charlie's tongue. He glanced at her. She frowned severely at the other man.

"He's innocent of the charges against him in that poster."

"You know that for sure, miss?"

"Yes, I do."

"How?"

"Because he told me so."

"Uh-huh. Well, you'll pardon me, miss, if I don't take his word for it." The man turned and headed back toward the whorehouse.

Angelina stepped forward, her mouth opened to speak further.

"Don't." Charlie stopped her with a hand on her arm.

"Why not? I can't believe you're going to let him get away with calling you a liar."

"What would you have me do, Angelina? Shoot him? That's what it'll take to make him shut up. Then I'd be exactly what he accused me of bein'."

Angelina remained silent. He could see his words had made her think. Maybe now she'd understand he wasn't the hero she thought him to be. Charlie reluctantly removed his hand from her arm and finished readying the horses.

"Come on," he said gruffly when he was done.

She obeyed stiffly, and when Charlie put his hands on her waist to help her onto the horse, the shocked hiss of her breath proved her mind had been elsewhere.

So small, Charlie marveled. His hands spanned her waist, even though he had seen for himself she wore no corset. He could feel the warmth of her flesh beneath the horrid brown dress Luanne's cook had given her. She smelled like warm woman—a scent somewhere between earthy and sweet. He had to grit his teeth to keep from turning her around in his arms and nuzzling her neck. Such thoughts had only gotten him into a mess of trouble before.

With a sudden movement, Charlie hoisted Angelina into the saddle, then released her immediately. She landed on the horse with a surprised squeak and scrambled to sit up as he walked off toward Gabe.

He had promised not to touch her. No, that wasn't right. He had promised not to touch her unless she asked him to. Charlie was sure he could make her ask him if he put his mind to the task. But he had a feeling he would be sorrier than he'd ever been about anything in his life if he seduced Angelina. Not only would he hurt her; he'd destroy what was left of himself.

With a curse, Charlie swung onto Gabe's back and kicked the horse into a gallop. He didn't look back to see if Angelina followed.

The way his luck was running, he knew she did.

Chapter Five

"Thieving, murdering Reb traitor," Drew shouted at the night sky. His horse shied, and he cursed, under his breath this time, while he soothed the animal with his hands. For the past hour he had tried to avoid admitting the truth. But he couldn't any longer.

He'd lost Coltrain.

If it hadn't been for that damn white horse, he would have caught the man. But there was nothing he could do. The outlaw had the better mount, and Coltrain seemed to know the area north of Blue Creek very well.

Drew stopped his horse and prepared to make camp. He would have to retrace his steps in the morning to find out where he'd gone wrong. At worst he could return to Blue Creek and talk to the pretty brown-eyed whore. If he didn't miss his guess, she was hiding something. Maybe she was the mysterious link to Coltrain. Even if she wasn't, he wouldn't mind paying for an hour of her time. All that tumbled dark hair and wide-eyed innocence intrigued him.

Drew sighed. He hadn't been interested in a woman since. . . .

"Aw, hell. Let's not start that now," he muttered as he started a fire and put the coffee on to boil. He would have to remain awake all night since he wouldn't put it past Coltrain to double back and try to surprise him. If he started to think about Claire, his mind would not be on the danger at hand.

Instead, to keep at bay the memories that fueled his desire for vengeance, he sat down near the flames and leaned back against his saddle. Drawing forth a piece of paper from his pocket, Drew settled in to read.

January 15, 1873

Dear Capt. Winston:
Your request for information regarding Charlie Coltrain and his brother Bill was forwarded to me from the Pinkerton Detective Agency. Bill Coltrain was shot and killed by myself and another Pinkerton agent in Second Chance during the summer of 1870. As far as I know, the remaining members of the Coltrain Gang, including Charlie, have left Missouri. Since many of the former members of the Confederacy, especially the guerrilla fighters, have taken up residence in Texas, I suggest you search there for Charlie. If I hear anything more, I will contact you.

Sincerely,
Jake Parker
Second Chance, Missouri

Drew stared at the creased-and-folded paper for several moments, then carefully returned it to his pocket. He had taken Parker's advice and come to Texas, eventually joining the Rangers when his funds and his information ran out.

Drew had spent years seeking Coltrain over the vast reaches of Texas. But outlaws always turned up somewhere—either dead or alive—and Charlie had finally turned up robbing trains and shooting engineers. What Drew couldn't figure out was why a smart man like Coltrain had not hightailed it to Mexico and disappeared along with his money. Why had Charlie joined a cattle drive, using his own name, and begun a trip to New Mexico?

Maybe the outlaw was even smarter than everyone thought, since he had managed to leave the drive and disappear into Texas despite the sizable bounty on his head. Since Drew had lost him, there was no telling where Coltrain would turn up next—and who he would hurt in the meantime.

The coffee was ready and he leaned forward to pour himself a cup, grimacing at the first taste of the bitter liquid. If he kept drinking, he knew the coffee would start to taste better as the night slept on, growing colder and darker and lonelier. He didn't want to sleep anyway. Until he brought Charlie Coltrain to justice—by the law or his own hand—Drew would only dream of Claire and what might have been.

As soon as the day grew light enough for him to see the ground, Drew packed up and mounted his horse. A few hours later he picked up the trail of Coltrain's big white horse and began to follow it.

As the sun neared its zenith, Drew peered at the horizon and frowned.

Blue Creek. What the hell?

Coltrain's trail led straight back to town. Drew kicked his horse into a gallop. Maybe the outlaw had finally made a fatal mistake. Drew would just hunt up that innocent-eyed working girl, and if he was lucky, Coltrain would be right beside her.

Drew thundered into town, drawing curious glances from the townsfolk. He ignored them all, pulling his horse to a stop in front of the whorehouse and jumping to the ground. Throwing his reins over the hitching rail out front, he slammed through the front door.

The lower floor was empty. Drew glanced up the staircase, then took the stairs two at a time. His gaze lit on the door to the room he'd been in only the afternoon before. Without a second thought he kicked it open.

The woman in bed sat up and shrieked. Drew ducked as a table lamp flew toward him, shattering against the door.

"Hold on. I just want to talk to you."

"Get out. Who the hell do you think you are? Joseph!"

Drew stepped inside and slammed the door behind him. Then he took a good look at the woman. She was naked to the waist, her full breasts rising and falling with indignation. Blonde hair tumbled over her shoulders. His gaze flicked up to hers. Her eyes narrowed, then lighted with a cynical, knowing expression in a face worn by years of hard living.

Drew sighed. Wrong woman. This one was the owner. He'd talked to her about Charlie when he'd first come to Blue Creek.

"Where's the girl that was here yesterday?"

"What girl?"

"You know the girl. She was in here with a man the size of the Rio Grande. Dark hair and eyes—Mexican maybe."

"I don't have any girl like that."

"You sure?"

"Listen, Ranger. I own the place. You know that. I think I'd know if I had a girl workin' for me that fits your description. Hell, I'm a businesswoman. I wouldn't let an opportunity pass me by." She smiled and stretched her arms over her head, pushing her impressive chest out for his perusal. "If you close your eyes, lawman, I can be anyone you want."

"No, thanks. I—"

The door behind him suddenly burst open, and the mountainous man he'd spoken with the day before entered the room. The man took one look at Drew and frowned.

"You want me to throw him out, Luanne?"

Luanne smirked. "Well, he hasn't been too friendly."

Joseph took a step toward Drew. Drew held up his hand. "I'm leaving. You don't have to strain yourself."

The big man shrugged. "Fine by me."

Drew nodded to Luanne and went out the door. Joseph followed right behind, and Drew turned to him with a curious look.

"I'll just make sure you find your way out," Joseph said with a grin.

Knowing argument would be useless, Drew said nothing. When they reached the front door, he paused.

"Who was she?"

Joseph raised an eyebrow as he leaned his massive frame against the wall. "She?"

"The woman in bed with you yesterday."

"I don't kiss and tell."

"Obviously she doesn't work here. I assume she's a friend of Coltrain's, and she stayed behind to trick me so Charlie could get away. Did she leave with him when he came back here?"

Joseph didn't answer, just continued to stare at Drew with an amused expression.

"Have it your way then," Drew muttered. "I'll find her myself."

He walked out of the whorehouse, the sound of Joesph's chuckle grating on his nerves. Swinging into the saddle, he glanced up and down the single street of Blue Creek. He'd been in the general store the day before, and the owner had not been very forthcoming. Drew's gaze lit upon the livery stable.

"Aha." He turned his horse in that direction.

Five minutes later he rode toward the edge of town, his destination the church. The man at the livery stable had been adamant. The man who had ridden out and then back in on the big white horse had delivered the animal to the church before returning to the whorehouse. And that man had not been Charlie Coltrain. Drew was beginning to see he had been duped.

Entering the church, he blinked at the sudden loss of light compared with the bright shine of a Texas afternoon.

"May I help you?"

Drew focused on the priest who walked warily up the aisle toward him. The man's eyes were riveted on Drew's guns. Drew raised his hands in a gesture of peace and the priest met his gaze.

"I hope you can, Father," Drew answered. "I'm looking for a woman—small, dark haired, maybe Mexican."

The priest was already nodding before Drew finished his description. "Yes, I know her."

"She was with a man?"

"Yes. Tall, light hair." The priest frowned. "Very worldly. Dangerous."

"That's him. Do you know where they went?"

"Not for certain. They rode west." He shrugged. "But they could have been going anywhere."

"They didn't say where?"

"No, I didn't ask. I know better than to question such as he."

Drew nodded his agreement. "Thank you, Father." He turned away.

"Young man."

Drew turned back.

"Are you a relative of hers?"

"No, I'm looking for the man."

"Oh." The priest's voice reflected his disappointment.

"Why, Father?"

"I just hoped that perhaps you could return her to her people in Corpus Christi."

"She's from there?"

"She is now. I got the impression she would have preferred to return to the convent."

Drew had to remind himself to close his mouth, which had dropped open at the priest's words. "The convent?"

"Why, yes. I assumed you knew. The man you seek is traveling with a postulate. Though I have no idea what she's doing out here, so far away from where she belongs."

"Did she tell you her name?"

The priest's brow creased. "No, now that you ask, I realize she did not. An interesting oversight."

"Yeah, ain't it." Drew handed the priest some coins from his pocket. "Thank you, Father. You've been very helpful."

Drew was halfway out of town when he started to laugh. The sound echoed in the dusty, oppressive air of a Texas afternoon.

"Charlie Coltrain and a nun," he said out loud, though no one but his horse could hear. "What next?"

They had traveled well into the night before making camp; then they were back on the trail before first light. Charlie had to admit Angelina was a good traveler. Despite her small stature, she had a will of steel. She kept pace with him without complaint, and she wasn't a chatterbox. He appreciated that in a woman.

He figured they might be a day ahead of the Ranger, depending on how good the lawman was at tracking. They would have to keep going longer and faster than the man behind them if they wanted to escape over the border.

Charlie glanced over at Angelina for the hundredth time that morning. Her lips were compressed into a tight line, the only visible sign of her fatigue. The ugly brown dress was not the best item of clothing for riding a horse. The material had ridden up above her high-topped nun's shoes, and Charlie could see a tantalizing glimpse of honey-toned calf. He yanked his gaze away from her legs and his attention wandered upward, pausing at her head. In Bakerstown she'd bought a fascinator. She'd explained to him that

the triangular shawl would be more practical than
a sunbonnet. She could drape the cloth over her
head during the day and at night use it for protection against the chill. Charlie conceded the point,
though he privately held the opinion that the knit-
ted black shawl was near the ugliest excuse for a
head covering he'd ever encountered.

"Is there a reason you keep staring at me?"

Her cool, calm voice interrupted his musings,
and he returned his gaze to the increasingly desolate land in front of them. The rolling green hills
were gradually giving way to flatter land filled
with chaparral and cactus.

"Do you know how to use a gun?" he asked,
uncertain of where the question had come from.

"I can shoot one. Just don't ask me to hit anything or reload the thing when I'm finished."

"Beautiful," he muttered. "I think we should
stop awhile."

"Now? I'm fine, Charlie. Really." She glanced
back over her shoulder uneasily. "Don't you think
we should keep going as long as we can?"

"We'll ride for a while after dark to make up
the time. Right now, I'd feel better if I gave you
a little lesson in the art of gunfightin'."

Charlie pulled his horse to a stop and dismounted. Angelina paused as well, but did not
get down from her mount.

"I don't understand why you think I need to
learn how to shoot. Of what possible use would
such knowledge be to me in the convent?"

"You're not in the convent now, Sister. You're
with me. And you might need the skill sooner
than you think. If that Ranger catches up with us,
I don't aim to return with him just to be hanged.
I'm goin' down fightin'."

Angelina remained silent and Charlie looked over at her. She bit her lip, a gesture he'd come to recognize as a byplay of indecision.

"I don't want you to hang, Charlie, but I can't help you kill someone to stay alive."

"I'm not askin' you to. If something happens to me, you'll need to know how to use a gun to save yourself. I would think you'd know by now that most of the men out here aren't as hospitable as me."

Angelina chewed on her lip for a moment longer, then slid from her horse and joined him. "All right. I suppose it wouldn't hurt to know how to defend myself."

"Would have helped a few days ago, I'm thinkin'." Charlie drew one of his pistols from the holster and checked it for bullets.

"I don't know if I could actually shoot a human being, Charlie."

He held the gun out to her. She stared at the weapon as though it were a live snake, then reached out a tentative had to accept it.

"When the stakes are your life or theirs, you'll shoot, Sister. I guarantee it."

Her gaze met his over the pistol, and she shivered, then looked away. "What do you want me to do?"

She held the gun as though she might drop it at any second, and Charlie sighed with exasperation. This might take longer than he'd thought. He moved around behind her and reached around her shoulders to place his hands over hers.

At the first contact of flesh against flesh, she tensed. "Settle down," he whispered in her ear. "I just want to show you how to aim the thing."

She nodded her assent, the movement of her body causing her shoulders to rub against his chest. He shifted away from her and bit back a curse. In his business, control—over oneself and over others—was everything. He had never before had a problem controlling the urges of his body. Old age was hitting him everywhere.

Unbidden, an image came to him of another time he'd taught a young woman to shoot. His half sister Annie had only been six years old when he'd left for the war. Knowing his stepfather was the lowest form of life upon the earth, Charlie figured Annie might need a way to defend herself from her own father. Remembering, he fought back the disgust that flooded him every time he thought of that no-good Yankee Jayhawker. A childhood spent in the same house with Richard Bakker had succeeded in turning both Charlie and his brother Bill into avid Rebels. They'd left to join the Confederacy as soon as the news had reached Missouri that the war was on. The only good thing to come from Bakker had been Annie, and she hadn't lived to see her fourteenth birthday. God, he hated Yankees.

Angelina's behind bumped against Charlie's thighs as she attempted to get a good grip on the gun, and his memories fled. Gritting his teeth, he forced himself to show her how to fix her sights on an object, adjust for the recoil and pull the trigger. Despite the long night and day of traveling, he could still smell the scent of soap that clung to her skin. He was used to women who scented their bodies with perfumes to cover up other odors. Angelina merely used plain lye soap and managed to smell more erotic than the most practiced whore.

"I think that's enough," he said tightly and took the gun from her now steady hand.

Angelina glanced at him with a frown. "Are you sure? I don't feel as if I know what I'm doing."

"It takes a lot of practice to be a good shot. As long as you can load a gun and look like you know how to use it, you might be able to fake your way through a situation without having to actually shoot."

She smiled. "I like that idea."

"But you always have to be prepared to shoot. And remember, it's you or them. Don't go all soft and nunnish when your life's on the line. Aim dead center, and you should hit somethin'. At the very least, you'll slow 'em down a bit."

She looked uncertain, but finally she nodded.

"We'd best eat somethin' and then get back on the trail."

They shared a meal of dried biscuits choked down with tepid water. Angelina didn't say a word. She just ate what she was given and then returned to her horse.

"You don't complain much, do you?

Angelina looked at him in surprise. "Why would I complain?"

"Most women wouldn't appreciate bein' dragged somewhere they didn't want to go at the pace we're goin' there."

"I'm not most women."

"So you've told me." A question had been bothering Charlie for a long time, and he decided now was a good time to learn the answer. "Angelina, why don't you want to go home?"

Her sharp intake of breath was the only indication she'd heard his question. She continued to stare straight ahead, focusing on a point near the rapidly darkening horizon. She didn't answer for so long Charlie figured she wouldn't.

"My father," she said, so low he had to strain to hear her.

Charlie froze. Her words, coming so soon after his own remembrances of Annie, made him think the worst.

"What did he do to you?" he demanded.

Angelina's head turned sharply in his direction. He could just make out her frown beneath the shadow of her ugly black scarf.

"He would say he did nothing. He's probably right. It's not his fault. He was raised to believe that women are to be used in any way men see fit."

"Did he use you?"

Angelina might have looked innocent, but she wasn't stupid. Her gasp of horror told him she'd picked up on the undercurrents of his question.

"That's disgusting," she hissed. "He's my father."

Charlie shrugged. "Don't be naive. That means nothing to certain men."

"I take it you've known such men."

"Yes." The word was clipped and final—a warning against any more such questions.

Angelina took the warning. "My father wanted to sell me into a marriage that would have doubled his landholdings."

"What was the problem with that?"

She threw him a glance filled with anger. "I have a calling. But he cared nothing for my beliefs. He only cared about owning the most land in Mexico and advancing his political career."

Charlie shrugged. "I can understand your father wanting you to marry. Maybe he just wanted you to be happy."

"I'm happy at the convent."

"How did you get him to let you go there if he was so set on your marrying?"

"He had no choice."

Charlie raised an eyebrow. "Your father don't sound like a man who gives in easy. Why didn't he have a choice?"

"I really don't want to talk about this," Angelina muttered.

"Somethin' to hide, Sister?"

A hiss of irritation escaped her lips before they tightened into a thin line. "Since you insist on returning me to my family, you'll no doubt hear the story anyway. My father made arrangements for me to marry the oldest son of our nearest neighbor. When I refused, my father locked me in my room until the wedding."

Charlie frowned. "How long?"

"A month. I was allowed to see no one but my father when he brought my meals. Every day he asked me to give in. I merely prayed and ignored him."

"Stubborn," Charlie said.

Angelina shrugged. "I knew what was right. To marry a man for his land is not right. Especially when God meant me for the church. I had no doubt things would work out in the end."

Charlie smirked. "What did you do?"

"The day of the wedding I went to the church. Everyone came from miles around. There had to be over a hundred people there. When I was asked to give my assent to the marriage, I told the priest of my calling and put myself in the protection of the church." A sound suspiciously akin to a laugh came from her throat. "My father had no choice but to give in. Too many people had heard me, and no priest would marry me once he knew of my calling. But my father was able to turn everything around to his advantage. He always does. Now he tells any who will listen about his daughter the postulate in Texas. He's discovered that, in a religious country like Mexico, it helps to have a daughter in the church."

"What about the man you were supposed to marry?"

Angelina's fingers clenched on the reins. "Juan was very angry. I embarrassed him. I tried to explain, but he wouldn't listen. Maybe someday he'll forgive me."

"Maybe," Charlie said, but he didn't agree. He could imagine the faceless Juan's anger at the loss of Angelina. But he couldn't pity the boy. Charlie had learned young to take what he wanted. If he'd been the man at the altar with Angelina, he would have made sure she left the church as his wife and no one else's.

Not even God's.

They didn't stop to rest until nigh on to midnight and then only because her horse was exhausted. Angelina nearly slept in the saddle, but she would never admit such a weakness. Since childhood, she had learned not to complain in any situation. Being the only girl and an obvious favorite with her mother, her brothers had always been jealous of her. They watched for the first sign of weakness and then circled like the scavengers they were. Angelina understood now that she had become a stronger person as a result of their jealousy and thanked the Lord for His foresight.

The night was chilly, and Angelina shivered as she wrapped herself in a blanket and sat down to eat their cold meal.

"Sorry we can't make a fire," Charlie said.

"I understand. The light might give us away. You don't have to worry about me, Charlie. I'm fine."

"I don't think that Ranger's on our trail yet. But I could be wrong. Doesn't pay to take chances."

"No, I agree."

"I wish I could figure out—" Charlie began, then drifted off as he stared into the darkness.

Angelina waited a moment for him to continue, then asked, "What?"

He started at her words, as though he'd forgotten her presence, then shrugged. "Oh, nothin' much. I just can't figure out why a damned Yankee is in the Texas Rangers."

"I've heard men come from all over to join them."

"Yeah, but I'd think mostly Southerners would come to Texas. Why a Yankee?"

"I don't know. Does it matter?"

"I suspect not, in the long run. If he catches me I'll hang. I'd just hate goin' down because of a Yankee."

His voice deepened on the last word, and Angelina flinched at the amount of hatred he managed to convey in a single declaration.

"Was the war so bad," she asked softly, "that you'd hate someone you don't even know just because of where he was born?"

She heard him shift uneasily in the darkness and wondered if he would refuse to answer. Then his voice came, rough and ruined, and her arms prickled with awareness.

"My hatin' Yankees started long before the war. The war and—" He trailed off as though remembering something that pained him. When he spoke again his voice was softer, gentler, if only for a moment. "What came after only made that hate a permanent part of me."

"I can't believe that. You must learn to forgive."

He snorted. "No way, Sister. Some things don't deserve forgivin'."

"But—"

"No, you know nothin' about me. Don't start tryin' to save me. I ain't worth it."

"I disagree. People can change, if they want to badly enough."

He sighed, the sound long and hollow, drawn deep from within him. "I tried to change. Got sick of the runnin' and the killin' and tried to take an honest job. Look where it got me. I'm wanted just the same."

"Charlie, the change has to come from within you. Out of a genuine desire to be a better person. Running away from what you've done, what you were, won't help."

"How'd you get so smart? Are you speakin' from experience, Angelina? Runnin' away from your family didn't help, did it? You're still a woman inside, not a dried-up nun."

Angelina's back stiffened at the taunting tone of his voice. "We're not talking about me."

"Why not?"

"We already did. I told you about my father, my wedding. Why don't you tell me about the hatred that overflows your voice every time the word Yankee enters the conversation."

"Why don't you go to hell, Sister?"

Angelina's gasp was not so much shock at his profanity as a reaction to the sudden realization that flooded through her like a heavenly light. She had heard others tell of such visions of purpose, but she had never experienced one for herself until that moment.

Suddenly she knew that purpose as well as she knew she was meant to be a nun. The father in Blue Creek had been right. God had sent Charlie to her for a reason. Charlie's hatred was eating him from within. Someone had to save him from himself.

Angelina smiled and wrapped her arms around her body, rocking back and forth to contain her inner delight.

God had given her a mission, and that mission's name was Charlie Coltrain.

Chapter Six

Charlie rarely slept. When he did, he never slept deeply. He couldn't remember a time when he'd been able to relax his vigilance enough to lose consciousness without at least part of his mind remaining alert.

Tonight was no exception. The anger consuming him when he'd told Angelina where to go had only increased when she'd sweetly wished him good night and fallen into a deep and easy sleep.

Charlie stared into the night and listened to the silence. Why, he asked himself, did Angelina's pious words infuriate him so deeply? The poor kid was only trying to help him.

Kid. He laughed at himself. Maybe if he kept calling her that he'd start to believe it and his body would stop responding to her whenever she came near him. Hell, calling her Sister sure wasn't working.

Maybe he wasn't so much angry at what she

107

said as with what he'd remembered. The stage accident, the screams and the death. Usually his mind only treated him to that memory when he could hold sleep at bay no longer. But tonight, when he'd spoken to Angelina about his reasons for turning away from crime, he'd remembered the occasion when he'd last broken the law in painful detail.

A rustle to his left made Charlie jerk his head up. Had he dozed off for a moment? He didn't think so, but if not, then why had his chin been resting upon his chest?

The noise came again, closer this time, and Charlie slowly moved his hand toward his gun. He glanced over at his horse. The animal slept, undisturbed.

Odd.

Charlie got to his feet quietly, putting himself between the noise and Angelina. Clouds shrouded the night in blackness. Despite his excellent night vision, he could not even make out a shadow in the dark. Well, he wasn't going to sit and let whoever or whatever was out there come and slaughter them without a fight. He'd learned as a youngster that surprise was the best defense.

Holding his gun at the ready, Charlie charged into the night.

Immediately he felt a shift of movement and leapt toward it. His lips parted in a grimace of victory when he connected with a body and drove the intruder into the dirt beneath him.

He straddled the wriggling, kicking form and pinned flailing fists to the ground.

"Who the hell are you? And what do you want?" he demanded.

"I want to go back to bed," Angelina said. "Now get off me."

Charlie was so surprised to hear her voice, he almost missed deflecting the knee that came up between his legs with lightning speed and deadly accuracy. But years of dealing with dirty fighters had honed his reflexes against such sudden moves. He shifted, pressing her legs tighter between his own and the rock-strewn ground.

"You know an awful lot about where to hurt a man for a nun."

"I have six brothers. I know how to defend myself."

"Maybe against them, but not against me."

Angelina arched her back and yanked on her wrists. The movement only served to make him achingly aware of each inch of feminine curve beneath him. She grunted with effort as she tried to pull free once more. Then she went still.

Charlie's eyes had adjusted to the darkness, and he could just make out her face. She glared at him, her lips pressed into an angry line.

Not scared, he thought, just spitting mad. Wonder if she acted like this at the convent.

Remembering how her pious tone had angered him earlier, he smiled. She wasn't so superior now.

"What's so funny?" she demanded.

"I'm not laughin'."

"You'd better not. Let me up."

"Not until you tell me what you were doin' out here. Were you tryin' to take off again?" A brief flare of anger shot through Charlie. When was the woman going to get it through her head that she had no choice but to accompany him to Mexico? "You should have learned by now that you'll only get yourself killed ridin' alone. I may not be the best company, but I won't let anyone hurt you."

Angelina shook her head. "I wasn't trying to leave."

"Then what were you doin' out here?"

She turned her head to the side, the movement disturbing the rocks beneath her head and causing them to make a shuffling sound. "I had to—"

"Oh." Charlie's momentary anger faded and he grinned wide at her embarrassment. He liked her much better embarrassed than preaching at him. He also found the timid squirms and shifts she was making against him to be more arousing than any seduction practiced upon him by the most skilled professional. He leaned closer and inhaled the fragrance that was unique to Angelina. The reaction of his body was immediate.

I'd better quit teasin' myself before I'm really uncomfortable.

Charlie shook his head ruefully. He was in bad shape when he couldn't stop lusting after a 20-year-old virgin. He cleared his throat and brought his attention back to the questions at hand. "How did you get past me?"

She had kept her head averted self-consciously. But at his words she turned back, her startled eyes meeting his. "You were sleeping."

Charlie frowned, any remaining thoughts of Angelina's soft body and enticing fragrance fleeing his mind. "I rarely sleep."

"Well, tonight you were. I got up and walked away. You never moved."

Impossible. Or is it?

Uncertainty flooded through Charlie. This slip of a girl had walked right by him and he'd never heard her? Obviously so, since she'd been out in the dark when he'd still believed her asleep in her bedroll. Anyone could have come upon them and done near anything, and he wouldn't have heard the intruder until too late.

In one quick movement Charlie lurched to his feet and yanked Angelina with him. He listened intently to the night sounds. As far as he could tell, they were still alone. He was just damn lucky that Yankee Ranger hadn't caught up with them yet.

Fine time to start sleepin' like a baby. My ears are failin' right along with the rest of me.

"Charlie?" Angelina broke into his thoughts. "What's the matter?"

"Nothin'. Just get back to camp, and don't go anywhere unless you tell me first," he growled. "Anyone could've grabbed you. You're just lucky it was me."

"I don't understand why you're so angry."

"You don't have to understand. Just get back to camp."

Angelina opened her mouth to argue, then snapped it shut with a click of her teeth and spun away. She'd only gone a few short steps when she whirled back to face him. "Aren't you coming?"

"Not right now. Just go back to sleep. I can see you from here. Don't worry. No one else will get by me tonight."

She stared at him for another moment, her forehead creasing into a puzzled frown. "I wasn't worried, Charlie. You are right. I know I'd die out here alone. But when I'm with you, I know I'm safe." She turned and disappeared into the darkness.

"Hellfire," Charlie muttered. "I was never that young."

He bent down and retrieved his pistol from the ground, checking the weapon carefully before returning it to his gunbelt. Then he took a brisk walk around the camp in the cool night air, alone with his thoughts. By the time he returned, the steady whisper of Angelina's breathing told him she slept.

Charlie stood over her. When he'd forced her to come with him, he'd honestly thought she would be safer. Now he wasn't so sure. He was losing his edge. That razor sharp awareness that had kept him alive for 37 years in an endless variety of dangerous situations was slipping away. But then he'd never had anyone else to protect before, at least not since Annie and his mother. And look what his protection had gotten both of them—side-by-side plots in the family cemetery.

With a disgusted sound, Charlie swung away from Angelina's sleeping form and returned to where he'd sat leaning against his saddle. He spent the rest of the long night watching Angelina sleep and wondering what on earth he was going to do with her.

The dilemma succeeded in keeping him awake, but when morning arrived he was no closer to a solution. He could leave Angelina in the nearest town, but he had no doubt the Ranger was no more than a day behind. Could he take the chance that the man would not hurt her? And if not the Ranger, then someone else without scruples. He'd been such a man himself once upon a time—still was in many ways. He understood the world too well to leave Angelina alone in it. Even his dubious ability to protect her would be better than nothing. He would just have to hope he could deliver Angelina to her family safely before their luck ran out.

Too bad the only kind of luck he ever had was bad.

Angelina stirred, groaned and sat up. After blinking at the rising sun—once, twice, three times—she got to her knees and squinted into the distance.

"Charlie?"

"Yeah. Good mornin' to you, too, Sister. Think you can make the coffee? I'm not up to it today."

She didn't answer; she just squinted harder at the horizon. Her hand came up to rest at the base of her throat in a gesture of unease. "Does dust signal a horse and rider or just wind?"

Charlie swore and jumped to his feet, peering at the tiny puff of dust in the distance. He'd seen enough dust like that to know what was coming. Bad luck, as usual.

"Mount up and let's move." He was already throwing the saddles onto the horses as he spoke.

Angelina didn't flinch. She merely packed up their belongings and did as she was told.

"Do you think it's him?" she asked as he tied down the last item. "The Ranger who's after us?"

"Yep."

"Couldn't it be someone else? Someone like us, just traveling?"

"We're not just travelin'."

"True. But how can you be so sure it's him."

"Bein' sure in situations like these has kept me alive so far. If you still want to be breathin' tomorrow you'll listen to me and ride as hard as you can."

Charlie swung onto his horse and turned to

look one final time at the increasing dust cloud.

"Do you think we can outrun him?"

He returned his attention to Angelina. Her face was tight and pale, but her gaze met his head on. She wanted the truth.

"I could outrun him on Gabe. But with you and that horse—" Charlie shrugged. "Don't worry about it none. I never planned to try to outrun him anyhow."

"What are we going to do then?"

"You'll see. Just follow me, and don't look back."

Angelina had thought they set a fast pace the day before. By midmorning she knew what fast really was. Despite Charlie's warning, she did look back—several times. To her anxious eyes it seemed as though the dust behind them was getting closer. But she couldn't be sure.

Charlie looked back only once, and he nodded in satisfaction at what he saw, which soothed Angelina's nerves somewhat. Then he veered his horse off the trail. Angelina was right behind as Charlie and Gabe wove a path through the cactus and mesquite. The sharp edges caught at her skirt and tore it in places, but she ignored the tugs and pushed onward.

She wanted to ask where they were going. But she knew better than to slow them down with questions. Charlie was riding for his life and perhaps hers as well. She trusted him to do what he thought best for both of them. She was certain he'd been in situations like this before and was far better equipped to handle the planning of their escape. She'd just continue to do as she was told and keep her mouth shut.

After about an hour of riding, they reached a stream banked on one side by a rocky hill. Charlie walked his horse to the stream and allowed the animal to drink. Angelina did the same.

"What now? she asked.

Charlie didn't answer. He merely turned Gabe away from the water and led the way to the top of the hill. There he dismounted.

Angelina heaved a sigh of relief. Her teeth felt as though they were loose in her head from all the jarring her horse had put her through that day. She slid to the ground, holding onto the saddle until her legs were steady enough to support her. When she glanced around for Charlie he was headed back down the hill on foot.

"Where are you going?"

"Just stay put. I'll be right back." He disappeared from view.

Angelina looked around the hill, noting the area would not be a very comfortable camp. She walked to the top and peered over. She had a perfect view of the stream below. Charlie appeared and she watched as he used a tree branch to obliterate the tracks their horses had made when they had left the stream and gone uphill. He left the tracks leading to the stream intact and returned.

Charlie lay down at the top of the hill and peered at the stream. His face held an expression of concentration. He did not seem to be aware of Angelina's presence any longer.

"Should I unsaddle the horses?" she ventured.

"No," he snapped without glancing in her direction. "We'll be leavin' soon enough."

Angelina sat down next to him. "Do you think he'll pass by?"

"Not if he's any kind of tracker."

"But—" Angelina bit her lip in confusion. "Then why did you get rid of our tracks leading up here? I thought you wanted him to think we walked our horses down the stream."

"I do want him to think that. At least for a minute or two. No lawman worth his salt would be fooled for very long by what I did."

"I don't understand."

"Shh!" Charlie hissed. "Get back. Go to the horses and make sure they don't call out to his horse."

When Angelina hesitated, he turned the full force of his black gaze upon her. She flinched away from the coldness in his eyes—an expression she had never seen directed at her before. Now that she'd seen it, she knew why others feared his wrath. Stumbling to her feet, Angelina did as she was told without further argument.

Seconds later the sound of a horse being ridden fast and furious reached her ears. As the Ranger rode closer, the sounds slowed. By the time he reached the stream, the steady clip-clop told Angelina the lawman's horse now walked. She kept her hand over the noses of their two animals and murmured soothingly to them. But neither seemed very interested in what was going on just over the hillside below them.

She risked a glance at Charlie and her stomach lurched sickeningly. He was crouched at the very apex of the hill—his gun drawn and trained on the stream below.

Forgetting the horses and her orders to keep them quiet, Angelina ran toward Charlie.

He can't. He won't.

He will if you don't stop him.

She threw herself onto her knees next to him

and Charlie turned toward her with a look of fury.

"Get back there!" he snapped.

She shook her head vehemently, knowing she had to be quiet or risk all their lives. She pointed at the gun and frowned, then shook her head again.

Charlie ignored her and returned his attention to the man below them. Angelina followed his gaze.

The Ranger had dismounted and was kneeling on the ground next to the water. He studied the tracks there intently, his mind well occupied.

Charlie cocked his gun and Angelina flinched. She turned toward him, a small gasp escaping her lips at the sight of his face. She had thought that she knew this man—that inside him there was goodness just waiting to be released with the right help. Yet now he crouched next to her with cold-blooded murder on his mind, his face as still, his eyes as emotionless as a snake preparing to strike.

"Rattler," Charlie muttered and leaned forward.

Angelina's mouth fell open at his echo of her thoughts. But she had no time to ponder the curiosity. Charlie's finger tightened on the trigger. She dove forward, knocking him sideways and causing the gun to discharge harmlessly into the sky.

A cry of pain from below made her scramble to her feet and peer over the edge of the hill. The Ranger lay on the ground, clutching his thigh. As she watched, he drew his own gun and shot the rattlesnake that had just finished sinking its fangs into his flesh.

She leapt to her feet and turned, prepared to run down the path and help the injured man. Charlie's iron grip on her upper arm spun her back toward him.

"What the hell did you do that for?"

"You were going to kill him."

Charlie frowned. "How do you know I wasn't goin' to kill the snake?"

She hesitated. Could she have been wrong about the look of murder on Charlie's face? Had he really meant to murder a lawman or merely a snake?

She didn't have time to consider Charlie's true motives. She had to get to the Ranger before it was too late. Living in Mexico, she had learned how to care for snakebites, and time was of the essence with a poisonous injury.

"I have to help him. He'll die without help."

"Fine. Then he'll be off our trail."

She gasped at the coldness of Charlie's voice and eyes. Maybe she had been right after all. Without bothering to answer him, Angelina jerked her arm free of his grip. He let her go.

"If you want to leave, then leave," she shouted. "I'm not stopping you. But I won't stand by and let a man die." Realizing she sounded slightly hysterical, Angelina took a deep, calming breath before looking into Charlie's eyes. "I can't let him die," she said more quietly.

Charlie looked at her for several seconds, then glanced up at the sky and closed his eyes as though praying for patience. But Angelina knew better than to believe Charlie would pray for any reason. When he returned his gaze to her face, the odd coldness had retreated from his expression, and she breathed a sigh of relief. This was the man she knew. The other frightened her.

"All right," he said. "But as soon as you're done helpin', we leave him somewhere and move on. Agreed?"

"You mean I have a choice?"

"No."

"That's what I thought." Angelina turned away. Charlie's hand on her arm stopped her once again.

"Let me go first," he said. "The Yankee needs to give up his gun before I'll let you anywhere near him."

She wanted to argue, but she could see the sense to his words. The man was, after all, hunting them. With another nod, Angelina allowed Charlie to proceed her down the path.

The Ranger, Drew Winston as she remembered him telling her in Blue Creek, lay on the ground next to his horse. Propped up on his elbows, he eyed the injury with disgust. At their approach, he tilted his weight onto one arm and pointed his gun at them with the other.

"Drop it, Coltrain."

"Don't think so, Yank. You're the one who'd better do the droppin'. If you don't let the Sister here take a look at your leg, you'll be one dead lawman."

Winston's bright blue gaze switched to Angelina. "I found out when I went back to Blue Creek that you don't know anything about whoring. Do you know more about nursing?"

Angelina let his offensive words slide over her without anger. She understood their cause. She had, to be truthful, deceived the lawman in Blue Creek. "What else do nuns do, Mr. Winston, except teach and nurse and pray?"

"Not much," Charlie muttered beside her.

She shot him a quick, sideways glance of irritation, but his gaze remained focused on the Ranger.

"Are you gonna drop the gun, Winston, or am I gonna have to make ya? I won't let the Sister here anywhere close if you're armed."

Winston looked as though he wanted to argue further. Then his face contorted with pain, and his leg began to twitch as though it wanted to run, leaving the rest of the man's body behind. With a shrug and a groan, Winston threw the pistol toward Charlie.

Charlie walked closer and picked up the weapon. "Now the other one."

With some difficulty, the Ranger withdrew the second pistol from his gunbelt and held the weapon out to Charlie.

"Stay back," Charlie growled to Angelina. Then he cocked his gun and advanced on the wounded man.

By the time Charlie reached him, Winston had drawn inward upon himself as severe cramps wracked him, and Charlie was able to retrieve the pistol without mishap.

"All right, Sister," Charlie called. "Since you're so all fired interested in savin' him, get to it."

Angelina hurried to the wounded man's side and dropped to her knees. His usually sharp blue eyes, now glazed with pain, stared back at her. He tried to lift his head, but he was too weak.

"Lie back, Mr. Winston. I've seen this before. I know exactly what to do." She looked up at Charlie. "See if he has any whiskey in those saddlebags. And give me your knife."

Charlie pulled the evil-looking blade from his belt and handed the weapon to her hilt first, then went to do her bidding. Without wasting any more time or words, Angelina slit the Ranger's pant leg from ankle to midthigh. Fang marks stood out against the swelling located above his knee. When she touched the leg gently, Winston jerked involuntarily from the pain.

"Here, Sister."

Charlie handed her a bottle half filled with whiskey and she nodded her thanks. After dousing the wound and the knife, she handed the bottle back to Charlie.

"Make him drink it," she ordered.

"Now?"

"Now. Some say alcohol will dilute the poison. Either way, he may as well have something to occupy his time while I do this." She glanced at the Ranger again. He still stared at her warily through half-open eyes. "It doesn't look as though he'll be kind enough to pass out and leave me to my work."

"Not likely," he mumbled.

"This won't feel very good, but I have to do it." Angelina nodded at Charlie, and he sat down next to the Ranger and lifted the man's head. Winston obediently drank from the offered bottle, and Angelina turned her attention back to his leg.

Before the Ranger knew what she was about, Angelina cut into his leg, enlarging each fang mark minutely. Winston's leg twitched, but he did not pull away. Angelina didn't spare him a glance. Saving time was what mattered right now. She couldn't spare a moment to worry over his pain. Lowering her head, she placed her mouth over the wound. With all her might she sucked. Blood filled her mouth, and she immediately spat the fluid onto the ground at her side and returned her mouth to the wound.

"What the hell?" Charlie roared, starting up from his position as if to stop her.

Angelina spat another mouthful of blood onto the ground and glared at him. "Shut up and sit down," she ordered, then returned to her work.

She didn't look at him again until she was finished. When she did, Drew Winston slept the sleep of the highly intoxicated. Charlie sat next to the lawman, an empty whiskey bottle in one hand and his pistol in the other.

"Are you going to shoot me with that thing?" Angelina nodded at the pistol.

"Huh?" He looked down at his hand, surprise spreading over his face at the sight of the gun in his palm. "Oh, I forgot." He stood and reholstered the weapon, then turned his gaze upon her.

Angelina self-consciously wiped the back of her hand across her mouth. "Is there anything left in that?" she asked.

"This?" He held up the whiskey bottle. At her nod he handed it to her. "Maybe a swallow or two."

"Good enough." She took the burning liquid into her mouth, swirling it around and around to rid herself of the taste of blood. Then she spat the whiskey onto the already soaked earth at her feet.

"Where'd you learn to do that, Sister?"

Charlie's voice, soft yet rough, made her pause in the act of raising the bottle for one final sip. She shrugged and lowered her arm. "Where I come from, snakes are everywhere. I learned as a child what I needed to do. And I've had to do it on several occasions."

"Your father let you."

Her eyes widened in surprise. "My father made me. The first time I cried all the while I worked over one of our ranch hands. I was terrified I would swallow the poison and die. My father stood over me and forced me to finish what I'd started."

"Bastard," Charlie muttered.

Though Angelina had to agree with the sentiment, her lips pressed together at the profanity. Still, to be truthful. . . . "In this case, my father was right. I needed to know what to do, and the only way to make sure I did the job right and didn't hurt myself in the process was to stand over me while I learned. I don't agree with my father on most things, but in this case he was right to insist. What would have happened to Mr. Winston if I hadn't known what to do and been able to do it?"

Charlie didn't answer her. He merely took a step closer and reached up to cup her cheek in his rough palm. Startled, Angelina froze.

"You're somethin' else, Sister. What you are, I don't know. Half woman, half child, part nun, part nurse. Hell, you've got me so confused, I don't know which way is south anymore."

"I don't mean to confuse you," she whispered, afraid he would remove his hand from her cheek, afraid he would not. The only other person who had ever touched her so tenderly had been her mother, and this was not the same—not better or worse—just different. Angelina craved that difference. Despite herself, she rubbed her cheek against his hand.

For a second, Charlie's palm cradled her. She looked into his eyes and smiled. Tentatively she raised her own fingers and reached toward his face.

Suddenly, the warmth was gone as he jerked away with a muttered oath. She stood with her hand still up in the air where Charlie's face had been, watching in amazement as he stalked away from her. He stopped at the edge of the creek, staring out over the water. His shoulders were stiff with tension. Slowly Angelina lowered her hand back to her side.

"You've got to stop that, Angelina."

His voice echoed in the night stillness. Far away, a coyote howled, long and mournful, the sound perfectly matching the ache within Angelina at that moment.

"Stop what?"

"Stop looking at me as though you could see into my soul. It's mighty black in there. You don't want to get inside my soul, Sister. You'd be lost— lost forever, just like me."

Chapter Seven

No louder than a mumble—still the first word awoke Angelina. The firelight flickered, partially obscuring Charlie reclined against his saddle.

After his depressing observation on the state of his soul, Charlie had refused to speak any more on the subject. Instead, he'd insisted they drag the Ranger and all his belongings up the hill to make camp. Remaining by the stream was out of the question in case a passerby decided to water his horse during the night. There were, Charlie reminded her, the bounty hunters still to consider.

The mumble came again, this time louder, though not coherent, and Angelina sat up. Her patient began to thrash and moan violently.

"I'll take care of him." Charlie's voice drifted across the wavering flames. "You've had enough for one day."

"No, I'd better look at him. Though if he's got a fever, I'll need your help."

Charlie grunted, a sound Angelina took for grudging assent. She got up and walked the few feet to her patient. Bending, she touched his forehead.

Too hot.

"Claire?" Winston muttered. "Is that you?"

"No, I'm sorry, it's not. I'm Angelina Reyes." She brushed his half-blond, half-brown hair away from his face in a soothing gesture reminiscent of her mother's. "Don't worry. I'll take care of you."

"So hot," he rasped. "Want to go skinny-dippin' at the creek like we used to?"

Angelina stifled a smile. Could the illusive Claire be the Ranger's wife?

"Not for me, Mr. Winston, but a swim is definitely in order for you."

She looked up. Charlie had come closer and now stood just on the other side of the Ranger, his beautiful features twisted into a dark frown.

"What?" she asked.

"He's not bein' respectful."

"As if you'd know respectful when you heard it. He's delirious. Help me get him undressed and into the creek. The water will bring down the fever."

She began to unbutton Winston's shirt.

"No way, Sister."

Startled at his flat denial, Angelina lifted her gaze to Charlie's determined face. "What do you mean? I need help. I can't get him to the stream. He's huge."

"I didn't say I wouldn't take him to the stream. But you're not undressin' him, Sister. You've done all you're gonna do with him for one night. Git out of the way. I'll do it."

She sighed and returned to her task. "I've done

a lot of nursing, Charlie. Undressing a man isn't something I haven't done countless times before."

"You never had me around to do it for you. Now if you want my help, you'll git out of the way."

Angelina paused. The mutinous set of Charlie's mouth told her he meant what he said. She was only wasting time arguing with him. The Ranger needed to get into that cold water as quickly as possible.

"All right," she said and rose to her feet. "You win. But the only reason I'm agreeing is because this man needs help right now."

One side of Charlie's mouth tilted up. "Don't worry, Angelina. I won't get used to your bein' agreeable. I know it's not natural for you."

It was Angelina's turn to scowl. Her expression only made Charlie give his coughlike imitation of a laugh. She turned on her heel and returned to the fire.

"Let me know when you're ready to take him to the stream," she called.

"I'll take him. You just stay here. When I bring him back and get his clothes on, you can take over."

Angelina sighed. There was really nothing she could do for Winston at the stream. "Fine. Just make sure you keep him in there until he's cooled down."

"Don't worry. I'll take care of him."

Angelina frowned at the tone of Charlie's voice. Maybe she should go with them after all. She hated to push Charlie too far in case he refused to carry the Ranger down to the stream. She could probably drag the man down the path, but by the time she got them there it would be too late to do any good.

When Charlie finished undressing Winston she heard him hoist the Ranger over his shoulder with a grunt of effort. Angelina risked a glance in their direction as Charlie headed down the path, then as quickly averted her eyes from the expanse of naked flesh in Charlie's arms. She hadn't lied when she said she'd undressed men before. She just hadn't mentioned they'd been old men and children. Drew Winston did not qualify in either category.

The low rumble of a male voice reached her ears, and she turned her head toward the sound. Angelina smiled. She could watch and make sure Charlie was doing as she asked from the top of the hill.

Quietly she made her way to the crest and peered over. The moon shone bright and silver upon the still water. Now that she was away from the crackle of the flames, she found she could hear the men's voices distinctly.

"Claire, I don't understand why." Winston's voice cracked with the fever—and something else.

"I'm not Claire, and I don't know. So just shut up and quit thrashin' around."

"Why did you have to die?"

Angelina's heart stuttered at the pain in Winston's voice. Poor man. He must have loved her very much.

"Can't answer you there, Yank. Must have been her time to go."

Angelina's fists clenched. She very much wanted to smack Charlie in the nose for his callous words and tone. She opened her mouth to call down and berate him. Then the Ranger spoke again, and she fell silent.

"I'll get Coltrain for you, Claire. He won't get away with it."

Angelina leaned forward, the sharp stones on the ground cutting into her palms.

"Which Coltrain?" Charlie's voice held a deadly warning, but the Ranger was too far into his delirium to notice.

"I heard he's in Texas. I'll head down there. I'll find him. He won't be able to stay on the right side of the law forever. Then I'll be there to take care of him."

"You're after the wrong man, Yank. I don't kill women. At least not on purpose."

"The house burned. Everything I'd worked for, everything you worked to save for us. Gone. I searched the ruin. Would have been our house. Nothing but ash and black wood. But I found the locket I gave you for Christmas before I left for the war. You wore it around your neck. Never took it off. Never."

The Ranger's words brimmed over with the agony inside him—an agony that twisted Angelina's stomach as the sense of his mutterings sunk into her mind. Feeling slightly sick, Angelina sat back and crossed her legs in front of her, then put her face into her hands. She shook her head back and forth, trying to erase the image Winston's words created in her mind. No matter how hard she tried, she could not.

The man believed Charlie responsible for such a horrible crime. Charlie said he hadn't done it. Who should she believe?

The ruined tones of Charlie's voice broke the cool night stillness. "Who told you Charlie

Coltrain killed your woman?"

Silence met Charlie's demand.

"Yank? Who told you?"

Still silence.

"Aw, hell. Fine time to go to sleep."

The swish and plop of the water as Charlie waded from the stream caused Angelina to raise her head from her hands. Quickly she backed away from the edge and returned to her position by the fire. Until she knew the truth of this matter, she would prefer not to let Charlie know she'd overheard his conversation.

Charlie had told her he'd killed, and she had waved away his confession with platitudes. It was easy to dismiss his life of crime when she had never been confronted with any of the victims. But now, hearing the pain in the Ranger's voice at the loss of his Claire, Angelina understood for the first time how others had been affected by Charlie's misdeeds. She had told him what he'd done before didn't matter, as long as he was willing to change. Perhaps she was mistaken.

She truly believed God had sent her to help Charlie; but could someone like her, whose exposure to the dark side of life had only been her bully of a father, help someone with secrets such as those contained in Charlie Coltrain's soul?

"He's sleepin' now."

Charlie's voice came from behind her, and Angelina started violently. Then she scolded herself for the racing beat of her heart. If Charlie Coltrain had wanted to hurt her, he had had plenty of opportunity before now. Repeating that fact over and over, she turned to face him.

He had deposited Winston on the bedroll and covered the sick man once more. Now he stood waiting her instructions. If she didn't want him to suspect what she'd overheard, she'd best pretend everything was the same as it had been only moments before—even though she knew such behavior was a lie.

Angelina smiled her most innocent smile and walked briskly toward the patient. "Thank you for helping him. It couldn't have been easy for you." She bent down and placed her palm to Winston's forehead. He was cool to the touch, and she sighed in relief.

"I didn't do it for him."

"No?" she asked absently as she checked the bandage on the patient's thigh and then gave a brisk nod. No redness, no infection—perhaps she had saved him after all.

"No, I did it for you."

She raised her gaze to his face. The fire flickered behind him, casting a red-orange halo around his golden hair. She could just make out his face, cast into shadow by the light. He was so beautiful he made her ache inside. Just like Lucifer—a resplendent angel fallen from grace, fit only to rule in hell for eternity. Would Charlie's fate be the same?

No!

Her mind shouted the answer so loudly she flinched and looked away from Charlie's prying gaze. No, she wouldn't let him suffer that way, not if she could help it. He was her mission, and she would do everything in her power to succeed.

She stood and moved away from the Ranger, intent on finding her bed and getting some rest before dawn. Charlie stepped in front of her.

"What were you thinkin' just now?" he asked.

She couldn't tell him. She wouldn't. Instead, she shrugged and tried to move past him.

He sidestepped, blocking her way once more. She looked up into his eyes again and froze. Though he didn't touch her, she was trapped just the same—trapped by the wealth of feelings that filled her whenever he came near. How could she wonder if he was a murderer one minute, then question how his lips would feel against her flesh the very next?

Sinful, the wind whispered.

Satan, the fire answered.

Heaven or hell, her mind taunted.

Unable to break the allure of Charlie's gaze, Angelina stood so close to him every breath he took brushed her hair, and the warmth of his body called out to hers. Despite her doubts, she would have done anything he asked if only he hadn't taunted her once more.

"Are you beggin' yet, Sister?" he asked. When her spine stiffened at the insult, he smirked, then turned away and disappeared into the shadows that threatened the firelight.

Charlie stayed on the outskirts of the firelight watching until Angelina slept; then he returned to his bedroll. Near dawn he dozed for a short while. For once he did not dream. Odd in itself, but especially odd considering the conversation he'd had with Drew Winston only a few hours before. Still, he found himself thanking a God he hadn't believed in since he'd stood over the graves of his sister and his mother for the brief respite and the badly needed rest. Maybe Angelina was getting to him after all.

The way she'd looked at him in the firelight the

night before had almost been his undoing. He'd wanted her with a desperation he'd never experienced in his life—and wanting someone that bad could never be good.

Despite the challenge he'd issued to her that he could make her beg for him, Charlie knew in his heart he would never force a test of that boast. He used the words to make her angry whenever she sidled too close to what remained of his heart. Last night she had gotten closer than ever before.

A metallic clank drew his attention, and he rolled over, sitting up and pushing his hair out of his eyes. Angelina stood over the fire making coffee. At his movement, she glanced at him. Her face held a weariness that betrayed her exhaustion.

"Good morning," she said.

"Mornin'." Charlie stretched and got to his feet. He looked over at the lump in the remaining bedroll. "How's the Yank?"

"Still asleep. But his fever's gone. I think he needs the rest for his body to recover from the poison and the fever."

"Well, he can sleep it off somewhere else. We've got to get a move on. We'll rig up some way to haul him and drop him at the first house we find."

Angelina slammed the lid onto the coffeepot and set it on the fire with a clatter. "He needs me. After all I went through to save him, I'm not going to leave him now."

"Yes," Charlie said, "you are. We saved his life. That's more than enough. We've got to get over the border before he's well enough to come after us."

"Won't do any good, Coltrain."

Charlie looked away from Angelina's angry face and met the laconic gaze of Drew Winston. The Ranger had managed to hoist himself up on one elbow, but the effort had caused his face to pale to a shade resembling clay.

"Why not?" Charlie said, walking around the fire to put himself between Angelina and the lawman. Though Winston had no weapon, Charlie didn't trust him not to use Angelina to get what he wanted.

"Because I'll follow you wherever you go, no matter how long it takes."

"Rangers aren't allowed to pursue over the border."

Winston's lips thinned, turning up at the edges into a smile that held little humor. "I'm on leave. Right now you can consider me under the same rules as any one of the bounty hunters on your tail, which means I have no rules but my own."

"Hellfire," Charlie muttered.

"I hope you roast in it soon," Drew said.

"Stop it!" Angelina cried out.

Both men turned to her in surprise.

"What's the matter?" Charlie asked.

"I don't want to hear any more about hell and death. I've spent a whole night trying to save your life"—she shot a glare at Winston—"and I've done nothing but help save your hide"—she glared at Charlie—"since you saved mine."

"I would like to thank you for saving my life," Winston said.

Angelina nodded, her shoulders held stiff and her hands twisted together tightly. "I'm just glad we were here when you needed us."

"I don't know about the we part, ma'am. But I'm glad you were here."

She lifted her chin and stared the Ranger in the eye. "You'd be dead this morning if Charlie hadn't been here."

"How you figure?"

"I suspect you don't remember since you were delirious, but Charlie carried you down to the stream and bathed you in the water until the fever broke. I couldn't have managed that on my own."

Winston frowned darkly. "I'm not going to thank him."

"I don't expect you to," Charlie snapped. He could think of little he would have liked less than thanks from a Yankee. "I didn't do it for you anyway. I did it for her. It would have suited me just fine if you had died."

"Feeling's mutual, Coltrain."

Angelina made a disgusted sound and turned away. She stomped down the path toward the stream without glancing back. Charlie watched her go. She'd come back when she calmed down, or he'd go get her. Right now he had some questions to ask the Ranger, and he'd prefer Angelina didn't hear them.

Charlie turned back to Winston. The lawman eyed him with ice-cold hatred. After what he'd heard the night before, Charlie understood why. He didn't like it, but he understood—all too well.

Well, the best defense was always a good offense, so he dove right into the Ranger with the question he knew would throw the man off balance. "Who's Claire?"

Winston's eyes narrowed. "You're the one who killed her. But I suspect you didn't know her name. Names don't matter to men like you. Only the killing."

"Listen, Yank. You did a lot of accusin' while I was swimmin' with you in the steam down there. But whatever you might have heard, I don't kill women."

"Right, and I'm Frank James. Don't try to fool me, Coltrain. I know what you did."

"Where did this happen?"

"Where the hell do you think? Bloody Kansas. Your territory."

"When did I supposedly do this deed? If you did your homework you'd know I left for Second Chance, Missouri, at the end of 1868."

"In November. Before you left for Missouri. I'm not a complete idiot, Coltrain. I checked with Jake Parker in Second Chance. You arrived there in December. I plan to see that you pay for killing Claire with your life."

Charlie sighed. He could tell by the set of the man's chin he would get no more out of Winston. But there was something about the situation that didn't ring true—something at the back of his memory that nagged at him. He knew from past experience, if he let it go for a while, the answer would bob to the surface of his mind eventually like a dead fish in the river.

"And just where were you when your woman died?"

The lawman scowled. "In the army. Remember the war?"

"Yeah, it was over in 1865."

"Some of us had to stay on and finish the job. The country was a mess."

"So you stayed in the army, went south and made the Rebs follow the rules. And whilst you were bein' patriotic, someone up and killed your woman?"

"Not someone," the Ranger said through his teeth. "You."

Charlie glanced down the path toward the stream. Nothing was being accomplished trading insults with the Yank. Time to get Angelina and be on their way. Whether she liked it or not, the Ranger was going to be off their hands as quickly as Charlie could find a little piece of civilization.

"What's the story with her?"

Charlie brought his gaze back to the lawman. "None of your damn business. Just remember who saved your life and leave her out of this. It's between you and me."

"Oh, I remember who it's between. Just because you wage war on innocents doesn't mean I do. Does she know about you?"

Charlie scowled. "All she needs to."

"How the hell did you get a nun to help you out?"

Charlie's gaze sharpened. He didn't like this line of questions. "How do you know what she is?"

"The priest in Blue Creek was pretty talkative. If it hadn't been for him, I'd've still thought she was a whore. Though there was something about her eyes when she was in that big bed—she made me think of—" The lawman trailed off with a grimace.

"Listen, Yank. I've got her with me because I can't leave her alone out here. You've seen how she is. She wouldn't last a day. She's got nothin' to do with me otherwise."

"For her own good, huh? I find that hard to believe. What's in it for you, Coltrain? Who is she really? Some kind of heiress? You plan on collecting a ransom for her?"

"You don't know me, Yank. You know nothin'

about me. I'm leavin' you first chance I get, and then I don't plan to see you again in this lifetime. But if I ever find out you touched her"—Charlie jerked his head in the direction of the stream— "I'll come after you, and then we'll see who pays for what with his life."

"You're never going to be free of me, Coltrain. For the rest of your life, I'll be right there, one step behind, maybe two. And one day, you'll find me out in front, just waiting for you to catch up."

Charlie had no doubt the Ranger spoke the truth. It was a fact of life—old age slowed even the best. He might be able to run for a few more years, but eventually he was going to get caught. If not by this young man, then by another. He was destined to swing at the end of a rope. His stepfather had often told him as much. Now it looked as though, at least in one case, the useless bastard had spoken the truth.

Angelina stayed by the river until Charlie came for her. She could hear the two men talking, though, unlike the night before, she could not hear what was being said.

When Charlie walked up behind her she could tell by the staccato crunch of his boots on the ground he was not happy. Neither was she.

"Time to go, Sister. I've got the Ranger loaded on a travois. We can go slow so he doesn't get jostled too bad. We should reach a town or a house some time today."

"I don't want to leave him."

Charlie sighed. "I know. But I don't see no other choice. As soon as he's well enough, he's gonna come after us. We need to get away."

Angelina frowned and turned to face him. "Rangers can't come over the border."

"Didn't you hear what he said before? He's on leave. Took off work just to get me. I suspect he didn't want to abide by Ranger rules in this case."

Angelina muttered an expletive that made Charlie's eyebrows rise and his mouth quirk up at the corner.

"My, my, where did you learn that one? I'm shocked."

"Shut up. I don't like this. Not one bit."

Charlie sobered at her sharp words. "You think I like draggin' a lawman who's out for my hide along behind my horse? We've got to get rid of him. Now maybe you'll quit fightin' me over leavin' him. I may be losin' my edge, but I still know how to take care of myself—and you if you'll just let me."

Angelina didn't answer right away. Fatigue and melancholy threatened to overwhelm her. Though the lack of sleep from the night before undoubtedly contributed to such a state, she didn't understand the sinking despair within her. She hadn't suffered such sadness since being locked in her room to await her wedding.

The revelations she'd overheard about Charlie the previous night weighed heavily on her mind. She did not like being uncertain of herself. She was a woman who had always had a plan for her life. When that plan did not go correctly, when she wasn't in control, her entire world tilted. Maybe that was why she kept fighting Charlie despite the fact that she knew he was only trying to do his best for the both of them. But until her life was back on a course she understood, she would continue to feel a creeping sense of catastrophe haunting her every move.

She began to walk back up the path to their horses and her patient. "I suppose you're right, Charlie. We have to leave him. But it still goes against everything I've been taught."

"I know, and I'm sorry."

Angelina glanced at him in surprise. He wasn't looking at her. Instead he studied the tips of his boots intently as they walked. If she hadn't known better, she'd have thought he actually was sorry. She'd always thought Charlie held her beliefs in barely veiled contempt. He had said once he respected her, but she'd taken that as a compliment to her courage, not her calling. Maybe she'd been wrong.

He was more subdued than she'd ever seen him. Could the revelations of last night be preying on his mind? Did she truly believe Charlie capable of what the Ranger had accused him of? Did his guilt or innocence matter to her mission?

The last question made Angelina falter, and Charlie reached out a hand to steady her. She smiled her thanks absently as her mind contemplated the truth.

Her mission was to save Charlie from himself. Whether or not he had killed the Ranger's Claire did not alter her plans. In fact, if he had killed Claire, he needed saving all the more. Angelina did not believe Charlie would ever hurt her. Even if she did, would she put her mission aside?

No.

The answer was as clear to her as the bright sunshine beating down upon her uncovered head.

They reached the top of the hill, and Angelina

left Charlie's side to go check on her patient. The Ranger smiled at her when she approached, and she returned the expression. He lay on a hastily constructed apparatus hitched to Angelina's horse. A blanket lay across his legs, his injured leg too swollen and sore to allow his pants to be put back on, despite the slit Angelina had made in their seam.

"I just want to check your leg one more time before we go, Mr. Winston. If we're going too fast for you, be sure to let us know." She flipped away the blanket, exposing a long, heavily muscled thigh, and pulled back the piece of petticoat she'd used to bind the wound. Pleased with how the bite had progressed toward healing, she nodded briskly and rebound his leg.

"You know I'll come after him." Winston's voice was so soft Angelina found herself straining to hear him. "And you, too, if you're still with him."

Angelina nodded and glanced over her shoulder. Charlie had already mounted Gabe. He could not hear them.

"I know you believe you're doing the right thing. But I believe I am as well. We all have our callings in this life, Mr. Winston."

He frowned. "What does your calling have to do with Coltrain?"

She smiled gently and stood. "He needs my help. You don't know all the demons that torment him. He was trying to turn his life around when you caught up with him."

Winston gave a snort of laughter. "Sure he was."

"He didn't rob that train, and he most certainly did not shoot that engineer."

"You seem awful sure, ma'am."

"I am. As to your Claire—" She broke off when he gave a quick start of surprise at her knowledge, then continued, trying to soothe away the flash of pain that lighted his eyes. "You must have been terribly hurt to lose her, and I understand that grief makes us do things we wouldn't otherwise. Perhaps you should check into these situations again and make certain you have the right man. After all, you're talking about his life."

Winston scowled and turned his head away. "What has he done to you to make you believe all his lies?"

"Nothing." She turned and looked toward Charlie again, her earlier doubts coming back full force. She hesitated, then straightened her shoulders. If she trusted Charlie, then she trusted him. She could spout her faith in him for days, but the only way to make Charlie believe in himself would be for her to believe in him, too—not just with words, but with actions. Angelina turned back to the Ranger for one final comment. "I believe that he's done many things that the Lord would not approve of, but I also believe he's willing to change his ways. We must learn to forgive, Mr. Winston."

His eyes pierced her with a burning glare. "No way, ma'am. Some things don't deserve forgiving."

"I think Charlie has the same opinion on forgiveness. You two have more in common than you think."

Before the Ranger could retort, she spun away and mounted her horse.

Charlie glanced over at her. "What were you two jabberin' about?"

"Just a short discussion on forgiveness."

He laughed and turned in his saddle to get a look at the Ranger. "Him? You're crazy. What are you tryin' to do, Sister? Save the world?"

"Not the world." She patted her horse's neck with a smile. "Just my little corner."

Chapter Eight

"I still don't like the idea of leaving him there," Angelina said, twisting around in her saddle to get a last look at the small shack they had just settled the Ranger into.

"He'll be fine. That woman was hoverin' over him like a bear with her last cub, and he'll be a helluva lot more comfortable in a bed than bein' dragged behind a horse."

"I know." Angelina sighed and forced her unease away. "You're right."

"I'm right?" Charlie laughed. "I like the sound of that outta your mouth. You just keep thinkin' that way, Sister, and the rest of the trip should go just fine."

When night came, they made camp. As Angelina was cleaning up the remains of their meal, Charlie spoke again. "Somethin's been eatin' at me all day. You've suddenly become awful agreeable to a lot of things. Like goin' to Mexico and leavin' the Ranger. Why the change?"

"I—uh—" She faltered to a stop. She couldn't tell him about her revelation. If he knew that she planned to cleanse him of his hatred for Yankees, that she'd discovered he was her mission from God, Charlie just might run away from her as fast as he was running from himself. She knew about stubborn men who didn't want to hear the truth. You had to make them see the truth slowly, as though any change were their own idea. Angelina had been taught that intricacy at the knee of her mother. Though, to be honest, Theresa Reyes had never had much success with her stubborn men.

"Angelina?" Charlie had crossed the distance separating them and taken the coffeepot from her stiff fingers.

"Yes? Oh, you asked me a question." His nearness flustered her. Whenever he came close, her body reacted with a wash of feelings—her stomach burned hot, her hands went ice cold, her mind was a mass of confusing sensations. The priest in Blue Creek had told her she must fight her weakness for this man and follow the way of God. She had never had a problem with such advice before. What on earth was the matter with her now?

She should be able to focus on her desire to help Charlie to the exclusion of all else. Instead, at odd moments, she found herself concentrating on the strength in his hands when he helped her onto or off of her horse, or the rasp of his ruined voice, which should not cause her flesh to ripple with awareness whenever he spoke to her. And, try as she might, she could not stop reliving the soft-hard texture of his lips against hers.

Angelina bit her lip. She was doing it again. Such imaginings must stop if she was to be any good for Charlie. Glancing at him, she saw he studied her with a frown, no doubt wondering if she'd been out in the sun too long again since she couldn't seem to work up an answer to his question.

Angelina sighed. She wasn't going to be able to get away without some kind of response. "When I spoke with the father at Blue Creek," she ventured, "he told me I should look for God's hand in what was happening to me. It seemed that no matter how hard I tried, I couldn't get away from returning to Mexico with you. So maybe God sent you to take me home."

There, Angelina thought, that was partly the truth. I do want to go home and see my mother. May God forgive me, I didn't tell the entire truth.

"God sent me to you?"

Angelina nodded.

Amusement lit his eyes. "Sister, you've really got the world backward."

"Why?"

"If anyone sent me to you, it wasn't God. He washed His hands of me a long time ago."

Angelina put her hand on Charlie's arm as he reached forward to place the coffeepot on the fire. He tensed, but for once did not react with violence to the suddenness of her touch.

Praise God for small favors, she thought.

Charlie turned his head toward her, and Angelina was struck once again by the incredible length of the lashes surrounding his black eyes.

"You're wrong, Charlie," she said softly, earnestly. "God never washes His hands of any of us. He's the eternal optimist. He'll never give up on you, and neither will I."

Charlie stared at her for a long time, his face as expressionless as his eyes. Angelina refused to back down, though she had a feeling stronger men often did in the face of such a stare. Finally his mouth quirked up slightly.

"Whatever you say, Sister. You're the expert in that department." He slowly withdrew his arm from Angelina's touch and went to check on the horses.

She gazed after him, wondering why she did not feel she had reached him, even though the words he'd uttered had agreed with her statement. With a sigh and a shake of her head, Angelina set about making her bed.

Later that night, Angelina lay in her bedroll and watched the stars. Charlie sat nearby, staring into the fire as he did every night. She couldn't understand how he continued to exist with virtually no rest. When she'd asked him why he didn't sleep, he'd fixed her with his black stare and informed her that she wouldn't sleep either if she saw the things he did whenever he closed his eyes. She hadn't mentioned the subject of sleep again.

The acrid smell of cigar smoke drifted to her, and Angelina frowned, raising her head. Charlie sat across the fire, a cigar in his hand. As she watched, he raised a bottle to his lips and took a swig. He grimaced as he swallowed, then tilted the bottle back for more.

Angelina sat up with a jerk, her single braid flipping over her shoulder with the motion. Charlie's gaze swung slowly to rest on that braid, then inched up to meet her eyes.

"Need to go behind a bush, Sister?"

She ignored that. "I've never seen you smoke or drink before."

He shrugged and took another swallow from the bottle, never letting his gaze wander from hers. "Things have been a little busy since I met you. I just didn't get a chance."

"Why tonight?"

"Why not tonight?"

Angelina shook her head in bewilderment. Where she came from, men drank in celebration or despair. What was Charlie's excuse? She asked him as much.

"God, you're young," Charlie said.

"You've told me that before. I'm getting sick of hearing it. Living with my father made me old for my years. Now, answer my question."

"Yes, Sister." He swallowed another mouthful and took a long draw on the cigar, blowing the smoke out in a gray stream of foul-smelling air. "I'm smokin' and drinkin' because I like it. No other reason. I'm not like your father and your brothers—upright, God-fearin' men with wives and families. I'm Charlie Coltrain—thief, outlaw and murderer."

"You have to quit thinking of yourself that way."

"Why? No one else thinks of me any other way."

"I do."

"Well, that makes one person in the whole damn world. I don't think you'll sway public opinion much."

Angelina thought hard. She had to get Charlie to believe in the goodness she was certain existed within him. But how, if no one had ever believed in him the way she did? Someone, somewhere must have seen something good in Charlie

Coltrain. A sudden thought occurred to her, and she blurted it out before thinking. "What about your mother? I'm sure she believes in you."

Charlie went very still, his body suddenly one mass of tension. He yanked the bottle up and took three large gulps, then wiped his mouth with the back of his hand. "My ma is dead."

Flinching at the cold finality of the words, and the pain they betrayed despite the coldness, Angelina bit her lip and continued on. "I'm sorry. But she must have believed in you when she was alive."

He was silent for a long time, staring into the flames.

"Charlie?" she said.

"Yeah, she believed in me." He looked up, and their gazes met through the flickering firelight. Angelina blinked away the tears threatening to spill free when she saw the despair in his eyes. He frowned and looked away. "She believed in me, and the only thing her belief got her was dead. Remember that, Sister."

A tear slid down her cheek, but Angelina ignored it, concentrating instead on keeping her voice calm. Now that she had got Charlie talking, she had to keep him talking. "Tell me more."

He shifted his shoulders as though to relieve their tension. She continued to gaze at him, but he avoided looking at her, staring instead at the night sky above them. When he spoke again his voice was gentler, though the anger still came through loud and clear. "Yes, my ma loved me—are you satisfied? But her husband, my stepfather, hated me. She wasn't strong enough to stand against that kind of hate, not even for her children. He told me every day of my life what a worthless, no-good, little Reb I was, and he turned out to be a whole lot righter than my ma in the end."

"But—" Angelina faltered to a halt, her mind trying to comprehend what Charlie was telling her. "I don't understand. How could you have been a Reb as a child?"

"You don't understand because you don't know the politics of Bloody Kansas. Ever heard of the Missouri Border Wars, Sister?"

Angelina was unable to speak as hope sprang to life within her. For some reason, maybe the alcohol, maybe the events of the past few days, Charlie had decided to tell her something about his past. She didn't dare speak and break the spell. Instead, she shook her head and pulled her bedroll tighter around her neck to ward off the increasing chill.

"I didn't think so. I suspect they skipped that lesson in Mexico—isn't a very pretty story. The wars have been goin' on for a long time on the Kansas-Missouri border. Some are still fightin' the good fight now and then, even though the big war's been over for ten years now. My family was right smack in the middle of it all. We didn't own any slaves, but my ma's family did once. And my pa's family was from Mississippi. He ran off when me and my brother Bill were just kids. Ma wasn't the type of woman to raise two hellions like us on her own, so she married the first man who asked."

Charlie took another few swigs from his bottle and a pull on the cigar as if fortifying himself for the rest of the story.

"Richard Bakker, his name was, and a more sorry son of bitch never breathed on this earth." He looked over to gauge Angelina's reaction. When she merely raised her eyebrows and nodded her encouragement, he continued. "Old Dick was a Jayhawker of the highest order. That means he was from the Kansas side of the fence and an antislavery fanatic. Now, I'm not sayin' that slavery was right. But slavery was never an issue at our house. We could barely afford to feed ourselves. Dick took it into his head to beat some sense into the two little Rebs under his charge."

Angelina shifted uneasily. She didn't like the way this story was proceeding.

"Should I stop, Angelina?"

Swallowing deeply, she twisted her fingers together and prayed a silent prayer for strength. "No, go on."

Charlie nodded and moistened his throat once again. "Bill didn't take too well to the beatin's. He turned mean as a cornered rattler. I—" He shrugged. "Well, I just decided to get even. When I was old enough, I sneaked out and rode with the guerrillas raiding over the border into Kansas. Ever heard of Quantrill?"

Angelina's eyes widened in horror. Stories of the atrocities of Quantrill's Raiders had even reached Mexico, especially after their attack on Lawrence, Kansas. "You didn't—"

"Not with him. The man was a lunatic. The James boys weren't much better. No, I rode with some friends from around home, and Bill, of course. Once he found out what I was up to, he had to come along, too. We had our own little band. Quiet, but thorough. Then Dick found out what we'd been doin', and all hell broke loose."

Charlie lapsed into brooding silence. Angelina waited a few moments, half afraid to hear what had happened. When she could no longer stand the steady swish-swish of the liquor in the bottle as Charlie tilted it up and down every few seconds, she spoke. "What did he do?"

Charlie's gaze flicked to hers, almost as though he'd forgotten she was there. He stared for a few more minutes, then lit another cigar before continuing. "He broke my ma's arm."

"What?" The word burst from her mouth. "What did she do?"

"Nothin'. He knew Bill and I were too big to beat on anymore. And it hadn't done much good anyway. So he broke Ma's arm while he held a gun on us to keep us away. We had a half sister Annie. He threatened to drag her out of bed and do the same if we didn't get lost. By then, the war had started, and we were itchin' to sign up anyway. Bill and I packed and left that night. Joined up with Mosby and spent the rest of the war learnin' how to be real guerrilla fighters."

"Did you ever go back? To Missouri, I mean."

Charlie laughed. "Oh, yeah, Sister. We sure did."

Angelina frowned at his laughter, so out of place in such a serious situation. "Did you come to see your mother and Annie?"

Charlie stopped laughing and took another drink. "I never saw my mother alive again. I saw Annie once more before she died. She was only thirteen years old."

Angelina gave a sharp gasp of pain. "Oh, no, Charlie. I'm so sorry. How did they die?"

He ignored her question as though she had not uttered a word. "After the war Bill and I stayed out east for a while. Ma was dead and there was no reason to go back. When we did—" He trailed off and leaned his head back to stare at the stars for several moments. Then he sighed, long and deep.

Angelina ached to go to him. But something in the way he held himself, tense, almost angry, told her such a movement would be a mistake. Instead, she sat quietly and waited for him to finish.

"We came back and found a town full of Yankees smack in the midst of Missouri. We spent a year there terrorizin' folks."

"Why?"

Charlie's head snapped back up, and suddenly she stared into angry black eyes. "Why not, Sister? The Yankees killed everything I ever loved. Doesn't the Bible say, 'An eye for an eye?' "

"It also says, 'Turn the other cheek.' I prefer that version."

"You would."

"You said Yankees killed everything you ever loved. Does that include your mother and sister?"

"That's right. Bill, too, though I can't say I loved him much. He was too deep down mean."

"How did it happen? Maybe I could understand better why you've done what you've done if you told me." When he continued to stare at her without speaking Angelina tried again. "You'd feel better for sharing you troubles with me."

"I've shared quite a bit with you tonight. But I don't feel none better." He shifted his body until his back was to her. The odor of cigar smoke reached her again, tinted with the scent of whiskey. "Go to sleep, Sister. Just go to sleep, and leave me alone."

Despite his words, Angelina got up and crossed the short distance between them. She reached out a tentative hand to touch him, but stopped only inches from his shoulder when his ruined voice broke the stillness. "I won't be responsible for what happens if you touch me, Sister. I've never been a mean drunk, but there's a first time for everything. If you know what's good for you, you'll go back to your own side of the fire and keep your mercy to yourself."

Angelina pulled her hand back, but she didn't move any farther. "Why can't you admit you're hurting?" she whispered.

"I finished hurtin' a long time ago. Now all that's left is hate. People who think there's anything else inside me wind up sorry in the end."

"I can't believe that."

"Believe it, Sister. Save yourself a lot of grief. Now get away from me. I don't need you and I don't want you here."

Angelina flinched at the ferocity of his words. She returned to her bedroll and listened to the night as thoughts filled her mind. Charlie had shown her a part of himself tonight, but not nearly enough. She now understood his burning hatred for Yankees. But there was more hidden within Charlie than the story of Richard Bakker. She sensed, if she could learn the rest of his secrets, she just might find a way to help him heal.

She glanced at Charlie again. He still sat turned from her, staring out at the darkness, keeping company with his cigar and his bottle. She snuggled deeper into her bedroll and closed her eyes. Charlie was right, he'd shared enough of himself for one night. She knew well the virtue of patience. Though her father called the same trait stubbornness, tireless patience and faith in what she believed to be right had stood her in good stead for most of her life. Relying on that trait, she would merely wait for a better opportunity to discover more about Charlie's past.

On that thought, she drifted off to sleep. Though she should have been exhausted past the point of dreams, such was not the case. She had only closed her eyes when the dream began. Sighing, she gave herself up to the images. This dream was familiar and comforting. She had been having such dreams since that first time, some ten years ago—the night she'd realized she would dedicate her life to God. Since that night, whenever she needed guidance, her angel came and spoke to her—the golden angel with the voice like sin.

Angelina shifted in her sleep and moaned. No, that was not right. Her angel was golden, but his voice always sounded like music—beautiful, ethereal music.

The angel stood before her, tall with long, shining hair. He wore white that was so bright it hurt her eyes to look at him, and when she looked into his eyes a sheen of holy light from within him shone directly into her soul.

"I needed you and you came," she said. "I don't know how to help him. He's hurting so badly inside I ache. Show me the way to make him whole."

"You must learn for yourself what is missing in his life. Only then will you be worthy."

Worthy?

Angelina wrinkled her brow in confusion. This dream was taking a new direction. In the past, the angel had always guided her to do what was right for everyone involved. He had never spoken of worth before. Even in the very first dream, he had only said she must follow God's path. Then he had shown her the convent in Corpus Christi.

"Worthy of what?"

"You will see. You believe God has given you a mission, Angelina?"

"Yes."

The angel nodded. "Do your best. Find your way."

"My way?" What was all this talk about her worth and her way? "What about Charlie?" she demanded.

The angel only smiled and disappeared.

Angelina awoke to the sun shining onto her face with a force reminiscent of the angel's holy light. Her head pounded, and her mouth tasted like Texas dust. If she hadn't known better, she would have sworn she'd been the one imbibing cigars and whiskey the night before.

"Thanks a lot, angel," she muttered. "I need help with Charlie, and you show me what it feels like to spend a night partaking of whiskey and cigars. Am I supposed to sympathize with him? If he feels like this, I certainly do."

Angelina glanced over to where she'd last seen Charlie. She caught her breath.

He was gone.

Throwing the cover off her legs, she jumped to her feet. The two horses turned their heads to look at her, placid eyes reflecting their lack of concern for her predicament. The sight of the animals gave her pause, though.

He can't have gone far if he's left Gabe, she thought.

Despite the increased pounding in her head from her too sudden movements, Angelina stalked over to Charlie's saddle. His saddlebag gaped open, exposing about eight cigars and a nearly full bottle of whiskey. The bottle Charlie had been indulging in the night before leaned against the saddle, only a small amount remaining at the bottom.

Angelina took another quick glance around. No Charlie. Without giving herself any more time to think, she snatched up the cigars and snapped each one in two, then tossed the fragments into the fire. She wasn't sure what the angel dream meant, but she was certain she had to save Charlie from himself. The first order of business was to get rid of the evils of smoke and drink.

The dry earth drank the rest of the whiskey without a whisper of complaint, and Angelina smiled as she shook the last drops from the bottles.

"There," she said in satisfaction. "That's the first step."

Hands clamped down on her wrists, and she dropped the bottles into the dirt with a shriek.

"And what's the next step, Sister," a gravelly voice whispered in her ear. "Gonna shoot me in my sleep?"

Chapter Nine

Beneath Charlie's fingers the bones of Angelina's wrists were fragile, almost childlike. He recognized that, even as his grip tightened.

Angelina winced slightly and turned her head to look at him over her shoulder. Her eyes, only inches away from his own, held no fear. Surprise flooded him. Most men cowered when his anger flared.

"Let me go."

Her voice was calm, level. She turned her entire body to face him and they stood, too close, his fingers still clasping her wrists. The thought shot through his mind that, to any observer, they might seem to be holding hands. Nothing could be farther from the truth.

"What the hell you playin' at, Sister?" he growled, still holding her fast. "Those cigars and that whiskey cost money. You gonna buy me some more?"

"Hardly. You don't need the evils of alcohol

and tobacco added to your other vices. I decided to do you a favor and get rid of temptation."

Shock rendered him speechless. His emotions must have shown on his face, for Angelina took advantage of his lapse in concentration to yank her wrists from his now slack fingers. She retreated several paces and put her hands behind her back. Charlie let her go, though he watched her warily.

"Since when did you become my keeper?"

"I—uh—" She trailed off and then looked toward the horses with a shrug.

"Don't tell me. I can figure some things out for myself. After the sad story I told you last night, you decided I needed motherin'." The anger he'd felt when he'd seen her destroying his property rushed back again at the thought of her pity. He wanted a lot of things from Angelina Reyes, and most of them would earn him the permanent place in hell he deserved, but her pity had never been on his list. "Poor old Charlie," he said in disgust. "Lost his mama, and now he needs someone to look after him. Well, I don't. I've been takin' care of myself for years, and a lot of others, too. You want to be a mama, find a nice young man to take care of that task. Don't look my way, 'cause I don't need you, Sister. I don't need anyone."

Her soft brown gaze slowly came back and rested on his face. "You're wrong. We all need someone. God sent you to me. To help you. All you have to do is let me."

This time his mouth came open in amazement. "What? You told me God wanted you to go home to your family. When did He change His mind?"

She took a step toward him, her hands coming forward to clasp together in front of her breasts.

Her face took on an expression of earnestness and hope that made him want to jump on his horse and ride, alone, for the border.

"I'm sorry I didn't tell you the entire truth before. I was afraid you wouldn't understand. But I'm here to help you. I wasn't sure at first if I was right about what I was supposed to be doing. I've never had to interpret God's will before. Usually my an—" She stopped and bit her lip as though considering her next words. "Well, you have to understand about visions and callings. Sometimes people not of the church have a difficult time understanding."

"Try me," he said, despite the clamoring of an inner voice to the contrary.

Angelina bit her lip some more and hesitated. Finally she let out a sharp sigh before speaking. "I saw my angel last night, and though I'm not exactly positive I understood everything he said, I do know I'm supposed to help you."

"Your angel?"

"Yes." She paused and swallowed hard, obviously uncomfortable with her revelations. When Charlie nodded his encouragement, she continued, a hesitant smile lifting the corners of her lips. "I-I've never told anyone but religious people about my angel. I don't know why I'm telling you. He—uh—he always comes to me in my dreams whenever I need guidance."

Charlie held up his hand and she stopped, her smile fading at the look on his face. "Let me get this straight. You say you see an angel?" She nodded. "In your dreams?" Another nod. "And he tells you what to do?"

"Yes."

Great, Charlie thought, not only am I saddled with a woman all the way to Mexico, but she has to be a nun-in-training who sees angels in her sleep.

"And this angel," he said "told you you're supposed to help me?"

"That's right. You're my mission."

"I'm your mission," Charlie muttered, the sick feeling at the back of his throat settling into his stomach. He did not like the sound of this.

"Yes, I'm very pleased. I've never been given a mission before. I had my calling, of course. But most of the Sisters have some sort of vision that tells them of their calling, unless their families forced them into the church."

Charlie's temper finally snapped. He'd had enough of her nonsense. He proceeded to let loose with the longest stream of words he'd spouted in years. "Listen, Sister. I'm no one's mission. I've got all I can do to keep us both alive and one step ahead of the law and the bounty hunters. I'm gonna get you to your family, and then I'm gonna disappear. God didn't send me to you. It was my own stupidity that wouldn't let me walk away from a woman in trouble. If you'd quit lookin' at me like I was some kind of hero, you might see what a low-down, no-good excuse for a man I really am. No decent woman would spend five minutes with me if she had a choice."

Angelina's face had whitened as his tirade lengthened. When he stopped for breath she whispered, "That's not true."

"You know it is. Deep down, below that sweet, serene I-love-everybody attitude, you know I'm worthless. My mother knew it. My sister knew it. Hell, I'm damn straight certain God knows it. You're the only one who hasn't got the message yet, Sister. So listen up, because I'm only gonna say it once." He walked over to where she stood looking up at him, wide-eyed and still. "It's not only impossible to save me; I'm not worth savin'."

Charlie spun on his heel and strode away from Angelina—strode away from her stricken face and her soft, pained gasp, and the small spark of hope she represented in a dark and dismal world.

The days were endless nightmares of heat and dust and a view of West Texas from the back of a horse. The nights were too short, filled with swirling remembrances of the horrid days and images too confusing to understand.

Since their last discussion, innumerable days before, Charlie had not spoken to Angelina beyond the necessities associated with their travels. She could tell he believed her half crazy. That knowledge wounded Angelina deeply. She had trusted him with one of the most important parts of herself, as he had trusted her with some of his secrets. But where she had tried to understand and support him, he had treated her like an escaped lunatic. She desperately needed guidance.

Angelina waited. But her angel did not return. She hoped, she prayed, and finally, she despaired. For the first time in her life, no guidance was forthcoming.

They crossed the Rio Grande into Mexico, and Angelina relaxed a bit, knowing they had escaped the jurisdiction of the surrounding law officials. If they were lucky, Drew Winston's injury had caused him to lose their trail, and he would give up on his quest. But in her heart, Angelina knew the wealth of hate she'd heard in the Ranger's voice would not allow him to give up so easily.

They made camp for the night in a valley shielded on three sides by rocky hills. A small stream ran nearby, providing fresh water for the horses and a welcome outlet for their own dwindling supply.

Dinner was once again a silent affair. As they had many times before during their days on the trail, they dined on dried mutton Charlie had taken from the Ranger's supplies. Whenever possible, Charlie shot a rabbit, and he cooked the carcass over the open fire. Still, after so many days of the same fare, Angelina found herself imagining the delicacies that would greet her once she reached home—fresh bread, fresh fruit, cool lemonade and any kind of meat, as long as it wasn't dried, boiled or killed only moments before eating.

Charlie got up, disturbing Angelina's reverie, and went to check on the horses one final time for the evening. Upon returning, he sat down on his bedroll and proceeded to stare into the flames and ignore her as he did every night.

Angelina considered trying to start a conversation, but the several attempts she'd already made on previous evenings had been met with sullen, if not outright rude, responses. The closeness she'd shared with Charlie was a thing of the past, and she was at a loss for how to reclaim it. For some reason her revelation of her mission had made him angry and cold. Since she couldn't take back her words, what was she to do? How was she to help him if he wouldn't let her?

Those questions filled her mind as she lay down on her own bedroll, keeping her eyes fixed on Charlie's beautiful profile until her lids grew heavy and sleep overcame her.

When she opened her eyes, dawn hinted on the horizon. Charlie no longer sat on the opposite side of the fire. Traveling with him, she'd learned he had a habit of walking around the camp at different times during the night, and Angelina did not worry about his absence. Instead, she got up, stretching the stiffness from her muscles. After looking through her meager supply of personal items, she gathered a small sliver of soap and a hairbrush Luanne had given her and headed for the stream, concealed from their camp by several shoulder-high rock formations.

Coming around one of those rocks, Angelina immediately froze at the sight before her. Without conscious thought she retreated several steps until she was concealed behind the rocks. Then, though she knew she should have returned to camp and forgotten what she'd seen, she peered around the edge one more time.

Charlie lay in the shallow stream; his long golden hair streamed free upon the water. He floated on his back, his face turned up to the encroaching sun. The newborn light drifted across his chest, casting shadows the shade of a ripe peach onto his bronzed flesh.

Angelina caught her breath, transfixed. She had never seen anything so beautiful. The allure of the forbidden drew her, and she found she could not stop watching him though her conscience shouted warnings. She blew out the breath she had been holding. Why was she suddenly so hot when the sun had not yet risen and a chill still pervaded the land?

She had often watched her brothers swimming. But her brothers had been boys, were boys still, she now understood. Charlie was a man. A man

in all his glory—strong, masculine, graceful—
and she was far too aware of him as just that—
a man.

Suddenly Charlie stood, slicking his wet hair
back from his face with his hands and starting
toward the bank of the creek. Angelina's eyes
widened as more and more of Charlie Coltrain
was revealed to her eyes. If she wasn't mistaken,
he was naked beneath the water. She might have
watched her brothers swim, but they had never
done so without some type of clothing covering
their privates. Curiosity warred with conscience
until embarrassment took over. Angelina averted
her eyes just as Charlie reached the shallow
water.

Now that he was done bathing, he would soon
return to the camp. Angelina prepared to back
away from her hiding place as quietly as she had
come. It wouldn't do for Charlie to know she
had watched him. He was angry enough at her
already. Though she wondered if he would really
mind if he learned what she'd been up to. She
wasn't sure. When it came to worldly things, she
didn't understand anything at all.

Before leaving, Angelina couldn't resist taking a
final glance through the concealing brush. Charlie
faced away from her as he buttoned his Levi's.
Angelina did not have time to be thankful he was
sufficiently clothed. Her gaze was riveted to the
flesh of his back. Where Charlie's chest had been
smooth, and bronzed and perfect, his back was a
mass of crisscrossing scars. Puckered and white,
they marred the rippling muscles of his back and
disappeared below the waist of his Levi's.

Angelina spun away and ran back to camp.
She fell onto her bedroll, her fist stuffed into her

mouth to stifle the sobs that threatened to erupt from her throat.

She had nursed men and women, young and old alike, at her father's ranch and during her time at the convent. She had seen countless injuries and she had treated them all. But the sight of the scars on Charlie's back caused a burning pain to flare in her stomach that threatened to choke her. She wanted to go to him and run her fingers over the scars; she wanted to soothe away the long-ago pain and murmur to him that she would make everything better. But such words would only have been a lie. Whatever had happened to Charlie to cause such scars could not be made better—not now, not ever. He had told her a few things about his past, but obviously not everything. She had no idea of the depth of his pain, and if she had, she was incapable of dealing with such atrocities. She had been so smug, so proud to have been given a mission by God. But never once had she considered the cost of failure until now. Charlie's life, his soul, hung in the balance.

The magnitude of her responsibility sent a shaft of terror through her to rival the anguish coursing through her at the remembrance of Charlie's injuries. Angelina yanked her rosary from the pocket of her dress, got onto her knees and prayed a desperate prayer to God.

"*Santo Dios,* send me strength. Send me wisdom. Show me the way to help him. I am not worthy of this mission you have given me. I know nothing about a man like him, about such secrets, such private terrors. How can I save him? What will become of him if I fail? *Santo Dios,* help me. *Por favor, Dios,* I must have your help."

The slight shuffle of a boot against dirt behind her had Angelina crossing herself hurriedly and replacing her rosary in the pocket of her dress. She would start this day by ending the silence between them. No matter what it took, she would make Charlie come out from behind his angry mask and talk to her again. Forcing a smile onto her face, she stood and turned to meet him.

Her face drained of color, and she faltered sideways a step.

Two men led their horses into camp. Both men and animals were dusty from the trail. They had obviously traveled all night, on the hunt for someone or something. Weariness showed on their faces, but watchfulness shone from their eyes. One was tall, thin but wiry, with an air of wickedness so strong Angelina had to swallow hard against her fear. The second was shorter, heavier, but he held himself as though he would be ready for anything whenever it came. Angelina disliked them both on sight.

"Ma'am," the tallest man greeted her. "Could we impose upon you for some coffee?"

The accent's American, Angelina thought. Do they know Charlie's here? Or do they merely want coffee as they say?

"Please sit down," she said, her smile stiff upon brittle lips. "I'll get you a cup."

Please, God, don't let Charlie come back now.

Angelina risked a quick glance around the perimeter of the campsite as she poured the coffee. No sign of him yet. She could only hope he'd heard the visitors and planned to stay out of sight until she got rid of them.

After serving the two men, Angelina retreated to the opposite side of the fire. "What brings you gentlemen to this side of the border?"

The two glanced at each other quickly; then the tallest man shrugged and took a sip of his coffee. "We're looking for a man. He's wanted for murder in the states."

"Really? How terrible. And you think he's come this way?"

"Yes, ma'am. We've been tailing him for a few weeks now. You haven't come across a big yellow-haired fellow on a white horse?"

Angelina had to grit her teeth to keep from glancing over the men's heads to where Gabe grazed, partially obscured by her horse. How was she going to talk her way out of this one?

"No, I haven't seen anyone like that. I can't say I'm sorry either since you say he's wanted for murder."

"Among other things. But murder's what the dead-or-alive bounty's for."

The taller of the two seemed to be doing all the talking, though the shorter man nodded his agreement every so often. The talkative one looked away from Angelina to glance around the camp. His gaze took note of the two bedrolls and two saddles. Then, very slowly, he turned his head and looked over his shoulder. He stared for a long time at the two horses while his companion drank coffee, and Angelina felt herself sweat. When he turned back toward her, his gaze went to her face. Taking another slow sip of coffee, he stared directly into Angelina's eyes. She wanted to scream for Charlie to run, to hide, to get the hell away and never come back. These men were dangerous. They meant to take Charlie back. And they meant to take him dead.

"Where's your man?" The tall one continued to stare at her.

"M-my man?"

"Uh-huh."

"What man?"

"The one who sleeps on this bedroll and rides on that saddle. The one who, unless I miss my guess, rides that big white horse over there."

"N-no. No man. Just the mother superior. She's a-a big woman. She needs a big horse."

The man choked on his coffee. "Mother superior? You're a nun? Wearing that dress?" He indicated her brown garment with a grimace.

"I'm a postulate. My habit was—it was ruined."

"And you want me to believe you're out here alone with only another woman?"

"It's the truth." Angelina bit her tongue at the lie. No sign of Charlie yet. If she could only make them believe her.

"Well, where's the other one then."

"She—she—" Angelina glanced at the creek. "She's bathing. Yes, that's right. She went to bathe, and then we were going on to our convent." She returned her gaze to the bounty hunter. One glance told her he wasn't buying her story.

"Well, I'm sure the mother superior won't mind if we drop in to say hello." He got to his feet. His companion followed.

"No!" Angelina ran forward. "She might be unclothed. I-I'll go get her."

The man hesitated, then gave a sharp nod. "All right. But hurry up." He unholstered his pistol. "And don't try anything funny. You won't get far without them horses, and we'll be waiting right here for you both."

Angelina didn't wait around for him to change his mind. She ran toward the creek, crashing through the brush and nearly stumbling down the small bank and into the water. Regaining her balance, she frantically searched the area for some sign of Charlie.

The creek was deserted.

She couldn't believe it. Though she'd been praying Charlie would get away, she couldn't believe he'd actually left her alone with those two men. But it looked as though he had.

Now what? How was she going to explain the disappearance of the mythical mother superior? Should she look for somewhere to hide until the bounty hunters left?

Angelina glanced around again, narrowing her eyes as she searched for a hiding place. No luck. The area was as barren as most of Texas.

"Hey, lady?" The shout made Angelina jump and whirl around. "We don't have all day. Bring her on out or we'll be coming to get her."

"She's getting dressed," Angelina called back, stalling for time.

Before the words were out of her mouth she heard the two men stomping toward her. Panic flooded Angelina's chest. There was nowhere to go, nowhere to hide. And her golden savior was nowhere to be found.

The shorter of the two men burst through the brush first, grabbing her arm in a painful clasp and yanking her toward him. He spoke to her for the first time, putting his face close to hers and grating out his question. "Where is he?"

"Who? I don't know who you're talking about."

He shook her then, so hard her teeth rattled together and her eyes felt as though they were going to fly from her head. "Coltrain. We know you're with him. Where is he?"

The taller man came into Angelina's line of vision. He shook his head sadly. "'Fraid when he gets riled I can't calm him down. Just tell him what he wants to know and we'll leave you go. We don't want to hurt you, lady. We will if we have to, but we don't want to."

"Speak for yourself," the man holding Angelina retorted. "She's Coltrain's woman. Seems to me we should get a taste of what he's been having before we go."

"I don't know who you're talking about." Angelina heard the desperate plea in her voice and swallowed hard against the terror. She had played this scene before. This time she had no doubt she would come out the loser. "Truly, I don't know. I lied because I didn't want you to know I was traveling alone. My father died last week and I buried him on the trail. I'm going home."

The man shook her again—only once—but this time so hard her neck snapped back and the sun exploded into stars before her eyes. "We don't believe you, lady. Tell us the truth or else."

The dull sound of something hard meeting flesh and bone followed by a grunt penetrated Angelina's dazed senses. Then she heard the click of a gun being cocked. She blinked to clear her head and focused on the man in front of her.

A gun was pointed at his temple. The surprised look on the bounty hunter's face caused a hysterical bubble of mirth to slide up Angelina's throat. The sound that erupted from her mouth was more akin to a sob.

"Let the lady loose," Charlie rasped. "Let her

go nice and easy, or I'll blow your brains out the other side of your head."

Immediately Angelina was free, and she stumbled away from the bounty hunter. The taller man lay on the ground at Charlie's feet, unconscious.

"Shit, Angelina, you don't lie worth beans, do ya?"

"Is that bad?" she stuttered, her teeth still chattering with fear.

"It is when our necks are on the line. Remind me to teach you how someday."

"No, thank you. Where have you been?"

Charlie frowned though he kept his gaze on the bounty hunter in front of him. "Where do you think I was? Tryin' to get a clear shot most of the time. But you couldn't seem to stay out of the way."

Angelina gasped. "You mean you were going to shoot these two men?"

"Sister, they'd have shot me and done the same or worse to you if we had given them half a chance. When are you gonna wise up?"

Angelina just stared at Charlie in amazement. He was serious. He flicked his glance her way, then, as quickly, returned his attention to the man he held at gunpoint. "Shut your mouth, Sister. The flies'll get in." She did with a snap of teeth and earned a quirk of his lips for her compliance. "Now get me a rope so we can tie these two up and get out of here."

"You aren't going to get away, Coltrain," the bounty hunter sneered. "There's guys looking for you from Texas to California and every place in between."

"I had that figured out for myself. I'm only

worryin' about you right now. Keep your hands where I can see 'em. I'd like nothin' better than to put a bullet in you after the way I heard you talkin' to the Sister here. In fact, maybe I will anyway, just for fun."

The bounty hunter turned pale and sweat rolled down one cheek.

"Would you quit taking about killing and shooting?" Angelina shouted, startling herself and the others with her vehemence.

Charlie frowned. "What's the matter with you?"

Angelina turned on her heel and walked away without answering. There was no reasoning with Charlie Coltrain. Stubborn men were always right. If she had to, she would admit he was the expert in handling dangerous situations. She just made a muddle of them. Still, he frightened her when he discussed murder as calmly as the weather. More and more she was coming to realize Charlie Coltrain was more man than she wanted to handle.

Within minutes Angelina returned to Charlie with the rope, ignoring his questioning look. Shortly thereafter, the two bounty hunters were tied securely, one still unconscious, though Angelina had checked his head and determined he would be all right. Then she and Charlie had returned to camp.

Angelina doused the fire and set about rolling up her bedding in preparation to leave. When she stood, the bedroll in her hands, and turned to go to the horses, Charlie blocked the way. She tilted her head back and looked into his face. His hat shaded his eyes, but she could still read the confusion within them as he stared down at her.

"Care to tell me what that was all about down by the creek?"

"No." She made to move past him.

He stopped her with his hand on her upper arm. "Yes, I want to know why you're so angry. Did you think I'd gone away and left you?"

"I didn't know what to think. I was frightened."

"You've got to know by now that I wouldn't have left you with them, Angelina."

Charlie's grip on her arm loosened, now more a caress than anything else. Angelina looked up at him again. "Why?" she asked. "Why would I know that?"

"I may be a lot of things, but I'm not a coward. I wouldn't walk away and leave a woman alone with two men like that, especially when she was doin' her damnedest to protect me."

He took a step closer and blocked the sun, throwing her into the shade caused by his shadow. Charlie's body brushed against hers, and Angelina caught her breath at the sensation. She couldn't seem to look away from his eyes. They held her in the same position, though she knew she should back away from him and the temptation he represented as fast as she could.

"Why'd you do it, Angelina?" His voice sounded somewhere between a whisper and a growl. "You lied for me. Isn't that a sin?"

A sin, yes, her mind answered. Her body answered a different call. When Charlie bent his head and touched his lips to hers in the softest of kisses, she leaned into him, raising her hands to cradle his face and pull him closer.

Suddenly all the fear that had been roiling in her stomach since she'd first seen the bounty hunters became an emotion of a different kind. If things had gone differently, if Charlie hadn't been who he was—the capable and dangerous outlaw—they would both be dead. But they weren't; they were alive. And she clung to him, to his heat and his passion and his life, as her mouth melded to his.

After his first initial start of surprise at her response, Charlie kissed her back with the same fervor. What had started as a gentle brush of lips became more as he coaxed her mouth open. When his tongue entered her, she met the caress with her own, shivering at the shaft of fire blazing from her mouth to her belly. She tangled her fingers in his hair and angled her head so she could experience the heat to its fullest.

Charlie wrenched his mouth away from hers and stared down at her, the confusion still present in his eyes. She took a step toward him, offering her lips again, but he shook his head sharply and put his hands on her waist, holding her back. Both of them were breathing fast, the sound harsh in the early morning stillness.

"What the hell are you doin', Angelina?"

"Kissing you. I thought that's what you wanted."

"I did. I do." He released her and ran a hand through the hair she had so recently caressed. "But you don't. Not really. I know what you're feelin' now. Sometimes when you think you're gonna die, and then you find out you're not, you want to prove you're still alive." He gave a short, harsh laugh. "I've been there enough times myself. But you shouldn't kiss me like that. You don't understand what you're doin'."

Anger flared along with the embarrassment. "I understand perfectly well what I'm doing. I'm not a child, Charlie Coltrain."

"Damn near." He held up a hand to stop her tirade. "You're young, you're innocent and you're goin' to be a nun."

"You told me once that you wouldn't kiss me again until I asked for it. Well, I asked for it."

"I think I told you you'd beg." A long sigh escaped him from somewhere deep inside. "Hell, I only said that to make you mad. I'm just a man, Sister, and not a very good one. I've done some awful things, but for most of 'em I had a reason, and I can still live with myself. Though just barely. If I ruin you, if I ruin your dream, I'll be doin' it for my own selfish need. That I can't live with." He looked straight into her eyes, and Angelina's breath caught in her throat at the earnestness of his gaze. "I'm the one doin' the beggin' now, Sister. Don't kiss me again. Don't touch me. I can't keep turnin' away from you forever. I want you too damn much."

Chapter Ten

The tense silence that had existed between Angelina and Charlie for the past week continued over the next few days. She was mortified she had allowed her emotions to run away with her usual good sense. What was wrong with her?

Charlie had said she was merely reacting to a frightening experience, and he should know. But if Angelina was being honest, she would have to admit the feelings that had rushed through her when she'd kissed Charlie had not been new feelings. She had experienced their pull nearly every minute since she had first seen him. She had told herself that the tiny bud of heat burning within her whenever she looked at him was a reaction to the danger she sensed in him, or it was a reaction to the danger all around them, or maybe just a residue of the excitement she was experiencing over her mission. It might be all those things, but the feeling was something else, too. Something frightening, strange and new, something that endangered everything she believed in, everything she wanted and held dear in her life.

Angelina sat up straighter on her horse, shaking her head and willing the disturbing thought away. She would not give a name to such emotions. She would not. There was no reason to. They would arrive at her father's hacienda outside of Chihuahua in about two days, and then Charlie Coltrain would be but a memory. Besides, he had told her himself—no, he had begged her—to leave him alone. Just the thought of his words made her cringe with embarrassment, though she was thankful he had said them. She had to concentrate all her energies on her mission if she was to succeed before her time ran out.

Charlie stopped at the top of a ridge and reined in his horse. He shaded his eyes and gazed downward.

"What's the matter?" Angelina asked as she pulled to a stop next to him.

"Ranch up ahead." Charlie's voice drew her attention forward, and he indicated the buildings below them with a nod. "Want to stop?"

"Oh, yes, please." Until the opportunity had become available, Angelina hadn't realized how tired and hot and dirty she was. The chance that they might be able to rest awhile and maybe clean off the top layer of dust was too much to resist.

Charlie gave her one of his rare half smiles and nudged his horse down the ridge.

They rode into the front yard of the hacienda and reined in their horses. The place looked quite a bit like her own home, though on a less grand scale. Her father had always made sure everything on his ranch was built to impress. This yard was circled by a barn, corral and two-story home. Several horses strolled leisurely around the paddock, nickering a welcome to Gabe and Angelina's horse.

Charlie jumped to the ground and helped Angelina from her horse. She swayed a bit, having been in the saddle since early morning, and Charlie put a steadying hand to her elbow. The flare of heat that always enveloped her at his touch sparked anew, and she gritted her teeth against the pleasure.

Noticing nothing amiss, Charlie released her and glanced around the deserted yard. "Looks like everyone's gone."

No sooner had he finished his sentence than the door to the house opened and a woman stepped forward. Just above five feet tall and obviously pregnant, she took slow and measured steps. The slant of the porch roof shaded her features as she leaned against the doorway and wiped her face with a languid gesture. At the movement her long black braid fell forward over her shoulder and smacked against her ample belly. She threw the hair back over her shoulder with an impatient gesture.

"Can I help you?" the woman called, shading her eyes and squinting into the sun. She focused on Angelina, then let out a gasp of delight and lumbered forward. "Angelina!" she shouted and walked down the steps to throw her arms around Angelina's neck, hugging her tightly.

"Maria," Angelina said, hugging the woman back despite the shock running though her. She stepped back, holding Maria at arm's length. "What on earth are you doing here?"

"This is my home. I got married." Maria smiled

shyly and ran a hand over the mound of her stomach. "Obviously. His father gave us this land and some stock, and we started our own ranch."

"I'm so happy for you. You always wanted to have dozens of children."

"So did you—" Maria broke off with a quick intake of breath. "I mean when we were children you did. I know that now you—uh—I mean—" She faltered to a stop.

Angelina laid a hand on her friend's arm to ease Maria's embarrassment. "I know what you mean. That's one of the best things about the convent, too—teaching the children."

Maria nodded, obviously relieved she had not offended Angelina. "What are you doing here? Your parents said you would not be home for many years." Her gaze went to Charlie and she frowned. "Who is this?"

Angelina turned to Charlie, who had stood patiently next to his horse while he watched their reunion. Angelina motioned for him to come closer and he did, removing his hat. Maria gasped out loud at the sight of his golden hair and beyond handsome face. Her gaze flicked to Angelina's face, then back to Charlie's, and she smiled slyly.

"Where is your habit and veil, Angelina? Is this why you've come home? To tell your parents you've given up the church"—she nodded at Charlie—"for him?"

"No!" The word burst from Angelina's mouth, sounding guilty even to her own ears. She took a deep breath and looked at Charlie. He raised his eyebrows and shrugged. She bit her lip to stifle a reprimand for the amusement she read in his eyes.

"This is Charlie Coltrain. I had a little problem returning to my convent after a short trip to nurse some other Sisters. Charlie assisted me and now he's taking me home for a visit."

"Hmm," was Maria's only comment.

Angelina chose to ignore the skepticism in her friend's tone. She knew explaining herself any further would only create more suspicion.

"Charlie, this is my dear friend from childhood. Maria—" She smiled at her friend. "I don't even know your married name. What is it?"

Just as Maria opened her mouth to answer, the sound of a horse being ridden hard and fast in their direction reached them. They all turned toward the house and seconds later a rider burst around the corner.

From the corner of her eye, Angelina saw Charlie draw his gun, but neither quickly nor desperately. He merely withdrew the weapon from the holster as though he didn't even realize he'd done it. He cocked the pistol and held the weapon at the ready. Stepping forward, he focused his eyes on the rider as he placed himself between the two women and the new arrival.

Angelina felt protected, safe and secure in the shadow of Charlie's capability and assurance. Warmth flooded her that had nothing to do with the heat of the sun or the heaviness of her old brown dress. The warmth sprang from deep inside and she didn't want the feeling to ever go away.

Then she looked up into the face of the man on the horse as he reined to a stop in front of them. The warmth died as icy-cold recognition jolted through her.

The man's eyes met hers and widened with recognition as well, before narrowing with dislike. He sported a thin mustache on his upper lip that had not been there the last time she had seen him. He was still tall, wiry, with blue-black hair and stunningly blue eyes that contrasted with his sun-browned skin. A handsome man—with a distinctly unhandsome personality.

"Angelina Reyes," he said with a nod and a thin, nasty smile. "What brings you and your—" He flicked a disdainful glance at Charlie, who continued to hold the gun ready while he observed the rider. "Would this be a gunslinger? What would a nun"—he spat the last word with obvious distaste—"want with a man of his caliber?"

"Seems to me," Charlie drawled, his ruined voice earning a start of surprise from everyone but Angelina, "from the looks of you, the Sister needs all the help she can get."

"Is that so? And just who the hell are you? And what are you doing on my land?"

Angelina stepped forward and placed a hand on Charlie's forearm. Though he looked perfectly calm and in control, the muscles of his arm were bunched tightly with tension. "Juan Alvarez, this is Charlie Coltrain."

"Juan from the church?" Charlie asked.

Juan grimaced and shot Angelina a venomous glare. He had obviously not forgiven her for refusing to marry him. Even though he'd married Maria and received land of his own, his pride had been wounded, and Spanish men did not easily forget such a blow. Angelina knew well the stiff-necked pride of the criollo male. She had lived with seven prime examples of that pride for most of her life.

"I can't believe you told this, this"—Juan waved

his hand dismissively at Charlie—"person about our private business."

"It was hardly private, Juan, considering everyone in the area was there. I'm sorry I had to embarrass you that way, but you have to admit we would have been miserable together."

Angelina took Juan's silence for acquiescence and went on. "As I was telling Maria before you came—" She glanced over at her friend, whose face had taken on a green tinge since the harsh words had flown between Angelina and Juan. Obviously stress was not good for Maria in her condition. Angelina paused long enough to lead her friend to a chair near the house before she continued. "As I was telling your wife, Charlie is taking me home. I had no idea you or Maria had settled here or we wouldn't have stopped. I have no more desire to see you, Juan, than you have to see me."

Juan swung his leg over the horse and jumped lightly to the ground. Before she'd left, Angelina had believed Juan the tallest man in these parts. Such was the case no longer since Charlie topped him by several inches. But it was not the height that made Charlie seem so much larger. It was the hint of menace sizzling in the air around him with the ferocity of a midsummer lightning storm.

"Do you want to call off your man, Angelina?" Juan asked. "That gun of his makes me a bit nervous."

"The Sister don't own me," Charlie growled, though he reholstered his pistol anyway. "Now that you've had your reunion, let's go, Sister." He turned and walked toward Gabe.

"Oh, no, please," Maria cried, getting up from the chair with a lurch. "Can't you stay the night?

It's been so long since I've seen Angelina, and the only women to talk to way out here are the servants. I—" She cast a glance at her glowering husband, then finished her sentence in a low-voiced rush. "Angelina and I were like sisters. Despite everything that's happened, I've missed her."

The thought of spending the night as a guest in the home of Juan Alvarez was anything but pleasant, despite the lure of a bed and a warm bath. Angelina could tell by Juan's face he loathed the idea as much as she. Charlie didn't look very happy either if the glance he sent her way was any indication. But the pleading tone of Maria's voice and the hope on her face had Angelina sighing in weary defeat before she nodded. "All right. Just one night. Then we must go on."

The thought occurred to Angelina that she had been hoping for a way to extend her time with Charlie, to learn how she was meant to help him. God had given her one more day. She would have to make use of the gift.

Maria's small cry of happiness warmed Angelina's heart. They had once been close. Though Juan might hold a grudge against her, Angelina knew Maria was too kindhearted to hold anything against anyone for more than a second. Maria possessed a saintly soul and everyone loved her. Angelina truly hoped Maria was happy with Juan. He was not really a bad man, just a man who had been raised to believe his will was one step below God's—and only that low when he chose to acknowledge it.

Angelina's attention turned to Charlie as he led the horses toward the barn. What was different about him that made her heart pound and her throat clench and her skin tingle whenever he was near? He was a man, but she did not feel the same distaste for him that she had for Juan.

Maria pulled on Angelina's arm and chattered rapidly in a mixture of English and Spanish as she drew her friend toward the house. Angelina glanced at Juan as she went by. He stared after Charlie, a curious frown on his face; then his gaze flicked to Angelina and he smiled knowingly. Angelina returned the stare without flinching.

"Is there something you wanted, Juan?" she asked.

"No. Have a nice talk, *muchachas*. I will be back for dinner. I have more work to do yet today. Perhaps your man will assist me?"

Angelina frowned. Juan was up to something, and it involved Charlie. "I don't think so. He needs to rest."

"I can speak for myself, Sister." Charlie spoke from the doorway of the barn, the command in his ruined voice stopping all conversation. "I'll help the man out. I know my way around a horse ranch."

"Splendid." Juan clapped his hands. "We'll get you a fresh mount and be off." He walked toward the barn.

Angelina scowled at Charlie, but she kept her displeasure to herself. He did not seem to appreciate any advice from her about what he was to do and not do. The side of his mouth turned up, and he shrugged, then followed Juan into the dark interior of the barn.

Maria chattered on as though the break in conversation had not even occurred, and Angelina turned away reluctantly to follow her friend into the house.

"We've got to get you another dress. Where on earth did you get that one?"

"A whorehouse," Angelina muttered absently.

"What? Oh, you can't be serious. Anyway, it's better than your habit, I expect. We'll find you something pretty to wear. You'll feel so much better with a pretty dress."

Angelina smiled. She was definitely home again if a pretty dress could fix everything. That had always been both her mother's and her father's answer to every problem. Unfortunately, for all of them, such tactics had never worked with Angelina.

"I'll never fit into one of your dresses, Maria. You're at least four inches shorter than me. And quite a bit wider these days, as well."

Maria waved her hand and led the way to the bedrooms at the back of the house. "Juan's *madre* left some things here the last time she visited, since she knew she would come back when the baby arrived. You can wear something of hers. She'll never miss one dress." They reached what was obviously the guest room, and Maria went to the French armoire, obviously imported from the United States or maybe even France. Angelina's father had installed the furnishing in every one of their bedrooms at home to avoid the sight of clothes hung upon the walls. Many of the wealthy families had followed his example.

Maria opened the doors of the armoire to reveal several dresses. "This"—she pulled one out with a smile—"will look beautiful on you."

Angelina had to admit the dusty rose shade would flatter her coloring, but the depth of the neckline made her flinch. "I'd better not," she said.

"Nonsense. You cannot wear that rag to dinner. I won't allow it. Now, take it off, and I'll send someone in with hot water."

The promise of a hot bath made the decision for Angelina. She would only wear the dress for one night, she assured herself; then she would be back on the trail again. Once she reached home, there would be more modest gowns at her disposal.

"All right," she agreed and smiled at Maria's delight.

"Wonderful. When you're dressed, join me in the parlor, and we'll have lemonade." She turned, and if her body would have allowed it, Angelina was sure Maria would have skipped out the door.

An hour later, after a languid soak in the tub, Angelina stood in front of the mirror. Luckily for her, Juan's mother was a bit thicker through the waist as a result of having children. Angelina no longer owned a corset, one of the many advantages of becoming a nun. Once she got home she supposed she would have to be strapped into that torturous device once more in order to fit into her own clothes. The prospect did not bring a smile to her face.

However, the dress she wore now did. She had not felt silk against her skin for a year, and the color was too lovely to be denied. If there was one thing she did not like about the convent it was the absence of beauty. The only place she could indulge her love for bright colors and differing textures was in church. There the paintings and tapestries and windows of colored glass warred with each other for precedence in a battle for the master of the exquisite.

She ran her hand over the skirt and sighed.

mother superior would have an attack if she could see Angelina now. Most of her chest was revealed, as well as the tops of her breasts. Her skin glowed like warm honey against the delicate shade of the fabric. She'd braided her hair and twisted it up while still damp. Loose tendrils curled against her neck, creating a soft frame for her face.

What will Charlie think?

The thought came unbidden, causing her to blink in surprise. She had never before cared what a man thought of her. Where had such a question come from?

Putting such vanities from her mind with an effort, Angelina walked briskly from the room and joined Maria in the front parlor.

"Oh, you look beautiful," Maria breathed. "Your man will be speechless."

Angelina plopped down on the settee, another import from the looks of the furnishing, and scowled. "Maria, he is not my man. I'm a postulate. I'm going to be a nun. I cannot have a man. Charlie is taking me to my parents. That's all."

"I've seen the way he looks at you, Angelina, and the way you look at him. I'm not blind. If there isn't something going on between you now, there soon will be."

Angelina grabbed a glass of lemonade from the tray and took a healthy gulp. Maria was too close to the truth for comfort. "You're mistaken," she said when she had her voice under control. "He is merely escorting me home."

"Maybe he is. But that doesn't change what I see." Maria leaned forward and placed her hand over Angelina's. "I wonder why you are not yet a novice? Shouldn't you have taken those vows already? I understood you would be a postulate for only six months."

Angelina took another swallow of lemonade to give herself a moment to think. Maria might act flighty, but she knew people. She could get anyone to talk to her just by asking quiet, concerned questions until the person gave in and told her everything.

"The mother superior did not think I was ready to become a novice yet. She wished for me to think on my calling a while longer. Then there was sickness, and I had other things to attend to that were more important than the ceremony that would make me a novice."

"I see. So the mother superior did not think you should be a nun either?"

"What do you mean either? You've known me all my life. You know how much I wanted to be with the Sisters. How can you ask me such a thing?"

"I want you to be happy. I understand your devotion to your beliefs. But I've also seen you with children. You won't be happy without them in your life." Maria laid her hand upon her distended belly with an absent gesture. Angelina's gaze followed her friend's hand, and she swallowed deeply against the lump of envy in her throat.

"I have the children I teach."

Maria laughed. "That's not the same and you know it. This man you are with. There is something between you. I sense it. You'll be happier with him than you ever could be in a convent. Believe me. I know."

"You're happy?" Angelina looked deeply into her friend's eyes. "With Juan?"

"Oh, yes. He's everything I ever wanted. Strong, manly, proud. We have this place"—she placed her hand over her belly—"and the *nino* on the way. I am in heaven on earth."

"You love him then?"

"Love?" Maria's face took on a puzzled expression before she said slowly, "I suppose I do love him. Now. Yes, of course I love the father of my child."

"You should have said something before, Maria. If you'd told your parents you loved him, then maybe he wouldn't have been promised to me, and we could have avoided all the embarrassment."

"Oh, I didn't love him then." Maria's eyes were round with shock. "When you went to the convent he was so hurt, so embarrassed, I felt sorry for him. We got to know each other and one thing led to another. We moved out here to avoid all the talk nearer home."

Angelina winced. She had always known she'd caused a scandal with her refusal to marry Juan, but once she'd gone off to the convent, she had forgotten all about him. She hadn't realized her actions would affect his life for so long. A wave of shame washed over her at her selfishness. But then, things had worked out for the best since he and Maria now had each other. Once she left again, they would forget about the past just as she had.

At the sound of several horses coming toward the house, they both stood and moved to the window. Juan and Charlie were back, accompanied by at least a dozen men.

"Let's go out and greet them," Maria said and led the way to the front door.

The men dismounted as Angelina and Maria approached. When the hands noticed them, something in the air changed. Angelina felt the change and hesitated. Strange, male faces turned toward her, one by one—some smirked, others snickered, several whispered to a companion under their breath.

She shot a confused glance at Charlie and Juan. Juan's eyes met hers first, triumphant, a smug smile curving his lips. He was too happy about something.

Angelina looked at Charlie. In contrast, his eyes were hard, angry, and his mouth formed a grim line. She crossed over to him and whispered, "What happened?"

Snickers erupted from the men, but she ignored them, concentrating instead on Charlie.

"You got trouble, Sister," he muttered. "Big trouble."

Trouble was too mild a word, Charlie thought, for what had gone on all afternoon at the hands of Juan Alvarez. Charlie had ignored the sly looks and the subtle innuendos all afternoon, though he had been hard pressed not to plant a fist in the middle of quite a few faces. He controlled himself only by remembering Angelina's face when she'd seen her friend. The presence of Maria had made Angelina happy. She had wanted to stay and talk with her friend. For that reason and that reason only, Charlie held his temper in check.

He didn't care what Alvarez and his cronies thought about him. But Angelina was a different matter. She had been the main topic of conversation throughout the afternoon. Though nothing was said outright, the speculation ran rampant.

Just what had Angelina Reyes been doing alone with a man in the wilds of Texas?

Charlie reasoned with himself that denial would only fuel the fire of rumor, so he kept his mouth stoically shut and kept working. He had hoped that, once they returned to the house, the men would depart and Alvarez would shut up before Angelina got wind of what was going on. But that was obviously not going to happen. Alvarez had a grudge against Angelina, and he meant to take whatever revenge he could while the taking was good.

The men departed to eat their meal in the combination bunkhouse and cookhouse. Angelina stood next to Charlie, a frown marring the usually smooth skin of her forehead. The one sentence he'd spoken to her before the men erupted into guffaws only hinted at the trouble brewing. He could not bring himself to elaborate with Alvarez's intent gaze capturing their every move. When Angelina tried to draw him aside to talk, he shook his head sharply and followed their hosts toward the house.

"Later," he hissed, and her worried frown deepened. If he had anything to say about it, they'd be on their way before daybreak tomorrow, and this issue would be left behind them.

As the four of them sat down to dinner, Charlie had a chance to notice what Angelina wore. How could he have overlooked it before?

He blinked, once, twice. She was lovely. He'd always known she was beautiful, even in the ugliest of clothes, but now he could see that beautiful was only a word when applied to Angelina Reyes. True, her features were delicate, her neck long and slender, and the tops of her breasts were revealed by the pink gown. Charlie stopped that thought before it went any further. Just the sight of her made him ache with suppressed lust.

He dragged his gaze away from her and encountered Juan Alvarez's smirk.

Damn. What he wouldn't give to smack such smugness from that Spanish gentleman's face.

"Well," Alvarez said expansively as he passed the china platters loaded with chicken and dumplings. "It has been quite a long time, Angelina. I never thought we'd see your face again once you entered the convent."

Charlie glanced at Angelina. She took the platter and smiled, though he noticed the smile did not reach her eyes. "I have not taken my final vows. I am allowed to visit my family before I enter the convent forever."

"Oh, I see. Then you are not truly a nun yet. Well, that makes things clearer, does it not?"

"What things?" Angelina asked.

"Just you and your amigo here." He toasted Charlie with his wineglass.

"What about me and my friend?"

Charlie winced. Why couldn't she just eat and be quiet?

"The way you two are traveling. Alone. An unmarried man, an Anglo, and an unmarried woman, a criollo. You know how people talk, Angelina."

Maria drew in a sharp, dismayed breath. Angelina glanced at her friend, pursed her lips and laid down her knife carefully beside her plate before turning her full attention to Alvarez.

"Exactly what are you implying, Juan?"

"I'm not implying anything. I'm simply stating facts. Your reputation is ruined, Angelina."

"And I'm sure I can count on you to spread the word. Can't I, Juan?"

He smiled and took another sip of wine before answering. "Of course."

"Juan!" Maria gasped. "How can you say such a thing to Angelina. You of all people should know of her calling to do God's work."

Alvarez's face darkened at the reminder of his humiliation. "Be silent, *mujer*. I do not need your interference in this." He turned back to Angelina. "I find it disgusting that a woman who has supposedly devoted her life to God would flaunt her lover in the face of good Catholic people. And to prefer that yellow-haired, pretty-faced Anglo to me is beyond forgiving."

Angelina didn't answer, but her face turned pale as Alvarez spoke. Her hand fluttered to her throat, then hesitated when her fingers met flesh. She flushed, obviously embarrassed by the amount of skin revealed by her dress. Her gaze flicked to Charlie's face, and he read the distress in her eyes before she got to her feet.

"I made a mistake in hoping you might have forgiven what I did to you, Juan. I thought maybe you would understand my reasons once I was gone. I believed that since you'd found Maria and started a life together you could get past your bitterness. But I was wrong. I am going to change my dress, and then we will leave."

Head held high, Angelina walked from the room. Sparing only a glare for her husband, Maria followed.

Charlie toyed with his wineglass. His hands, always capable with a gun or a horse, looked large and clumsy next to the fragile crystal filled with rich red liquid.

"And now there are only the two of us," Alvarez said.

"Looks that way. Do you like tormentin' women?"

"Only some."

"Pretty cowardly if you ask me." Charlie glanced up and caught the flash of anger in the man's eyes.

"I did not ask you."

"True enough." Charlie put down the wine, untasted, keeping his gaze on Alvarez. "I feel like a smoke. Should we go outside?"

Alvarez raised his eyebrows at the polite inquiry. But he nodded and led the way.

When they reached the middle of the yard, he paused and looked at Charlie with a puzzled expression. "You wanted to smoke. Where's your tobacco?"

Charlie chuckled, a gravelly sound that made Alvarez flinch. "I forgot. Don't have none left. The Sister burned it all."

"Then why—" Alvarez trailed off as the true reason for their trip out of doors came to him. "So you are finally going to stand up for the honor of your woman. To tell you the truth I thought you'd have done something before now. But you merely proved my theory that no-account Anglos have no respect for their women."

"I've got more respect for the Sister than a low-down excuse for a criollo gentleman like you could ever imagine. I just wanted to come out here to discuss respect with you. Before we go, you'll apologize to the Sister." Charlie took a step closer to Alvarez and lowered his voice to a whisper. "And you'll make her believe you mean it, even though you and I both know you won't."

"Like hell I will. I wouldn't apologize to that little *puta* for any amount of money."

"Care to make a bet on that?"

Charlie didn't flinch as he smashed his fist into Alvarez's stomach. When the man doubled over, Charlie brought his knee up to connect with Juan's chin. Alvarez landed on his back in the dirt. Charlie knelt next to him and grabbed the man by his shirt front. Though Juan was groggy from the blow, he focused on Charlie's face when Charlie shook him.

"Listen to me, Alvarez. You're one disgustin' excuse for a man. I don't want to hear one more word out of you against Angelina, and you'd better make sure your men keep quiet, too. Because if I ever hear any of that crap you were spouting about her out of anyone else's mouth, I'll come lookin' for you. And next time you'll be in a lot worse shape when I'm through"

Charlie stood and turned toward the house, intent on collecting Angelina and getting off Alvarez property.

"Charlie, behind you!"

Angelina's shriek from the bedroom window made him dive for the dirt. The report of a gun echoed, and a bullet whizzed past his cheek, close enough to sting. He rolled toward Alvarez and snatched the derringer from the man's fingers. Then he hauled back his fist and punched Juan Alvarez directly on his aristocratic jaw. The man lapsed into unconsciousness just as Angelina ran out of the house and threw herself into Charlie's arms.

Chapter Eleven

"Dear God, dear God," Angelina sobbed against Charlie's chest. "I thought he was going to kill you."

"He meant to. If you hadn't warned me, he would likely have blown my head off."

Just the thought made Angelina shiver and hug Charlie closer. The commotion had brought most of the hands from the bunkhouse and they stood in a semicircle around them. Maria sobbed quietly in the background.

"We'd better get a move on, Sister, before someone takes a notion to keep us here. I don't think we want to wait for Alvarez to wake up."

"No, you're right." Angelina forced herself to release him. He was alive, and that was all that mattered now. The fact that she wanted to go on holding him forever was a thought she pushed forcibly from her mind. She looked up into his face, and he gave her his half smile for encouragement. Something wet glistened at the side of his face, and Angelina reached up to wipe it away.

Charlie winced at her touch.

"You're hurt," she gasped, staring at the blood on her fingertips.

"Only a scratch. I told you, he'd've blown my head off if it hadn't been for you."

"You mean you're bleeding from a bullet?" A wave of dizziness washed over her and she swayed.

"Hey, Sister." Charlie grasped her arm. "What's the matter? I thought you were used to blood."

"Not yours."

"I don't like it much neither. But we've got to get out of here while we can. Faint on me later."

Angelina nodded. Luckily she'd been able to discard the rose-colored dress and change into a riding habit borrowed from Senora Alvarez before she'd heard voices outside and gone to investigate. There was no reason to return to the house now. Angelina crossed to where Maria knelt at the side of her husband.

"I'm sorry this had to happen. We'll be leaving now."

Maria nodded, but said nothing more. Angelina looked at Charlie. He'd drawn his gun and he watched the circle of men warily. She joined him, and together they backed toward the barn.

"Can you saddle the horses?" he whispered. "I don't think I'd better take my eyes off 'em right now."

"Certainly," Angelina said and did just that as Charlie stood guard near the door.

Juan was just starting to stir as they rode out. No one tried to stop them, and Angelina breathed a sigh of relief once they rode out of sight of the ranch.

They traveled hard for an hour, and then Angelina stopped her mount.

Charlie stopped as well, but rounded on her with fury in his voice. "What the hell are you stoppin' for? They could be right behind us. I got the drop on 'em once, but they'll be ready now. I'm no match for a dozen armed men, Sister."

Angelina dismounted and calmly ripped a piece of material from the dark trailing skirt of Senora Alvarez's riding habit. She would have to remember to send the woman a new one.

"What are you doin'?" Charlie jumped down from his horse and strode toward her.

"I'm going to clean your wound."

"Not now. I tell ya, I'm fine."

"I'm not moving from this spot until you let me see your face."

"Angelina." The word was a growl—a warning.

She ignored it, taking out her canteen and wetting the material in her hand. "They won't come after us, Charlie. Relax."

"How do you know? I'm sure Alvarez is hoppin' mad."

"I'm sure Juan is nursing a headache the size of Mexico City."

"He'll send his men out after us."

"No," Angelina said. "He won't. He might insult us on his own property, but he wouldn't dare send armed men after me—not when we're so close to my father's hacienda."

"Your father has that much power?"

"Yes," she said simply. "Believe me, no one is following us."

Her sincerity must have convinced Charlie, for the tense readiness of his body relaxed. He came a few steps nearer. "Get it over with then," he growled and turned his cheek toward her.

The moon shone bright above them, casting a blue-white light across his features. Blood had darkened to black as it dried across his injured cheek.

"You'll have to sit down. I can't see very well from here."

Charlie obeyed without comment, and Angelina joined him on the ground. He avoided her eyes, staring instead straight ahead while she ministered to him. Gently, she cleaned away the blood, allowing the slash to bleed for a few seconds to cleanse the wound.

"You might have a scar," she observed.

He didn't even look at her. "Good. I've always been too pretty."

"I wouldn't say that." Angelina pressed a clean cloth to the wound to staunch the flow.

He looked at her then, his black eyes boring into hers. Had she ever thought his eyes cold and empty? Impossible. Right now they flamed with a glow from within and brimmed with so much emotion that she caught her breath in wonder.

"You wouldn't?" he asked, his ruined voice affecting her like a caress. "What would you say, Angelina?" His hand came up and cupped hers where she pressed the cloth to his cheek.

"Not too pretty," she choked out past the sudden tightness in her throat. "Handsome."

"Too handsome?"

"Perhaps."

"I'm sure you've learned a pretty face doesn't reflect what's inside."

"Of course," she answered, though her mind was distracted by the way his thumb moved up

and down the back of her hand, stroking, soothing, arousing.

"Yeah, Sister, you know it's the soul that counts.
And mine's awful black."

She was drowning in his eyes, black pools filled
with too many emotions for her to name—longing, lust and a deep well of sadness that drew her
closer and closer.

"I can help you," she whispered, just before her
lips met his.

They had shared kisses of all kinds—hard, soft,
punishing, seductive—but this one was somehow
different. This kiss was all those things at once
and more.

His mouth on hers was warm, comforting. She
sank against him, somehow landing in his lap.
His arms went around her, cradling her body to
his. She urged his face closer and opened her
mouth to welcome him. Somewhere in the back
of her mind she remembered she was not supposed to kiss him, not supposed to touch him.
But the thought only lasted a moment before the
sensations destroyed it.

He groaned softly, and she moved her hands to
the back of his neck, half afraid he would stop
touching her. But he did not. Instead, his tongue
stroked the inside of her mouth, her teeth, then
finally met the tip of hers with a feather-light
touch. She pushed his hat from his head, and his
golden hair cascaded around their faces, drifting
softly past her cheek.

She moved her hands to his back, feeling the
ridged scars despite the covering of his shirt.
Tracing them with her fingers, she soothed his
movement of retreat with low murmurs deep in
her throat and long, slow strokes of her hands up

and down his spine. She remembered the livid white scars that had marred the perfection of his muscled back and spread her palms across his shoulders to hug him tighter.

Lost. She was lost in the wonder of Charlie. His mouth, his hands, his hair—every part of him enchanted her. She wanted to know more about this wondrous feeling that had been building between them since they'd first set eyes upon each other. She was tempted, so very tempted.

Charlie could teach her. All she had to do was let him.

With a strangled cry of dismay, Angelina tore her mouth away from Charlie's.

"What?" Charlie asked, holding her fast in his lap as she tried to scramble away. "What's wrong?"

His voice was even rougher than usual, laced with passion and need. Angelina winced and turned her gaze up to the bright moon above them. She couldn't look at his beautiful face. She would not look into his hot black eyes. He had told her not to kiss him, not to touch him. The lust between them was too great a temptation.

But the temptation was not all for Charlie. Just as Christ had been tempted in another desert, in this desert Angelina was learning the true meaning of the word, and without the benefit of Christ's divinity, she didn't know how to resist.

With Charlie's lips hot on her own, with temptation tasting too good to resist, Angelina experienced another revelation. The reason she couldn't discover a way to help Charlie, to fulfill her mission, was because Charlie was not her mission.

Oh, no.

He was her temptation.

*   *   *

The snakebite delayed Drew for two weeks. He had been delirious, probably calling for Claire as he always did in his sleep. Luckily the couple taking care of him understood very little English. He didn't have to explain his ravings to them as he'd been asked to do on several occasions in the past when he'd called out the wrong woman's name in bed.

When he was finally back on the trail, he found the nearest telegraph office and sent a message to Ranger headquarters regarding his accident, telling his superior he would be on leave indefinitely. Drew didn't really care one way or the other if he lost his post. Charlie Coltrain was going to get his punishment one way or the other.

Drew shaded his eyes for the tenth time that day and looked into the distance. Nothing. No one.

Where could they be? In Mexico by now, that much was certain. Drew had crossed over the border himself that morning. He figured Coltrain and the woman had quite a jump on him. But he did possess one fact they had no doubt forgotten, and he planned to make use of his information as soon as he found any place resembling a town.

Night approached as he reached a settlement called Villa something or other, the elements having erased half the sign. Drew left his horse outside the saloon and entered. Where there was alcohol, gambling and women, there was always information.

He approached the bartender and ordered whiskey. The man eyed Drew's Colt Peacemakers with interest before he complied. Drew tossed back the shot, but shook his head at the offer of a second.

He needed to keep riding tonight if he wanted to make up some time.

"Got a minute for a question or two?" he asked the bartender.

The man shrugged, but didn't move away. Encouraged, Drew leaned his elbow on the bar. "I'm looking for a man. Tall, yellow hair. His voice is wrecked from the war. Seen him?"

"No."

"Might have been with a woman. Small, pretty, Mexican."

"No."

Drew sighed. This was getting him nowhere. He put a coin on the bar and slid it toward the bartender. The money disappeared into the man's palm.

"Remember 'em now?"

"No, senor. If they came through this town, they would have come here. We have the only rooms and the only kitchen. They have not been here."

Drew nodded slowly. The few hours following his injury were hazy to him. But he did remember certain things. He remembered Coltrain carrying him around when he was too weak to protest. He remembered gentle hands and concerned brown eyes. Best of all, he remembered her name.

"Angelina Reyes," he said. "Ever heard the name Reyes."

The bartender's eyes widened in surprise. "*Si,* Senor. Miguel Reyes owns the biggest hacienda in northern Mexico."

Drew Winston smiled. The bartender returned the smile until he looked into Drew's eyes. Whatever he saw there made his smile fade as he backed away, wariness etching his forehead with lines.

"Where?" Drew's voice was taut with suppressed excitement. "Where in northern Mexico?"

"Near Chihuahua, Senor. Ask anyone when you get there. Anyone can tell you how to find the Reyes ranch."

Drew nodded his thanks and left the saloon. He mounted his horse and turned it in the direction of . . .

"Chihuahua," he whispered in triumph.

Angelina and Charlie stopped their horses at the top of a ridge that overlooked her father's ranch. They stared down at the bustle of activity below them.

Home.

The word slammed through Angelina's head like the crack of a whip. There was no going back now. She would have to face her father and everything such a meeting entailed. Her heart thumped faster in reaction to the thought.

Angelina slanted a glance Charlie's way. He was not looking at her. What else was new? Since the incident two nights past when she had realized Charlie's true significance and mumbled some stupid excuse for her withdrawal from him, Charlie had rarely looked at her.

Oh, he had been polite. Too polite. The closeness that had grown between them during their time together had been replaced by a distant civility she abhorred. Though she should be happy Charlie's changed attitude had removed temptation from her grasp, she wanted to beg him just to look at her once the way he used to.

She straightened in the saddle, wincing against the pain slicing through her back at the movement. What on earth was the matter with her? She should thank the Lord their hellish trip was nearly at an end. Once Charlie left, she would never see his face again, never hear his ruined voice, never kiss his sinfully clever lips. She would be out of temptation's clutches; she would pass God's test.

So why did she want to cry?

"Nice spread." Charlie continued to stare at the two-story house, barn, bunkhouse and corral below them.

The house shone in the sun, whitewashed to perfection. Miguel Reyes never allowed his home to look anything less than like the palace he considered it to be. "The largest hacienda in this part of Mexico," Angelina said, though the pride her father felt over that accomplishment remained absent from her voice and her heart.

"Hmm. All your brothers live here, too?"

"No. My father married every one off to an heiress and nearly doubled the size of Reyes land. All my brothers manage their own part of the empire."

"Your father sounds like an interestin' man."

"I wouldn't call him interesting."

"What would you call him?"

Angelina considered several terms, then regretfully discarded each one as unladylike. *"Padre,"* she answered. "I just call him *Padre.*"

Without further comment, she kicked her horse into a gallop and set off toward home.

She should have known that nothing would escape the notice of Miguel Reyes. By the time she dismounted in front of the house, he and her mother were already waiting on the porch. They had changed little in the year she had been gone. Perhaps her mother was a bit thinner, but no gray showed in the thick black hair and her face was still unlined and beautiful. Only her eyes revealed the old soul held within.

"Angelina," her mother said, joy coloring her voice. She started forward, her arms outstretched for an embrace. Her husband stopped her with a motion of his hand.

"What is the meaning of this, daughter?" His voice was as cold as his eyes. His muscular, stocky build had thickened minutely around the waist, though he still held himself stiff with the power of his own importance.

"The meaning of what?" Angelina asked.

"Why are you here? Dressed like that? Where is your habit?"

"It's a long story, *Padre*. Could we go inside and discuss this?"

The sound of hoofbeats approached, and her father's gaze focused behind her. Obviously Charlie had decided to join them instead of riding out of her life without a good-bye. Angelina clenched her teeth against the happiness flooding through her at his presence.

"Who is this?" Her father's lip curled in distaste, and his gaze flicked back to Angelina's face. She saw the speculation in his eyes and struggled not to turn away. She had learned long ago that any expression of weakness would only give him more control over her.

"Charlie Coltrain. He escorted me here from Texas."

"Alone?" Her mother's voice shook with shock.

"Yes, *Madre*. Alone."

"You had better have a good explanation for this, Angelina," her father said. "Come inside. I wish to hear everything." He looked at Charlie. "You can water your horse and then come around to the kitchen. The cook will feed you." He turned toward the house.

"No." Defiance resonated in the word. Angelina braced herself as her father turned slowly back to face her.

"Pardon me?" he said slowly.

"Charlie is not some hired hand you can order around like a slave. He saved my life many times over. You won't treat him like this."

"I won't?"

"Angelina, it's all right."

Her parents started at the sound of Charlie's ruined voice. They stared at him as though his horse had sat up and asked for tea. Her mother's hand fluttered up to rest at her throat, a sure sign of unease.

Angelina spared Charlie a glance. He stared at her father impassively. She knew that look. He was coldly furious.

"It is not all right," she told Charlie. He continued to stare at her father. "Put Gabe in the barn and then join us inside." She turned back to her parents. Her father must have seen the determination in her eyes and decided, for whatever reason, to let this act of defiance pass. He shrugged in agreement and went into the house. Her mother followed as always. Angelina turned to Charlie.

"There's no reason to get everyone in an uproar over me," he said, at last looking her in the eyes, though no emotion showed upon his face. "I told you I'd take you home. You're home, so I'll be goin'."

"No, wait." Angelina fought against the panic rising within her at the thought of his leaving. "You can at least stay the night, have a hot meal, a bath. I owe you that. And I'll have my father pay you right away."

"Pay me for what? You wanted to go to the convent. I dragged you here."

"You didn't have a choice but to bring me here. I'm safe. Alive. My father can afford to pay you."

Charlie hesitated as though he were going to argue. Then he nodded and slid down from Gabe's back. "I'd tell you I don't want the money. But fact is, I need it. I'll have to hide out down here awhile before I can make my way back to Texas and find out who's been pretendin' to be me."

"I want you to have the money. We made a deal, and though it didn't work out the way I planned, you did your best."

Charlie's black gaze swept over her face, and Angelina's mouth went dry. "What we have is much more than a deal, Angel, and you know it." Before she could answer, he turned and led Gabe away.

"Angelina." Her father's voice summoned, and she turned away from the sight of Charlie's retreating back with a sigh. She should have let him go. Life would be so much less complicated without Charlie Coltrain in it. But she couldn't bring herself to say good-bye to him. Not yet.

She faced her parents in the parlor. Miguel and Theresa Reyes sat together on the settee, though they took pains to avoid touching. Things had not changed between them since Angelina had left a year ago. Each existed next to the other with very little interaction between them. The example of her parents' loveless marriage had done little to endear the idea of an arranged union to Angelina. If she had to exist in the same house for the rest of her life with a person she detested, she'd rather be dead.

"Well, daughter." Her father folded his hands in his lap and stared at her. He had always done the same when doling out her childhood punishments. Then she had squirmed under his regard; now she merely stared back stoically. "We are surprised to find you on our doorstep when we thought you in a convent."

"Surprised and displeased, no doubt."

"I am not pleased to have you arrive with an Anglo gunslinger."

"He is not a gunslinger."

"No? Well, no matter. I wish for you to explain yourself. Immediately."

Since she could see no way out of providing an explanation, Angelina took a deep breath and dove in. She regaled them with the tale from the moment she'd left her convent in Corpus Christi, continued with a graphic rendition of the murders of her friends and her own near rape and finished with her rescue by Charlie. She left out the details of their trip and Charlie's wanted status, as well as her own vision of the angel and her confusing feelings for the man in question.

A soft, pained gasp caused Angelina to stop speaking and glance at her mother. Theresa was pale, her dark eyes round with shock. Sheltered first on her parents' hacienda, then on that of her husband, Theresa had never encountered anything more disturbing than Miguel Reyes. Though he was more disturbing than most, he did not compare to the tale Angelina had just told.

"I'm sorry, *Madre*," Angelina said. "I should not have told you all the details."

With an impatient wave of his hand, her father put aside her mother's distress. "Theresa," he barked, "go and see to your daughter's bath. She smells of the trail."

Without a word of protest, Angelina's mother quit the room.

"You told this man I would pay him to bring you here?"

"I had no other choice. I was alone; he was there. What would you expect me to do?"

"Why didn't you return to the convent?"

"I wanted to see my mother." Only my mother, not you or this place, she added silently. Angelina raised her chin and stared at her father. "Is that a crime?"

"No, I am just surprised. A year ago you couldn't wait to get away from here. Now you want to see your mother. I am curious."

"Don't be. I will stay for a visit and then I will return to Corpus Christi and take my vows."

"And that is another curiosity. When I sent you to the convent, I understood you would begin your novitiate after six months. Yet it is a year after you left here and you tell me you are still a postulate. Why?"

Angelina gritted her teeth and fought to remain calm. The way her father asked his questions lent an insinuation to the words that rankled her. "The mother superior wanted me to take a little more time to think about what I was vowing to become."

Her father raised his eyebrows. "The mother did not feel you had a calling?"

"She didn't know me as well as she knew some of the other women. Most of the postulates there are from the area. They went to the school the

Sisters run there. Once I enter the novitiate, I must take my religious name and wear the habit of the order. It is a very important step. One not to be taken lightly. The mother superior only wanted to be sure I was ready."

Her father nodded his understanding. "And what about this Charlie?"

"He will stay the night. Then it is up to him what he wants to do."

Something in her voice must have betrayed her true feelings, for her father looked at her sharply, his gaze narrowing in speculation. Angelina fought to keep from flinching against his prying eyes. He already acted too suspicious. If she showed any weakness, he would move in for the kill like a coyote with a maimed rabbit.

"All right," he said and stood. "I will pay your man. Go and find your mother. Wash, dress. I will see you at dinner." He strode out of the house without a backward glance.

Angelina remained where she was for a moment. She should be relieved the interrogation was over. As a child she often wondered if her father had learned his questioning methods from studying the Inquisition. He had let her off remarkably easy this time. Perhaps he had finally realized she was a grown woman who would not be intimidated as easily as her mother.

Angelina relaxed and took a deep breath. She had accomplished what she wanted. Her father would pay Charlie, and that would be the end of this short, frightening, exciting interlude in her life. She could return to the convent none the worse for her adventure.

Then in the dark, quiet, lonely nights she would dream about Charlie Coltrain and remember.

*   *   *

Charlie finished tending to Gabe and took care of Angelina's mount, as well. He knew he should join the Reyes family in the house, but he just couldn't bring himself to go inside.

There was something about Angelina's father that set his teeth on edge. Maybe it was the way the man spoke to Angelina, as though she were his property and not a human being with her own will. Or maybe it was the way Reyes had looked at him, as if he were lower than an insect crawling out from under the nearest rock. Either way, Charlie didn't relish joining them in the parlor.

"Can I have a moment of your time, Senor?"

Charlie looked up and met the slick, dark gaze of Miguel Reyes. Immediately he went on the alert. The man wanted something. But what?

"I suspect I've got a minute," Charlie said.

"My daughter told us how you saved her life. Her mother and I are very grateful."

"Forget it."

"Oh, but I can't. I owe you. What can I do to repay your kindness?"

"I just want the money the Sister promised. That's all and I'll be goin'."

"The Sister?" Miguel chuckled as though Charlie had made a joke. "Oh, Angelina. Yes. But of course I'll pay you the money. Before we do that though, I thought I might offer you something more. How are you with horses?"

"Good." Charlie frowned. What was the man getting at?

"I thought you would be. One of my hands was injured yesterday and won't be able to work for quite a while. Perhaps you would consent to take his place?"

"You want me to work for you?" Though he had meant to keep his voice level, some of his distaste for the idea must have come through, for Reyes narrowed his eyes.

"Would that be so bad? Or do you have a pressing engagement elsewhere?"

"No." Charlie thought a moment. He would make more money, which he could always use. The ranch was as good a place to hide out as any. And he could keep an eye on Angelina and make sure things with her father weren't even worse than she'd let on. He didn't trust the man, not a bit. Charlie had the feeling an ulterior motive lurked behind the job offer, though he couldn't see what it was. Yes, he would stick around and see just what old Miguel was up to. Once he was sure Angelina wasn't going to be hurt, then he could move on.

Charlie held out his hand to Reyes, smiling thinly when the man hesitated before grasping his fingers. "All right," he said as he met Miguel's gaze straight on. "You've got yourself a hired hand."

Chapter Twelve

"Where is he?" Angelina's voice echoed through the house.

Her mother flinched at the volume, but continued to sew without pause. "Lower your voice. The servants will hear."

"I don't care what they hear. I want to know where Charlie is. I haven't seen him for two days. Where is Father?"

"Away."

"Where?"

Her mother shrugged. "He never tells me where he goes. I am merely thankful he goes."

Angelina stifled her temper. Sometimes her mother's apathy about her situation made Angelina want to scream. But she knew from experience nothing would make Theresa Reyes see beyond the boundaries of life imposed by her husband. She was a deeply religious woman who believed in the vows she had made to Miguel Reyes. She would obey until death parted them— and probably beyond.

Angelina tried to take a deep, calming breath, but the pressure of her corset choked the attempt. As she had suspected, the only clothes left in her room were too tight to wear without the confining contraption. The dresses, most of them made for her wedding trousseau, were all in the latest fashion. Still, wearing them and living in her father's home once again, if only temporarily, made her feel like a child. The feeling preyed on her already tense nerves, making her short-tempered and snappish. "I've looked all over for Charlie, *Madre*." Angelina fought to keep her irritation and her nerves from her voice. "I can't find him."

"Perhaps he left."

"No. He wouldn't. Not without saying—" Angelina bit her lip against the flood of alarm at the thought. "I mean, his horse is still in the barn. He wouldn't leave without his horse."

Her mother nodded and continued to sew. "Is there something you want to share with me about this man, Angelina?"

Angelina had been listlessly examining the flower arrangement on the low table next to the sitting room door, wondering, as always, how her mother kept roses alive in the heat of Mexico. At her mother's words, she went still. "What do you mean by that?" she asked, keeping her eyes focused on the silky blossoms.

"I have never seen you so concerned about anyone before. For you, God has always been foremost in your mind. But since you've been back, I sense something else."

"Charlie is—" Angelina trailed off. How could she explain what Charlie had come to mean to her when she didn't know the truth herself? "Charlie saved my life. He is special."

Her mother looked up then, concern etching her features. "Special? Are you in love with him?"

"Love?" Angelina turned away from the flowers with a start. Her breath seemed to stick in her throat. "No, it's not that."

"He's a little old for you, *querida*."

Angelina shifted, uneasy with the direction of the conversation. "If I were in love with him, his age wouldn't matter."

"Did anything happen between the two of you while you were traveling together?"

Her mother studied her intently, and Angelina's face flushed as she remembered the times she and Charlie had kissed—and the pleasure she'd felt during each and every incident. "Nothing happened, *Madre*," she said. "Nothing I couldn't deal with."

Angelina looked away from her mother's probing gaze, the lie laying between them like thick river-bottom mud.

"I worry," her mother said as she returned to her sewing. "After all the trouble of last year, the wedding, Juan." She sighed, a sound of pain from deep within, and Angelina winced at the shaft of guilt that shot through her own chest. "Your father has finally come to accept your calling. You know how much your entering the convent has pleased me. I always wanted one of my children to go to the church."

"I went because I was called, *Madre*. Not to make you or *Padre* happy."

"I know. I would just hate for all the trouble to have been for nothing."

"How could that be?"

"Your father wants to go into politics, Angelina. He always has. The time has come for him to achieve his dream. He wanted all his children settled before he made such a step."

"You mean he wanted us all filed safely away where we could create no scandals."

"Honor thy father and mother, *querida*."

The admonishment held great strength despite, or perhaps because of, the softness of the tone in which it was administered.

"*Si, Madre.*" Angelina looked down at her hands. She had twisted her fingers together so tightly they shone white at the knuckles. "I am sorry."

"It will be good for your father's career to have a daughter in the church."

"I'm glad I can oblige him," Angelina muttered.

Her mother glanced at her sharply, but said nothing about her comment. "All I'm asking is that you stand by your decision. The scandal you caused by your refusal to marry your father's choice of husband has nearly died down. The fact that you went into the church was the only reason your behavior was forgiven. I'm begging you not to ruin your father's chances for advancement. He is counting on you to become a bride of Christ."

The sound of a horse approaching the house at high speed saved Angelina from telling her mother exactly what she thought of her father. Hurrying to the front door, Angelina opened it in time to see the man in question dismount his horse. He took the front steps in a single stride, then stopped with a lurch when he saw her standing in the doorway.

His cheeks flooded red, and Angelina took a step backward at the anger in his eyes.

"Get upstairs, daughter." He pointed his finger at her and jabbed it twice for emphasis. "Go to your room and don't come out until I call you."

"What happened?"

"Don't talk to me. Get out!" he bellowed.

Her mother came running at the sound of his voice. "Miguel! What is it?"

"I have been to town." He glanced at Angelina again. "Get out of my sight before I lose my temper."

If this isn't losing your temper, Angelina thought, what is? She kept the words to herself, but stood her ground, refusing to obey his command. His eyes narrowed and his lips thinned. He took a step toward Angelina, but her mother stepped between them.

"Go," she whispered. "I will calm him and find out what the trouble is." When Angelina continued to hesitate, her mother added the only word that could make Angelina give in, "Please."

Angelina turned and walked upstairs. As she went to her room, her father's voice carried up the staircase in her wake. "If I do not think of something quickly, all my chances for a position in the government will be destroyed. That girl has been nothing but trouble since the minute she was born. Why was I cursed with such a daughter? Why couldn't she have gone to that convent and stayed there? Why on earth did she have to show up here again to ruin my life?"

Charlie returned to the bunkhouse with the three hands he'd worked with over the past few days. As soon as he'd agreed to work for Reyes, Charlie had been sent to the farthest reaches of the property to ride the boundaries. No doubt the man wanted to separate him from Angelina. He couldn't fault Reyes for that. If he'd had a daughter, he wouldn't have let a low-down excuse for a man like Charlie Coltrain near her any longer than he had to. What Charlie couldn't understand was why Angelina's father would offer him a job at all if the man wanted to separate them.

Charlie yanked off his shirt and began to wash off the accumulated grime of two days' riding. When he'd done the best he could, he poured the rest of the bucket of water over his head. He'd set out for the stream later and taken a real bath. Right now, the clean wetness of the rainwater soothed away the heat of his skin.

"Senor, I need to speak with you immediately."

Charlie stiffened at the slick voice behind him. He was definitely slipping. He hadn't heard the man coming. Without turning around, Charlie reached for his shirt and shoved his arms into it. He'd be damned if he'd talk to the man half naked. He took his time buttoning the front, then finger combed his hair back from his brow and replaced his hat. Only then did Charlie turn to face Miguel Reyes.

Something was very wrong. Though Angelina's father's voice had been cool and deceptively calm, Charlie recognized banked fury in his eyes.

"Is Angelina all right?" Charlie demanded.

Reyes smiled thinly but the anger in his eyes remained in place. "I find it most amusing that you should ask that."

"Funny. You don't look like you're laughin'."

Reyes pretended to ignore the sarcasm, though his jaw muscles tightened and relaxed, then tightened again, betraying his irritation. "I discovered a bit of a problem in town today."

Charlie waited, uncertain why the man wanted to discuss his problems with the hired help.

"A problem that I hope you can help me with," Reyes said. When Charlie did not respond he made an impatient sound and said, "A problem that concerns my daughter."

"What problem?"

Reyes smiled again, this time with a glint of true amusement. "Yes, I thought that might get your attention. I've noticed my daughter and you are quite concerned about each other's welfare."

"Stands to reason after what we've been through gettin' here."

"How true. Since you are so concerned about her welfare, I felt I could depend on you to assist me in saving her from a very unpleasant situation."

"Get on with it," Charlie muttered, not liking the drift of the conversation.

"Ah, a man who likes to get to the point. An Anglo trait, but one I happen to admire. I took a trip into Chihuahua today, and you must imagine my surprise upon hearing my daughter's name bandied about as though she were a common *puta.*"

Charlie growled low in his throat. His hands clenched into fists. "Alvarez."

"Yes, I suspect you are right there. Juan has never quite gotten over the public embarrassment Angelina caused him at their wedding." Reyes looked at him closely. "I see she told you of her misbehavior. That is good. She saved me the time explaining her past."

"So what do you want me to do? Kill him?" Charlie's hand went to his gun.

Reyes chuckled. "No, *gracias*. That would only cause more trouble. No, Coltrain, I want you to marry her."

"Huh?" Charlie gaped. "She's a nun."

"Oh, no. Not yet."

"She wants to be a nun. She won't marry me. Besides, what does she care about her reputation? She'll be in a convent soon enough."

"She may not care about her reputation, but I do. I have a plan, Coltrain. A plan where we can all have what we want."

A sudden wariness made Charlie back up a step and lean against a fence post. Reyes was up to something. Charlie just had to figure out what. "And what do you think I want?" he asked, watching Reyes closely for any clue that might reveal what trick the man had planned.

"Angelina, of course. I saw the way you looked at her when you came here. You want her." He raised his hand to hold off Charlie's denial. "You don't have to pretend with me. I understand. You can have her. I want you to have her."

Charlie gripped his hands together to keep from putting them around Miguel Reyes's throat. "What you want doesn't interest me. What does Angelina want?"

"I will handle her. This time she will do as I say. Marry her and save her reputation. Then, if things do not work out between the two of you, disappear. Angelina will believe she is a widow, and she can return to the convent. I will pay you whatever you ask. Everyone will be happy."

"Everyone except Angelina."

"She will come to understand. And if she is truly unhappy she can return to her precious convent. Where is the harm?"

"Aren't you forgetting the little matter of her virginity?"

"Do not worry about that." Ryes waved his hand, dismissing the problem. "The convent will accept a widow of good reputation if she arrives with an impressive dowry."

"I don't want her forced into anything."

Reyes sighed, a sound heavy with irritation. "Fine. I will talk to her. She is a reasonable young woman. She will agree."

Charlie turned away and leaned against the corral fence. He should say no immediately. He knew that. But instead his entire body clamored for him to accept the offer.

He didn't deserve her. She was young, beautiful, innocent. He was old, scarred, dissolute. His stepfather had told him often enough that no decent woman would ever want him. Charlie was sure Angelina would agree.

But maybe, just this once, he could do something good for someone. If Charlie said no, old Miguel would find someone else to marry Angelina, and who was to say that someone would understand her and her dream the way Charlie did. At the very least, he could get Angelina away from her sorry excuse for a father and return her to the convent. Once she was Charlie Coltrain's wife, no one would treat her like a possession ever again.

Charlie turned. He met and matched the cold gaze of Miguel Reyes. "All right," he said. "I'll marry your daughter."

Night fell and still Angelina remained in her room. Her mother arrived, bringing dinner but no information. Though she might know what was wrong, she wasn't saying. Upon leaving, her mother locked the door. Angelina begged to be released, but, as always, Theresa Reyes followed the orders of her husband.

The moon rose, casting eerie silver shadows through the window and across the bed upon which Angelina lay. She stared at the ceiling and wondered what had made her father so angry this time. After countless minutes of wondering, Angelina realized her imagination was creating much worse scenarios than could possibly be the truth. If she had to stay in her room much longer without knowing, she would go mad.

The lock clicked, and her door swung inward. Angelina sat up quickly. She would not meet her fate lying down. In the doorway stood her father. His face was indistinguishable in the darkness, but the set of his shoulders revealed his barely suppressed anger.

He stepped into the room and shut the door behind him, locking it with a flick of his wrist. Angelina fought not to flinch as he walked toward her. Without warning he hit her, the back of his hand connecting with her cheek. Angelina absorbed the blow, biting down on her tongue to keep from crying out.

"That," he hissed, "is for your stupidity. Did you think news of your actions wouldn't reach Chihuahua?"

"What actions?"

He raised his hand again, then with obvious reluctance lowered it. "Did you think you could travel across the country with that man, stop at the Alvarez ranch and parade him in front of everyone and not cause gossip to run rampant?"

"I had no choice but to travel with him. I didn't

know Juan and Maria lived there until it was too late to leave, and I didn't realize people would be so small-minded. I am a postulate, *Padre*. I am near to taking my vows. Why is everyone so eager to believe I would lie down with a man just because he's available?"

Her father moved away, striding to the window and staring out at the darkened yard. Angelina breathed a sigh of relief. She couldn't think when he hovered over her, prepared to strike at any moment.

"Why they believe it is not the issue here," he said. "The issue is that they do believe. You told Maria Alvarez about your troubles at the convent. The fact that you are not a novice yet, that the mother superior did not feel you were ready for those vows, only added fuel to the murmurs. You nearly ruined my political career once with your willfulness. You will not do so again."

"I will leave tonight."

"No, you will not."

The icy finality of his tone chilled Angelina all the way to her toes. She took a deep breath and attempted to convince him of her sincerity.

"I will go back to the convent. The talk will die down very quickly once I am gone."

"Perhaps. Perhaps not. I am not prepared to take any more chances because of you, daughter. You will marry him tonight and cause their prattling tongues to cease wagging."

"Marry?" Angelina's mind groped for the missing piece to the puzzle. When had marriage entered the conversation? "Marry whom?"

Her father turned away from the window, and even in the darkness she could see the shine of his white teeth when he smiled. "Why your gunslinging friend, of course. You wanted him so much. Now you can have him."

For one second, happiness overpowered her shock. Then reality intruded. What about her calling? Her visions? She was to be a nun. Charlie was her test from God. If she gave in to her feelings for him, she failed. She must remember that truth above any others.

"I cannot marry him, *Padre*."

"I did not ask for your consent. You will marry him, and you will marry him tonight."

"I seem to remember having this conversation once before. You can't make me marry someone against my will."

To Angelina's surprise, her father merely laughed, crossed the room to unlock the door, then left without another word. The click of the bolt sliding home on the other side of the door sounded loud in the quiet darkness. Angelina fell backward onto the bed and resumed staring at the ceiling.

Her father was too happy by far. And when Miguel Reyes was happy, that usually boded ill for someone else. She had a bad feeling she was that someone this time.

Though it seemed like many hours, perhaps only one hour passed before the door opened once more. This time everyone held a kerosene lamp and they filled the room with light. Angelina sat up and blinked against the unaccustomed brightness. When her eyes adjusted, she recognized her mother, with her father just behind and the family priest next to him, a different man from the one who had given her sanctuary at the last wedding.

Her father stepped around her mother. In his left hand he held a shotgun. Angelina frowned and glanced at her mother, who would not meet her eyes.

Angelina stood and addressed the priest. "What is going on here?"

The priest took up a position in front of the window and opened his Bible, ignoring her question. Obviously she could depend on no help from that quarter. Her father answered her. "Time for a wedding, daughter."

"I told you—"

Angelina broke off as another figure came through the door. She caught her breath as the light fell across his handsome face. He'd dressed in Levi's and a clean black shirt. For once, he had no gunbelt, a state she had never observed before.

Odd, she thought, he still looks just as dangerous without a firearm.

The dark material of his shirt contrasted with his gold-silver hair as the strands glistened in the flickering light. His gaze seemed impossibly black as it swept the room and lit upon her. He smiled, the first true smile she'd ever seen upon his lips, and she couldn't help but smile in return.

Charlie took a step toward her with his hand outstretched. Angelina hesitated a second. Had Charlie agreed to this farce? How could he when he knew of her visions, her angel, her dream? He had to know she would not agree. Before she could give voice to her questions, they were answered in an unexpected way.

Miguel Reyes swung the shotgun upward and planted the barrel against Charlie's chest. The smile upon Charlie's lips faded. He froze and glanced down at the gun, then up at the man who held the weapon.

"What the hell do you think you're doin', Reyes?" Charlie growled.

"Just a little insurance." Her father's gaze never left Charlie, though his next words were meant for her. "Say the words, daughter. Marry this man without a fight, or I'll splatter him across the room."

Angelina gasped, her shocked gaze flicking to Charlie's. If possible, his eyes darkened even more. Black ice, she thought. He looks ready to kill.

"This wasn't part of the agreement, Reyes."

Agreement? Angelina looked back and forth between her father and Charlie. What agreement?

"You said you would marry her. Here she is. There is the priest. Now do it or I'll blow you into the next life."

"No," Charlie growled.

Angelina's father cocked the gun.

"I told you I wouldn't marry her unless she agreed. I don't want her forced into anything—especially by you."

Charlie's words warmed Angelina's heart. He understood her. He would never hurt her if he could help it.

Her father shoved Charlie with the butt of the gun, and Charlie stumbled backward a few steps. Angelina cried out and stepped forward. Her mother reached out and grabbed her elbow, but Angelina jerked her arm away from the restraining touch. The two men ignored her, intent on their own conversation.

"You'll do as I tell you, Coltrain, and keep your mouth shut unless you are asked to open it. Shall we see if you can still say your vows with your leg full of lead?"

"Stop it!" Angelina screamed. All eyes turned to her. "Just leave him alone. I'll do it. All right? I'll say anything you want if you just leave him alone."

Everyone in the room smiled at her compliance—except for Charlie. He frowned. Then her father moved behind him and shoved Charlie forward with the butt of the shotgun until he stood next to Angelina.

"Let's get on with the wedding, shall we?" her father said, obviously pleased to be getting his way. "Padre?"

The priest began to mumble in Latin. Angelina could feel Charlie's tension as a force in the air. She could tell he was desperately trying to think of a way to get them out of the situation. But her father stood behind them with the shotgun to Charlie's back.

Most of the ceremony was a blur. When she was required to speak her vows, Angelina glanced behind her. Her father cocked the shotgun again for emphasis, and she hurriedly repeated what she was asked to say. When Charlie's turn came, a prod with the butt of the gun forced him to comply, though his voice roughened with suppressed anger.

And then it was done. She was no longer Angelina Reyes, but Angelina Coltrain. Numb, she turned to her husband. Her words of apology never got past her lips.

With a growl of irritation, Charlie turned on her mother and father. "You've got what you wanted. Now take that gun and get out."

Her father smirked. "Can't wait to claim your rights, Coltrain?"

Angelina's mother gasped; then with a soft pat

on Angelina's hand she fled the room. Her father backed away from them, keeping his gaze on Charlie and his shotgun ready.

Charlie followed, and as soon as her father was past the threshold, he kicked the door shut. Then he locked it and leaned his forehead against the wood. A long sigh escaped him.

Angelina stood in the middle of the room. She was married now—one half of a larger whole.

Then why did she feel more alone than she'd ever felt in her life?

Chapter Thirteen

Charlie turned away from the door and Angelina flinched. What did he expect of her now? She had a vague idea of what went on between men and women from eavesdropping on her brothers, and being raised on a horse farm had taught her some things. Her mother had tried to talk to her the night before she'd been dragged to the church to marry Juan. But that conversation had consisted mainly of exhortations to trust in God, submit to her husband, and dream of her children. Not a very helpful bit of instruction, all in all.

Charlie took a step toward her, and Angelina took two steps backward in quick succession.

"Hell and damnation, Angelina. I'm not gonna attack you. Settle down." Charlie pushed his fingers through his long hair in an impatient gesture, then crossed the room to sit on the bed.

"Wh-what are you doing?"

"I'm goin' to sleep. This has all been a little tirin' for me." He yanked off his boots and let them fall to the floor—twin thuds against the wood planks.

"Y-you mean to sleep in my bed?"

"Yeah. It's the only one in the room. I don't relish meetin' up with your *padre* and his pet shotgun in the hall, so I'm not leavin' here until mornin'. By then we'll all have a chance to cool off."

"I'll sleep in the chair." She nodded at the rocker near the window.

Charlie shook his head. "You'll sleep in the bed, same's me. We're married now; there's nothin' sinful about it. Though, to my mind, makin' love to someone you care about is a long way from sinful. But then who am I to argue with the church?"

Sinful. How many times had her mind shouted that very word to her? Countless times—every single time she'd imagined herself and Charlie together. Like this. Charlie began to unbutton his shirt.

"No!" The word burst from between her stiff lips. "I can't sleep with you. I don't know—" She trailed off.

Charlie stopped what he was doing, though he had already finished unbuttoning his shirt. The garment hung open, framing his chest and giving her peeks of golden skin and hair as he shifted to look at her.

"I know you don't understand, Angelina." His tone was the softest she'd ever heard it. When he spoke so gently, she could barely distinguish anything amiss with his voice. "We won't do anything tonight but sleep. I promise. I didn't marry you for sex."

He stood and, moving around the room, blew out all the lights. The room became shrouded in silver moonlight and velvet shadows. Charlie returned to the bed and pulled off his shirt, carefully keeping his back turned away from her. He didn't know Angelina was already aware of the scars upon his back, but now was not the time to discuss her spying. When he stood to remove his pants, Angelina looked away, staring out the window until she heard him get into bed.

"Come to bed. You're tired. I won't hurt you."

Charlie was right. She was so exhausted from the emotions and events of the day the room swayed before her eyes. Moving to the bed, she sat, then reached behind her to unbutton her dress.

At the first touch of rough, masculine fingers, she stiffened. But Charlie brushed her hands aside and finished unfastening the garment with ease. The air of the room, which had before seemed stifling, now brushed against her exposed skin and made her shiver. Charlie's hands hesitated at the base of her spine, then withdrew.

Angelina breathed a sigh of relief until he began to pull the pins from her hair.

"No." She gasped, reaching up to stop him. "You promised."

"I promised I wouldn't hurt you. I won't. But let me take down your hair. I've always wanted to see it loose."

"If I don't braid my hair for the night I'll end up with a nest of tangles."

"I'll comb your hair for you in the mornin'. Please," he whispered, the word drifting across the exposed nape of her neck. "For me."

The thought of Charlie brushing out her hair in the morning after they'd spent a night in the same bed sent a shiver of anticipation down her spine. The intimacies of marriage had only just begun. Angelina released his fingers and sat stiffly on the edge of the bed until he finished unbinding her hair. The thick dark mass slid downward, tickling her neck, shoulders and back. Charlie ran his fingers through the strands for several seconds, then moved to rub her shoulders and neck.

"Relax," he said.

She did with a low moan of pleasure. No one had ever touched her so. It was wonderful. The sensation of his flesh against hers was like nothing she could ever have imagined. He gently pushed her head forward and proceeded to rub her neck.

When had his fingers slid her gown from her shoulders? She didn't notice until his magic touch reached her collarbone. But what he was doing to her felt so good, and she was so lethargic, any thought of resistance drifted away on a long river of thick need.

"Take off your dress and lie down." The whisper seemed to come from inside her head. She complied, removing her petticoats as well, but leaving her chemise in place. She lay back against the pillows. Charlie sat up next to her, a dark shadow against the indigo of the moonstruck bedroom. His golden hair created a halo of light around his head, and though she could not see his face, his eyes shone in the darkness.

Without warning, he leaned down and kissed her. His body hovered near, not quite touching, but close enough so the heat of his body reached her. His lips, hard at first, softened against her mouth. He stroked her compressed lips with his tongue, and the shiver his caress created rippled from her mouth throughout her body. Giving the rest of herself up to the river of longing within, Angelina wound her arms around Charlie's neck and pulled him to her.

He was naked. The hard, heavy length of his body pressed against hers, the heat of his flesh warming her through the fine cotton of her shift. He held himself very still, as though he didn't want to frighten her, but she could still feel the strength of his desire pressing against her secret woman's place.

The kiss went on and on, lips to lips, tongue to tongue. Charlie's large hand cupped her breast. Instead of being shocked, she moaned into his mouth and arched into his palm. Her nipple tightened to an almost unbearable peak. He removed his mouth from hers and lowered his head, taking the taut bud into his mouth through the material of her gown. The contrast of warmth and wetness rubbing the thin cotton against her straining flesh made Angelina clench her fingers into his hair. He trailed kisses across the valley between her breasts and took her other nipple into his mouth, at the same time he flexed his lower body against her. Angelina cried out from the shock and the pleasure. She knew she should put a stop to what they were doing. But she couldn't think past the incredible sensations that had sapped her will. Her body answered a different call.

Charlie pressed a kiss to the crook of her neck, then pressed his face there, his breathing harsh and fast. He arched against her once again, and the world exploded into a shower

of stars before her closed eyes. The ripples
of tension radiated outward, centering warmth
wherever Charlie touched her. She clutched him
to her until the waves receded, then stroked his
hair until he raised his head and kissed her
brow.

The bed creaked when he rolled away from her.
He lay, his hands behind his head, staring at the
ceiling. She lay next to him, stiff as a stick, and
observed the fascinating ceiling as she had done
all afternoon. She had done something wrong.
But what?

"I'm sorry," she whispered.

Charlie swore, and Angelina closed her eyes
and held her breath. Now she was certain she
had done something wrong.

"That shouldn't have happened, Angelina. I just
wanted to touch you and kiss you. Then when you
responded, I couldn't think. I should be able to
keep myself in control better than that. I don't
know what's the matter with me." His voice
roughened with anger and the bed shifted as he
tensed.

"I knew I did something wrong."

"No." Charlie's voice became gentle once again,
and he pulled her closer to nestle in the crook of
his arm, her head on his shoulder and her body
tight against his. "What we did wasn't wrong.
We're married."

"Are we, truly? I know enough about sex to
know we didn't make love, so the marriage isn't
consummated."

"That's right. And I intend for it to stay that
way."

"What?" Angelina tried to sit up, but Charlie
held her tight to him. After a second of useless

struggle she relaxed. "Why would you say such a thing?"

Charlie sighed. "Sometimes I forget how young you are. You act so damn self-sufficient all the time. Though now that I've met your father, I can see why you couldn't depend on him or your ma for anything."

"I don't know why you keep calling me young. I'm twenty. Most of the young women around here get married when they're sixteen. I'm an old maid, really."

"When you're thirty-seven, twenty is a lifetime ago. I can barely remember the man I was at twenty."

"I find that hard to believe."

"Believe it. That was before the war, before Mosby—" He trailed off. When he spoke again, his voice was so low Angelina had to strain to hear the words. "Before a lot of things."

Angelina bit her lip. There was so much she didn't know about Charlie, about his past and his family and why he had become who he was. Would she ever know the entire truth? Did she want to? And most important of all her questions . . .

"Why did you marry me?"

Charlie pondered for a moment before answering. "To protect you. I guess it's all over town about us travelin' together. Your father was in an uproar. He swore he'd make you marry someone. I figured you'd be best off with me."

She hated the thought he had gotten into this mess just to protect her. "I can take care of myself."

"Yeah, you've done a great job so far," he said sarcastically, then put two fingers to her lips to staunch the angry words trying to tumble forth "Listen to me a minute. Miguel Reyes holds all the power over you until you're a nun or you're married. Now you're married. He won't be able to tell you what to do ever again."

"What I want to do is become a nun."

"If that's what you want, you can have it. Angelina, I'm still a wanted man. There's no tellin' what'll happen to me in the future. When I'm out of the the way, you can go back to your convent."

Cold dread washed over Angelina at his words. "What do you mean by out of the way?"

His shoulder shifted beneath her cheek as he shrugged. "In jail. Missing. Dead."

"Stop!"

"You've got to face facts. You said yourself you don't want to be married. You want to be a nun. I took the easiest route to get you what you wanted."

"And what do you want, Charlie Coltrain? You say you won't make love to me, but you want to. You're my husband now. No one will stop you. Why didn't you take what you wanted before? I was more than willing."

"You sound like your father," Charlie muttered.

Angelina stiffened. "What do you mean by that?"

"Nothin'."

"No. I want to know. What did he say to you?"

"Just that I could have you. He would pay the convent a sizable dowry to accept you later if things didn't work out."

"Does he know who you are? That you're wanted?"

From Charlie's start, Angelina discerned he hadn't considered that question.

"I don't think so," Charlie said slowly. "If he'd known, he wouldn't have had to bribe me. He would've settled for threats. And I doubt if I would have been considered a suitable candidate to save his daughter's reputation."

"True." Angelina remained quiet as she mulled over the thought that kept returning to the forefront of her mind. After what she'd just experienced in Charlie's arms, she found herself wanting more. As he'd said before, they were married, they could make love and their coming together would not be a sin. In fact, the church would expect them to consummate the marriage. Charlie wanted her. Why had he stopped before teaching her everything? He had ignored the question before, but she wanted to know the truth. Gathering her courage, Angelina repeated her question. "Why didn't you make love to me? You said yourself we're married. I was willing."

Charlie turned his head toward her, and she felt a light touch to the top of her head, almost as though he had kissed her hair. "I'd like nothin' better than to show you what it's like to be a woman, Angelina. I've been burnin' every night and day since I first met you. Knowin' I couldn't have you only made me want you more. Right now I'm achin' worse than I ever thought I would in my life. But one thing I won't do is leave a child of mine behind without a father. I lived through that nightmare myself, and I wouldn't wish it on my worst enemy, let alone my own flesh and blood."

Angelina remembered Charlie's tale of his life with Richard Bakker and understanding dawned within her. At least he had enough sense to look ahead to the consequences of their actions. "You're right. I wasn't thinking. Forgive me."

"Go to sleep, Angelina," Charlie said, his voice old and weary. "Tomorrow looks to be a tough day."

He kissed her forehead and lay still. But Angelina's mind was too full of thoughts to sleep right away.

A child. She was so naive. All she had thought about when Charlie had touched her was continuing the glorious riot of pleasure she was experiencing. She had not thought ahead to the next hour, let alone the next life they might have created. At least Charlie had enough sense to avoid making such a mistake.

The thought of having a child, Charlie's child, caused a heavy warmth to settle at the base of her throat. She blinked back a sudden wetness in the corners of her eyes. She had always loved children. That was why she'd wanted to join a teaching order, despite her talent with nursing. She wanted children to be a part of her life, even if they could never be children of her own.

A picture appeared before her of the life she could have with Charlie. A true marriage— sleeping with him every night, holding him, touching him and learning more of the intense passion she enjoyed every time they kissed or touched. The fantasy beckoned, and she allowed herself a moment to contemplate the unreachable—bearing Charlie's children, loving them, teaching them, raising them. She wanted those things so much it hurt. Then reality intruded.

This man was her test. A test she was failing miserably. Instead of resisting his allure, she had married him. If she gave in to the passion he stirred in her, the dream of a normal life he represented, she would have to deny her calling. If she did that, then where would she be? She had believed in the truth of her life with God since the age of ten. Could she have been wrong? If her calling was not a true one, then what about her visions of the golden angel? What did they mean?

If she was not Angelina Reyes, postulate to the Sisters of the Incarnate Word and the Blessed Sacrament, then who was she? Angelina Coltrain, wife of a wanted man? Or just an out-and-out impostor in every aspect of life?

The questions came too fast for her already overtaxed mind. With the accusations and confusion still tumbling through her brain, Angelina cuddled against Charlie and gave herself up to uneasy sleep.

Charlie held Angelina as she slept, fitfully, her eyes and hands twitching, soft moans issuing from the back of her throat. He attempted to soothe whatever disturbing thoughts flitted through her mind by speaking softly and combing his fingers through her hair.

Nothing worked.

Finally he eased himself away, wondering if his nearness could be the cause of her unease. Moving across the room, he seated himself in the rocking chair. While he watched Angelina sleep, he had a much needed talk with himself.

For the first time in many years, someone had outfoxed him. During the last incident, in Second Chance, Missouri, he'd lost his brother because he had trusted a stranger too much. Charlie had seen in Jake Banner a ruthlessness to match his own and a gift for leading men he could make use of. He'd given Banner a trusted position in the gang. Then the man had turned out to be a stinking Pinkerton spy. Because of Banner, the majority of Charlie's gang had been shot in an ambush. The few who escaped had ridden off to Texas ahead of him, though, thinking on that fact now, Charlie realized that those men had never shown up in San Antonio. His brother Bill had returned to the town to settle an old score and ended up being shot like a dog outside the Second Chance Bank by Banner and his partner. That had been the beginning of many lapses in judgment for Charlie Coltrain.

Charlie returned his attention to Angelina. She slept peacefully; whatever had been bothering her had passed.

What on earth was he going to do about her? Had he ever believed he could disappear from her life and never look back? He wanted so much more from her than she was prepared to give. Looking at her he found himself, for the first time in his life, contemplating a normal existence—a home, a wife, a family. But to have those things he must convince Angelina she was better off his wife than a nun. How would he make a convincing argument when he knew just the opposite to be true?

He was no good. Never had been. He had no right ruining an innocent girl's life. Forget the fact that he'd gotten into this marriage to help her, he could see now he'd done nothing but make the situation worse.

Even if, by some miracle of her God, Angelina decided she would remain his wife, he still had a Texas Ranger on his trail, as well as countless bounty hunters. He could not subject her to such a life. He would not.

No. The best thing to do would be to disappear as soon as he could get away. For once in his miserable life he was going to do the right thing. Even if it killed him. And leaving Angelina just might accomplish that task, when countless lawmen and their guns had failed.

Charlie reached into his pocket and pulled out a long red piece of satin ribbon. He'd seen the guilty way Angelina had admired the bauble on Luanne's dresser weeks before. When she wasn't looking, he'd pocketed the item, not really sure why. At the time, he'd found the good Sister's weakness for pretty things amusing. Now he found it sad.

He'd planned to give her the ribbon after they were married, but the unanticipated nature of their wedding had driven the thought from his mind.

Charlie fell asleep, the ribbon twined about his fingers, and dreamed of Montana. Thousands of acres of land to roam free and easy. No one looking for him but ranchers with money to buy his horses. Sure, there were Indians to contend with, but he could handle them. Before, whenever he'd had the dream, the solitude of Montana had soothed him. This time, the loneliness of the endless grasses and the endless years alone settled as a physical ache within his soul.

"Charlie?"

The voice came from far away, soothing the ache and making him feel whole. He went toward the voice and awoke with a start. Angelina stood over him, fully clothed. The sun blazed through the window behind her.

"Wh-what time is it?" he rasped, reaching up to push his hair out of his eyes. The red ribbon in his fingers tangled with the strands, and he jerked his hand away in irritation.

"What's this?" Angelina asked and took his hand, unthreading the satin from between his fingers.

"Present for you." He stood, embarrassed to be caught sleeping with a woman's hair ribbon. "I wanted to give it to you last night, but—" He shrugged.

"Thank you. How did you know?"

Charlie shot her a glance. She was staring at the ribbon as though he'd given her gold. "Know what?"

"Red's my favorite color."

"I didn't know. Just thought it'd look pretty in your hair." He looked away again. Hell, he'd never been good at talking to women. Had never needed to be. They'd always flocked to him in droves, no matter how rude he was. Now he wished he'd paid better attention when his mother had tried to teach him some manners.

When he glanced at Angelina again, she'd tied her hair away from her face with the gift. She smiled at him, her face lighting up brighter than the red of the satin. He tried smiling back. It wasn't so bad.

The sound of horses in the yard below broke their gaze, and they moved to the window. Two men dismounted. Charlie narrowed his eyes. Both wore gunbelts and they walked as though they knew how to use them. Young men, in the prime of life, their reflexes at peak performance. And here he sat without a gun. What he wanted to know was how had the bounty hunters found him so fast?

Calm blanketed Charlie as it always did when danger beckoned. He scanned the room for a weapon, as he mind searched for a plan. Nothing came. No weapon, no plan.

"Gotta find a gun," he muttered, turning toward the door. "You stay here. Where does your father keep his guns?"

"Why?"

"I don't have time to argue with you, Angelina. I need a gun before those men find me."

"They won't hurt you. They wouldn't dare."

Charlie snorted, stopping at the door to shoot his wife a glance of disbelief. "I'm wanted. They'll dare anything to take me back."

"They don't know anything about you. That's Mark and Luke." Angelina frowned, looking out the window once more. "I wonder what my father's up to."

"You know those two?"

She nodded. "My brothers."

The breath Charlie had been holding came whooshing out of his mouth in a blast of relief, and he let go of the doorknob. "Where's the rest of 'em?"

"They all have their own ranches. Matthew, the oldest, lives the farthest away. Otherwise I'm sure he'd be right in the middle of whatever my father is planning. "Mark and Luke are next in line and then there's John, Timothy and Peter."

"Your father's disciples."

"Exactly."

"Why'd he stop at six? Hell, I'd've thought he'd try for the whole twelve."

"I'm sure he would have. But after I was born, my mother lost two babies, and then the doctor said she could die if she had any more. The two of them barely speak now."

Charlie nodded. He had seen the tension between the elder Reyeses. The example of her parents' marriage had probably influenced Angelina more than she realized into her opting for the church.

"Better go down and see what they want before they come up here and tell us," Charlie said. "Takin' the offense is the best defense."

Angelina turned away from the window. She touched her hair ribbon as though she wanted to make sure it was still there. When her fingers encountered the satin, she smiled softly to herself. "Did you learn that strategy from your Col. Mosby?"

"Sure enough. And I've lived by the rule ever since. Remember that, Sister."

"Is that your plan for today?" she asked as Charlie unlocked the door and led her into the hall.

"Yep. We'll go down, say *buenos dias* to your brothers. Then just as quick it'll be adios, and we're gettin' out of here."

"Where are we going?"

"Away. The sooner we're out of your father's house the better. Agreed?"

Angelina's gaze searched his face; then she met his eyes. With only a hint of reluctance, she nodded.

Charlie saw the trust in her face and fought not to flinch. He didn't deserve such a gift.

Together they went down the steps and found her family in the dining room. The three men had their heads together and spoke rapidly in Spanish.

Theresa Reyes sat calmly at the table drinking coffee. When they entered, she put down her cup and smiled. "Good morning, *querida*."

Immediately, all three men turned to face them, pulling their guns free of their gunbelts and pointing them at Charlie. He yanked Angelina behind him and glanced at her father.

"You always greet your new relations like this, *Padre?*" The emphasis he put on the final word made it into an insult. Reyes frowned. "I understand these two men are my new brothers. Good morning, gentlemen."

Mark and Luke Reyes stared at him obliquely, twins of their father in appearance, though they stood a half a foot taller, and their bodies were sinewy with work-hardened muscle. Charlie had learned early to look straight into a man's eyes when he held a gun on you. You could always judge his sincerity best that way. What he saw in Mark and Luke's eyes didn't bode well for him. They would not gainsay their father.

Charlie glanced at his mother-in-law. Theresa looked ready to faint at the show of force in her dining room. She would be no help.

"What is the meaning of this, *Padre?*" Angelina stepped around Charlie, placing herself between him and the guns. He tried to take her by the shoulders and move her out of the way, but she stamped down hard on his instep, and he had to clench his teeth to keep from grunting in pain. She put her hands up, holding his fingers upon her shoulders. The movement looked like a caress. When her fingernails dug into his flesh, he knew the gesture for what it was—a warning.

Miguel saw the movement and smiled. "Just a little insurance, daughter. I do not trust my new son."

"We did what you wanted. We're married. What else is there?"

"Oh, much more. Much more."

"Spit it out, Reyes," Charlie growled.

"Ah, yes. You are a man who likes to get to the point. I forgot." He nodded and put away his own gun, though Mark and Luke kept theirs pointed steadily at Charlie's chest. "You two will go to a small retreat for a few days. Just until we can spread the word of your marriage. Mark and Luke will take you, and since we wouldn't want to lose you, they will bring your horses back with them. In a few days they will return for you. Once you are home again, we will have a party to celebrate the wedding of my only daughter. You will both come, and you will act the part of a happily married couple."

Charlie grimaced. Outflanked again. Since there were still two guns trained on him, and Angelina stood in the way, he saw no way out of the situation. He would have to agree until he could find another way out.

"All right," he agreed. "We'll be ready to go as soon as we eat and pack."

Angelina gasped and turned to stare at him. "What are you saying? How can you let him manipulate you like that?"

Charlie raised his eyebrows at her. "From where I'm standin' he's got all the guns, Sister. You've got to learn when to cut your losses"—he smiled and leaned down to whisper for her ears only—"and when to regroup for another day."

Chapter Fourteen

The cabin was a day's ride away, situated at the outer boundary between the main Reyes ranch and the ranch of Luke Reyes, the third brother. The structure was used by ranch hands working far away from the main house for long periods. Angelina's father had assured them when they left the main house that no one would be in the vicinity of the cabin during the time Charlie and Angelina spent there. He had done so in a hearty voice, as though he were sending them on a lavish honeymoon trip. Unfortunately, the presence of her brothers and their guns ruined the happy picture.

Not much was said during the ride to the cabin. Angelina tried to reason with her brothers once they were out of earshot of her father, but as usual, they had their orders and barely acknowledged her existence, let alone listened to her arguments. Angelina lapsed into angry silence for the rest of the trip.

Charlie was also silent, but she could tell from the tension in his body and the way his gaze flicked from her brothers to their guns to the landscape that he was trying to determine some route for escape. Unfortunately, as he'd told her earlier, the opposition held all the guns, which gave them every advantage.

They reached the cabin right before dark. Angelina and Charlie dismounted, each removing his saddlebag, which contained the clothes and personal items they'd been ordered to pack. Without a word, her brothers took the reins of the horses, dropped a bag of food onto the ground and turned to leave.

"Hey, what about water?" Charlie asked.

Mark jabbed a finger at the full rain barrel next to the front door and kept on riding.

Angelina let out a hiss of irritation and sat down on the ground. "I'll pay you back for this, *hermanos*," she yelled at their retreating backs. "Just see if I don't."

The two men didn't look back. They just kept riding and eventually disappeared into the dusk.

"Revenge isn't a very charitable emotion, Sister," Charlie murmured as he sat down beside her.

"My brothers don't deserve any of my charitable emotions. They make me so mad I want to scream. They always have."

Charlie put an arm around her shoulder, and with a sigh she leaned against him. Anger was not an emotion she'd been rewarded for as a child or as a postulate. But right now it felt so good to be angry and to know that Charlie understood. He might joke with her, but he would always understand. She could be herself with him as she'd never been able to be with anyone else in her lifetime.

"To be honest," Charlie said as he stroked her hair. "I'm not much on my new in-laws either. But bastard that your father is, he still made you. I guess he can't be all bad."

Angelina turned her head and surprised something in Charlie's eyes—an emotion he quickly banked as he looked away from her toward the cabin. If she hadn't known better, she might have considered the hidden emotion love. But since she had no idea what love looked like in a man's eyes, she must certainly have been mistaken.

Charlie removed his arm from her shoulders and stood. He held out a hand to help her up. "Let's take a look at where we'll be livin'. I wouldn't put it past old Miguel to send us to a leakin' shack."

Since Angelina wouldn't put it past her father either, she followed Charlie with trepidation. She hoped the place was habitable. She knew where they were, and without horses it would be next to impossible to walk from the cabin to civilization. They were stranded here until her brothers returned.

Charlie opened the cabin door and peered inside. "Too dark to see a thing. You stay here until I find a lamp," he said and went in.

He stumbled over something and cursed, but a few moments later a soft orange glow came toward Angelina, and Charlie reappeared in the doorway holding a kerosene lamp. He beckoned her inside.

The cabin was rough, but not as bad as she'd feared. From what she could see in the semidarkness, the place was clean. A stove stood in one corner; a table with several rough hewn chairs occupied the middle of the room. A small bed covered by a faded quilt resided under the single window, which consisted of a hole cut into the log wall and covered with canvas. Some bedrolls were stacked at the foot of the bed.

"I've seen better," Angelina said.

"I've seen worse," Charlie said.

He set the lamp on the table and stepped outside. When he returned he plopped the bag of food onto the table next to the flickering light.

"Hungry?" he asked.

"No. Exhausted. Even that bed looks good right now."

"Yeah. You take it. I'm used to sleepin' on the ground."

Angelina stared at him in surprise. After what had happened between them the night before she'd assumed. . . . Well, she understood why he didn't want to consummate the marriage, but she'd half hoped at the back of her mind they could repeat the wondrous experience of their wedding night.

"You don't have to sleep on the ground. We can share. Like last night."

"No," Charlie said firmly. "We can't. I'm not sayin' I didn't enjoy kissin' and touchin' you. But there's only so much of that a man can take. It's goin' to be bad enough bein' alone with you here for a week. I'd better not test myself any more than I already have.

At the mention of the word test Angelina froze. There it was, when she wasn't even thinking about it. A message from God. A reminder that Charlie was her test. She was failing so far, but she must stand firm and not fail the ultimate test. As long as she and Charlie kept their marriage in name only, she could still follow her calling. If she conceived a child there would be no going back to the life she had coveted for so long.

"Of course. You're right." Angelina crossed to the bed and started to unbutton her dress.

"Ahem." Charlie cleared his throat, and she looked up at him in surprise. He was turned away from her. "I'll just go outside and give you some privacy." Without waiting for her answer, he went out and shut the door.

Well, she'd certainly changed if she could begin to undress in a room with a man and not even realize she was doing it—and then embarrass someone like Charlie Coltrain, who had probably seen hundreds of naked women. Angelina wanted to crawl beneath the covers and hide for the duration of the week.

When Charlie returned, she lay under the quilt in her chemise, pretending to be asleep. He took one of the bedrolls and spread the covering out on the floor a few feet away. When she opened her eye a crack she saw him remove his shirt and lie down. He glanced her way, and she hurriedly snapped her eyes shut.

"I'm sorry this turned out the way it did, Angelina," he said. "I underestimated your father. I've been doin' a lot of stupid things over the past few years. Just goes to show that age creeps up on a man."

Angelina gave up pretending and turned on her side, staring across the darkness separating them. There had always been a sadness in Charlie, something she sensed hovering just under the surface that had scarred him even more deeply than the marks on his back.

"Tell me," she whispered.

For a moment she thought he would ignore her. Then he began to speak, his ruined voice lending a rough emotion to the words that tore at her heart.

"My half sister Annie."

"Yes, you told me about her a bit. She died."

"Yeah. She was always such a little thing, all eyes and hair and bony elbows and knees. When she was real small, she used to play with my hair when I held her." His voice lowered, sounding almost shy as he continued. "When she got older she made me promise not to ever cut my hair. Might be silly, but I kept that promise at least. She idolized me even though I didn't deserve it."

"I wish I could have felt like that about at least one of my brothers. Annie must have seen something in you worth loving."

"I suspect so. But I failed her, just as I failed my ma. When they needed me the most, I wasn't there. I was off fightin' the war and killin' Yankees when the one Yankee I should have killed was back home killin' my ma and violatin' my sister."

"Bakker," Angelina breathed.

"Yeah. The night Bill and I went off to join up with the Confederacy, Bakker got drunk and—" He stopped and drew in a shaky sigh. "He beat Ma to death."

Angelina caught her breath, but refrained from saying anything. After a moment, Charlie continued. "Bill and I heard she was dead while we were fightin' the war, but we never found out how she died until we came home. We heard the fascinatin' details in the local saloon. Of course no one had seen anything. No one could be bothered to interfere in family matters, so Bakker got away with killin' her. For a little while. Annie was still livin' with him, so we lit out for the house to get her." Charlie paused again, as though he hadn't spoken of the incident for so long he had to dredge the facts from the depths of his memory. Perhaps he did. "When we walked in, we thought no one was there. I heard somethin' in the back bedroom and I opened the door." He made a garbled sound, halfway between a retch and a sigh. "The son of a bitch was rapin' her. And it wasn't the first time. I pulled my gun, but Bakker had one, too. He held it to Annie's head. I tried to talk to him, to get him to give us Annie and we'd leave. I talked so hard I forgot about Bill behind me. Just when I thought I was makin' some progress, Bill shot Bakker in the shoulder. Old Dick wasn't bluffin' when he said he'd blow Annie's brains out if we tried somethin'. Before I could do anything, he pulled the trigger."

"Dear God," Angelina said on a sob.

Charlie ignored her, deep in the pit of his hellish past. "I emptied my gun into the bastard before Annie hit the floor. Then I buried her next to my ma and headed for Second Chance."

Tears running down her face, Angelina threw back the covers to go to him.

"No." The word cracked in the tense air between them and she froze, sitting on the edge of the bed, her feet just touching the dirt floor. "There's more. Now that you know that much, I may as well tell you the rest."

"You don't have to tell me any more. I understand now. I understand your hatred for the Yankees. I understand why you became what you did."

"You're goin' to hear it all, right now. Then maybe you won't look at me like I'm a damned fallen angel anymore. I told you about Second Chance. How we spent a year terrorizin' the folks. The Pinkertons broke up the gang, killed Bill, and I headed south. On the way, I couldn't resist robbin' one more stage. I was spittin' mad and just achin' to prove I could still do a job. God, I was stupid." He sighed, more of a groan than anything else. "Happened in Arkansas. Things were goin' just fine until a little girl ran away from her mother. She was between me and the stage. She looked so much like Annie when she was little, I froze. One of the drivers saw his chance and took a shot."

Angelina closed her eyes against the pain. She knew what was coming even before Charlie's raw voice spoke the words. "He killed the little girl. She fell right at my feet." He shifted and must have brought his hands up to cover his face because his next words were muffled. "Every night I dream of the mother's screams. Every damn night."

"What happened then?"

Charlie's next words were clearer, as he recited the rest of the story. Where the earlier words had been filled with feeling, what followed was as devoid of emotion as a dead fish. "I shot the driver, then got on my horse and rode away. No one else tried to stop me. They were too busy takin' care of their dead. I stayed in San Antonio for five years. I played cards and drank myself half to death tryin' to forget. Couldn't bring myself to start another gang, even though I had plenty of opportunity. I just wanted to be alone. Finally I decided to sign on with a cattle drive, earn money the honest way for once and buy a ranch. Then, on the first day of my new life, I came across this woman—"

"I know the rest."

"Yeah, I guess you do. Even though I haven't done nothin' outside the law for five years, I'm still wanted. I didn't rob that train or kill that engineer, but I guess it don't really matter. I've done enough other things I never got punished for. I'm sure some of those were hangin' offenses. If I hang for the one thing I didn't do, I guess it will be a twisted sort of justice." He laughed without humor, and Angelina flinched at the harsh sound. "The only kind of justice I deserve anyhow."

Angelina's head ached with the tale Charlie had just related. She desperately wanted to go to him and soothe away the pain. But he would not accept her sympathy. Right now the depths of his past had arisen to trap him in memories and guilt.

Angelina lay back on the bed, flipping the quilt over her legs and closing her eyes with determination. But she found she could not go to sleep without at least telling him what she thought.

Opening her eyes, she stared into the darkness. Her eyes teared as she spoke, though her voice remained calm and soothing. "What you did, Charlie, was nothing worse than what most men would have done in your place. Your hate is understandable. If you can get past the hate and see the way to forgiveness, your guilt will leave you."

"Don't prophesy to me, Sister," he growled. "I know what I am. What I'll always be. A no-good thief and murderer."

Angelina bit her tongue against the angry denial that sprang to her lips. Charlie wouldn't hear her now. He would argue with anything she said. But how would she ever convince him to let go of the past and look forward to a brighter future?

As she did whenever she had a question of great importance, Angelina folded her hands and gave her problem up to the contemplation of her God.

For the third day in a row Drew Winston stared at the ranch below him. Unless Coltrain was hiding inside, he wasn't staying at the main ranch in the Reyes empire. The girl Angelina wasn't there either. He had a hard time believing he wouldn't have seen either of them outside in three days if they were hiding out at this ranch. Which meant only one thing.

He would have to check all six ranches belonging to her brothers. Charlie and the girl had to be somewhere, and he'd bet his horse Angelina had run to her family.

Drew had asked at a few ranches and learned the extent of the Reyes holdings. But no one had seen Angelina or Charlie pass by. Those he had spoken to knew nothing about Charlie Coltrain, and Drew did not inform them. He wanted to catch Coltrain himself. Only then would his thirst for revenge be satisfied. It wouldn't do to let someone else step in and take care of Charlie before Drew got his hands on him again.

Next time, Charlie Coltrain would not get away.

Charlie had finally figured out what Miguel Reyes had been trying to do when he sent them to the cabin. He had been trying to drive Charlie insane.

The plan was working.

Four days had passed since he and Angelina arrived at the cabin, and each day Charlie's lust mounted. He couldn't be in such close proximity to Angelina and not want her. That they were man and wife, and living as such in all ways but one, made his body rebel.

To Angelina's credit, she did her best to avoid him, as well as she could when they lived in a one-room cabin. Since the night he'd told her his secrets, she had kept her distance. When he'd started telling her his past, he'd only wanted to get everything out in the open, to have her see what he was really like so she could understand him better. When he'd gotten halfway through the tale, he'd realized he'd lit on a good way to keep Angelina at a distance. After what he'd done, no woman would want to remain his wife—not even one as forgiving as Angelina.

The way she was avoiding him proved he'd been right about that. Deep down, he had to admit he was disappointed. Angelina might have saved him if she'd tried. But he knew she was destined for the church, and a nun could not help him in the way he needed to be helped. He needed someone to love him for himself, to understand him with all his faults and forgive him his legion of mistakes. He'd come to see over the past few weeks that Angelina was the only woman for him. Just his luck, her heart belonged to Christ. Which put him right back where he'd started—an aging outlaw with too high a price on his head and nothing to live for.

He told himself over and over he needed her to keep her distance so he could leave her when the time came. If she continued to look at him as if he was some kind of hero, he might start to believe the fantasy himself. Such a belief could be dangerous—to both of them. He had to remember who and what _he was and who was after him.

Getting soft would only get them both killed.

Angelina came out of the house, wiping her hands on a towel. Charlie assumed she'd just finished washing the dinner dishes, one of the few tasks available during their enforced solitude. One of the worst things about the situation was the lack of anything to do—anything but thinking and wanting and dreaming of what could never be.

For the first time in several days, Angelina approached him. She sat down next to him where he leaned against the cabin wall. A sidelong glance showed him she sat much farther away from him than she once would have.

"I've been thinking," she said.

"Haven't we all."

"Well, I've been praying, too. But I can't seem to come up with an answer. I was wondering if I could ask you some questions."

He shrugged. "After what I told you the other night, I've got nothin' to hide anymore."

"I was wondering why you told me so many things, but you never mentioned what the Ranger accused you of. What do you know about his Claire?"

Charlie frowned. He hadn't been expecting that question. Then he remembered something and scowled even harder. "How did you know about that? He told me about her when you weren't around."

Angelina flushed and looked away. "I have to confess, I eavesdropped on the two of you at the stream."

"So you've known all this time, and you've never said anything?" Anger flared in him anew at her unfounded trust. The woman was going to get herself killed if she kept depending upon the good in all men. "How could you travel with me and trust me not to kill you? Accordin' to the Ranger, I murdered his woman. What makes you thing you're so special I wouldn't do the same to you?"

"According to him, you killed Claire. I want to hear what you have to say about it."

"And you'll believe me?"

"Of course. You've never lied to me."

She said it with such conviction, Charlie almost believed it himself. Thinking back on their relationship, he started in surprise. She was right. He had never lied to her. Fancy that.

"I don't know nothin' about no Claire. Yes, I raided in Bloody Kansas, but I took pains not to kill women. Never had the stomach for it. And I did my best to make sure my men followed my rules."

Angelina nodded, as though pleased with herself. "I didn't think you could do such a thing."

Charlie sighed in irritation. "I didn't say I didn't kill her. I said I tried not to kill women. In the mess of the Border Wars, a lot of people got killed who shouldn't have." Charlie rubbed his forehead, trying to remember a point that kept tickling at his brain whenever he thought of the Ranger. "There's somethin' though. Somethin' about what he said that makes me think he is wrong about me bein' the one who killed her. I just wish I could remember what it is."

"Don't think about it and then you'll remember. That always works for me." Angelina patted his hand like an elderly schoolteacher. Charlie flinched away. Even though she'd meant the touch as a comfort, his body reacted in anything but a comforting way.

Angelina frowned at her hand as though her flesh had suddenly turned an odd color. Then she shook her fingers. When she noticed Charlie staring at her, she stood and brushed off the back of her skirt.

Charlie watched her movements, wishing he were the one dusting off her bottom. Then he pulled his gaze away with an effort before she saw the direction of his thoughts. It was too demeaning to have a woman-child like his wife know just how much he wanted her.

He cleared his throat, and she looked at him with her eyebrows raised in question. "Angelina, I hope you aren't this trustin' with everyone. You could get hurt."

"I'm not a total fool, Charlie. I know you're trustworthy. I felt it in my soul the first time you looked at me."

He hated it when she talked like that. No matter what he said, she'd never change her opinion on that score. He could only hope once he was gone, she didn't take the notion into her head to trust a cold-blooded murderer.

He still sensed a hesitancy in her that had not been there before the revelations of his past. Though that hesitancy pained him a bit whenever he saw the shadows in her eyes, he had to admit her withdrawal from him was for the best.

"I'm going to bed." Angelina's voice brought his attention back to where she stood at the door to the cabin. She smiled at him, all womanly softness and sultry Spanish eyes, even sexier because she had no idea what she did to him. Charlie swallowed, hard. "I'm sure my brothers will show up tomorrow or the next day to take us back.

We'll have a long day's ride ahead. Then if we can get away, I'm sure we'll have a long ride after that. I know you can make the trip, but I'd better rest up."

Charlie nodded and said good night, his voice even more hoarse than usual. Little did she know she would not be riding away with him when he left. The plans had changed. Though he had thought to take her with him when they escaped her father's ranch and return her personally to the convent once he could safely do so, Charlie knew he couldn't. He had to get away from her as soon as he could or he would never be able to let her go. Every day she showed him how much she believed in his essential goodness—a goodness that didn't exist beyond her own imagination. Because of her belief in him—a belief no one else had ever shown for him throughout his life since Annie—he would make sure she achieved her dream. And the only way to be certain she forgot about him and returned to the convent thinking herself a widow was to disappear from her life without a trace.

If he did things right, then maybe, just maybe, she would hate him enough to go on with her life.

Chapter Fifteen

Two men approached the following evening. Charlie automatically reached for his gun, cursing profusely when his hand encountered only his Levi's. He hated being helpless. Never before in his life had he been caught without his gun. He vowed never to let the same thing happen again.

The sound of his curses must have reached Angelina, for she emerged from the cabin and squinted into the distance.

"My brothers," she said. "See? There are four horses."

Charlie squinted as well and then relaxed. She was right. Two horses trailed behind the mounted men.

When the Reyes boys got closer, Charlie saw they were not the same two who had brought them to the cabin. Though these men looked almost exactly like the others, they were younger. Too bad they still held their guns with obvious intent.

"More disciples?" Charlie murmured.

Angelina nodded. "Timothy and Peter. The youngest ahead of me."

"Any chance we can get by these two?"

"I doubt it. They were all trained by my father. They know too well the sting of his displeasure. They won't fail in carrying out their orders, even for me." She was silent for a moment, then added, "Especially for me."

The sadness in her voice tugged at Charlie, and despite his vow to keep his distance, he could not resist putting an arm around her shoulders to pull her close. He told himself the movement was only to assure her no-good brothers of his protection. But Angelina's slight body against his side felt so good and so right he knew he lied to himself once again.

The two men stopped in front of them. They held their guns on Charlie. One of the two threw the reins of the horses toward him. He caught them with his free hand.

"You must think I'm a pretty dangerous fella since I keep starin' down the barrel of a pistol every time I meet a new brother-in-law."

Timothy and Peter merely stared at him, their dark eyes as emotionless as the eyes of every other Reyes male Charlie had encountered thus far. Charlie hugged Angelina tighter, thinking how awful it must have been to grow up in a household full of snakes. He'd never had much use for his brother, but at least Bill had possessed some emotions that made him marginally human, and he'd been loyal to his kin. Charlie couldn't think of one redeeming quality he could apply to the disciples.

"Nice to see you, too, Timothy. Peter," Angelina said, nodding to each in turn.

The two nodded back slowly, their heads going down and up in perfect imitation of each other.

"Mount up," Timothy ordered.

"Now?" Angelina asked.

"Father wants you two back by morning. There's a wedding party and a dance tomorrow night. You can sleep all day and be ready to appear when the party begins."

Clever, Charlie thought, old Miguel makes sure we ride all night so we sleep all day and are too tired to argue about appearing at his blasted party.

Charlie glanced at Angelina. He could tell from the mutinous expression on her face she would love to argue. But the unwavering guns of her brothers made her swallow her words. She moved away from the protection of Charlie's arm and turned toward the house.

"I'll get our things," she muttered.

When Angelina was out of earshot, Charlie turned his attention back to Timothy and Peter.

"So, boys, tell me what it's like to be a disciple. I always wanted to know."

Four black eyes stared at him without a flicker of emotion. Neither man answered.

"Not much for conversation? Well, I suppose you wouldn't be. You probably never learned to say much beyond what your pa tells you to. That's all right. I'll do all the talkin'." He moved his lips upward into a thin smile. The disciples continued to stare. "I just want you to know, and you can tell the rest of the boys, too, I think the way you treat your sister is disgustin'. And somewhere down the line, when things are a bit more even between us"—he nodded at their guns—"I'll make sure you pay for it."

The horses showed more emotion than the men, pricking their ears toward Charlie. Neither man gave so much as a blink to indicate they had heard him. But Charlie knew they had.

Angelina came out of the house, and he helped her onto her horse. She looked down at him and smiled her thanks. He squeezed her hand and went to his own horse.

Yes, sir, he would make sure the disciples had a lesson in brotherly love as soon as the opportunity presented itself. He was looking forward to that day more and more with every passing second.

By the time they reached home, Angelina could barely hold herself upright in the saddle. For the last several miles, Charlie had ridden next to her, obviously worried she would fall to the ground. His quiet strength and concern warmed her heart. Usually she only experienced such warmth after the angel visited her in the night. This was the first time such a feeling had come to her from another human being.

When the horses stopped, Charlie jumped down and hurried over to lift her from the saddle. Angelina thought he would put her down. Instead, he carried her against his chest up the porch steps. He paused a moment at the front door, shifting her so he could open it, then strode with her into the house.

Inside, everyone slept, dawn just moments away. Outside, Angelina heard her brothers ride away. Charlie started up the stairs to her room.

She really should insist upon walking, but being surrounded by Charlie's strength and warmth felt too good, she found she could not bring herself to ask for release from his embrace. Instead, she let her cheek rest against his shoulder and wrapped her arms around his neck.

As he drew near the top of the steps, he slowed. His arms and chest tensed.

"Reyes," he growled, the rumble of his voice tickling her chin.

"Coltrain," her father answered, the word dripping with contempt.

Angelina fought to raise her head, to tell her father to show some respect for her husband, but the world was made up of little black dots that danced in front of her eyes whenever she opened them.

She must have made some sound of protest, for Charlie whispered, "Hush, I can handle 'im."

Since she knew he could, she subsided, cuddling closer to his chest.

"My sons told you? Tonight we are having a party to introduce you and celebrate your marriage to my daughter."

"Yeah, we heard."

"Excellent. You can place my daughter in her room. There's a place for you in the stable."

Charlie laughed, his chest shaking with his amusement. "She's my wife, Reyes. I go where she goes. I married her, and one of the things I recall vowin', with a gun to my back, was to protect her. To my way of thinkin' the one she needs protectin' the most from is you."

Her father's anger seemed to shimmer over Angelina and Charlie with the heat of the sun in the midst of August. Her fingers clenched against Charlie's neck, and he murmured soothing nonsense under his breath until she relaxed against him once again.

"Bring my daughter to the party at precisely eight o'clock." Her father's voice was tight with his anger. "Once everyone there hears of her marriage and sees that she indeed has a husband, I will give you the money we agreed upon, and you will leave. Angelina will be my problem once again. You need not concern yourself any longer about your vows."

Angelina tried to raise her head and ask what on earth they were talking about, but Charlie took the remaining steps in quick succession, shouldering past her father without further argument. Once inside her room, he kicked the door shut and placed her gently upon the bed.

Fighting against the thick fog of sleep, Angelina opened her eyes to meet Charlie's gaze.

"You married me for money?" she whispered.

Charlie sighed and looked away. But the guilt on his face was all she needed to answer her question. She turned on her side and closed her eyes. She could understand Charlie marrying her to save her reputation. Such a reason was even noble to her mind. But to marry her for money? He was no better than her disgustingly greedy brothers or even Juan Alvarez for that matter.

The bed dipped as Charlie sat next to her. He put his hand on her shoulder. She refused to move. He swore softly and removed his hand. "Angelina, it's not what you think. I wanted to help you. But you know I need money for my ranch. Your father insisted, and I figured . . . well, I figured—"

"It's all right," she said before he could say anything more and possibly make her hurt even worse. "I understand." She didn't, but she would never admit such a thing to him. "I'm tired now. I need to sleep. Could you tell my mother to wake me at seven so I can dress for our party?"

Charlie remained silent for a moment; then he stood. The bed swayed with the loss of his weight. "Sure, Sister. Whatever you want."

The door closed quietly behind him, and Angelina opened her eyes, staring out the window. Charlie had called her Sister, a name he used when he wanted to put some distance between the two of them. He was right. She had to remember just what their marriage was made up of: vows taken by force, lies made legal by the church. Just because she cared for him didn't mean he cared for her. Charlie Coltrain had had a life before he met her—a life he would return to just as soon as he got his money and got rid of an excess wife. She should not fault him for looking out for his own interests, even as he was forced to look out for hers.

As Angelina watched, dawn arrived, painting the sky outside the glass with all the colors of a summer day—red, orange, bright yellow against blue and white.

A new day. The same old problems.

Angelina closed her eyes against the joyful array, but despite her exhaustion, a long time passed before sleep claimed her mind.

Hellfire.
Charlie wanted to roast Reyes alive for telling Angelina of their money arrangement. To be truthful, he'd forgotten about the agreement until Reyes had brought it up. His main reason for marrying Angelina had been to get her away from her father's clutches. But she'd never believe him now, and that was fine. His greed would just be another mark against him. When he left, she

would hate him all the more. Even if she eventually came to believe he was dead, as her father had suggested, it would be easier if she had good reason to hate him first. He didn't want her pining away with guilt because she hadn't been able to save his lousy hide.

Even though what he had planned was the right thing to do, Charlie still detested himself for plotting the step-by-step erosion of her faith in him. He had come to count on that faith more than he cared to admit.

After giving Theresa Reyes her daughter's message, Charlie checked on Gabe, then returned to Angelina's room. She slept, dark lashes feathering honey-hued skin. He trailed a finger across her cheek, committing to memory the texture of her skin. She stirred, murmuring something that sounded suspiciously like his name, and he froze, his breath catching in his throat at the bolt of desire that shot through his body. Curling his fingers into fists, he forced himself to turn away. After locking the door, he stripped. Wrapping himself in a blanket from the foot of Angelina's bed, he lay down on the floor.

Charlie awoke to tapping on the door. A glance at Angelina showed she was still sleeping. Quickly he yanked on his pants and opened the door. Theresa Reyes stood on the threshold. Her eyes widened at the sight of his naked chest.

Charlie moved away and shrugged on his shirt before returning to the door. "Tell her I'll be back at eight." He stepped into the hallway, stifling a smile as Theresa edged past him into the room. She nodded and closed the door behind him.

Charlie went to the barn, where he found a set of borrowed clothes lying over his saddle. The brown frock coat was somewhat out of style, but it would be presentable once paired with the snow-white shirt, linen braces and tan trousers that made up the rest of the outfit. He considered refusing the implied order and showing up for the party in his guerrilla raider outfit just to spite Reyes, but he knew such an action would only reflect upon Angelina. This entire performance was for her benefit. He would see the farce out to the end.

When eight o'clock arrived, he was washed, combed, shaved and dressed to within an inch of his life. Charlie had to admit, as he gazed down at himself, he'd never looked so good. But then, looking good had never been much of an asset in his profession. In fact, his looks only made him more identifiable to the law.

At the thought of the law, Charlie remembered Drew Winston. Had the Ranger died from his snakebite? If not, Winston might show up any time. Though Charlie hadn't felt the itch at the back of his neck that indicated he was being followed or watched, such a lack did not mean the Ranger wasn't back on his trail. His instincts had been failing him with regularity for the past few years, and he expected that telltale itch to go the way of his other gifts right quick. He'd better get on down the trail soon just to be on the safe side. But first he'd have to find his gun and gunbelt. A thorough search of his belongings and the barn had unearthed nothing resembling a firearm. Reyes must have hidden the Colts inside the house somewhere. Perhaps, during the dance, Charlie would peek around the place and take back what belonged to him. The long, loose frock coat would be helpful in concealing any weapons he was able to retrieve.

Wagons and carriages had been arriving for the past half hour. When Charlie walked across the yard separating the barn and the house, curious stares followed him all the way.

The front door stood open; he walked inside. Theresa and Miguel greeted guests at the foot of the staircase. At Charlie's entrance, Miguel detached himself from the couple to whom he was talking and came toward his son-in-law.

"Angelina will be down in a moment. I'll introduce the two of you and then you can start the dancing."

Charlie frowned. "I don't dance."

"You will tonight. It's tradition."

Miguel began to turn away, but Charlie stopped him with a hand on his arm. "You don't understand," Charlie said. "I don't mean I won't dance; I mean I can't dance."

His father-in-law's eyes reflected his amusement. "Ah, I see. Interesting, though I won't say I'm surprised at your lack of such a basic social grace. Fine. I'll introduce you, and then Theresa and I will start the dancing."

Charlie nodded. Miguel walked away, and Charlie stifled the desire to kick his father-in-law in the seat of his pants. The man's snide superiority grated on Charlie's nerves.

At Miguel's urging, the guests filed into the parlor, which had been cleared of furniture to make way for dancing. Charlie stood alone in the front hall. He fought the urge to fidget in the confines of his borrowed coat and the stiff-necked shirt.

A sound at the top of the stairs made him glance up. His breath caught in his throat.

An angel, all in white, hovered above him. Dear God, she's so beautiful. He had always known it, but now, with the sun setting behind him and the candles in the hallway lending an artificial golden light to the staircase, she was even more lovely than he'd dreamed during the many long, sleepless nights since he'd first seen her face.

Her dark hair had been braided and then wound around her head in the shape of a crown, leaving her neck free to the night breeze. The gown hugged her breasts and waist, emphasizing her fragile bone structure. A conspicuous lack of frills and flounces only served to make her look more elegant. The long, full skirt circled her lower body, held out from her legs with the aid of a small hoop, and a single flounce created a train at the back that slid slowly down the stairs in her wake. The red ribbon he had given her was her only adornment, wrapped around the braided crown of her hair.

Angelina descended the staircase, holding her head up regally, avoiding Charlie's eyes. She looked cool and calm in her ice-white gown, but the shade of her fingers, which had turned the same pale shade as the material swirling about her ankles, told him of the tension she held within.

She reached the bottom step, and Charlie moved forward to offer her his arm. Without looking at him or speaking, she placed her fingertips atop his coat sleeve. She had not forgiven him for accepting money to marry her. Though the urge to explain himself one more time was strong, Charlie bit down on that urge sharply. He had to let her go and her disgust with him would be for the best in the long run. Without a word of greeting, Charlie led Angelina toward the parlor.

At the door, all eyes turned to them. Conversation dwindled to a murmur. Angelina's fingers tightened upon his arm, and he reached across his body with his free hand, covering her cold fingers with his warm ones. She glanced up, startled, then gave him a small smile of thanks before returning her gaze to the room in front of them. Like the hallway, candles also illuminated the parlor, the use of kerosene lamps being kept to a minimum because of their tendency to smoke and make the room stink of the oil. The decorations consisted of the paintings upon the walls and the women in the room. A long table with light refreshments had been set up near the band at the front of the room. Servants milled through the crowd, distributing champagne for the ladies and stronger spirits for the men.

Miguel motioned for Charlie and Angelina to join him in front of the band. As they walked through the room, the crowd parted. Charlie glanced at the faces, absently looking for anyone he recognized or anyone who might be looking at him too closely. Old habits died hard. All the gazes he encountered were curious, but open and friendly, not cautious and sly. He relaxed slightly. So far, word of his notoriety had not reached Mexico.

"Honored guests." Miguel's voice interrupted Charlie's thoughts. He and Angelina paused next to her parents and faced the crowd as Miguel continued. "My wife and I have asked you here tonight to celebrate the marriage of our only daughter, Angelina Theresa Reyes. Please join us in welcoming Charles Coltrain to the family."

Charles? Charlie stifled a laugh. He hadn't been called Charles since his baptism, and maybe not even then. Interesting old Miguel neglected to mention where his daughter had been married and when. He also neglected to address the fact that, the last anyone had seen Angelina, she was throwing herself on the mercy of the church and begging to become a nun. Miguel just announced his daughter was married and produced a groom, and everyone was supposed to fall into line and cut out the gossip. Well, for once, Charlie hoped his father-in-law was right.

With a great show of pleasure, Angelina's father shook Charlie's hand and clapped him on the back. Then Miguel kissed his daughter. Charlie was the only one close enough to hear Angelina's outward hiss of breath as her father's lips met her cheek. He would have bet Gabe she couldn't remember the last time her father had kissed her.

A cryin' shame, Charlie thought. If I had a daughter, she'd be my little girl all her life. She wouldn't forget the last time her daddy kissed her.

The thought of a child, a little girl with Angelina's eyes and smile, made Charlie start. Children had never entered his mind before. And they shouldn't now. Old outlaws did not contemplate having children with young nuns. Even if the nun in question happened to be the outlaw's wife.

The band began to play a waltz, and Angelina turned to him expectantly. Before he could explain his sad lack of the necessary social skill, Miguel and Theresa nudged them aside to take their place on the floor. After a moment filled with stares and whispers, the rest of the crowd turned away from Charlie and Angelina and joined the dancing.

Angelina stood next to him, staring at the swirling dancers. She held her body stiff with tension, her face a mask of studied uninterest.

Charlie leaned over. "I'm sorry you're embarrassed," he said, softly. "But dancin' wasn't one of the skills I picked up in my youth."

Angelina glanced at him in surprise. "I'm not embarrassed. I'm disgusted. My father will do anything to keep his reputation intact. This is just another example of how far he'll go to further his political career." She reached for Charlie again, this time curling her fingers around his arm and stepping closer to his body. "Now that we've made our requested appearance, let's go outside so I can breathe. I haven't worn a corset in a year. The Sisters definitely have the right idea there. I'm afraid I'll faint if I don't get some air soon."

Charlie nodded, her pained expression and shallow breathing would have told him the tale even if she hadn't. He led her toward the open door and allowed her to precede him outside. Since the party had only just begun, the garden was deserted.

Angelina walked until they reached a secluded area. She sat down on a low bench hidden from sight of the house by some rose bushes. A light breeze, warm but better than nothing, wafted across the yard, bringing along the smell of the barn. Angelina wrinkled her nose with a sound of disgust.

"I guess we can't get away from the fact that this is a horse ranch, no matter how hard my father tries to disguise it," she said.

"Hard to disguise nature." Charlie moved into the clearing. If he stood just so, he could still see the door of the house over the tops of the bushes. Large crowds full of strangers made him nervous. Though no one had watched him with anything beyond normal curiosity, he was still a wanted man and could not afford to relax with his back to the unknown.

The band struck up a new song, a love song. It sounded like "Sweet Genevieve" to Charlie, and Angelina closed her eyes, listening intently. "I love this song," she murmured, swaying with the music. Charlie watched, fascinated with the movements of her body, the smooth perfection of her skin, the innocence of her face.

Suddenly her eyes snapped open and she stood. Charlie tensed, wondering if she saw something behind him to cause her sudden movement. His hand automatically reached for his gun. He swore when his fingers met the material of his suit coat and not cool metal. He had to find his Colts and fast.

"Calm down," Angelina said and came toward him. "I just wanted you to dance with me."

"I don't dance."

She stopped only inches away from him and placed one hand on his shoulder. She took his other hand in hers. "You can with me."

"I wasn't bein' difficult just to spite your father." Charlie looked into her hopeful, upturned face and sighed. "I really don't know how to dance."

"I believe you. But you can pretend, just for a few minutes. It's only the two of us out here. No one will see. You only have to follow me."

Without waiting for his agreement, Angelina moved to the side in time with the music. Charlie stumbled after her. He tried, as hard as he'd tried to do anything for a very long time, to feel the music the way she did. But to his ears, the notes were merely a jumble of separate sounds. Her closeness did little to increase his concentration.

The smell of fresh soap—a scent he'd never found particularly arousing before he'd met Angelina—tickled his nostrils, and he had to fight for control of his thoughts and his body. Charlie tripped over his feet and stepped down hard onto her slippered toes.

"Ouch." Angelina stopped dancing and moved back.

"Sorry. Guess it's a good thing no one tried to teach me to dance before. I'm hopeless."

"No, you're not." Angelina took two steps toward him, coming even closer than before. "Let's try this," she said and slipped both arms around his shoulders, clasping her fingers together behind his neck. She placed her lips next to his ear. "I'll count; you listen."

Charlie went still. Her breath against his earlobe shredded the remains of his self-control. A glance toward the house showed him that their attempts at dancing had moved them out of sight of the open door. They were as alone as they were going to get. So, instead of listening, Charlie turned his head and pressed his mouth against her neck.

Angelina's soft gasp of surprise aroused him even further. He kissed a path up to her softly parted lips. After looking into her eyes and seeing his need reflected in their darkened depths, he put his lips to hers. His hands, which had hung limply at his sides since she approached him for the second part of their lesson, found a home against her waist. The hard corset underneath her gown made him growl with impatience. Whenever he'd touched her before, there had been only Angelina beneath the material of her clothes. He had to admit that he'd take the nun's way of dressing over the lady's any day.

There was one part of Angelina though that had
been tantalizing him since she'd walked down the
stairs. The bodice of her gown dipped so low, he
wondered if her ample breasts might spring free
of their confines if given any encouragement.
His palms spread across her rib cage, caressing
upward until his fingertips touched the edge of
her bodice. With only the slightest tug, the gown
slipped down, freeing her breasts.

Eagerly he filled his hands with her soft flesh,
his thumbs rolling over her already hardened
nipples as he teased her lips with his tongue.
She moaned into his mouth and arched against
his hands. He broke the kiss, lowering his head
as he brought her breast up to meet his tongue.
Her fingers tangled in his hair, pulling him closer,
showing him she wanted what was happening as
much as he did.

He took one dark red nipple into his mouth,
sucking gently while he rolled the other between
his fingers. Angelina's lower body pressed into
him, and he thought he would explode just from
the touch of her stomach against his hardened
shaft. He moved his mouth to her other nipple
and bit it gently, laving away the small pain with
his tongue. With the tip of his finger he skimmed
a trail down between the hardened globes and
then cupped her in his palms. She caught her
breath, watching him seductively through half-
open eyes.

"Isn't this a pretty sight?"

Charlie stiffened at the low-voiced question
behind him and shifted his body to shield
Angelina from prying eyes. After biting back
a startled shriek, his wife's hands flew to her
bodice. Charlie's fingers were there before hers

pulling the fabric up to cover her. He took her shaking hands in his and looked into her eyes, calming her with a steady gaze.

He let her go and turned, keeping Angelina behind him. The barrel of a gun hovered only a few feet from his chest. His gaze flicked up to meet the eyes of the man whose finger rested confidently against the trigger.

Charlie smiled. "I was wonderin' if you'd have the guts to show up, Alvarez. Now that you have, we've got unfinished business."

"Yes," Juan said, "we do. Me and you and the law. A thousand dollars is too good to pass up."

Charlie hesitated. News of his wanted status had finally crossed the border. "I'm sure you need the money, Alvarez. You can't be much of a rancher."

To Charlie's disappointment, the man ignored the insult. His gaze and his gun remained steady. "There are very few people in this world who could not use more money. Since the offer is for you, dead or alive, I have to decide how I want to deliver you. Dead would be my choice, but I hate to kill you here. Angelina's father is powerful in Chihuahua. I can't afford to ruin his party by killing his new son-in-law."

"No, that wouldn't be neighborly."

"Glad you agree." Juan's gaze flicked over Charlie's shoulder. "Angelina," he snapped, "get in the house."

"That's my wife you're talkin' to," Charlie growled. "I'll tell her what to do, and when to do it."

"That's right," Angelina said, trying to step around Charlie. "I'm not leaving."

Charlie shoved her behind him, none too gently. "Angelina, get in the house."

"What?"

He turned just in time to see the stricken expression on her face. "I can't do anything with him if I have to worry about you, too," he whispered. "Get help."

"Quit that love talk and get her out of here, Coltrain," Alvarez snapped.

Angelina looked into his face and slowly nodded. With a last lingering caress of her finger across his cheek, she turned and ran for the house.

Charlie watched her until she disappeared, then turned back to meet his fate.

Chapter Sixteen

Just as Angelina raced into the brightly lit room, the band began to play "The Wabash Cannonball." She flinched at the contrast of the lively tune with such a desperate situation. Frantically, she searched the crowd for a sight of one of her brothers. Though they were pretty much useless in most cases, any one of them would do to deal with Juan. She spotted Timothy nearest the door, flirting with one of the servants. His wife glowered near by.

Angelina started toward him. Then a gunshot froze her in her tracks. Most of the couples on the dance floor kept dancing, the music and the conversation blurring other sounds. A few people near the door to the garden glanced outside with a frown.

Her heart beating the rhythm of panic, Angelina didn't pause to ask for help. She leapt forward, grabbed her brother's gun from its holster and yanked the weapon free. While he was still gaping, she spun around and ran back outside.

The gun weighed more than she had expected. Her corset pushed all the breath from her lungs. The air hung heavy with heat. Her face flamed, but whether from tears or exertion, she didn't know. The trip back to Charlie took far too long.

She burst into the clearing. Charlie lay on the ground. Juan stood over him. As she watched, Juan cocked the gun and pointed the weapon at Charlie's chest.

Angelina raised Timothy's pistol and fired. Juan cried out and fell to the ground, clasping his leg. She ran forward, stopping next to Juan and pointing the gun at him again. "Give it to me," she ordered.

Juan looked at her, his face gray with pain, and held out the weapon without argument. She snatched the pistol from his fingers, then cocked her own gun again. "Did you kill him?"

"What—" He broke off and groaned. "What if I did?"

"Pray you didn't," Angelina said. Her sincerity must have reached Juan, for he paled even further and fell back onto the ground with another groan.

Angelina left him in his own blood and fell to her knees beside Charlie.

His shoulder was a bloody wreck. But the steady rise and fall of his chest proved he still lived. With a cry of relief she leaned down to press her wet, hot cheek against his.

"Nice work, Angel." Charlie's voice was quieter than usual, barely above a whisper. "When I taught you to shoot, I didn't think I'd need you to save my life."

"Lucky for you, you did." She smoothed his tangled hair away from his face.

Charlie's eyes opened at her touch and he smiled. "Tough talk. What were you gonna do to old Alvarez there if he'd killed me?"

Angelina glanced at Juan, who seemed to have fainted. "I honestly don't know. At the time, I was mad enough to shoot him again." She sighed and let the guns slide from her tense fingers onto the ground. A sob welled up in her throat, and she fell forward onto Charlie's chest, hugging him tightly, careful not to jar him too much. "You scared me to death." She wept into his shirt.

When her brothers and parents arrived moments later with most of the guests behind them, they found Angelina draped across her husband's chest, his blood staining her white gown while he attempted to calm her tears.

"What is going on here?" Her father's voice echoed in the night stillness.

Angelina drew in a deep breath and raised her head. She got to her feet, wiping away the tears from her cheeks with the back of her hand. Charlie struggled into a sitting position. But when he attempted to stand she glared at him, and he subsided with a lopsided smile. Angelina turned to her father. "Juan shot Charlie. Then I shot Juan."

Her father's eyes widened; then his frown deepened. Turning to the gaping onlookers he snapped, "Boys, take everyone back inside. Send them home. Now." He looked at his wife, who swayed with shock as she stared at all the blood. With a sound of disgust, he caught his wife as she pitched forward, then hoisted her up like a bag of flour and handed her to his nearest son.

"Take your mother to her room," he said before turning away.

Angelina stood protectively in front of Charlie. Her hands had begun to shake, but she clasped them behind her and fought to appear calm. Once she'd dealt with her father and gotten rid of Juan, she could tend to Charlie. Right now, that was all she cared about. The most important thing was not to show weakness. Her father preyed on weakness. Since Charlie did not look capable of protecting either of them right now, she had to be the strong one—for both their sakes.

Her father walked over to Juan, who had just regained consciousness. He lifted the man to a sitting position. "What is the meaning of this?" he demanded. "How dare you come to my home and cause such a scene?"

Juan's lips compressed into a thin, pale line. He glared at Angelina and Charlie, hatred spilling from his eyes. "Miguel, don't tell me you don't know who he is?"

"Who?"

"Coltrain. He's wanted for murder in the states. There's a thousand-dollar bounty on his head."

Angelina bit her lip. Damn, Juan Alvarez. She'd known he was trouble the first time she met him. And she'd been right—twice over.

Slowly her father turned toward Angelina. She fought not to flinch at the suppressed anger in his eyes. "Is this true, daughter?"

"Yes."

"And you didn't tell me?"

"You didn't ask."

He stared at her for one long moment, then turned away. Angelina knew she had not seen the last of his anger. She and Charlie would have to leave as soon as possible. She wouldn't put it past the man to turn his new son-in-law in just to teach his wayward daughter a lesson.

Her father helped Juan to his feet and led him away. With a sigh of relief Angelina turned back to Charlie.

"I think we'd better—" Her voice drifted off at the sight of her husband unconscious upon the ground. "Hellfire," she muttered, then ran toward the house shouting, "Matthew, Mark, Luke, John, Timothy, Peter."

And for the first time in her life, when she needed her brothers' assistance, they actually came running.

Charlie floated in the limbo between consciousness and unconsciousness. He heard the commotion around him when the disciples arrived to carry him inside. He heard Angelina's voice stridently ordering them to hurry up and be careful. He felt the softness of her bed when they laid him upon it. But when Angelina began to probe at his shoulder to remove the bullet, he took the easier road for both of them and surrendered to the fluffy darkness.

He'd been there once before, during the war. The darkness wasn't half bad, especially when compared to the pain on the other side. During this visit, Charlie remembered his last sojourn into the land of dreams.

He'd been on a raiding mission with the rest of Mosby's Rangers, harrying Union supply lines, doing their job. Suddenly, from out of the darkness, thundered a herd of cavalry wearing the Union Blue. The battle was short and bloody, the enemy retreating before the ferocity of the Confederate Rangers' assault.

One of their men fell, and Charlie rode into the woods a ways to retrieve the body. The rest of the Rangers regrouped several yards in the distance. He jumped down from his Gabe. Just as he bent to lift his dead comrade, a horse and rider burst from a dense area of bushes to his right. Straightening up, Charlie reached for his gun. Before he could withdraw his pistol from the holster, a rifle butt smashed against his throat. Pain exploded throughout his head. As he fell, Charlie heard the report of a gun and decided the blackness descending upon him would last throughout eternity.

When he awoke, he lay in a makeshift Confederate hospital—in reality a sympathizer's barn—alive, but unable to speak. Within a week he was back on his horse and raiding once more. The scar tissue in his throat thickened, and his voice became a permanent growl. He never learned who shot his attacker. Since no one owned up to it, Charlie had always believed his savior to be Col. Mosby himself. But he had never dared ask. If the Gray Ghost had wanted Charlie to know, he would have told him. The one person in his life Charlie had ever respected was John Singleton Mosby—until he'd met Angelina.

When Charlie came out of the fluffy blackness this time, her anxious face hovered above him. He reached up and smoothed away the worry line between her eyes with his finger. She smiled, a tense shift of her lips that didn't reach her eyes.

"Am I gonna make it, Angel?" he rasped, the thickness in his throat reminding him of the last time he'd woken up after an injury.

"Yes, you'll be fine. No thanks to Juan."

"No, I'd say it was thanks to you. And I do."

She nodded an acknowledgment of his gratitude and turned away, fussing with a basin of bloody water and equally bloody towels. He noticed she still wore her party gown, so he must not have been unconscious for too long.

"How is old Juan anyway?"

"He'll live."

"Lucky man."

"Yes." She sighed and stopped what she was doing, staring into the mirror above her dresser as though the sight of her own strained face fascinated her. "I could have killed him, you know? I wanted to."

"Yes."

"Does it always feel that way?"

"What way?"

"The ice-hot rage. It sweeps over you a second before you pull the trigger. I was so angry I wanted to explode, and when the gun went off I felt—"

"Good," Charlie said.

Angelina didn't answer for a second; she continued to stare at herself in the mirror. Then with a suddenness that surprised him, she snatched a bottle from the nightstand and threw it against the glass. The mirror shattered into hundreds of tiny shards, raining down onto the floor. She spun back toward him, the train of her dress swirling with her movement. His blood showed stark red against the white satin of her bodice; matching spots of red stood out against the bright paleness of her face.

"Yes," she shouted. "It felt good. He hurt you. I wanted to kill him." Her chest heaved with the force of her emotion. Her eyes glittered with unshed tears. "Dear God, what's happened to me? I wanted to kill another human being because of you. When does this stop? I don't even know myself anymore."

Charlie sat up and reached for her, but she shrank back, staring at him as though he were a stranger. Then without another word or touch, she ran from the room.

Angelina successfully avoided another confrontation with her father by hiding in the attic. Not very courageous behavior on her part, but she didn't care. She'd watched from the window as he'd supervised Matthew and Mark loading Juan into a wagon. Then he'd gone inside to bed, and her brothers had driven away with Juan into the night.

Despite Charlie's wound, they would have to leave at dawn the next morning. Now that most of the countryside knew her husband was a wanted man with a sizable bounty on his head, he wouldn't last another day at the Reyes hacienda.

Angelina sighed and turned away from the window. She had cried so hard her eyes ached. She was so very tired, both in body and in soul, but all her tears and her anger did not change the truth.

She had failed God's test. She loved Charlie Coltrain—as a woman loved a man.

When she'd seen him on the ground and feared he was dead, the truth had come to her in a flash. She loved him. She would always love him.

She could return to the convent and become a nun as she had always wanted, but would such an action be right? Mother superior had always told them they must believe in the life they vowed to enter with all their hearts. There was no going back. That was one of the reasons the good woman had insisted Angelina wait a while longer before entering the novitiate. She wanted all her Sisters to be certain the convent was meant to be their life.

Though Angelina still loved God, part of her heart belonged to Charlie. She could deny her love and follow her calling, but would it be right to become a bride of Christ when what she truly wanted was to remain with Charlie for the rest of her days?

If only she had someone she could talk to about the dilemma. Her angel had been stubbornly silent ever since his last visit, and her mother was next to useless when conflict of any kind might be involved. And Charlie. . . . Well, this was not something she could discuss with him. Yes, he'd married her, but that didn't mean he loved her or wanted her to remain his wife. According to her father, Charlie had married her for the money. While she had not believed such an explanation for long, she knew Charlie hadn't married her for love. Maybe out of gratitude, or to protect her, but not for love. With all the things he'd told her about himself and his life, she had serious doubts he knew the meaning of the word.

Angelina leaned her head against the window-pane. The smooth, cool glass soothed her hot, aching forehead.

Her angel had said she must find her way. She should learn what was missing from Charlie's life. Then she would be worthy.

Could love be what was missing from Charlie's life? If she loved him, might her love save

Charlie from his self-destructive path? If so, then she would need to stay with Charlie and be his wife in every way, forever. Such a thought sent a spark of joy through her despair, and she raised her head from the window, her brow creasing in concentration.

Was that what her angel had meant about being worthy? Not worthy of becoming a nun, but worthy of being Charlie's wife. Worthy enough to turn him away from the path of destruction and toward a life he could be proud of.

Angelina fell to her knees and clasped her hands together. "*Santo Dios,* I need a sign. Am I right? Will my love for Charlie save him? Is this what I am supposed to do? Or am I supposed to resist this feeling and return to the convent? I was so arrogant in my certainty that I was destined for the church. I don't understand anything anymore. Help me. *Por favor, Dios.* Help me to see the truth."

The attic remained silent, the echo of her voice fading away into the darkness. Angelina listened, straining her ears for the slightest hint of an answer. Several moments later she gave way to her exhaustion and lay her head down on the floor. Sleep claimed her soon after.

And the angel came.

"Praise God," she whispered. "I needed you desperately and you came."

"Calm your fears, child. You have chosen the correct path. You were never meant for the church. For everyone there is someone, and for you there is Charlie Coltrain. Marriage is a sacred vow, as well. Honor yours."

"I will. But why did you show me the convent? Why did you make me think I should go there?"

"You were supposed to go there. Your sojourn with the Sisters was part of God's plan. Would you have met Charlie if you had not gone to the convent?"

"No, I suppose I wouldn't have. I would have been married to the wrong man."

"Precisely. God has a plan for all his children. Your vow of marriage to Charlie is just as sacred as your vow to the convent would have been. Trust in God as you always have, Angelina. There are still dark days ahead for you. Keep your faith. Strengthen your love. With love and faith, you can win against all adversaries."

With those final words ringing in her ears, Angelina awoke. A glance at the window showed the night was at its darkest. She couldn't have slept for more than half an hour.

Hurrying from the attic, she went toward her room. When she'd left it last, her emotional state had been the worst she could ever remember. Now, upon returning, she was once more at peace.

Opening her bedroom door, she quietly slipped inside and approached the bed. Charlie slept, his face relaxed in slumber. He looked younger, less forbidding, but still sinfully handsome. Careful not to disturb him, Angelina walked around the bed and sat in the rocking chair.

Though knowing she trod the correct path helped her peace of mind, there were still many obstacles to overcome before their lives could be peaceful. Charlie was still wanted. Drew Winston would show up eventually. Either Charlie had to prove his innocence, or they must travel far enough away from Texas to leave his past behind them.

And that problem wasn't even the worst of her worries. The hardest task of all would be to convince Charlie they were meant to be together. After his reaction the last time she had told him about her angel, she didn't think informing him of the latest visit and message would do much good. No, she had to find another way to make him understand that their marriage should not be dissolved.

He thought he was too old for her. He believed himself a no-good outlaw whose failure to protect his mother and sister had resulted in their deaths. Angelina knew better, but she had to make Charlie see the truth and believe those truths as deeply as she did. Convincing him was her true mission, and she would not fail. Charlie might be ready to learn how to love if he could forgive himself and come to recognize his own worth.

Charlie muttered something in his sleep and shifted, throwing the covers back. Angelina got up and moved across the room, drawing the blanket over his bare chest. For a moment her fingers lingered against his flesh, warm but, thankfully, not fever hot. He had a beautiful chest—firmly muscled, tanned to a golden brown with a light dusting of blond hair.

He mumbled something again, a word that sounded suspiciously like Annie, and her heart shifted in sympathy. He had suffered so much and so long for his sister. She started to turn away but Charlie spoke, and what he said was as clear as a hot summer sky, though he was still sound asleep.

Angelina returned to the rocking chair. She smiled to herself as a tiny kernel of hope sprang to life within her.

Charlie had not been muttering his dead sister's name. Instead, the word he'd murmured in his dear, ruined voice had been her own.

Charlie awoke, his shoulder on fire. Groaning, he tried to sit up in bed, then fell back with a curse.

Angelina appeared in his line of vision. She rubbed her eyes and tried to smooth her rumpled dressing gown. He was glad to see she'd gotten rid of the bloody ball gown. If he'd had to see it one more time, he might have been tempted to yank the gruesome thing off her.

When she moved her head, she flinched and reached up a hand to massage the side of her neck. Obviously she'd fallen asleep in the rocking chair while watching over him. The thought warmed Charlie inside. No one had cared in a long time whether he lived or died.

"Mornin', Sister." He smiled and she smiled back, a radiant smile somewhat out of place in the situation. Immediately, Charlie quit smiling and wrinkled his brow in confusion.

"What happened?" he asked, watching her walk around the edge of the bed and sit down beside him.

"You don't remember?"

"Hell, yes, I remember last night. How could I forget with my shoulder hurtin' like you dug out a cannonball. I meant, why are you so all fired cheerful this mornin'?"

She shrugged and smiled at him again. Instead of answering she reached for his bandage. "Let me take a look at that shoulder."

Charlie caught her wrist before she could touch him. "I'm fine. Thanks to you. What I need to do is get outta here. Everyone in the area's gonna show up soon lookin' to make a thousand dollars."

"I know. As soon as I change, we'll leave."

Charlie looked at her closely. He had the feeling he was missing something in this conversation. "No, we won't," he said slowly, clearly. "I'll leave. You're stayin' here."

The eager look on her face disappeared. She swallowed and yanked her wrist from his grasp. "I'm your wife. I go where you go."

Charlie shook his head, uncertain he had heard her correctly. She was his wife? Where had this sudden determination to be his wife come from? Before last night she had wanted to be a nun. The last time he had seen her she'd run from the room in tears since she'd almost killed a man because of him. Now, here she was this morning, all smiles, insisting she was his wife. Did she feel guilty because he had nearly gotten killed while masquerading as her husband for the benefit of her reputation? Or was she back to pitying him for the sorry life he'd led? Either way, he had to disabuse her of the notion she was going anywhere with him. Not only would the situation be getting too dangerous, but he couldn't continue to traipse all over the countryside with her at his side, night and day, and not make love to her. And once they made love, he didn't think he could let her go. He had to turn her away.

Now. Forever.

"You are not my wife, Angelina. You know as well as I do our marriage was just for show. And there's no way on God's earth you're goin' with me. There'll be a hundred men after me now. It's too dangerous. Your father will see that you get back to the convent."

She stood and planted her feet, putting her hands on her hips. "I'm not going back to the convent," she said through her teeth. "I'm going with you."

Charlie sighed and ran his fingers through his hair. He hated to be downright mean, but she was being stubborn as his ma's old mule. "Sister, you wanted to be a nun. You've been screamin' it at me since the day I met you. Now I'm leavin' here. Alone. We didn't consummate the marriage. Have the damn thing annulled and go back to Corpus Christi. Your father will be thrilled to help you now that he knows what I am. It's as simple as that."

"Is it?"

The sound of a horse below echoed Charlie's growl of irritation. They both tensed and glanced toward the window. Charlie started to get out of bed but Angelina waved him back and went to look out herself.

"Just one horse. Whoever it is already went inside. Must be one of my brothers come to see father."

She came back and sat down again on the bed. Her closeness tempted him, but he tried once more to convince her. If being ornery wouldn't work, maybe reason would. "Listen, Angelina," he said in what he thought was a reasonable voice. He couldn't be sure since he'd never tried to reason with anyone before. He usually just growled and glared and everyone fell into line. Angelina obviously didn't know the rules yet. "I appreciate what you've done for me. But I think we can call things even between us now. We've both got to get on with our lives. You know what you want. Now you go on and fulfill your dream. I have a dream, too. I want to go to Montana. I want to start my ranch. By myself."

He waited, holding his breath. He didn't know what he'd do if she kept insisting that she was going with him, that she was his wife. The thought of taking her with him, making her his wife in truth, living out the rest of their days together in Montana was almost too enticing to resist. But even as he let himself contemplate such joy, one look at her young, innocent face forced him to see the truth.

He could never do such a thing to her. She deserved better than a life on the run. Even if they got to Montana alive, one day his past would come knocking on their door. Life in a convent would be much safer than life with Charlie Coltrain. She couldn't really mean what she said anyway. What young woman would want to tie herself forever to an old outlaw? Certainly not a beautiful woman like Angelina Reyes, who had her entire life in front of her. If she really wanted to be married, she could do much better than Charlie.

Angelina opened her mouth to argue, but before she could speak, the door slammed open, hitting the wall with a thud.

Charlie narrowed his eyes at the person who stood in the doorway and again reached for a gun that was no longer there.

Angelina jumped up and spun toward the sound. Her gaze darted around the room as she looked for a weapon. Finding none, she placed herself between Charlie and the intruder.

"Move aside, Miss Reyes," Drew Winston drawled. "No matter what you do, I'm takin' him back to Texas to be hanged."

Chapter Seventeen

Angelina stared at the gun in Drew Winston's hand. A movement behind him made her glance into the hallway. Her father hovered outside. Anger flooded her at the sight of his smug face.

"You," she shouted, pointing a finger at her father. "You led him here. You could have gotten rid of him if you tried. But you saw a way to get what you wanted, and you sold my husband out." Fury propelled her forward. Charlie grabbed the skirt of her nightdress and yanked her back. She sat down heavily on the bed, her rear end bumping against Charlie's legs.

"Sister," he growled, amusement lacing every word, "the lawman there is holdin' a gun on us. I don't think he'll take too kindly to your runnin' at him like that."

"I wasn't running at him. I was running at my father."

"I know that and you know that." He nodded toward the hallway, now empty of anyone but the Ranger. "I think even your father knows that. But old Winston there might not. I don't want you splattered all over your bedroom. Wouldn't be pretty."

Angelina swallowed. She hadn't thought of what the Ranger might do. She'd only thought of what her father had done. She glanced at Winston. He shrugged and continued to hold a gun on Charlie.

"Did I hear you right, ma'am? Did you say this man is your husband?"

"Don't answer that," Charlie growled.

She shot him a perplexed look. "I don't see why not. I'm not ashamed of it. Yes, Mr. Winston, I'm Charlie's wife."

"Hmm. Sorry to hear it, ma'am. You know the story. He's going back to Texas with me."

"You can't take him now," she said, a bit desperately. "He's hurt. He can't travel."

"I'm sure he was planning on leaving here today. If he can run away, he can go to Texas."

"I don't run away from nothin', Yank."

"Then what are you doing in Mexico? If you're as innocent of that train robbery as you claim, why didn't you stay and prove it?"

Charlie snorted. "Right. With a thousand-dollar bounty on my head? I'd be lucky if I lived long enough to see the judge. I don't count on my life bein' worth beans once I'm out of sight of this ranch neither."

Angelina gasped and jumped to her feet. She had to do something to keep Charlie out of the Ranger's hands. She looked back and forth between the two glowering men. Then she marched up to Drew Winston.

"I saved your life, Mr. Winston."

He looked down at her, his blue eyes startling in his sun-darkened face. "Yes, you did, ma'am. I'm grateful, but I'm not letting him go if that's what you're thinking."

Angelina bit her lip. She had been thinking exactly that. She should have known better than to hope for such a concession.

Angelina tried another tactic. "You blame Charlie for Claire's death. I understand your pain. But he would never have done such a thing."

Winston's face became closed and cold at the mention of his dead fiancee. "You don't know anything about it. You're blinded by him. Most women are once they get a good look at his face."

Angelina laughed, startling the anger from the Ranger's eyes. "I hardly think I'm one to be turned by a pretty face, Mr. Winston. But I do know Charlie. You do not. Believe me. He didn't do what you're accusing him of. He didn't kill your Claire, and he didn't kill that engineer."

"He'll have his day with the judge to discuss the engineer. Claire," he said and shot a glance of hatred Charlie's way. "Claire he'll discuss with me."

Angelina stifled her flare of anger. The Ranger was as stubborn as Charlie. But she wouldn't give up. She'd dealt with stubborn men before and prevailed. She would not allow Drew Winston to take her husband away to be hanged.

"Could I say somethin' here?" Charlie asked.

"No!" Angelina and the Ranger answered in unison.

"I think I'd better," he said.

Angelina rounded on him. "You'd better keep quiet while I handle this. You heard him. He's taking you back to Texas. If he does, you'll be hanged. No one will believe you there."

"I know that, Angelina. But I just remembered something—something about Claire."

Angelina froze at the name on Charlie's lips. Icy-cold dread swept through her. She glanced at the Ranger, who had also gone still at the mention of his fiancee.

"Spit it out, Coltrain." He cocked the gun. "Now."

"Relax," Charlie said in disgust. "I'm tryin' to tell you. I remembered where I was when you say I was burnin' your place and killin' your woman."

"Where?" Angelina asked through stiff lips.

"First I was at a funeral; then I was in jail. I can prove I didn't kill Claire. I've got witnesses."

"What are you talking about?" Angelina demanded.

Charlie looked at the Ranger, ignoring the gun trained upon him as though it weren't there. "When was your woman killed? What month?"

Winston frowned, obviously confused at the question. "November."

Charlie nodded. "Yeah, that's what I thought." He turned to Angelina with a crooked smile. "Remember, I told you that somethin' about what the Ranger was sayin' sounded kinda off to me. I finally remembered what. Before I left for Second Chance, I buried my sister." He took in a deep breath after those words before plunging ahead. "Then I spent a month in jail for killin' my stepfather. The judge decided what I already knew. Richard Bakker needed killin'. He let me go at the beginning of December. I spent the entire month of November, when the Ranger's woman got killed, in jail."

"And you just remembered this now?" Angelina asked.

"Yeah. That whole time was kinda a blur to me. But talkin' about it all so much lately with you—" He shrugged. "Well, it must have brought everything back. When the Ranger came in, I suddenly remembered."

Angelina scowled at Charlie. He hadn't made things very easy for the Ranger, forgetting something so important. She glanced at the lawman. Winston looked as though someone had just kicked him hard in the stomach. He uncocked his gun, but kept the weapon pointed at Charlie. "I can check this out, Coltrain."

"Fine. Go ahead. Check it out."

The Ranger stared at Charlie for another moment. Then he glanced at Angelina. Her hope must have shown in her eyes, for he flinched away from her gaze and returned his attention to Charlie. "I'll still have to take you back to Texas."

"What?" Angelina shouted. "Why? He told you he can prove he didn't kill Claire."

"He hasn't proved it yet. And unlike you, ma'am, I don't trust him. He still has to stand trial for the train engineer's murder and the robbery."

"Why? You were wrong about him once, couldn't you be wrong about him again?"

"Possibly. But I doubt if I'm wrong on both counts. Either way, he's going back with me. He can talk to the judge."

"No!" Angelina heard the hysteria in her voice and, for once, didn't care. She was past the point of being good and calm and angelic. Being all those things had gotten her nowhere so far. Maybe being difficult would. "I won't let you take him. I won't. Not now. Not when I've finally found out what—"

"Angelina!" Charlie's voice stopped her in mid-tirade. "Calm down. He's right."

"Huh?" The Ranger gaped at Charlie.

"What are you saying?" Angelina's heart thumped a fearful cadence at the unnatural note of despair lacing Charlie's voice.

"I've got to go back. If I can prove my innocence, then I can get on with my life. If not—" He shrugged. "I've gotten away with plenty of things in my life I deserve to be hanged for. It's kinda fittin' I be hanged for somethin' I didn't do."

"If you insist upon going, then I'm going with you."

"No, you're not. You're goin' back to that convent, and you're gettin' on with your life. I'm no good for you. I'm no good for any woman."

"Listen to him, ma'am."

"You stay out of this," she snapped. "In fact, get out of my room. You can watch the door from the hallway."

The Ranger shrugged. "I'll be right outside." He shut the door behind him.

"I'm sure you will," she muttered. Turning, she ran straight into Charlie's concerned gaze.

"What's gotten into you, Sister? I've never seen you so worked up."

"How can you sit there and calmly discuss your own hanging? If we think, we can get you out of this. There's got to be a way."

"No. No more thinkin'. No more plottin'. I'm goin' back with him. I'm not gonna let you throw your life away because of misguided loyalty to me. You're goin' back to the Sisters, and I'm goin' to Texas with the Ranger."

Angelina bit her lip, panic racing through her at the finality in his tone. He wanted her to go back to the convent. He planned to leave today—without her—to ride merrily toward a near certain death. All her carefully laid plans and her newfound hopes and dreams were shattering around her with every word Charlie uttered.

Angelina took a deep breath and forced herself to be calm. There was a way out of this situation. Her angel had told her to hold fast to her faith and her love. She would do just that, and somehow she would find a way to save them both from disaster.

Outside in the hallway, Drew listened to Angelina's voice rise and fall. Coltrain's ruined tones answered her.

He could almost feel sorry for the girl. She obviously loved the bastard, though he couldn't understand why. When she'd tended his rattlesnake bite, Drew had thought her pretty, sweet, full of an inner strength that lent maturity to her face despite a lack of years. How on earth had Coltrain gotten her to marry him? She hadn't seemed the type to fall for a handsome face, as she'd pointed out. And that father of hers obviously couldn't wait to get Coltrain out of the way. What was the story here?

The door banged open and Angelina came out. Drew caught a quick glance of Coltrain, still propped in the bed, before she closed the door behind her.

"He insists on leaving with you tomorrow."

"Tomorrow? What about now?"

"He was just shot last night, Mr. Winston. He's staying here until tomorrow."

Her voice and her face brooked no argument, and though Drew knew he could force the issue, he decided he didn't have the heart right now.

"All right, ma'am. Tomorrow then."

She gave a sharp nod and went downstairs. He watched her go, the slump of her shoulders reflecting the dejection within his own heart.

He'd spent the last several years of his life hating Charlie Coltrain, and now it looked as though he just might have been wrong. His entire existence over those years had been geared toward one thing—making Charlie Coltrain pay. If what the outlaw said was true and he wasn't guilty, Drew was in quite a bind. At this late date he would never be able to determine the truth about who had murdered the woman he loved. And if he could not avenge Claire's death, then what did he have left to live for?

Absolutely nothing, his mind taunted.

Drew shook his head against the melancholy sweeping over him. He still had to return Coltrain to Texas and then make certain the man was telling the truth about his whereabouts when Claire had died. If not, Drew would kill Coltrain himself.

A sound at the head of the stairs made him turn sharply, gun at the ready. He relaxed only slightly at the sight of Miguel Reyes.

"Well?" Reyes asked. "Are you taking him away?"

Drew nodded. "Tomorrow. As soon as the sun's up."

Reyes walked toward him, nodding. He stopped directly in front of Drew. "Good. The sooner the better. Angelina is being difficult, not that her being difficult is anything unusual for her." He shrugged. "You say Coltrain will most likely be hanged."

"Most likely. He says he didn't rob the train. Wasn't anywhere near the place. He could go free. Who knows? That's for the judge to decide."

Reyes frowned. "That's no good. I have to be certain he is gone forever." He peered at Drew, speculation ripe in his eyes. "Young man, I sense your distaste for Coltrain. Perhaps you would accept a proposition?"

"What proposition?"

"I am a very wealthy man. I can make this worth your while. Name your price."

"For what?" Drew had no idea what Reyes was talking about, and his irritation with that fact was reflected in the sharpness of his tone.

Reyes chose not to notice. Instead he smiled, leaning toward Drew with an unmistakable air of secrecy. Despite himself, Drew tilted his head to listen.

"Make sure Coltrain dies before he reaches Texas, and I'll pay you anything you ask."

Angelina searched the house for a gun. Not only were there none to be found, but her parents and her brothers had become conspicuously absent. She let out an exasperated breath. She was wasting her time. Even if she had been able to find a weapon, she doubted if she could have used it to overpower Drew Winston. He looked too blasted capable. If by some miracle she had been able to disarm the Ranger, she would still have had to face the problem of Charlie's attitude.

She had witnessed the stubborn set to his mouth. She knew very well what that meant. He planned to go back and face the judge. She doubted if she could have convinced him to run again, incapacitated Ranger or not.

Heart sinking, she returned to the attic. She had found answers within these walls only the day before. Perhaps the answer of how to avoid impending doom could be found there as well. Anything was worth a try.

Night fell but no answer came. Her knees ached from kneeling on the hardwood floor throughout the day. The panic she'd kept at bay through prayer returned, stronger now and becoming worse with each passing minute that brought Charlie's departure closer.

When dawn came, the Ranger would take her husband away. And there wasn't a thing she could do about it. The more she thought of Charlie's leaving, the more clouded her mind became. She couldn't think; she couldn't reason. All she could do was feel, and what she felt was want and need and desire.

There was every chance she would never see Charlie again after this night. She would spend the rest of her life in a convent, remembering, dreaming of him. She planned to take with her whatever memories she could. For one night, she would be a woman. He was not going to refuse her tonight with platitudes about her innocence. She would make love to her husband.

Tonight.

Still in her nightdress, she made her way downstairs. The house remained silent, still empty. She went to her mother's room by the servant's staircase leading from the kitchen. Once there, she washed from the pitcher of water on the nightstand. Then she brushed out her hair, leaving it loose except for the red ribbon Charlie had given her. She tied the satin around her head, gently pulling the dark mass back from her face.

Barefoot, she padded down the hall to her room. The Ranger still stood outside the door. At her approach, he straightened up.

"Ma'am." He nodded. "I was worried about you."

"No need. My husband, he's all right?"

Winston glanced at the door and shrugged. "He asked for you. I told him I didn't know where you'd gone. He wasn't happy."

"I can imagine."

"He asked for a bottle." Winston winced at her frown. "I figured what the hell and got him one from downstairs."

"He's drunk?"

"Maybe. I brought him the whiskey about an hour ago."

Angelina held her breath. She wouldn't know the truth until she went into the room. Even if Charlie was already passed out, she planned to stay with him tonight. She looked up at the Ranger. "Since this is our last night together, Mr. Winston, I'd appreciate it if you'd go downstairs so we could have some time together."

He looked at her for several moments, a thoughtful expression on his face.

"Please." Angelina allowed the fear she'd banked all afternoon to creep into her voice. "I need this night. You can sit on the porch. My window is right above. There's no way we can get out. And the barn will be in your sight as well. We can't leave without horses."

The Ranger sighed, then nodded. "All right. I guess I owe you. But I'll be knocking on the door at dawn. No excuses then."

"No, I promise."

He turned away and started for the stairs.

"Drew?" Angelina called. He glanced at her over his shoulder, raising his eyebrows at her use of his Christian name. She smiled shyly. "Thank you. You don't know what this means to me."

"But I do, ma'am. I remember what it's like to be in love." His face saddened momentarily before he tipped his dusty, broad-brimmed hat and retreated to the porch.

Angelina stood with her hand on the doorknob, gathering her courage. Once she went inside, there would be no going back. With a deep breath, she opened the door and stepped into the room.

Before she could close the door behind her, Charlie's ruined voice came out of the semi-darkness. "Well, well, well. If it isn't the nun-in-training. Where've you been all day, Sister? Prayin' for my immortal soul?" He laughed his coughlike laugh. "Too late for that, and you should know it."

Crossing to the nightstand, Angelina lit the kerosene lamp and turned to face the bed. Charlie toasted her with the half bottle of whiskey in his hand. Sometime during the day he must have convinced Winston to retrieve a pair of Levi's from his belongings, for the lower half of his body was once again respectably covered. But the rest of him—Angelina caught her breath as she stared. No, the rest of him was not respectable at all.

He looked sinfully handsome, his chest bare, tanned skin glowing against the white sheets and long, silver-gold hair hanging in a tangle. She wanted to run her fingers through the strands and smooth them into place. Instead, Angelina ignored the sarcasm in his words and returned to lock the door.

Charlie raised his eyebrows. "Oh, oh. Why'd you lock the door? A locked door won't stop the Yank if he really wants to come in. Ain't that right, Yank?" he shouted, then took another swig of the liquor.

"He won't answer you. I sent him away."

He glanced at her speculatively over the rim of the bottle. "How far?"

"Downstairs. To the porch."

"I'm not escapin' if that's what you're thinkin'. I've decided to face the judge. I'm sick of runnin'."

"I know. I understand. I'm not here to talk you out of it."

"No?" Charlie frowned at her and took another sip of whiskey. "Then what do you want?"

Angelina swallowed. She had no idea how to go about seducing a man. Such lessons had never been included in any of her schooling. To be truthful, she wasn't quite sure of the actual technicalities of the final procedure. She hoped that by the time that problem arose, Charlie would compensate for her lack of knowledge.

Slowly Angelina moved forward to turn down the lamp. Then, before she could lose her courage, she turned toward Charlie and shrugged her robe from one shoulder.

Charlie scowled. "What do you think you're doin', Sister? Tonight's not the night to disrobe in front of me. In fact, we'd both be better off if you slept in another room."

Taking a deep breath, she shrugged the robe from her other shoulder. The stiff white covering slid to the floor without a whisper of protest. Charlie's gaze, which had been focused on her face, drifted downward, pausing at her breasts before moving lower. From the way his eyes widened and his breathing quickened, Angelina could tell that her thin nightdress, combined with the wavering light of the lamp behind her, revealed the nakedness barely hidden beneath the white cotton.

She traversed the three steps between the dresser and the bed, then sat down next to him. "I'm not going anywhere tonight, Charlie," she said firmly and took the bottle from his hand. Leaning down, she placed the whiskey on the floor. When she returned to an upright position, Charlie stared at her as though she were the first woman who'd ever accosted him in his bedroom. Angelina was certain that was not the case. The thought of the other women who had been with Charlie—skilled, mature, knowledgeable women—made her lick her lips nervously.

Charlie watched the movement of her tongue, then slowly reached out and tugged the ribbon from her hair. The satin came loose, gliding across the back of her neck, then falling forward to rest on the tops of her cotton-covered breasts.

"This is a mistake," Charlie said, his gaze focused on the red satin. "You should run away now, little girl. You're playing big-girl games you don't understand."

"I understand more than you think, Charlie Coltrain." She reached up and began to unbutton her nightdress. He watched her fingers for a moment. His gaze flicked up to meet hers. He let the ribbon slip from his fingers to the bed between them and leaned forward to push away her fumbling fingers.

She allowed him to move her hands aside, but when he rebuttoned the buttons, she reached up and caught his hands. "What do you think you're doing?"

"Keepin' us both from makin' a big mistake." He removed his hands from under hers as though he couldn't stand her touch. Then he looked away. "Now pick up the rest of your clothes and get the hell out of here."

Angelina hesitated, uncertain, confused. Then, while he continued to stare stoically away from her, she reached up and yanked her nightgown open once more.

When she had opened the garment to the top of her breasts, she put her fingers to Charlie's chin and forced him to look at her.

"I won't leave." She stared into his eyes for a long moment. "I can't."

Almost as though he could not stop himself, Charlie's hands came up. "Oh, Angel, my sweet Angel," he murmured. "You have no idea what you do to me."

His first tentative touch made her draw in a sharp hiss of breath. One by one, with agonizing slowness, the rest of her buttons came free. Reaching inside her gown, Charlie's palms skimmed across her collarbone as he pushed her nightdress over her shoulders. She shrugged the garment away, and the bodice pooled around her waist.

His hands, rough from the years of working with horses, stroked her with amazing gentleness. As though she were made of the most fragile glass, he trailed his fingertips across the tops of her breasts, stroking, teasing, cupping her fullness in his palms, then rubbing callused thumbs over hardened nipples. Her head fell back as she accepted and relished his touch. Then his mouth closed over an aching peak, and he eased her backward onto the bed.

While his lips worked magic upon her, she reached up, smoothing her hands down the hard, defined muscles of his back. She traced his scars with her fingertips, soothing him with murmurs from deep in her throat when he stiffened.

He raised his head, looking deeply into her eyes. "There are a lot of things you don't understand about me."

She smiled a tremulous, tentative smile, then curved her hand around his neck and brought him closer. Just before his lips claimed hers she whispered, "I know all I need to know. Right now and for always."

He tasted of despair and desire, a combination as intoxicating as the whiskey he'd sipped moments before. She answered his desperate caress with one of her own, opening her mouth and welcoming him inside with an eager sound of acceptance. As he kissed her, she touched him, impatient to experience everything she had believed forbidden to her forever.

When her hand moved lower, tentatively stroking a finger up the hardened swell of his Levi's, Charlie gasped and grabbed her wrist.

Angelina's eyes snapped open. His face, so close to hers was tense, his eyes closed and his mouth a thin line. As she watched his eyes opened.

"Are you tryin' to kill me, Angelina?" he rasped.

She reached her free hand up to stroke his cheek. "No, I'm just trying to love you." She raised her head from the bed to capture his mouth with hers and kiss him deeply. His naked chest pressed to her breasts, and she rubbed the aching tips against him. He moaned and kissed her back. Seconds later he released her wrist. Wasting no more time, she applied her fingers to the metal buttons on his pants.

He started in surprise when she touched him, flesh to flesh, and he tried to pull away. "No," she murmured against his lips. "Let me touch you. Please."

He sighed and shifted, his rigid member springing free of his Levi's. Angelina pushed him back onto the bed and sat up, pulling the pants down his legs and discarding them on the floor. Then she stared in amazement at the beauty before her. Never had she seen a naked man. Charlie might believe that he was old, but his body revealed the lie. Strong, bronzed, firm, he was a living testament to the beauty of the male animal.

Unable to keep herself from touching such a sight, she ran her fingers up his legs and over his hard, flat stomach. Then, as she caught his gaze and held it with her own, she took him in her hands and learned every inch of the part that made Charlie a man.

He had been conspicuously silent throughout her examination, but as she continued to stroke him, he growled a curse and pulled her down on the bed next to him. A quick yank and her nightdress joined his Levi's on the floor. With a single shift he lay atop her, her face captured between his palms, her body immobile beneath his.

Angelina looked into his black eyes alight with desire and regret. Her heart lurched. He was going to refuse her again. This time she couldn't bear it. She wanted him. She needed him. This might be her last chance.

Just as he opened his mouth to speak, the lamp flickered and went out.

The room plunged into darkness, and Angelina took the advantage. She arched her neck and captured his lips with hers. Putting everything she had learned since their first kiss into this caress, she stroked, nipped, teased, allowing all she felt for him to come rushing forth. For a single second Charlie held back; then with a sound mixed of anguish and disbelief, he responded.

The darkness added fuel to their passion, their true feelings coming alive with the loss of the light. The hesitation she'd sensed in him from the beginning disappeared, and he met her innocent caresses with ever bolder touches of his own. Now that she didn't have to think so hard about how to seduce him, Angelina was able to close her eyes and experience all the incredible sensations shooting through her like a thousand falling stars.

He kissed her like a starving man who suddenly comes upon a banquet. His hands touched her reverently, sliding up her waist and cupping her breasts, teasing them until she pressed his mouth to the aching peaks. Only when he drew her nipples into the warm cavern did she know relief.

An uncomfortable emptiness raged out of control inside her and she shifted. Charlie groaned and pushed against her, his hardness pressing against her secret place. Without really knowing why, she opened her legs and arched against him, gasping at the flood of pleasure sweeping through her. She remembered one other time when she had felt the release of tension after Charlie touched her just so. How wonderful that feeling had been, though a strange sense of emptiness had come over her after the joy faded.

Shifting, she went still as the head of his shaft probed against her opening. Charlie raised his head from her breasts and buried his face in the crook of her neck. The sudden tension in his arms and back worried her, and she lifted her hands to soothe it away. As she did so, her lower body bumped against him, and his shaft slid inside her a bit further.

"Oh!" she gasped. He felt wonderful. He filled the emptiness inside her. She wanted more.

"Don't, Angelina," Charlie ground out between his teeth, raising his head slightly away from her neck. "Don't move. I should never have let this go so far."

"I wanted this. I want you," she whispered, smoothing his hair back from his damp face. "You told me you'd make me beg. So I'm begging. Please love me tonight."

"No, I didn't mean that. We can't do this. You can't undo such a thing. If we go on, you won't be innocent anymore. There might be a child. We talked about this, Angelina. I won't do this to either of us."

He began to withdraw from her body and Angelina panicked. She had to do something now or she would lose him forever.

"I'm your wife," she said. "Your wife." Biting her lip against the expected pain, she thrust herself forward. Charlie, not expecting the move, was unable to withdraw in time and, instead, found himself buried firmly inside the body of his wife.

"Hellfire," he shouted. "What have you done?"

"What we've done. I'm your wife now." The small stab of pain had faded quickly and warmth flowed through her instead. She thrust up against him again. "The deed's done. Show me the rest, Charlie. Teach me passion."

Though Charlie's arms were still stiff and unyielding, the rest of his body had begun to react on its own. Slowly he slid out and into her again. Angelina gasped and clutched him closer.

"God help me," he muttered, "but I can't stop."

He came into her again, harder this time, deeper, filling her completely. The tension built within her once more. She moved her body in time with his thrusts, and this time when she called out his name, he answered with his own cry of release.

Charlie collapsed on top of her, then rolled to the side, cradling her in his arms. Spent, Angelina drifted on a warm river toward sleep.

"I love you, Charlie," she whispered as consciousness ebbed away.

In her dream, he kissed her forehead and said, "I love you, too, Angel." Then he took her with him to Texas. Together, they convinced those who mattered that he was innocent and rode off to a life together in Montana.

Angelina awoke with a smile. They could do it. Now that they were husband and wife in truth, he would not leave her behind. They would face everything together, and together they would triumph. She had held fast to her love and her faith. She had followed the angel's advice. A life with Charlie would be her reward.

Rolling over, Angelina reached out a hand for her husband.

The bed was empty.

Chapter Eighteen

Charlie awoke before dawn. His head ached—from the whiskey or the woman, he didn't know. What he did know was that he had made a big mistake. He could only hope Angelina wouldn't pay for his lapse in judgment.

When she'd come to him the previous night, she had caught him at the worst possible moment. He'd just reached the stage of drinking when he got maudlin, seconds before he became angry and then passed out. If she'd only arrived a few swigs later, he would have insulted her until she left. As it was, her wide, doelike eyes and trembling lips had turned his resolutions to mush. He wanted her, had always wanted her. Hell, he wanted her still—over and over again until he memorized every inch of her body and she did the same with his. He wanted to wake up every morning with her by his side and to look forward to every night in her arms. During the night he'd even dreamed of children, a luxury he'd never allowed to cross his mind with the life he'd led. But that life was what had brought him up short of his dreams in the end. Someday his past would catch up with him. If not in a few weeks, then in a few years. He would pay for his crimes—no one else. Not Angelina and not his children. The sins of this father would never be visited upon his sons and daughters. Not if Charlie Coltrain had anything to say about it. The kindest thing he could do for the woman he loved was to leave her.

He should have been on his way before last night. What had happened between them spelled disaster, but he hadn't been able to help himself. No excuse, his ma would have said, but the truth nevertheless. Still, deep down where the memory of Angelina's touch would warm him for the rest of his life, he couldn't regret the few precious hours he'd spent in her arms. Nothing in his life had ever been quite so good as making love to Angelina, his wife.

When he slipped from her bed like the thief he was, she turned over, looking even more young and innocent in sleep than she did when awake. He wanted to reach out and touch her one last time, but he didn't dare. If she awoke and he had to look into her eyes again, he wouldn't be able to leave her.

And he had to leave her.

There was no way in this hell of a world he was going to take her to Texas with him. Once there he'd either twist at the end of a rope or be run out of town like a half-mad dog. If he had to die, he would do so alone. If he lived, he couldn't bear to have her see him for what he really was.

For some reason she believed in him. She thought he had an essential goodness, some aptitude for heroics buried beneath his outlaw exterior. Lord knew where she'd gotten that idea, but he had to admit he kind of liked it. If he was going to be hanged, at least he'd carry the memory of her belief with him to the grave—along with the memory of their one night together.

After gathering up his few things, he scribbled a quick note and tossed it on the dresser. At the door, he paused and looked back.

Angelina still slept. A scrap of red on the floor caught his eye, and Charlie crossed the room to pick it up. Her ribbon dangled from his fingers. After a final, lingering glance at his wife, Charlie stuffed the satin into his pocket and quietly left the room.

He didn't make it two steps onto the porch before he heard the click of a gun being cocked.

"Going somewhere, Coltrain?"

Charlie stopped and glanced at the Ranger lounging against the porch rail, gun aimed at Charlie's head.

"To Texas with you. That is, if you can make it, Yank."

"Ready when you are."

Charlie glanced up toward Angelina's window. "I'm ready now. And let's make it quick and quiet."

Winston followed Charlie's gaze, and his eyes narrowed in speculation. Then he nodded his agreement and motioned for Charlie to precede him to the barn.

Minutes later, they rode out to the east.

They traveled throughout the day in silence, two men at odds for so long suddenly forced to travel together over a long distance. When they stopped just after dark, Charlie found they worked well together, making the camp and scraping out a meal.

After dinner, Winston approached with a length of rope. "Have to tie you for the night."

Charlie shrugged. "I'd do the same if I were you." He was surprised to find the hatred he'd harbored in his soul for anyone he considered a Yankee had faded to a dull burn. He couldn't summon up the fierce bitterness. Every time he attempted to bring back the hate, he saw Angelina's face and heard her words of forgiveness. Life was too short, and his was getting shorter with every mile they rode closer to the border. He didn't want to spend his last few days hating a man who was only doing what he believed to be right. Charlie wanted to spend those last days remembering Angelina and every moment they'd shared together.

The next several days passed in much the same way. Charlie slept little and ate less. Sometimes he caught the Ranger watching him with an almost concerned expression on his face. Charlie ignored the man. He had no reason to engage in either activity. Soon enough he would have no need for food, and he could sleep for all eternity.

"You really love her, don't you?"

Winston's question startled Charlie out of a half doze beside the fire, where he'd been dreaming of the first time he'd kissed Angelina. Sitting up straight, he blinked a few times to clear the fog from his eyes and stared across the wavering flames at the Ranger.

"What if I do? Won't help me now, will it?"

"Might. Love can accomplish amazing things for a man."

Charlie snorted. "You're an expert?"

"Not an expert. I just know what it's like to love someone so young and innocent. Someone who looks at you as if you could save the world, even though you know you're not fit to kiss her toes."

The sincerity in Winston's voice made Charlie smile grudgingly. The Ranger had it right there.

"It was like that with you and your Claire?"

Winston shot him a dark glance at the mention of his dead fiancee. Charlie thought the Ranger might remind him of his supposed part in her death, but after a moment's consideration Winston nodded and stared into the fire.

"When you lose someone you love the way I loved her, in the way I lost her, there's nothing left. That part inside of you that belonged to her is suddenly empty. The only way to fill that hole inside you is to make certain someone pays for that loss."

His gaze locked with Charlie's again. Charlie nodded slowly and looked away, thoughts of his ma and Annie crowding into his mind. He and the Ranger had a lot in common. They were both being eaten from the inside out by hate and grief and guilt. Maybe he could help the man out, though God knew why he should give a damn.

What the hell? he thought. Got nothin' better to do with my time anyway.

"It doesn't help," he blurted, earning a frown of confusion from Winston. "Even if you find that person and kill him with your own hands, it doesn't help. The one you love is still dead, and nothing will bring them back."

The Ranger nodded, considering Charlie's words. "So how do you go on living?" Winston asked, his eyes full of an earnest desire to learn the answer.

"You don't live. Not really. You exist. You hate the world and everyone in it. You blame a group of people for the evil of one. And you die alone and lonely."

"Pleasant prospect."

"Yeah, ain't it?" Charlie said

They both stared at the dancing red-orange glow of the flames between them, and Charlie wondered when the hate within him had withered and died and when tolerance had taken its place instead.

Sister,

If the worst happens and you carry my child, I'm sure you'll be able to find me in the Dallas jail. At least until they hang me. What happened between us was a mistake. For what it's worth, you have my name, which is more than I ever got from my pa. If I had anything else to give you, I would. Good-bye.

Charlie

"Hellfire," Angelina muttered and threw the paper back onto the dresser where she'd found it. "If he thinks I'm staying here until he's hanged for something he didn't do, he's made a bigger mistake than making love to me."

While she stuffed clothes into a bag and changed into a riding habit, she talked to herself, her anger flaring higher with every word. "If I'm carrying a child, he's darn well going to hear about it. I'm not going to let him sacrifice himself for the wrong reasons. No, sir. And how dare he say having a child would be the worst that could happen? Wait until I get my hands on that man."

Whirling away from the bed, she threw her pack over her shoulder and headed for the door. She reached for the knob and jerked it toward her, then stumbled forward to bump her nose against the immobile door. Frowning, Angelina rattled the doorknob.

Locked.

Fury, hot and fresh and blinding, raced through her blood. Throwing the pack to the floor, she banged on the door with all her strength.

"Let me out of here," she shouted.

No one answered. Angelina's gaze swept the room as panic set in. She had to get on the trail or she'd never catch Charlie and the Ranger. Once she did, she was going to have a word with her husband about locking his wife in her room.

She ran to the window and threw it open. Below, her father had just stepped off the porch.

"I'm locked in," Angelina called. "Can you come up and open the door?"

He stopped and turned to face her, tilting his head up. "I don't think so, daughter. Since I locked you in, I don't believe I'm going to let you out just because you asked me to."

Angelina's heart stuttered. Her father had locked her in, not Charlie. "Why did you do lock me in?"

"To prevent your doing exactly what I can see you planned to do: going after your outlaw. You're going back to the convent, daughter. They'll accept you with a sizable dowry and forget your unfortunate marriage. The people around here won't be so forgiving. I have to get you out of sight of my political companions so they can forget about you and your scandalous behavior. Then I can take my rightful place in our government."

Angelina bit her lip, trying to think of a way out of the predicament. Perhaps the best course of action would be to agree. If she could get out of this room and off of this ranch, she might have a chance to thwart her father's plans. "Yes, I see your point. Why don't you have one of the boys take me back to the convent today?"

Her father smiled, white teeth flashing against bronzed skin. "I'm not an idiot, daughter. You'd find a way to get word to your outlaw. Besides, I can't send you to the convent with a brat in your belly."

Angelina flinched at the distaste in his voice, but she bit back the words of anger. She had to find a way out of this, and alienating her father would not get her the information she needed. But she needn't have worried. Now that he'd begun to talk, her father seemed to enjoy telling her his entire scheme.

"You will stay in your room until I'm certain you don't carry a child. If you do, you will go to your aunt's in Mexico City and leave the baby with her. In any event, by the time such a problem is resolved, your husband will be dead. Then your brothers will take you back where you belong."

"How can you be so certain they'll hang Charlie? He did not kill that man or rob that train."

"Whether he did or did not hardly matters. If the law doesn't take care of him one way, the Ranger will take care of him another. Either way, he'll be just as dead."

Angelina went very still, smelling a rat somewhere close. "What are you talking about? Charlie did not kill Drew Winston's fiancee. He has proof. Winston wouldn't kill him."

"Really?" He laughed. "You are so naive. Men will do anything for money. And I offered the Ranger quite a bit of cash to make sure Charlie Coltrain dies, one way or the other."

Her father turned away, a smug smile upon his lips. Angelina sank to the floor as despair washed over her.

Charlie was gone and she was trapped. When her father set his mind to something, a way around him rarely presented itself. She would not get out of this room until he had the answer he sought. By then it would be too late to save her husband. And without Charlie, she really didn't care what happened to her.

Dallas

Not the place Charlie would have picked to die, but then one was as good as the next in his situation.

He and Winston rode through town. As they approached the jail, the Ranger pulled up and stopped.

"What the hell?" Winston muttered as he stared at the crowd milling in front of a hanging platform.

"How'd they know I was comin'?" Charlie asked. "Thought I was gonna get a trial."

"You will." Winston shook his head. "This isn't for you." He pointed at the platform. "Look."

Several law officers mounted the steps both before and behind a tall, blond man. The prisoner's hands were bound behind him. One of the officials led the man to the noose in the middle of the platform that swayed slowly in the dusty breeze.

Charlie narrowed his eyes. "Hellfire," he murmured.

Winston glanced at him sharply. "Know him?"

"Yeah. Neil Hansen. Rode with me in Missouri before and after the war. Never cared for him much. He had a nasty streak of mean—kind of like my brother, Bill, only worse. Didn't follow my rules, so I told him he wasn't welcome in my gang." Charlie frowned, remembering. "Hansen didn't take it well at all. As I recall, he swore he'd pay me back someday."

Charlie fell silent as one of the lawmen stepped forward. "You have been convicted of train robbery and murder. Your sentence is to hang by the neck until dead." The lawman raised his hand, and seconds later, Neil Hansen was twisting and kicking from the noose. While he watched the man's final struggles, the lawman said, "May God have mercy upon your soul, Charlie Coltrain."

"Son of a bitch," Winston swore.

"Yep," Charlie said. "I'd say he didn't get his revenge quite the way he planned. Looks as if he got himself hanged, usin' my name."

Winston looked around the town square as though he could find someone to tell him what had happened. His gaze came back to Charlie, and Charlie almost smiled at the confusion in the Ranger's eyes.

"Told you I didn't do it."

Winston grimaced. "I know. Listen, I'm gonna have to put you in the jail until I check this out."

"Don't forget to wire Missouri and check the dates on my bein' in jail there."

"I will," Winston said, though his voice held an absentminded quality.

They rode around the crowd, Gabe on a leading rein tied to the Ranger's horse. At the jail, they both dismounted. Charlie followed Winston inside.

"Got a man I need you to hold," Winston told the officer on duty.

"Name?"

"Uh—" Winston turned to Charlie with a question in his eyes.

"Reyes." Charlie supplied the only name he could think of at the moment. "Charlie Reyes." He didn't feel like explaining why he had the same name as the man who'd just been hanged. Until he found out just what crimes Neil Hansen had committed in his name, Charlie figured he'd better keep his true identity to himself. Obviously Winston agreed since he nodded and left Charlie with the jailer. Shortly thereafter, Charlie entered a cell and joined a raucous poker game already in progress.

Night fell before Drew found all his answers. He sat outside the jail and thought about what he had learned.

The man Charlie knew as Neil Hansen had been on a crime spree throughout Texas, robbing and killing with great abandon under the name Charlie Coltrain. As far as the powers-that-be knew, Charlie Coltrain had died upon the hanging platform. Drew did not set them straight. For the life of him, he couldn't figure out why.

He had sent a wire to Missouri and received his answer not more than an hour before. Charlie Coltrain had indeed been confined when Claire was killed. Drew had spent the last several years chasing an innocent man. More than likely; someone from Charlie's gang had done the burning and the killing. Since Neil Hansen had used Charlie's name in Texas, perhaps he had done the same in Missouri. If that was the case, then Claire's killer had died in front of Drew's eyes that morning. Or maybe Charlie's brother Bill had been the culprit. The man had had an evil reputation. But revenge on Bill was out of the question as well, since the man had fallen under Pinkerton gunfire in Second Chance.

Drew felt as though his entire existence had shattered around him. All he had lived for since he'd learned of Claire's death was the day when he could bring Charlie Coltrain to justice. Now he found out he had been wrong, and there was no way to learn for sure who had killed Claire.

Drew had a feeling Charlie was right, too. Even if he did kill the culprit with his bare hands, it wouldn't help ease the desolate emptiness inside him. Claire was gone. Forever. He was alive and he had to go on. Somehow he had to discover a way to make something of his life. He had to find a place where he belonged.

He did not belong in the Texas Rangers. Remaining a small part of the large unit protecting Texas from Comanche renegades, Mexican bandits and American outlaws was not for him. He had joined the Rangers as a means to a personal end—an end that had turned out to be false. After receiving the wire confirming Charlie's confinement in a Missouri jail during the dates in question, Drew Winston had resigned his post in the Texas Rangers.

Now he had to decide what to do about Coltrain. According to all the information Drew had been able to come up with, the man wasn't wanted for anything anywhere. Though he was sure Charlie had committed enough crimes to keep the man in jail for many years, Drew had to let him go if someone didn't want him for something somewhere.

He didn't know when it had happened, but somewhere between Mexico and Texas, his hate had faded. Now that he'd learned the truth, he almost liked the man. They had a lot in common. If their lives had been different, they might have been friends. For certain, Drew felt sorry for the ex-outlaw. Coltrain obviously loved his wife, and Angelina loved Coltrain. They should be together. Drew was ashamed that he had been the instrument to separate them. After losing Claire, he knew what it felt like to be deprived of the woman you loved. And Angelina sure as hell shouldn't be left with that father of hers; the man was a snake of the worst sort.

Drew stood and went into the jail. He'd get Charlie released and send him on his way back to his wife. The woman needed a little rescuing—from her family and from the convent. Maybe helping two people find their way to each other would make him feel better about his own loss.

Half an hour later, he and Coltrain sat together in the nearest saloon.

"You've got me confused, Yank. Now I'm not complainin', but why am I out of jail and sippin' whiskey with you?"

Drew took a deep pull on his drink before answering. "You were telling the truth. You didn't rob the train, you didn't kill the engineer and you didn't kill Claire."

"Yeah, so?"

"No one else is looking for you anywhere. There's no reason to keep you in jail. Either your notoriety is greatly exaggerated, or you're one careful criminal."

Charlie raised his eyebrows. "I was a careful criminal. Now I'm just an out-of-work cowboy." He downed the rest of his whiskey. "Did you tell them who they hanged today?"

"No, I figured we could do that together tomorrow. Though I don't suppose you have any proof of who you are?"

"Nope. If it's all the same to you, Yank, I'd just as soon leave Charlie Coltrain dead."

Drew choked on the sip of whiskey he'd just attempted to swallow. Charlie banged him on the back until he had his breath back. "What for?" he demanded.

"Let's just say it'd be for the best. I've gotten a reputation, as you say. Sooner or later someone's gonna come lookin' for me. If I'm already dead, there won't be anyone to look for. I can start over. I'm too old to go back to thievin'. I plan to start a ranch in Montana. I'd just as soon start my life fresh."

Drew nodded. "Not a bad idea. It'll protect your wife, too."

"I don't have a wife." Charlie's ruined voice was heavy with warning.

"What are you talking about?"

"Charlie Coltrain had a wife. I don't."

"Wait just a minute. That woman loves you. You can both start a new life now. Get your butt back to Mexico and get her."

"Nope. She deserves better than me. Just because I have a different name doesn't make me a different man. I'm old and sour and broken.

She wants to be a nun. The least I can do for her is to let her follow her dream."

"How do you know her dream isn't you?"

Charlie laughed, a coughlike sound that reflected no humor. "I'm not a young girl's dream, Yank. I'm every woman's nightmare."

Chapter Nineteen

Three weeks passed. Three weeks when all Angelina's hopes were pinned to the single possibility that she carried a child. If her prayers were answered, she would somehow get word to Charlie from her aunt's, and he would come for both her and his child.

She didn't for one moment believe he was dead. He had not committed the murder; therefore he would not hang for it. Once the Ranger learned for certain Charlie had not killed Claire, he would do the right thing and let Charlie go free. Drew Winston was an honorable man. He would not take money to kill the innocent. She clung to that belief. It was all she had.

Despite her husband's stubborn insistence he was not good enough for her and she should return to the convent, he would not desert his child. If she could just get him to come back to her, she would find a way to make him love her. She had faith in the power of that love.

When the irrefutable evidence arrived that she did not carry Charlie's child, Angelina crawled into her bed and wept for a day.

When she felt as bad as she looked, she got up, dressed and demanded to be released from her prison. She would go to town and send a wire to Dallas. Charlie would come for her if she told him she was in trouble, and she was definitely in trouble.

Her father smiled at her good news and graciously gave her permission to go into Chihuahua with her mother to buy a few things for her trip back to the convent. Once he got his way, Miguel Reyes could be very generous.

Angelina found it amazingly easy to slip away from her flighty mother. She left Theresa Reyes in the midst of the dry-goods shop and headed across the street to the telegraph office.

"I need to send a message to Dallas, Texas," she told the operator.

He nodded, avoiding her eyes, and handed her a piece of paper to write upon.

To Charlie Coltrain Stop
I need you at the Reyes ranch immediately
Stop
Please come Stop Angelina

She read over what she had written and nodded, pleased. Good enough. Short. Vague. Charlie would have to return if he cared anything about her. She was betting her life that he did.

The telegraph operator collected her paper and her money. "Umm," she flushed, knowing the way her instructions would sound, but she was unable to avoid giving them. "You might tell the operator in Dallas to look for him in the jail."

The operator merely nodded and turned away. A few moments later he returned to hand her a sheet of paper containing a short message.

Charlie Coltrain tried convicted and hanged for murder Stop

Angelina stared at the paper, then watched as it drifted slowly downward. The words continued to scream their horrible message at her from where they rested on the floor.

"No, no, no!"

The words, high pitched, hysterical, startled her until she realized they were coming from her own mouth. Clasping her fingers to her lips, she tried to stop the horrible keening cries, but could not.

As the telegraph operator hurried toward her, fear etched across his usually placid face, she crumpled to her knees on the floor. Retrieving the fallen message, she crushed the paper in her fingers just before the entire world faded to black.

Charlie stayed in Dallas a few days. He drank, he played cards and he drank some more. What he tried not to do was sleep. Every time he did, he dreamed of Angelina.

The night they had been together before he left had been the most beautiful night of his life. He might pretend to be angry that she had seduced him and he might tell himself he had been half drunk, but he had no such excuses for the second time they had made love.

When he'd awoken in the night, his head had been totally clear. His body was on fire. Angelina had lain curled against him, her back pressed to his front, her naked buttocks nestled to his hardened shaft. He had buried his face in her hair, kissing her neck. She'd moaned his name and pushed herself more tightly against him.

He thought she slept, unaware of her actions, but when she had taken his hand and placed it on her breasts, he knew she was as awake as he. Her scent, soap and fulfilled woman, drifted to him, and his body responded against his will.

He stroked between her breasts, cupping their fullness, then teasing at the already hardened nipples. She whispered his name on a sigh of desire and he was lost.

The damage had already been done, he told himself. He had failed her. But he could love her one more time before he left—one more time so that he would have another memory to take to his grave.

Gently he adjusted her body so he could slide within. Her surprised gasp was filled with pleasure and wonder. Pulling her closer, he groaned when she clenched herself around him.

He clasped her hips and began the movement. Her head fell back onto his shoulder, and he kissed the soft skin at the crook of her neck. She reached up to pull his head forward, turning her face toward him and taking his lips with her own. Her cry of release mingled with their kiss as he plunged into her one last time. He filled her with his love, the only thing he had to give her, though she would never know of its existence.

"Coltrain."

Charlie's eyes snapped open. He hadn't been asleep exactly, just resting his head against the bar. He looked at the man taking the stool next to him and relaxed.

Lucky for him the new arrival was Winston. If he wasn't careful he'd end up dead anyway, despite his narrow escape from the noose. Charlie looked around the smoke-filled room, his gaze grazing several characters who watched him slyly from beneath lowered hat brims. No, it wasn't a good idea to lose his edge in a place like this.

His hands went to the new pair of Colts strapped to his hips—not the same as the one's he'd lost to Miguel Reyes. Those he'd had since the war and missed like a dead comrade. The guns he'd bought to replace his own were Colt Peacemakers, 45s like those the Ranger carried. Newfangled contraptions, but he'd get the hang of them. The pistols worked and that was all that mattered right now.

"Winston." He nodded to his companion and motioned for the bartender to bring another glass. "Thought you'd be back out with the Rangers by now."

"Nope. I quit."

Charlie gulped down the mouthful of liquor he'd just taken into his mouth, burning a path of fire down his damaged throat. "How come?"

Winston shrugged. "Never was much of a lawman. I joined the Rangers to get at you. Now that's done and I'm out."

Charlie nodded. "What next?"

"Don't know. Thought maybe I'd join a cattle drive and head up to Kansas. Last I heard some people from home lived there."

"Hmm, funny you should mention that. I won a dance hall during a friendly poker game in jail. Located in a small town outside of Dodge called

Last Chance." Charlie chuckled. "With a name like that, I thought I had to take a look at the place. Maybe I'll just join you."

Winston turned toward him, and Charlie had the impression the ex-Ranger wanted to argue. Charlie stared at his companion with a frown. He didn't need to hear again Winston's views on love, life and marriage. They glared at each other for a moment; then Winston slammed his whiskey glass onto the bar and stood. "You want to go to Kansas. That's fine with me. There should be one more drive headed out on the Western Trail this year."

Winston strode toward the door without looking back. Charlie sighed and pulled a tattered length of red ribbon from his pocket. He held the satin to his face, feeling for just a moment the softness, smelling the faint, lingering essence of his wife. "Good-bye," he whispered and replaced the memento back in his pocket before following Drew Winston out the door and onto the trail.

Winston was quiet as they rode out of Dallas, which sat just fine with Charlie. He was in no mood to travel with a chattering companion all the way to Kansas. But from what he'd seen of Winston, the man only spoke when he had something important to say.

Drew cleared his throat. Charlie glanced his way.

"There's something you should know about Miguel Reyes."

Charlie stiffened at the mention of Miguel's name. His father-in-law always meant trouble. "Spit it out, Yank. Now."

"Before we left the ranch, he offered to pay me anything I asked to make sure you died."

Charlie raised his eyebrows and returned his attention to the dusty road in front of him. His hands tightened on the reins, and Gabe yanked his mouth away from the tension, snorting in disapproval.

"So you brought me out of town to take care of things without witnesses." Charlie nodded his approval. "Never said you weren't a smart Yank. How much am I worth dead these days?"

"Nothing to me. I turned him down flat." Drew chuckled. "He was hopping mad."

"I bet. He likes to get his way." Charlie turned his head to look at Drew in curiosity. "Why'd you turn him down? You wanted me dead at the time. You could have picked up some money for doin' it."

Drew shrugged, keeping his attention on the trail. "I don't kill for money. Besides, something about that man rubbed me the wrong way."

"You and me both."

Drew's gaze shifted toward Charlie and then back to the trail again. "If you feel that way, why are you leaving your wife with him? You know he'll force her to do what he wants, whatever he wants."

"Nobody forces Angelina into anything."

"She married you of her own free will?"

Charlie frowned at Winston. Obviously during the short time the man was at the ranch he had learned the story of Angelina's two trips to the altar. "What's your point, Yank?" he growled.

"I wouldn't leave anyone I love with that man. He's dangerous. At least get her away from him and then decide what to do."

"I've already decided. I'm out of her life. I'm goin' to Kansas with you."

"You might have decided, but what about her? You keep saying she's young and you're old. You're not good enough for her. But from what I saw, she loves you. She should have a chance to make up her own mind. You're just like her father, telling her what's good for her and what's not."

Charlie frowned. He didn't like the direction of the conversation, especially if he was being compared to Miguel Reyes. "I'm just tryin' to do somethin' right for once in my sorry life."

"What if you're doing something wrong for the right reasons?"

"Quit jabberin' and tell me what you're after, Yank."

"I'm just thinking you should give each other a chance. That woman was not meant to be a nun. I've seen how she looks at you. Some of the hired help at her parents' place told me how much she loves children. Children are the reason she went into a teaching order. She wanted to be near them even though she'd never have any of her own. She'll be miserable in the convent for the rest of her life. Is that what you want?"

Charlie didn't answer. He just scowled at a point between Gabe's twitching ears.

"What if she's pregnant?"

Charlie started at Winston's bald question. "She never tried to get in touch with me in Dallas."

"How do you know? In Dallas you're dead."

Ice-cold fear flooded through Charlie as he thought of all that might have happened in Mexico during his absence, and he'd left Angelina to face everything alone.

"Hellfire," Charlie muttered and yanked Gabe to a stop.

"What are you doing?"

"I'm goin' to Mexico to get my wife."

Drew grinned. "Need some company?"

Charlie grinned back. Despite himself, he was starting to like the no-good Yankee lawman. "Sure thing, Yank." Charlie touched Gabe with his heels, and the massive white animal reared onto his hind legs, pawing the air with sharp front hooves. "Try to keep up," he called over his shoulder as the horse settled into a run.

Angelina remained in bed for a week. When she finally managed to get up, she searched for her red ribbon, the only tangible item Charlie had ever given her. Unable to find the scrap of satin, Angelina tore apart the room, throwing everything she owned onto the floor and sorting through it again and again.

The gift was nowhere to be found.

A maid appeared in the doorway, alerted by the strange sounds coming from the room. "Where is it?" Angelina shouted at her.

"What, senora?" the young girl asked, cringing back from Angelina's anger.

"My ribbon. A red ribbon. I wore it at the party, and now it's gone. I have to find my ribbon."

Angelina heard the hysteria in her voice, and even before the maid ran down the hall calling for Angelina's mother to come quickly, she knew she was overreacting. She couldn't seem to help herself. The ribbon was the only thing she had left of Charlie and she wanted that ribbon back.

Her mother arrived and tried to soothe Angelina's temper. But the gentle woman could do nothing beyond questioning all the servants. No one had ever seen a red ribbon in Angelina's room.

Angelina threw everyone out and locked the door. She then went back to her bed, where she cried herself to sleep. The next day she refused to leave her room. The doctor came and went without doing anything more than cluck over her in Spanish, the same as he'd done the first week she'd lain in bed. There was nothing wrong with her, nothing a doctor could cure anyway.

Her heart was broken. She wanted to curl into a ball and die. Alone. The way Charlie had died. Even though he had been hanged in the midst of people, he had still died alone and lonely, away from the one person who loved him, who would love him for all time.

Every night she lay in the bed she'd shared with him and remembered. She lamented the fact that their one night together had not produced a child. She would have at least had some little part of Charlie to keep with her forever. Despite what her father had said, no one would have taken Charlie's child away from her.

No one.

Her father stayed out of her sight. Once the doctor decided she would recover, he went back to running the ranch and making political maneuvers. He left the care of Angelina to the family physician and his wife, who hovered over her only daughter with a vague, worried air, mumbling nonsense and doing little.

Therefore, when he showed up in the doorway to her bedroom several weeks after she'd fainted in the telegraph office, Angelina knew he had come to impart his decision on the rest of her life. She could have cared less.

"Tomorrow, daughter, your brothers will escort you back to the Sisters in Corpus Christi."

Angelina didn't bother to look at him. She continued to lay on her back in the bed and peruse the ceiling. "All my brothers? Why call out the disciples now?"

"You will ride in an enclosed carriage. Your brothers are for protection."

"Against what?"

"In order to smooth your way back into the convent after the scandal you've brought down upon the Reyes name, I had to promise an extremely large dowry."

Angelina knew her father well enough to hear the anger in his voice, though a stranger would not have been able to distinguish any emotion. He might pretend all was well between them in public, but he would never forgive her for the trouble she had caused him. She didn't have the will to care what he thought of her, nor the will to care where he sent her.

"Why bother with the money?" she asked. "I don't care where I go. Send me where no one's ever heard your precious name."

Her father finally stepped into the room, and Angelina looked at him for the first time. His face flushed with fury as he stood over the bed. Angelina raised her eyebrows at the uncommon show of emotion. "I care where you go," he spat. "How do you think it will look if the Sisters to whom you were pledged do not take you back? And if they do not, do you think you can stay here? No, we don't need your wan face drifting around this house, reminding everyone who visits of your unfortunate attachment to an outlaw. And there is no man in Chihuahua who would marry you now." He paused and drew in a deep, shaky breath. "No, daughter, you are leaving. You are returning to that convent, and I don't expect to see your face again in this lifetime. Take your vows, the vows you were screaming to take during your first wedding, and live out your life as a nun. The scandal will blow over soon enough if you aren't here to remind everyone. I've been advised that having a daughter in the church looks good for a government official in a Catholic country. Everything will work out fine in the end."

Angelina stared at her father for a moment, wondering at the flood of distaste flowing through her. It was the first emotion she'd felt since reading the message informing her of Charlie's death. "As you wish, Miguel," she said. No longer would she refer to the man before her as her father. He had never cared for her, only for what she could bring him. "I will leave tomorrow. But only because I choose to go. I have no reason to live in your world. The church will suit me. I will go anywhere I don't have to see you again."

Angelina stared into her father's cold black eyes and wondered how her mother had endured being married to such a selfish human being for so many years. Even after his only daughter had stated she never wanted to see him again, he merely smiled, pleased at getting his way. "Then we understand each other?"

"Perfectly." Angelina returned her attention to the ceiling as her father left the room.

She didn't care where she spent the rest of her life, though she wondered momentarily how she'd fare back at the convent. She was sure the Sisters would welcome her with open arms, perhaps even pamper her a bit to make up for her horrible experience at the hands of the real world. But she would forever be different from them. She had known love and passion for a man. She would ache for that man every night. In the eyes of every child she taught she would see the promise of what might have been.

She had trusted in her angel's words of advice. She had held fast to her faith and her love.

Where had things gone so wrong?

Charlie and Drew pulled their horses to a halt at the top of the ridge above the Reyes hacienda.

"Got a plan?" Drew asked.

"I'd like to go down there, punch my father-in-law in the nose, grab my wife and hightail it outta here. But somehow I don't think that would be a good idea."

Drew's mouth twitched. "No, I reckon not."

"So how about I go down there and talk to my wife. You stay out of sight and cover me in case Reyes and his disciples decide to shoot me before I say my piece."

"Disciples?"

"It's a long story. Just watch for six men who are younger versions of Reyes. They know how to ride, and the guns they carry ain't for show."

Drew nodded and moved off to take up position behind a few strategic trees.

Charlie rode down the hill, but before he could get near the house, Reyes rode up from another direction, accompanied by two ranch hands. All three men had their guns drawn and pointed at Charlie. Not a disciple was in sight, but the two men with Reyes held their pistols with confidence. Charlie kept his hands away from his own guns. His father-in-law would shoot him with very little provocation, so Charlie would take pains to be agreeable for the moment.

The look of surprise that had appeared upon Reyes's face when he'd first seen Charlie faded fast. "I heard you were dead," Reyes said.

"Hardly." Charlie stared at his father-in-law without flinching. He meant to get what he wanted, one way or another. "I've come for my wife."

Miguel's thin lips curved into a satisfied smile. "She's not here."

"Where is she?"

"You think I'll tell you?"

Charlie sighed. This situation called for tact, which was not something he possessed in abundance. He probably should have sent Winston to talk to Reyes and stayed up on the hill himself. But he'd been so anxious to see Angelina, he hadn't been thinking smart.

"She's my wife, Reyes. I want her back. You have nothin' to say about it."

"Oh, but I do. I know where she is and you don't. I'm holding the gun on you. Now get off my ranch." He cocked his pistol for emphasis. The other two men did the same.

Charlie tried another tactic. He lowered his voice to a conspiratorial level. "You never cared about her. I know our marriage has been an embarrassment to you. I promise I'll take her where no one has ever heard of either of us. You'll never have to be embarrassed again."

"You're right. You have been an embarrassment. And Angelina—well, she's been nothing but trouble all her life. I'll admit I'm glad she's gone. But I've finally arranged things just the way I want them, and I don't plan to let you foul them up again. You can look all you want, but you won't find her here."

Charlie opened his mouth to argue, and Reyes pulled the trigger. The earth in front of Gabe's hooves spit dust and the horse reared. Charlie calmed his mount with murmured words and soothing strokes. When he glanced at Reyes once more, the man and his companions had ridden away.

"Son of a bitch." Charlie glanced up at the hill and waved to let Winston to know he was all right. The man stepped out from behind a tree and waved back his understanding.

Charlie turned his attention to Angelina's bedroom window. Could she be up there despite Reyes's assurances to the contrary? He doubted Reyes would have left him on the property if such were the case. Still, he couldn't leave without knowing for sure his wife was not trapped inside.

Charlie walked Gabe up to the house and dismounted. A glance into the distance revealed Reyes and the other two men had nearly disappeared into the dust created by their mounts. His boot perched atop the first step, Charlie froze when the front door opened. His head whipped back toward the house just as Theresa Reyes stepped outside.

She smiled, a trifle fearfully. Charlie did his best to smile back without scaring her any further. He failed. She took a step backward, her long, pale fingers fluttering at her throat.

"Don't be afraid," Charlie said. She flinched at the rasp of his voice. "I just want to know where Angelina is. Can you tell me?

Theresa glanced around the empty yard.

"He's gone," Charlie supplied. "Rode out to the west with two men. He'll never know you told me. I swear."

After another moment's hesitation, she nodded. "He sent her back to the convent in Corpus Christi yesterday. All the boys went with her, heavily armed."

"Why?" Charlie frowned. "He thought I was dead. Who was he protecting her from?"

"Anyone. Everyone. He had to send along a substantial dowry so the Sisters would accept her back. It's the money he's protecting, not Angelina."

"Figures." Charlie turned away and mounted his horse.

Theresa followed, perching on the top step like a frightened bird set for flight. "Mr. Coltrain? Tell her I just want her to be happy. That's all I've ever wanted. I was never strong enough to protect her. But you are. You'll make her happy, won't you?"

"Ma'am, I'll do my best."

She smiled. "I thought so. Be careful, won't you? My sons can be dangerous."

"So can I." Charlie tipped his hat and nodded to his mother-in-law before spinning Gabe around and riding up the hill.

Drew met him at the crest. "Sorry about that shot Reyes got off. Since he didn't hit you, I figured I should let it pass. Didn't want to start a small war with you in the middle."

Charlie nodded. "He was just showin' off."

"So where is she?"

"On her way to the convent in Corpus Christi."

Drew nodded. "How far ahead of us?"

"A day.

"No problem. We ride through the night and we'll catch up by midday."

"You don't have to tag along, Yank. Reyes sent all six of his disciples with her. They're packin' a lot of money and a lot of iron. Could be dangerous."

Drew shrugged. "Life's dangerous. I don't have anything better to do. And besides, I'd love to pull one over on Senor Reyes."

Charlie smiled. "My father-in-law doesn't make friends too easy."

"Not with me anyway. So how do two men take one woman away from six armed guards?"

"Why do I get to do all the planning?"

"Because you're the outlaw. I'm the ex-lawman. When it comes to kidnapping women from armed protectors, I'll leave the planning to you. If you need some advice on how to catch the culprit or rescue the woman, then I'll take over."

"Fair enough." Charlie's mouth twitched upward at the corner. He was starting to like Winston. The man's sense of humor tickled him.

"So what's the plan?"

"I'll let you know," Charlie said and kicked Gabe into a run. "Just as soon as I think of one," he muttered to himself.

Despite being inside her family's private coach, Angelina was covered in dust. She would have preferred to ride, but Miguel had given her brothers orders that she stay inside, out of sight. Since her lethargy over the past few weeks had sapped her strength, she didn't particularly care enough to argue with her brothers. Instead, she snapped closed the heavy curtain, effectively closing off the sight of dirt-dry northern Mexico.

Angelina shifted uncomfortably on the hard seat, her foot knocking against the carpetbag on the floor. With a childish gesture, she kicked the bag, and it skidded across the few feet of floor space. Inside rested a few personal items, some medical supplies and the substantial bribe for the convent.

The coach lurched, then slowed and Angelina straightened. It was too soon to stop for the night. Why were they slowing down? She reached for the curtain covering the window. Pushing the material aside, she glanced out.

Luke and John rode directly outside the window. They both peered into the distance, focused on a sight out of her view.

"What's the matter?" she shouted.

Luke glanced at her and shrugged. Angelina grimaced. Her brothers dolled out conversation like misers hoarding gold. Sometimes she wondered if they could speak at all beyond a few necessary words.

The coach jerked to a stop, and she pitched forward onto the floor. Muttering words she never would have used two months before, Angelina righted herself. After smoothing her plain gray dress back into place, she kicked the door open and stepped out into the hot, dusty air. Luke, John, Timothy and Peter, all mounted, stood at the front of the coach where Matthew and Mark sat atop the driver's seat. All six stared straight ahead.

Angelina squinted into the sun. Maybe a mile in front of them, black smoke drifted upward.

"What is it?" she asked.

Six sets of shoulders shrugged. No one spoke.

"Indians?" she said.

Six heads shook a negative reply.

"Shouldn't we check and see if anyone's hurt?"

Five pairs of eyes turned to Matthew, the eldest, for a decision.

Instead of a verbal answer, he drew his gun and motioned for Angelina to get back inside. Once she did, the coach started forward at a sedate pace. A glance out the window revealed all her brothers approached the scene with guns drawn, black eyes twitching suspiciously.

Minutes later the coach stopped again. "Stay there," Luke hissed at her through the window when Angelina made a move to get out. Once he rode away, she ignored the order and stepped outside once again.

Black smoke continued to swirl upward from the burning remains of an unknown item. Two bodies lay on the ground next to the fire. Not a horse was in sight.

"Robbery and murder," Matthew observed, returning his gun to the holster. The rest of the men followed suit. "Get a shovel, boys, and bury 'em."

Angelina tilted her head, frowning. Something about one of the bodies looked familiar. She shook her head. Grief had made her fanciful. But she would check to make sure the men were truly dead and not just badly injured before her brothers commenced with the burial.

Reaching inside the coach, she snatched her carpetbag from the floor and headed toward the closest body, gray skirts swirling around her ankles with every step.

"Angelina, get back inside the coach," Matthew ordered. "Our father gave strict orders."

"No."

"Angelina!" Her brother's voice held a note of warning.

She stopped and turned to face her brother. "What are you going to do to me, Matthew? Shoot me? I don't care. The only thing I have left to live for in this life is helping others, and if I can help these men at all, I'm going to do it. So if you want to stop me, then shoot me." Turning, she strode to the first fallen victim. None of her brothers made any further attempt to dissuade her.

The man lay on his stomach, face in the dirt. Angelina could see no sign of an injury on his back, and she reached for his shoulder to roll him over. As she did so, he suddenly turned and grabbed her wrist.

Angelina opened her mouth to scream for help. Then her eyes met those of her captor and she gasped. "You."

Drew Winston smiled, blue eyes crinkling in amusement as he jumped to his feet. He kept a tight grip on her wrist so he could drag her in front of him.

The cold barrel of a gun pressed to Angelina's temple, and she tried to flinch away.

"Just relax and go along with this, ma'am," he whispered in her ear, holding her tighter as she struggled. "No one will get hurt, and you can be on your way."

Angelina opened her mouth to ask where he thought she was going. But Drew was already shouting orders to her brothers.

"Put down the guns. All of them. Unless you want your sister's brains separated from her pretty, little head."

Her brothers froze. They all looked to Matthew, who was in charge as long as Miguel wasn't there. He scowled at Angelina for her stupidity, then threw his pistol and rifle to the ground. The others followed his example. Angelina struggled with her surprise. She never would have expected Matthew to choose her life over money.

"Wise choice," Winston said. "Now all of you line up over here where I can see you."

The six men did as they were ordered.

Angelina's mind spun. What was the Ranger doing here? Why was he kidnapping her? How dare he show his face to her after he'd dragged her husband away to be killed?

With that thought in mind, she stomped down hard on his foot with her boot. Winston's hold loosened enough for her to break free and spin around to face him.

"Ouch!" he exclaimed. "What did you do that for?"

"I'd kill you if I could," she hissed. "You—"

The angry tirade froze in her throat as the other man, the one she had assumed dead since he had not entered the fray, sat up. She fought to catch her breath as the man's long golden hair swung forward over his shoulders. Black eyes, which she had once considered hard and emotionless, locked with hers. The love in Charlie's gaze reawakened her cold and dead soul.

Angelina swayed, and Drew reached out a hand to steady her. "Whoa, there, ma'am. Don't go fainting on us now. We have too much to do yet."

She nodded weakly, accepting his help until she was able to stumble forward on her own.

Charlie stood, brushing the dust from his Levi's absently as he started to move toward her. One, two, three strides and they were together in each other's arms. She held him tightly, afraid if she loosened her grip he would disappear into the land of her dreams once more.

He smoothed her hair gently, almost reverently, and she looked up into his face.

An angel fallen to the earth, she thought. Then his lips came down on hers, and she thought of nothing beyond his embrace.

She had believed she would never feel such things again—passion, desire, all-consuming love. Those emotions, which had died when she thought she'd lost Charlie, leapt to life again within her at his kiss. She clung to him, pouring all her needs and fears and wants into the caress.

When they finally broke apart, Angelina's eyes were moist with tears. "How? Why?" she asked. "They told me you were dead."

Charlie sighed and ran his hand through his hair, keeping one arm wrapped around her waist as though afraid she would leave him if he let her go.

"It's a long story." He glanced over her shoulder at Drew. "And one I'd best save for when we're far away from here. Grab your things and let's go, Sister."

"Where?"

"I'll tell you that later, too. Right now I want to get away from your brothers as fast as we can. No one's takin' you away from me again without a fight. But I'd rather not have to shoot one of your relatives if I can help it."

Angelina turned slightly to observe the situation behind her. All six of her brothers had been tied and now sat on the dusty Mexican earth. Drew stood in front of them, gun drawn. He grinned at her and tipped his hat.

"Have a nice life, Angelina. You saved mine. Now I'm happy to give you a chance to find yours."

Angelina smiled back. "I'm sorry I stomped on you before. I didn't know."

He shrugged. "I've had worse injuries. I'll live."

She glanced at her husband. "I thought you hated Yankees."

"Certain Yankees. This one turned out all right in the end."

"I see." Angelina peered at her husband closely. There was something different about him, a relaxed air in place of his usual tense readiness. She would have to explore this change further when they had the time.

Detaching herself from Charlie's embrace with reluctance, Angelina went to retrieve her carpetbag from the ground where she'd dropped it. When she turned around, Charlie and Drew had their heads together in deep discussion. She joined them.

"I'll stay here for a day," Drew was saying. "Then I'll go into Chihuahua and send someone out for them. You'll be long gone by then. By the time they're let loose, so will I."

Charlie nodded. He reached into his shirt and withdrew a creased-and-torn paper. He shoved it into the lawman's hand. "The dance hall I told you about. You take it. We won't be needing the thing."

Drew looked down at the paper in his hand, then up at Charlie. He nodded his thanks and stuffed the parchment into the pocket of his pants. The two men looked at each other for a moment, hesitancy in every movement. Then Charlie stiffly stuck out his hand. Drew clasped it and they shook, looking into each other's eyes for a long moment.

Angelina bit her lip against the catch in her throat. Not more than a month ago the two men had been mortal enemies. What had happened to make them forgive one another and become friends?

Charlie and Drew parted. "If you ever need a hand, you'll know where to find me," Drew told him.

Charlie nodded and turned away. Within minutes, Angelina and Charlie retrieved Gabe from his hiding place and rode away to the north.

Night fell and they made camp. They had ridden too hard and fast since leaving Drew and her brothers to have any kind of conversation. Though Angelina's curiosity was near to bursting, a need of a different kind took precedence over her questions.

No sooner had they made a fire and laid out the bedroll than she was in his arms. Impatient to feel his flesh against hers, she yanked his shirt open, spreading her palms across his chest, then lowering her lips to press kisses across the broad expanse.

"I never thought I'd see you again," she whispered between kisses.

"I know. But I'm here now. No more talk, Angelina. I need you too much."

With that statement, issued in a rough, urgent tone, he quickly stripped her clothes. His own garments landed in the pile on top of hers.

He lay in the hollow between her legs, his hardness pressed against her pulsing center. Cradling her face, he kissed her deeply. She moaned against his mouth, arching into him, clasping his taut buttocks and urging him closer.

"Please," she begged. "Don't wait. I want you inside me now. I need to know for sure I'm not dreaming. That you're really here with me. That you're really alive."

With a single movement he came into her, filling her completely. The tears she had put off all afternoon flowed freely down her cheeks. He leaned down and kissed them away.

"Don't cry, Angel. Please. It tears me up when you do that."

"I'm all right." She smiled and blinked back the last of her tears, then reached up to cup his cheek in her palm. "I was just so afraid that none of this was real. That I might wake up and be in the convent forever, and you would still be dead."

Charlie smiled a wicked smile and pulled slowly out of her body; then he thrust into her once more. "I'm definitely alive and well." She reached out and pulled him back into her again. Charlie groaned. "Though you may kill me yet."

Then there were no more words for a long while, just the sound of lovers loving, making new promises for a lifetime together and fulfilling the vows they had made not so very long ago.

The stars rose above them, clear and bright in the dark Mexican sky. Angelina and Charlie lay together, fingers linked, and watched the twinkling array.

"Why did you come back?" Angelina asked.

Charlie sighed. "I wasn't going to. Winston and I were on our way to sign on with a drive to Kansas."

"And?"

"And something he said made me realize the truth."

"What truth?"

"That I love you."

Angelina caught her breath in wonder and turned onto her side so she could see his face. She had known he desired her. She had hoped she could teach him to love her. Eventually. Maybe years in the future. She had been willing to wait, to teach him with her patience and her love the joy of such an emotion. But now, with one sentence, he made all her careful plans unnecessary.

Angelina reached up and ran a finger over his lips. He kissed the tip, looking into her eyes, the love in his gaze reflecting her own.

"I also wondered if the one night we spent together made a child." He looked at her, a question in his eyes.

She sighed, all her disappointment evident in the small sound.

Charlie brushed his knuckle over her cheekbone. "Don't worry. We'll get it right yet." He smiled at her and she smiled back, hope lighting her heart. "I used to think you would be better off without me. I'm old, and I've never been anything more than an outlaw. But I realized that with you I'm more than I was. With you I can be something better."

Angelina nodded, hearing the beliefs she'd held in her heart put into words for the first time.

"And selfish bastard that I am, I decided to come and take you away from the convent. You don't belong there, Angelina. You belong with me."

He shifted so he rested on his side also, and they lay face-to-face, heart to heart. "You should have children. My children." He placed his large hand over her stomach, and she reached up to cover his fingers with her own. He looked deeply into her eyes. "I'll make you happy. You won't regret bein' my wife."

"I've never regretted being your wife. I never will."

"I'm sorry about the convent. I know that was your dream."

"Yes, it was my dream. The dream of a naive young girl who wanted nothing more than to get away from a father who had no use for her. I thought I could make a difference there, and I might have. But I've made a difference somewhere else—with you. I was right all along. You were my mission, Charlie. And I succeeded beyond every dream I ever had."

He smiled at her then, a true smile, one full of joy and promise that reached all the way to his eyes—a smile she never would have believed possible when she'd first met the cold, hard man with the beautiful face and the fathomless soul.

"I have somethin' for you," he said and reached over to pull an item from his discarded Levi's. He raised his hand into the air.

A red satin ribbon—stained, ripped, destroy-ed—dangled in front of Angelina's eyes. She sat up and snatched it away with a gasp.

"You stole my ribbon! And you ruined it!"

"Sorry." He tried to take the satin back, but she held it out of his reach. "I'll buy you another, though funds are gonna be pretty tight until I get a job somewhere."

Angelina froze. "Money." She gasped and jump-ed to her feet. Naked she ran around the fire and snatched up her carpetbag. Returning to the bed-roll, she upended the bag. Clothes, bandages and money poured out, landing all over Charlie.

He sat up, staring at the pile of cash in his lap. "What's this?"

"My dowry." Angelina grinned. "You're my husband. The money belongs to you."

Charlie started to laugh. "When your father finds out I got this much of his money it'll give him apoplexy."

Plopping down next to Charlie, Angelina scooped up some of the bills and then let them flutter back down to rest on the bedroll. She looked up at Charlie, who continued to chuckle. The sound of his happiness caused joy to spark to life within her. "What are we going to do with it?"

"Ever consider bein' a rancher's wife?"

"I have now. Where?"

"How does Montana sound?"

Angelina took Charlie's hand. "To paraphrase a woman named Ruth, wherever you go, I go." She drew him toward her and placed a soft kiss upon his lips. "Wherever you are is my home."

"I kinda like the sound of that."

"I thought you might."

They lay down upon their bed beneath the stars and fell asleep holding hands.

The angel came one last time.

"Will I ever see you again?" Angelina asked.

"Not in this life. But I'll be watching over you—over you, your husband and all your children. Be happy, Angelina."

With a wave of his hand, the angel showed Angelina her future.

And it was good.